The Truth About Unicorns

Bonnie Jones Reynolds

FELONY & MAYHEM PRESS • NEW YORK

THE TRUTH ABOUT UNICORNS

A Felony & Mayhem mystery

PRINTING HISTORY
First U.S. edition (Stein and Day): 1972
Felony & Mayhem edition: 2010

ISBN: 978-1-934609-65-1

Manufactured in the United States of America

Library of Congress Cataloging-in-Publication Data

Reynolds, Bonnie Jones.
  The truth about unicorns / Bonnie Jones Reynolds. -- Felony & Mayhem
ed.
    p. cm.
  ISBN 978-1-934609-65-1
  1. Witches--Fiction. 2. Unicorns--Fiction. I. Title.
  PS3568.E887T78 2010
  813'.54--dc22
                        2010036199

To Harwood Hamlin Jones, my father;
to Guy Endore, my teacher;
to Henrietta Endore, my friend.

ACKNOWLEDGMENTS

A difficult task. There have been so many who have given their support. If I forget, please forgive.

My husband, Gene Reynolds, whose enthusiasm made it possible for me to go to the typewriter with a clear conscience; Leona Jenkins, who made it possible for me to stay there; Leonardo Bercovici, who pointed me in the right direction; Stephanie Post, Leila Rosten, Marge Rogers, Gail Andrews, and Linda Becker, who typed and retyped; my parents, Harwood and Deanie, my Grandmother Jones, and my Great-Aunt "Kitty-Belle" Cash, who allowed me to pick their brains for details of the period and for anecdotes; Dr. Klaus Hoppe, who was kind enough to read the manuscript and supply his comments; George Wilner, who paved the path to my agent, Roberta Pryor; Roberta herself.

Then there is Guy's Group, composed nowadays of Martha Axelrod, John Davis, Blossom Elfman, Henrietta Endore, John Harrington, Gita Endore Kaiser, Betty McKenzie, and myself. The results of our Thursday night meetings could never be unraveled from this book.

The final word of thanks must be to my editor, Renni Browne, and to the entire organization of Stein and Day. Seldom has an author been more fortunate.

The Truth About Unicorns

They say that, in a certain place in America, in a dark and strange wood, there is to be seen, if you look at the right moment, a fleet and solitary white animal appearing as a horse, with a mane that sweeps toward the ground. It has a beard like a goat and a tail like a bull, and a fine long horn in the middle of its forehead. Some call it a Unicorn. But Unicorns do not exist. Except in the finest reaches of our minds.

PROLOGUE

SPRING FARM

June 6, 1910

"I'M GOING TO have to sacrifice the baby, Tobin—and even then I can't guarantee Hitty." Tobin knew Doc Barnes was trying to be gentle, but he wore red gauntlets. "Do you understand what I'm saying, Tobin?"

Tobin nodded, then turned toward the room of Hitty's labor, thinking he'd heard a sound—her voice, calling his name.

But no. After thirty hours, there was silence. Only to her father, Frank, had she called, "Daddy! Daddy!"

Tobin crossed to the window, stared out at the blackness, and heard Doc Barnes go back to Hitty's room. If only, he thought, she'd leave me with the memory of just one "Tobin!"

Doc Barnes's forceps on the tiny head were not sentimental. It's only a lump, he told himself as he wrenched the baby from Hitty and laid it, dead, on a nearby chair. Life was oozing from Hitty. Barnes and the nurse turned their attention to staying the flow.

Dawn mottled the darkness of the woods surrounding the small red farmhouse; in the barnyard, the cattle were bellowing, past their milking hour; Tobin still stood at the window. For some reason he kept thinking of Carrie. He wondered if Frank, and Hitty's mother, Flora, were thinking of her, too, so silent in their chairs.

The bawling of the cows became more insistent. Tobin heard his father, Thomas, get to his feet. "I'll see to the milking, son."

Tobin nodded.

Then—a baby's cry.

From the bedroom came a muffled exclamation. "Flora!" Doc Barnes called. "Get in here! Tend this baby!"

If neither doctor nor nurse had a free hand, then Hitty must still be—

"I'm going to faint," said Flora, and did.

The baby cried again.

Suddenly Tobin was running. He pulled open the door, and searched out the figure of Hitty upon the bed. Then, quickly, he averted his eyes, trying to erase what he had seen. He had to remember her as she'd been till now. Dresden.

"Flora fainted again?" said Barnes. "Well, wrap the baby in something warm, Tobin. Rock it. Damn it, nurse, hold that candle steady!"

But the candle fluttered and died, as though blown by some breath.

Tobin turned cold. A candle snuffed. A life—

Barnes swore. "That's the third time, nurse!"

"I'm sorry." She fumbled with matches. "It's that draft. I don't know where it comes from."

The windows of the room were closed. The air was short and still.

"Is Hitty dead?" said Tobin.

"Take care of that baby like I told you."

Tobin walked to the chair and looked down at his son. Bruised; bloodied of his mother and of himself; skull lopsided; umbilical twisting from belly to afterbirth. Tobin fought back tears and extended trembling hands.

Then he stopped, blinking at the afterbirth. Couldn't lift the baby with that thing there. He poked at the cord, pulled at it, found that the fibers tore under gentle pressure. Pretend it's a calf, he told himself.

They were doing something to Hitty. He wouldn't look. He lifted the baby, and as he laid it against his chest, it made a sound. His arms tightened around it and he walked back to the parlor.

Wrap it in something warm, Barnes had said. Tobin wrapped it in the afghan and sat down in his chair. Then the baby grew still. Tobin shook it. It moved. *Rock it*, Barnes had said. Yes. Rock it. Remind it to live.

It. Not even a person. And it had killed Hitty.

But it hadn't killed Hitty. Hitty lived. It was christened Harley Franklin Westcott and Tobin was proud of the tiny bundle that seemed so determined to live.

At first. At first he was proud.

CHAPTER ONE

THE WESTCOTTS

June 6, 1926

THE SOFT THUD of Polly's hooves became a sharp click-clock as Harley turned out of the woods and started down the newly macadamed road. There'd been no *reason* to pave this road. Didn't go anywhere except past Aunt Carrie's, then on around the woods past Cole's and Grampa Parmalee's—the whole country would be macadamed before the town engineers got finished. Not that engineers gave a damn about horseshoes.

The real source of Harley's concern was not, however, the wear and tear on horseshoes.

He'd used to be able to approach Carrie's house quietly.

Harley did not understand his desire to pass Carrie's house unseen any more than he'd ever understood his desire to go there in the first place.

It was always the same.

The Victorian cottage would look deserted and forbidding, no matter how sweet the day, for the woods seemed to hold that cottage as a part of themselves. Harley would hear

Carrie in the little walled garden she had built for herself, humming as she worked, always the same tune. He heard the haunting notes now.

The song stopped at the clickclock on macadam. Harley drew in his breath and watched the door in the wall swing slowly outward.

It always did. And that, perhaps, was why he came. Each time he swore he'd speak to her. And today he would. Today—his sixteenth birthday. What would be so difficult, after all? He'd say, "Good morning, Aunt Carrie."

At that moment Carrie's dark eyes met his.

The down on his neck prickled. He touched Polly's flank and clickclocked away, Carrie's eyes following, his brain urging more rapid retreat, till he rounded a curve and halted behind the screen of trees.

Always the same.

He sighed and turned Polly back into the woods, toward Spring Farm. The phantom hooves joined him at the forest's edge, falling into step some distance behind and to the right. Harley did not look around. Always the same echo—another of the sounds of these woods, a phenomenon of a different dimension.

It was not until Harley reached Westcott pastureland that he thought to look at his watch. Then he clucked in annoyance. When Upjohn had excused him early from class the day before, he had promised to make it up this morning. As usual, he was late.

He touched Polly and released the reins. The gray jumper broke into a smooth gallop and the two streaked toward home, taking the potholes with ease, comfortable with one another as two old friends should be.

"Always off on his horse," neighbors would say of Harley.

"Well, can you blame him?" others would say. "Tobin's too busy to give him the time of day, and Hitty hardly tolerates him for more'n an hour at a time."

"I guess. But he's a strange one. Prowls those woods. Talks to himself."

"Good-looking though."

"Yeah, but he's got them moony gray eyes—never looks straight at you. Gives me the creeps."

"Maybe it's because his head's a little crooked. Got mashed when he was born."

"That so? Funny I never noticed."

The thing that disturbed neighbors was not, however, to be found in the set of Harley's skull or in any single attribute. It was the solitude of Harley which aroused the distrust of the pack.

Toynbee Upjohn waited patiently in the Westcott library. He was not a man to waste time and life, so he sat on a window seat where he might read and still savor the air of the June morning. He wore a tailored white pinstripe with a pearl-gray vest, and a silver fob bearing the imprint of a serpent entwining a long, straight object and the head of a dog in a six-pointed star. His nails were manicured, and he smelt of his habitual musky cologne, a scent so strong one always knew that Upjohn was soon approaching or lately gone. His features were thin and alive with interest; he was not old, yet he did not seem young.

The sound of hoofbeats. Laddie's welcoming bark. Harley burst into the room, smoothing his thick, dark hair—so like Tobin's, so unfriendly to combs. "Sorry. I forgot the time."

Upjohn finished a paragraph and placed his bookmark. "Someday soon," he said, "you will have to remember the time." He looked long and seriously at Harley. He did that often, and it always drove Harley's eyes to the floor. "So. You are sixteen today. The number of perfection."

Harley tilted his head. "Really?"

"So witches and kabbalists and numerologists insist. How does it feel, being sixteen?"

The question was not the something-to-pass-the-time it would have been from another. But Harley was still considering the specialty of the number sixteen. He shrugged. "I don't know."

"You don't know?" Upjohn sprang to his feet with a litheness he seemed to reserve for startling his pupil. "Come, Harley, articulate! Or I shall know that my ten years of labor in the Westcott vineyard have been for naught."

"Well…" Harley lowered his eyes. According to his grandmother, who claimed she had looked at the clock just as she fainted, he had let out his first cry at 6:26 in the morning. Today was the sixth of the sixth month, 1926. Harley guessed he was the only one who'd ever been impressed by those numbers. He'd been waiting for this day for years, hoping—no, expecting—that something cataclysmic would occur. But nothing had occurred. He hadn't even spoken to Carrie. And if he mentioned his numbers to Upjohn, Upjohn would lecture him on the subject and make him write an essay entitled *A Critical Evaluation of the Merits of Numerology.* "I don't really feel any differently than I did when I was fifteen." He hoped that sounded reasonable enough to satisfy Upjohn. "And being sixteen isn't really special, is it? I don't think Mother is even giving me a party this year."

"No birthday party? What a shame. Well, don't let it worry you. I'm sure nothing bad will come of it."

"Why *should* anything bad come of not having a party?"

"It's just a superstition. There are those who consider a yearly observance of the birthday necessary to ensure life for another year."

"That's crazy!" said Harley. Lots of people didn't get birthday parties. Why last year, Dad—no, there'd been a cake for Dad, and for Mother and Grampa and everybody he could remember, actually.

Old people! There were thousands of old people in the world, family and friends dead, deserted, or uncaring. *They* didn't have parties. But then, old people died like flies. "Do you think there's any truth to it?"

"I don't know. I've always managed to have, for myself, a party of sorts."

Harley, searching his tutor's face for a glint of humor, found it. "You're pulling my leg."

"You're right," said Upjohn. "I'm sure parties aren't that important. Though some people would say not having a *cake* is a dangerous thing—especially for you."

Harley sighed, refusing to bite the second time. He got his books and seated himself at the desk. "Sixteen's too old to be upset about not having a party."

"My boy, I understand perfectly." Upjohn stopped behind Harley's chair and placed his hands on Harley's shoulders. "Have you finished reading Montague Summers?"

"I've got a few pages to go."

"Finish them and we'll discuss it."

They fell into silence, Upjohn reading on the window seat, Harley at the desk with Summers' *History of Witchcraft and Demonology*—until Upjohn glanced up and caught his pupil staring into space.

"Harley?"

Harley jumped. "Sorry."

"Have you finished? Where were you just now?"

"Nowhere."

"Harley, you are not a Yogi—I refuse to believe that your mind was a blank."

Harley shrugged. "I was just thinking about this morning. I rode by my Aunt Carrie's place."

"I know."

"You do?" said Harley.

"I was taking a stroll and happened to be near there."

Harley frowned, remembering Upjohn—cool, collected, and reading when he'd arrived for his lesson. Upjohn certainly could not have been "strolling" at Carrie's and then beaten him and Polly home. "Why didn't you say hello if you saw me?"

"I appreciate the solitude of my strolls. I assume that you also appreciate the solitude of your rides. You don't ever go into your aunt's home, do you?"

"Heck no, she'd never invite me in. I've always had the feeling..."

"What feeling?" said Upjohn.

Harley was silent, then he drew his breath. "That she hates me. That she's—evil." He stopped, then went on slowly. "Mr. Upjohn, do you believe there are evil things? I mean people *born* evil?"

Upjohn didn't smile. "I take it you think your aunt may be."

"I guess I do. Have you ever seen Aunt Carrie?"

"From a distance."

"Well, I guess you couldn't tell from a distance. The evil is in her eyes. But I'm not sure it is. I mean, I'm not sure I really see it in her eyes or whether I think I see it because Mother says it's there."

"What, exactly, does your mother say?"

"She says her papa always said, 'You gotta watch Carrie. She's evil. Born evil.' Exactly like that."

Upjohn smiled. "You're right. We can't be sure that what you sense is anything other than your mother's opinion, which is her *father's* opinion—and thus the world so often goes."

"But maybe Grampa Parmalee has good reason to believe that Carrie was born evil."

"Very possibly. Let's get on with our discussion of Summers. What do you think of his book?"

"I guess I think it's crazy. According to him all the people ever burned for witches were really witches, and everything they confessed was really true!"

"Well?"

"Well, you don't think that's the truth, do you?"

"Harley, according to Democritus, truth lies at the bottom of a well. Were I to look into that well and report to you what I saw, I would be describing my own image, my own truth. I want to hear *your* truth—and preferably in decipherable English."

Harley sighed. "I've read a great many opinions, both pro and con, on the subject of witchcraft—including facsimiles of actual documents and trial proceedings—and, after weighing the evidence, it's my opinion that the vast majority of persons killed during the persecutions were innocent of the charges leveled against them."

"I'll accept that. And well spoken! How did it feel?"

"What do you mean?"

"You uttered a sentence of more than ten words with no 'wells' or 'I guesses' or 'hecks.' How did you feel as you were speaking?"

Harley hesitated. He'd felt good. For a moment he had sounded, to himself, like Upjohn. "I felt...like a round, smooth stone, exhilarating down a hill."

Upjohn grimaced.

"What'd I do?"

"Besides inventing a new verb, you've mixed a metaphor. Stones cannot exhilarate, Harley. I'm willing to go along with your persistence in crediting animals and plants with feelings, but I draw the line at stones! Couldn't you have said that *you* felt as if you were 'exhilarating' down a hill?"

"No. Because I felt like I was a *round, smooth stone* exhilarating down a hill." Harley cocked his head. "I kind of like it. It's picturesque."

"It may be picturesque, Harley, but it is incorrect. Now. Where were we?"

Harley lowered his eyes, chastened. "Montague Summers."

Despite the increasing heat of the afternoon, they remained an hour past their classtime, Upjohn reading, Harley working on an essay.

At last Upjohn rose and went to the bank of bookcases to replace his book. He stopped just after he had done so, and, with a puzzled expression, waved his hand through the air before him.

Harley chanced to look up. "What's the matter?"

"There seems to be a draft here," said Upjohn.

Harley joined him and waved his own hand about. He shivered. "Where do you suppose it's coming from?"

"I don't know," said Upjohn. He started for the door. "I'd stay out of it if I were you. You might catch cold—or something worse."

Harley moved away from the cold spot. "Mr. Upjohn?"

Upjohn turned.

"What did you mean before, when you said it was especially important for *me* to have a birthday cake?"

Upjohn smiled. The humor was back in his eyes. "Some would say it is especially important for you to have a cake because you were born on the sixth of the month."

Did Upjohn know about his numbers? "What's so special about the sixth of the month?"

"The ancients believed the sixth of each month to be the birthday of the goddess of the moon, Artemis. And on that day they placed honeycakes upon her altar, round like the full moon, with lighted candles. You are a child of the moon, Harley. Do you sometimes feel odd when the moon is full?"

"Gosh, I don't know!"

"At any rate, your failure to have a cake might be taken as an affront to Artemis. And Artemis, when angered, is rumored to be less than reasonable. Of course, it's mythology." Upjohn smiled. "Don't work too late, Harley. Remember, it's your birthday."

There was, to Harley's relief, a party in the Westcott house that night. It was not really a birthday party. It was simply Grampa and Gramma Parmalee coming to dinner as they did almost every Saturday night, Gramma still clinging to floor-length dresses, high collars, and a massive, rat-filled pompadour; Grampa still stern and firm of opinion, but looking worse and worse from the "miseries" which had eaten at his vigor for six years.

It was Grampa Westcott, tipsy from sneaking "boot" throughout the day and everyone pretending not to notice.

It was Tobin, sitting impatiently through the main course and then excusing himself before dessert to go work in his office.

And it was no birthday cake, but a rhubarb pie, iced with ice cream and aflame with sixteen candles. "Grampa had his mouth set for a pie," Hitty explained. "I knew you wouldn't mind, Harley."

"'Course he doesn't mind," said Frank. "He's got a whole life of cakes in front of him. *I* might be dead tomorrow, the way I'm feeling lately."

Harley swallowed his resentment. "No, I don't mind." After all, the pie was round, like the full moon.

They retired to the drawing room after dinner. As usual, Harley was asked to play the piano.

A short, fast version of the "Blue Danube." Chopin would be a waste. Gramma Parmalee would say, "My, wasn't that a pretty tune," and Grampa Parmalee would grumble that he "didn't know a damn Polack could be so talented."

"Play Gershwin for an encore," urged Hitty as he finished.

"God damn it," said Frank, "doesn't he know any *American* music?"

Harley rose. "I'd rather not do an encore, Mother. May I be excused?"

"Let him go." Frank went to the piano and got his violin from its case. He smiled at Hitty. "We know what's a nice tune, don't we, daughter?"

The first notes of his grandfather's tune followed Harley into the candelabra-lit foyer—"My Beckoning Fair One," a haunting English folk thing in a minor key. Frank often played it for Hitty. It was "their" song, hers and Frank's, since Hitty had been a small girl. And it was the song that Carrie hummed over and over to herself as she worked alone in the walled garden she had built for herself.

Harley stopped. There was a dim light beneath the library too—and it was dancing. Tobin? Couldn't be—nothing could drag him away from his "cow-work." What, then? He went to investigate.

As he stepped into the room, he saw something by the bookcase, where the cold spot had been. A black form? face?—surrounded by a glow.

The door closed behind him. Harley reached for the handle. It wouldn't turn! He shot a look over his shoulder, flattened himself against the door.

"Harley, am I that frightening by candlelight?" It was Mr. Upjohn, his face distorted by the candle he carried. "Good heavens, Harley, you're pallid! Forgive me, there was no intent to frighten."

"You didn't."

Upjohn turned back to the bookcase and withdrew a book.

"Is that cold spot still there?"

"As a matter of fact, it is." Upjohn walked to the door, turned the handle, and opened it.

"Why didn't you turn on the lights to look for your book?" said Harley.

Upjohn flicked the light switch. Nothing happened. It was not unusual for a section to go out. The electricity that served Spring Farm was from Tobin's homemade power plant, and the mechanics of the system were, to say the least, erratic.

The strains of "My Beckoning Fair One" floated through the hall. Upjohn tilted his head. "A lovely tune," he murmured. "Your grandfather's health is no worse?"

"I don't think so."

"I'm glad. Well, good night, my boy. Sleep well." He disappeared through the door behind the stairs which led through the pantry to the servants' wing.

Could at least have said Happy Birthday, thought Harley. He mounted the stairs and rounded the gallery, reached his bedroom, and started to open the door—

There was a glow in the darkness of his room, too! He stretched out a toe and pushed the door completely open.

On his desk was the source of the glow. A cake, alight with sixteen candles. It was plain with no frosting, but it was round and it was definitely a cake. Harley opened the envelope propped beside it:

My boy,
I may not be a superstitious man, but I am a man who believes that a rhubarb pie is not grand enough for a boy's sixteenth birthday. You may eat this cake without trepidation, for I am not an unaccomplished baker (though Henrietta and the cook

feel I leave much to be desired). With it, I wish you and Artemis
another happy, healthy year.

And here is my gift to you. It is a parable on the subject
of personal truth—the kind of truth I would like you to
find—not accepting another's report of what lies in the well.
"One day Soshi was walking on the bank of a river with a
friend. 'How delightfully the fishes are enjoying themselves in
the water!' exclaimed Soshi. His friend spake to him thus:
'You are not a fish, how do you know that the fishes are
enjoying themselves?' 'You are not myself,' returned Soshi:
'how do you know that I do not know that the fishes are
enjoying themselves?'"

Your friend,
Toynbee Upjohn

Harley broke off a piece of the honeycake, then sat down
and read the parable again. At the end of the second reading, he
seized pen and paper:

Dear Mr. Upjohn,
I'm sure you know how grateful I am for the cake and for the
parable. I feel compelled to return the favor, not of the cake,
which would be a gastronomic disaster, but of the parable. It is
my gift to you upon the subject of personal truth, and it goes
thus: "One day Harley was walking through the fields with his
teacher. 'Did you see that round, smooth stone exhilarating
down the hill?' exclaimed Harley. His teacher spake to him
thus: 'You are not a stone, how do you know that a stone can
exhilarate?' 'You are not myself,' returned Harley. 'How do you
know that I do not know that stones can exhilarate?'"

Your pupil,
Harley Franklin Westcott

CHAPTER TWO

JUNE 6, 1926, moved on toward midnight. Hitty waved her parents off at the door and retired to her lavender-canopied bed. In his office, as usual, Tobin busied himself with paper work as he waited for Sailor, his overseer, to arrive with the butterfat and poundage reports from the last milking. The herd of champion Holsteins that Tobin had bred over the past two decades was milked four times a day, at five, eleven, five, and eleven.

In his room, Harley lay sleepless—or so it seemed to him. Yet at eleven when the putt-putt of the milking machine sounded, no flicker of awareness crossed his face.

Then his eyes opened. He'd heard a voice. No—a bell. "Harley. Listen to me."

Harley sat up. There was no one in the room.

He ran to the open French windows. Beyond the lawn, beyond Hitty's lilac jungle in the middle of the cobblestoned court, the main barn blazed with lights; and he heard the familiar sound of machinery being washed and put away. Funny he hadn't heard the milking machine running.

Then he heard the bell again.

"Harley. Listen to me."

It was coming from the lilacs in the middle of the court! Without thinking, Harley hopped over the balustrade, scaled the ivy to the ground, and ran toward the lilac bushes.

He stopped, suddenly uneasy.

He glanced toward the light coming from his father's office, toying with the idea of enlisting Tobin's aid. "Dad," he'd say. "I just heard a bell. It called my name. It's out in the lilac bushes. Would you please come help me look?"

But Tobin would get that disgusted look on his face. And he'd be thinking what Harley had heard him say to Grampa Westcott one day: "How I ever got such a sissy dreamer for a son, I'll never understand."

No use telling Tobin.

Harley brightened. "Sailor." The overseer was striding toward him.

"Mr. Harley? What are you doing out?"

"You see anything in the lilac bushes when you came past?"

"I didn't look."

"There's something in there. I heard it calling me just now."

Sailor laughed. "You been dreaming, Mr. Harley."

"Come on, help me look!"

Sailor followed and lit a cigar as Harley scoured the bushes. "Find anything?"

"What's going on here?" Tobin stood in the door of his office.

Harley stepped dutifully into the light. "I was sleep-walking, sir."

Tobin hesitated. Then he laughed. Harley shuffled uneasily. Tobin was not a laugher—a friendly Tobin was an ominous unknown. Like the bobcat Harley had surprised in the woods one day. Instead of running or acting mean, it had trotted toward him, purring. Harley had run away. But after a hundred yards he'd stopped. If that bobcat was acting friendly, it must be a friendly bobcat. Someone's pet, even—lost, lonely, maybe disappointed now. So he'd run back. But the bobcat was gone, and he never saw it again.

Now, Tobin leaned in the doorway, watching Harley—bobcat-friendly. "Better get back to bed," he said.

Cautiously, Harley mounted the stoop. Tobin did raise a hand, but only to touch Harley's shoulder. "Good night, son."

Harley didn't look back as he crossed the office, but once in the parlor, he stopped, nagged by remorse. Maybe the old man really wanted to be friendly.

Then he became aware of the dark silent parlor behind him. He turned, wondering if the cold spot in the library moved through the house at night. Suddenly he was eager to reach his bedroom. No use listening at Tobin's door. It didn't matter why the old man had laughed, or why he'd been friendly. He couldn't be trusted. Harley might have made friends with that bobcat; he could never make friends with his father. What's more, he didn't care to.

Tobin sat at his desk long after Sailor had gone, but his mind was not on business. He hadn't let on to Sailor—it would never do to let a hired hand see the hurt. But he wished Harley would come to *him* when he had a problem.

Where had it started, the strangeness between him and Harley? When had strangeness become so common that it was just the way things were?

It hadn't been there when—bloody, helpless—lost in the afghan...

Tobin had got a tea towel, dipped it in water, tried to clean him off. Flora had a conniption when she came to. *Darn fool man! Not supposed to use water!*

She'd taken Harley away, emptied his arms. She got a pot of bacon grease and smeared it on the baby.

You sure water wouldn't get him cleaner, Mrs. Parmalee?

Get out of here, Tobin. Leave babies to women.

Hitty. Sick and nervous so long after. Too sick and nervous to have either the baby or him sleeping with her. *We got to get a woman to tend after me and the baby and the house, Tobin—just temporary, till I get my strength back.*

Sixteen years Henrietta had been with them now. Maybe without her...

So nice, at first, to carry Harley into Hitty's room. To just sit and visit, Harley a mite in his arms.

Don't know what drives me up a tree most, that baby's fussing or watching you hold him. Henrietta! Come get Harley!

Should have argued. So many times he should have argued. But, hell, Harley had always been sick with one thing or another.

Farm was growing. Building the new house, the new barn. Tired most of the time. Of course, he could have taken him along more often when he worked, but Harley was always knocking something over or getting the stock worked up. That meant bawling him out and sending him back to the house.

Then Tobin would watch him walking away. He always looked so small—a little kid walking away like that, the loneliest-looking thing in the world.

And that's when the strangeness had started. Because he'd wanted to call him back. Instead he'd lied to himself. *There'll be time when he's older.*

Now, he ought to tell Harley—*Next time, son, come to your father.*

"Sleepwalking!" Tobin laughed out loud. "Damn, but he gets more like his mother every day!"

He pictured her upstairs in that grand canopied bed, adorable in lacy white, sleeping without covers.

"Sleepwalking!"

He rose and hurried to his room; put on his nightshirt and splashed on cologne. Maybe she wouldn't be angry when he woke her. Maybe she'd laugh when he told her about Harley. Maybe she'd even let him make love. It had been April, last time.

She lay just as he'd imagined. He drew up a chair. For a while, he'd just sit and look.

Tobin had never quite recovered from marrying Mehitable Parmalee. After nineteen years he still acted as though she was an art treasure on loan.

The social elite of the village of Oriskany Forks consisted of eight Founding Families—the Hortons, Coles, Coopers, Hamlins, Arnolds, Comstocks, Woodins, Parmalees. It was accepted that the offspring of these families would find mates inside their own circle. Only the Parmalees and Coles, as a result of long-standing animosity, never intermarried; until the marriage of Tobin and Hitty, only one couple in one hundred and thirteen years had broken that tradition—Hitty's parents, Flora Cole and Frank Parmalee, of the feuding families.

The gossip had, no doubt, been true. Nothing in the world would have forced Jason Cole to give his daughter Flora to a Parmalee unless Flora was in the family way by that Parmalee. And though Hitty's sister Carrie was born an almost-respectable seven and a half months after the marriage, and though claims of prematurity clouded the calculations of village matrons, the actions of the principals in the affair spoke for themselves. Frank Parmalee never made any bones about the resentment he bore his wife, his first daughter, and the whole parcel of Coles—especially Jason, though no one could be sure whether that resentment was because he'd found himself stuck with Flora or because of Jason Cole's curse.

The curse had been pronounced the day Carrie was born.

Doc Barnes, Sr., heard it when he came down to the parlor of the old Cole home with the newborn Carrie in his arms. Flora's mother heard it, thin and pale after months of illness, tucked beneath a crazy-quilt comforter in the old parlor rocker. So did Flora's best friend, Hadassah Horton, and Flora's second-best friend, Sarah Cooper.

They were there, the two girls and Flora's parents, in a little knot on one side of the Cole parlor. Frank Parmalee was on the other side, staring out at the early November snowstorm enshrouding the woods.

As Hadassah told the story, Doc Barnes hesitated as he came into the room, not knowing who should see the baby first. Then he went to the father. "It's a girl, Frank. Flora's just fine."

"And Frank hardly even looked around, just mumbled something nasty." Though old Doc Barnes always claimed that what Frank had mumbled was "Thank God," and that he'd kept his back turned because he was crying, Doc Barnes had not been the talker that Hadassah Horton was and his version didn't get much circulation.

Then, according to Hadassah, Doc brought Carrie to her grandparents. "Jason Cole reached out and took that baby in his arms. Well, you know, the Coles and Parmalees are cousins to start with—and they're all fair, every last one of them. But there was Carrie. Dark! I got goose pimples all over my arms before Jason even spoke, that's how spooky-looking that baby was!

"Old Jason just stood there, looking down at her. 'This is a child of darkness,' he finally said. Then he turned and looked right at Frank. 'You've killed my wife,' he says to Frank. I don't know how poor Mrs. Cole liked hearing that. It's true she got sick right after hearing Flora was in the family way, but she wasn't exactly *dead* yet, and when she did die a few weeks later, it was like she was doing it so as not to make a liar out of Jason.

'You killed her with the shame you've visited upon her,' he said, 'and you've blackened the honor of our daughter.'"

Sarah Cooper, who was the second-best friend of Flora, maybe with good reason, was not exactly charitable when she came to this particular part of the story. Sarah stood up for Frank. "If Flora's father had known how Flora schemed to get Frank. Meeting him in those gloomy old woods and all. If you ask me, Flora Cole blackened her *own* honor."

At least Sarah and Hadassah were in accord when it came to Jason's curse. "This child will be my vengeance," he said. "This child will be your death, Frank Parmalee."

"Didn't even make a dent in Frank," said Hadassah. "He just laughed. Then he got his coat and charged out into the storm. An hour later he was back with Tom Edwards' covered delivery wagon. 'I'm taking my wife and daughter home,' he said. And he did—in the middle of a snowstorm, Flora just delivered and Carrie barely oiled. Could of killed them both. Oh, he's a hard man, that Frank Parmalee," Hadassah would say.

But though Jason's curse intrigued the villagers, it really hadn't mattered to them whether Frank and Flora were in love, whether Carrie was premature, or how Jason Cole might curse. Flora and Frank were both of Founding Families. The social balance remained undisturbed.

So it was that when twenty-year-old Tobin Westcott— already on the way to being a successful farmer, but not of the Founding Families—attended a dance in Marve Short's new barn in the fall of 1906, took a long look at his seventeen-year-old neighbor Hitty Parmalee, and fell in love with her, he regarded his adoration as a disease that must be borne but never cured.

The dance was held in the hayloft, fragrant with the newness of pine. The glow of kerosene lamps lit cider and dough-nuts at the perimeter of the dance floor. Laughter and sounds of dancing feet filled the loft. But the loudest and most energetic sound of all was the sound of Frank Parmalee's yellow violin.

Tall and lean, with a hooked nose and stinging blue eyes, Frank laughed and stomped, his bow arm a blur. Dancers ignored perspiration and fatigue, determined to keep up with Frank as long as he could keep up with himself.

But Tobin, alone on the edge of the floor, heard not a note.

Always after, when Tobin tried to recall how Hitty had looked that night, he couldn't. He remembered only a lilac-and-white glow under honey-colored hair; bobbing, swaying, lighting the room more successfully than all the kerosene lamps put together.

Her dance card was filled, not a name repeated. Yet not once did she dance with Tobin; not once that he could be sure of did she even look at him.

And by not doing so, he thought, she displayed her good taste. Oh, he was taller than most, and well-built. Some people called him handsome. But it was an unfaceted handsomeness that failed to interest even Tobin.

Into his line of vision came Hitty's eighteen-year-old sister, Carrie, crossing from her chair to the punch table and—he never knew quite how it happened, he must have asked her—she was dancing with him, bringing him closer to Hitty.

And then—again, unaccountably—he had asked Hitty's sister if he might come calling, and she was leading him through the crowd to the podium where Frank was preparing to strike up another tune.

Why, Tobin still wondered, had he asked to call on Carrie? He hadn't wanted to. But there were her eyes on him, paralyzing if you looked too long...

"Papa," she said, "Tobin would like to come calling on me. Is it all right?"

Frank's eyes swept Tobin. "Evening, Tobin. Your father well?"

"Still got the arthritis pretty bad."

"Sorry to hear it. You sure you want to call on Carrie?"

He said it in a way that Tobin found cruel—as though Carrie wasn't even standing there, as though she had no feelings—and Tobin answered with more gusto than he'd planned, "Yes, sir! I do."

Frank shrugged. "You got my permission." And without another glance he put his bow to the violin and began to play "My Beckoning Fair One."

Carrie stiffened and turned away.

She's crying, thought Tobin.

Then she looked up at Frank. Her eyes were glittering, but not from tears.

"Shall we dance again, Miss Carrie?"

"No," she said. "Never to this tune until those two are dead."

Tobin followed her to the punch table. He'd misunderstood; she couldn't have said that. Besides, without Carrie...

For nearly a year, Tobin made a weekly trip to the Parmalee house on the other side of the woods, looking forward to each visit with anticipation and guilt. It wasn't fair to visit Carrie just to catch some glimpse of Hitty's face.

As the year wore on, it began to seem even more unfair. Where at first Tobin had been only one of several young men who called on Carrie, he found now that he was the *only* young man who called on Carrie. She began to pronounce his name differently. Flora began to greet him with so much warmth that it embarrassed him, and he was invited to dinner once a week.

It was obvious that Flora and Carrie expected him to propose. Would Frank allow it? And did he *want* to marry Carrie?

Those were the questions in Tobin's mind as he rode away from the Parmalee home one night in late summer of 1907. The moon was full, the night warm. He settled back, put his feet on the dash, and let Jefferson head for his stall.

Carrie. Beautiful, quiet, a listener. A man wanted that in a wife. Of course, he didn't *feel* anything for her, except...He looked over at the woods. Carrie's eyes were like those woods.

Jefferson shied. "Whoa!"

"Evening, Tobin." Hitty Parmalee stood square in the middle of the road. "Goodness, Tobin, close your mouth. You'll let the flies in." Hitty executed a pirouette. "Isn't it the most beautiful night you ever saw?" She swung around again, arms raised to the stars, oblivious to Tobin and to the fact that she wore nothing but a nightgown.

"Miss Hitty, you oughtn't to be out like that. You'll catch cold."

Hitty swayed in the moonlight, her hair tumbling over her breasts, her eyes amused at Tobin's furtive glances. "I might catch something, I just might at that." She extended her arms in a stretch and began to spin again; waltzing, humming, a marble Venus come to life.

"Miss Hitty! What in hell are you doing?"

Hitty stopped. "I'm taking a walk, if it's any business of yours."

"Miss Hitty, ladies don't take walks in their nightgowns."

"Tobin Westcott, you implying I'm not a lady?"

"Of course not, Miss Hitty, but—"

"But nothing!" Hitty's hands went to her hips. "You come charging up the road interrupting my solitude, then you insult me. A body hasn't any privacy anymore!" She turned and flounced down the road. Then she squealed. "You made me turn my ankle!"

Tobin's throat went dry.

"Well, for goodness sake, don't just sit there, Tobin. Come get me and put me in the buggy!"

Slowly Tobin climbed down and walked to Hitty's side. Slowly he lifted her, slowly carried her to the buggy and set her upon the seat.

"Now drive me home," said Hitty. She crossed one leg over the other and began to bounce her foot.

Tobin turned Jefferson back toward Parmalees'. Hitty's foot kept bouncing, her naked ankle flashing. Tobin pulled at his collar and kept his eyes on the road.

Hitty began to hum.

"Shut up."

Hitty drew in her breath. "Tobin Westcott! Don't you talk to me that way."

She was playing games with him. She knew damned well he wouldn't touch her, so she was having her fun. "You weren't out for a walk. You came out just to tease me!"

"I did not."

"You did so."

"You calling me a liar?"

"Yes."

Hitty's foot pumped angrily now. "All right. If you're going to call me names I'll tell you a thing or two. You're deceitful, Tobin Westcott."

"Me?"

"Yes *you!* You've been in love with me since the night of Marve Short's barn dance!"

Heat attacked Tobin's collar at its tightest point.

"You've been courting Miss Icy-Eyes when all the time it was me you wanted. If that's not deceit, I don't know what is."

"I haven't been deceitful," Tobin said. "I'm planning to ask for Carrie's hand."

"Well you're a fool if you do. She's evil. Papa says so."

"Who the hell *do* you want me to marry? You?"

"Ha!" said Hitty. "I wouldn't marry you if you were the last man on earth. Let me out of this buggy!"

Tobin pulled Jefferson to a halt. "I thought you had a sprained ankle."

"I wished it away," said Hitty, and leaped nimbly to the ground. She walked a few feet, then turned back. "The moonlight drive was lovely, Tobin. Carrie's going to be very interested."

"Don't you dare tell Carrie!"

Hitty laughed and started up the road.

Tobin sprang from the buggy; Hitty took to her heels at a most unfeminine speed.

Tobin finally caught her just at the spot where woods met Parmalee lawn. He spun her about.

"Don't you dare kiss me, Tobin. I'll call my papa if you do!"

Tobin tried to slow his breathing. "You're not going to get kissed," he said. With a deft movement he lifted her, knelt, and swung her over one knee.

"Tobin!" cried Hitty.

"What the hell is going on here?"

In the door of the outhouse stood Frank Parmalee, in nightshirt and stockingcap, staring at Tobin's hand poised over his daughter's nightgowned backside.

Then Frank began to laugh. "Tobin, I should shake your hand. I been meaning to tan that girl's behind for years now."

"But Papa!" Hitty wiggled free. "You don't understand. I was sleepwalking and Tobin found me and he tried to kiss me—"

"Very sensible of him."

"Sir, she's lying. I was on my way home and—"

"You don't have to tell me, Tobin. I know my daughter well enough to piece it together. And in a way I'm glad it happened. I've done some checking on what you've been up to since you bought your dad's place, young man. You're a good match. You'll be able to support a wife in real style. I'll be honest with you, I'd rather not waste you on Carrie."

"Papa!"

"You mean you'd let me marry *Hitty?*"

"If you love her."

"I do! I do love her!" And then Tobin stopped. Carrie stood in the shadows of the porch.

"Tobin," she said.

"Get back in the house," said Frank.

Carrie stepped off the porch. She was wearing a gown like Hitty's, but Carrie was no marble-Venus-come-to-life; she was a stark silhouette. Her face was in darkness, and Tobin felt, rather than saw, her eyes. "I love you, Tobin. Don't do this. I won't be responsible for what happens if you do."

"Don't go threatening Tobin," said Frank, but his voice held fear.

"You don't love Hitty, Tobin," said Carrie. "You love me."

Her eyes! Tobin could see them now, and the warmth of the night turned chill.

"Tell them. You love *me*, Tobin."

And then Hitty took Tobin's arm. "You already heard him say who he loves, Carrie. And I think Papa's right. He'll support me in real comfort. I'll marry him if he wants me to."

Carrie turned those eyes on Hitty. "Do you love him?"

"I guess I could put up with him," said Hitty with a toss of the head.

Carrie turned to Tobin. "Is that what you want? Someone to put up with you for your money?"

"I love Hitty, Carrie." Tobin's voice was barely a whisper. "I'll take her however I can get her."

Carrie smiled. "Then I guess you've got her. Enjoy it while you can." She turned and walked, not back to the house, but toward the woods.

"Caroline! Get into the house!" She disappeared among the trees.

The woods had seemed especially silent as Tobin drove home that night. They had seemed to have eyes.

But they'd been watching now for nineteen years, and Tobin had never once regretted his choice. Oh, maybe Hitty wasn't the most loving wife in the world, but *his* love made up for her lack. And Hitty was happy. He'd built her this house and given her everything she ever asked for. She, in return, was Hitty, and Tobin was content with that.

He leaned forward now, and touched her shoulder. She stirred. "Tobin, mmmmm, you smell good. Oh-h-h!" Her hand went to her forehead. "I have such a headache."

"I'm sorry," he said. "Go back to sleep."

"Tobin?"

"Yes."

"You can sleep here and rub my back if you promise that's all. I really do have a dreadful headache.

Tobin got into bed. It would be something, at least. Her back was warm and lithe.

"That's nice." Hitty wiggled. "Don't stop till I'm asleep. You have such gentle hands."

He rubbed patiently. A sliver of moonlight fell across the cascade of Hitty's hair—no longer honey-colored, for it had turned pearl-white just after Harley's birth.

Tobin didn't mean to fall asleep, but he did. He was awakened by Hitty's small hand passing down his chest. He jumped.

"Tobin? I've been trying to wish my headache away."

For a moment that made no sense. Then it did. "Is it still there?"

"Yes."

He rolled over and kissed her gently. "Any better?"

"Maybe a little."

Tobin grinned. "We'll get that headache wished away if it takes all night!"

CHAPTER THREE

"MORNING," SAID HENRIETTA.

Harley paused at his mother's door and eyed the breakfast trays being removed from the dumbwaiter. "Any cinnamon buns?"

"We'll see." Which meant there were. Harley smiled and opened the door.

Then he stopped.

Tobin, in dressing gown and slippers, was lounging on the newly made bed.

"What are *you* doing here?" said Harley.

"I live here," said Tobin.

Harley went to the dressing table and kissed his mother's cheek. All the good, familiar scents were there—the lilac, the smell of her warm hair and the curling iron.

But there was something else this morning. A smell or a feeling? Either way, it was Tobin—his presence, clinging to Hitty.

From the open French windows came a familiar squawk. Genevieve, the blue jay.

Hitty's cat, Fluffy, glanced up and yawned. As a kitten, Fluffy had made the mistake of trying to catch Genevieve; she bore the scars still and ignored the bird even when it joined her for a bowl of milk.

"Good morning, Genevieve!" Hitty's voice was uncommonly cheerful. "What would you say if I told you I shan't give you a crumb this morning?"

The blue jay cocked its head and squawked something nasty.

Hitty laughed and began to hum, never taking her gaze from the mirror as her small white hands twirled the curling iron, and her fingers scampered through the mass of curls. Twice a day, before breakfast and supper, Hitty curled her hair. It was at these times, and only these times, that Harley was welcome in her room. He had always been allowed to sit and watch or talk, or, as he'd grown older, play an occasional game of chess when she finished—so long as he did not touch anything breakable, or Hitty's hair.

This morning it would all be spoiled.

He glared at Tobin. Tobin's pasty white legs were sticking out beneath his dressing gown. How could Hitty have done it? How could she have let Tobin and those hairy legs into bed with her? For he knew his mother and father had slept together last night. He'd heard Tobin enter this room, and he *hadn't* heard him come out.

And he knew what they'd been doing all night long. He'd first read about it in the *McCauley's Marriage Manual* he found in the attic, and Sailor had confirmed the disgusting truth.

"Of course your Ma and Pa do that," he'd said. "What's the matter? Can't stand to think of your Ma taking off her clothes and letting your Pa stick his dinglehopper inside her? Gets us all at first. Don't go walking away now. You asked me, and I'm answering. Though your Pa should have tended to this long ago. I guess he thought you'd have it long-figured, what with all the animals doing it before your very nose."

"But—"

"I know," Sailor had said. "Animals are one thing, parents another. Especially mothers. You don't look at Locust Leaf Aaggie Veeman staggering under old Cornie and figure that Ma and Pa would do something like that for the fun of it. But, Harley, I'm sad to tell you—"

How, Harley wondered now, could Hitty and Tobin face him without embarrassment if they'd done that last night? How could Hitty giggle and feed Genevieve? He headed for the door.

"Where are you going?" said Hitty.

"To saddle Polly. Will you be ready soon?"

"Yes. But don't you want your eggs at least?"

"Give them to Genevieve."

Hitty cast a doubtful glance at Genevieve. "I'm sure she wouldn't eat them. That would be cannibalistic."

"Hitty," said Tobin, "when you're not feeding her crackers, she likes nothing better than some other bird's eggs."

"Genevieve wouldn't do a thing like that!"

"Lots of things do things you never think they'd do," said Harley.

That would fix them, even if they didn't know what he was talking about.

Harley descended the stairs, testing the banister for dust. In the library Thomas Westcott and Mr. Upjohn stood before a table littered with books.

"Harley," said Mr. Upjohn. "I'm trying to explain to your grandfather that unicorns have no being on the plane of reality."

"Don't tell me they got no being," said Thomas. "I *seen* one of 'em once, right here on this farm."

"You must have seen it after an attack of arthritis, Thomas."

"I hadn't had a drop!"

"You probably saw a drawing and then only thought you saw a real one. I, myself, have often seen drawings of unicorns."

"Well, that just shows you," said Thomas. "How could anybody draw it if nobody's ever seen one?"

"Harley, should we try to convince your grandfather that unicorns are purely spiritual creatures?"

"Oh, I don't know," Harley teased. "That may be *your* truth, but I thought I saw a unicorn up on the Crazy Lizzy just last month."

"Hah!" said Thomas. "How do you like that, Upjohn? Must've been the same one I seen."

Upjohn shrugged. "I see you have arrived at a truth of your own, Harley. You believe in unicorns. If Tobin is raising horse-like cattle with horns on their foreheads, then so be it. Are you and your mother going into town?"

"Yes. Want a ride?"

"No. I'll walk. The exercise will do me good."

Harley watched him go. Each Sunday morning Mr. Upjohn asked the same question, and each Sunday morning he declined the ride, saying the walk would do him good. Where he walked to, in his white pinstripe and derby and the dangling fob, was a mystery that had never been solved to anyone's satisfaction.

"You and your mother leaving soon?" asked Thomas.

Harley's grandfather was a wisp of a man with wild gray hair, a drooping moustache, and sad brown eyes. They were sadder than usual now, for, as Harley knew, Thomas was waiting for everyone to leave the house so he could ease his arthritis. To do that, he had to get his bottle of boot out of the springs of Hitty's parlor settee.

"Go in and get it," said Harley. "I'll keep watch."

"Can't," Thomas said. "Colleen's in there, chatting with her wee people and dusting. Fool woman. Such a thing as being too clean." He sighed. "I'll wait until your mother leaves, then Colleen will go upstairs to dust."

"But Dad's still upstairs," said Harley.

"Oh," said Thomas. He winked. "Must've been a jim-dandy to keep Tobin out of the barn."

Harley turned to go.

"Harley? Could you take your camera along next time you go up to the Crazy Lizzy? It would sure fix Upjohn's little red wagon if we got a snapshot of that unicorn. There's got to be a first time for everything, you know."

The morning air was comfortable, but heavy white clouds hung in the sky. There would be thundershowers before evening. Laddie rose from his post by the front steps, wagged his tail, and followed his master down the court to the cow barn.

It was an imposing structure, built to Tobin's specifications fourteen years before, as the new house had been built to Hitty's. At the right of the main door were twin silos; to the left, Tobin's power plant. The main nave beneath the second floor haymow was divided into two sections. First came the milk house and the stalls—fifteen-foot cubicles with padded walls, straw-covered floors, and polished oak doors bearing brass nameplates. Here were kept Pontiac Lass, who'd set a world's record of 44.15 pounds of butterfat in seven days, and seven of her sisters and cousins. The farthest section contained fifty stanchions for the rest of the herd, pure-breds all, differing from their pampered sisters only in a pound or even a fraction of a pound of butterfat production.

The right side of the barn was buttressed by the bull shed. Ten pens, like those which housed Pontiac Lass and her sisters, stretched its length. Doors on the rear wall opened into hundred-foot runs with high concrete walls, each with an iron gate at the end. At one end of the corridor that stretched along the front of the pens, a fenced walkway led to the paddock Sailor called "Hump Hollow," where the bulls met their appointed mates; at the other was a chute for loading bulls into trucks.

Harley entered and walked the length of the corridor, greeting each bull in turn; grand, thick animals with mean eyes, and noses continually running where the iron ring passed through.

Harley had always loved the barn. When he was little, it had seemed the most wonderful place in the world—maybe because he was so seldom allowed in it.

There'd been Sailor, milking, pointing the teat at Harley's open mouth, filling it with warm milk, and never a dribble or a miss; the tester with his funny little jiggers and scales; the clank of the stanchions and the rustling of the cattle in the straw; the banter of the men as they went about their work; the scent, warm and strangely comforting; the champions, curried till they shone, munching endless alfalfa and grain, with a man standing by to remove their manure as it dropped.

He had loved those cows. He wanted to pet them. *Keep away from those cows, Harley. You rile them up and they'll go off their milk.*

He'd wanted to play with the calves. *I catch you near those calf pens again, I'll tan your hide. That's valuable livestock.*

But the bull shed had always been the best part of the barn. There was the thing he'd seen coming out of Spring Farm King Cornucopia's belly one day—red and wet and throbbing, over a foot long. *Get away from those bulls!* Harley, sent in to his mother, had sneaked back again and again to watch.

Then, when Harley was ten, he'd made friends with Cornie's grandson, K.P. Spring Farm King. King was a two-year-old at the time, gentle, with small mustard-colored eyes and, as Harley found out the day King snatched a candy bar from his hand, a sweet tooth.

Harley stole candy, cookies, anything he could lay his hands on, and he gave them to King when his father wasn't watching; until one night as he was feeding King jawbreakers, a hand closed on his shoulder and spun him around. *How long you been feeding King candy?*

Harley began to cry.

Your mother's right. You don't belong here. That bull's worth ten of you, and I can't have you feeding him candy.

But Harley had never stopped slipping sweets to King. It was one of the few ways he could get back at his father.

This morning, he took especial pleasure in his treachery.

Sweets for the horses had never been forbidden. At the stable, Harley made his way down the aisle, favoring each. Rose, Hitty's former carriage horse, was the favorite. Jet black, with a streak of mischief that at times seemed human. You never simply handed Rose a lump of sugar. You braced yourself, and proceeded with caution. Today Rose merely accepted it with a flip of velvet lips. "How polite we are!" said Harley.

Rose nickered.

Harley turned to go, then stopped in his tracks as Rose sank her teeth into his jacket. He looked up into the limpid eyes. "Let go."

Rose shook her head, tugging at Harley's jacket until the buttons strained.

"Let go, Rose!"

It would be easy enough to unbutton the jacket and slip out, but the last time he'd tried that, Rose had dragged it into the stall, dropped it on a clump of manure, and stomped on it.

Harley waved a cube of sugar. "Want it?"

Rose eyed the sugar, eyed Harley, then made a grab. Harley, the jacket, and the sugar moved quickly out of reach.

"You about ready?" Tobin stood in the door of the stable.

"I'll have Polly saddled in a minute."

Tobin nodded and disappeared.

The stable was quiet as Harley slipped the bridle with the silver "P" into place. The saddle was on and the girth tightened when Harley looked up to find Tobin standing there with his hands in his pockets. "She still got the sore on her fetlock?"

"That healed a month ago."

"Oh. Good."

Harley led Polly from the stall. Tobin followed.

"Is something wrong?" Harley asked.

"Everything's fine." Tobin kept following. "What time you think you'll be back from town?"

"About three, I guess." Harley mounted. "Why?"

"I'm gonna paint the storage shed at Crazy Lizzy this afternoon. Thought you might like to come up and talk when you get back."

"Why?"

Harley suddenly wished he hadn't said that.

"No reason. Forget it. I'll get the car for your mother."

Tobin brought the Stevens-Duryea around front; Hitty came down the steps, her parasol raised for the brief trip in the sun. She kissed Tobin's cheek. "Don't work too long, dear."

"I won't."

He would. He always did.

Hitty put the big black automobile into gear. It lurched away down the avenue of maples, with Harley behind. They'd gone a hundred feet when Harley reined in.

Tobin was still standing by the porch. "If it's not too late when we get back," Harley called, "I will come up." Without waiting for a reply, he cantered after the Duryea.

Polly rarely had to exert herself to keep up with the automobile. Hitty's maximum cruising speed of fifteen miles per hour was attained only when she was late, which she almost never was. She allowed herself a good hour to drive the four miles to town and then chat with the ladies at the Presbyterian Bench before church.

The drive, at this time of year, was always a pleasure for both of them. Hitty drove with her window open, waving to friends, exclaiming over flowers, driving now on the right, now on the left, now in the middle as the fancy took her. There was little danger; in 1926, there were fewer than fifty motorcars among the 5,021 inhabitants of Oriskany Forks, and on College Road only the Westcotts and Carrie owned one.

So it was that when Hitty spied a model-T now approaching, she said, "Well! I'd like to know who's that gallivanting around on a Sunday morning. A body's not safe on her own road anymore."

The model-T, however, seemed to be making arrangements for Hitty's safety. It pulled to the side of the road.

Suddenly Harley spurred Polly ahead of the Duryea, placing himself between his mother and the other car. It was silly, of course. Why should he fear for his mother? Carrie would just sit there and stare at them until they passed.

Which is exactly what she did. Her gaze did not falter, not even when Hitty waved.

But as Harley and his mother continued toward town, he knew without looking back that Carrie's car was still at the side of the road, that her gaze was still following them, and that her expression *had* changed.

Franklin College crowned the hill on the west side of the valley in which Oriskany Forks nestled. It was a school for young men of means; in two years that would include Harley, who would automatically become one of those "fast" college men from whom village daughters were so zealously guarded.

Hitty and Harley wound their way down the steep hill, past the rambling Victorian fraternity houses with the Greek letters and spacious gardens. At the edge of town, College Road widened. Here the side walks began, and the two- and three-story frame houses emptied their inhabitants into the tree-lined streets for the weekly stroll to the churches on the square.

Until a few years back, the ritual stroll had been unexciting, especially for the men who attended church. But that era came to an abrupt end the Sunday that Hitty Westcott parked her Stevens-Duryea at the curb, opened the door, extended two shapely legs in silk stockings, and sauntered toward the Presbyterian Bench wearing a sleeveless lavender chemise *an inch above the middle of the knee.*

No one, of course, dared condemn Mehitable Parmalee Westcott to her face, and few of the women could stand to let Hitty be the town's only fashion plate. So, one by one, in the months that followed, hemlines, with the exception of Maybelle Horton's and her clique's, crept upward from midcalf. Harve Woodin was rumored to have made fifty dollars in bets by predicting whether a woman would have knobby or shapely knees.

"Did you see Sally Cooper?" Hitty said as Harley handed her from the car. "Just below the knee. Maybelle will be fit to be tied!" She peered back down College Road. "When Sally gets here I'm going to raise the roof about how marvelous she looks. Are you coming to church with me?"

"No." Hitty asked every week, but she had long ago resigned herself to the fact that Harley was practically agnostic. "I'll meet you at the library," said Harley.

Hitty smiled. "I think you'd better give me an hour, then pick me up at Sally Cooper's house," and she hurried toward her friends, bearing the news of Sally's approaching hemline.

Despite the stir among those ladies, despite the quarreling church-bells, the village square was peaceful. Trees canopied the walks and benches, the Founders' Stone, and tablets to the Civil War dead, the Spanish War dead, and the Great War dead. The fountain, a product of the cultural campaign of 1899, boasted a nymph, naked but neuter, who spouted water from her laurel leaves whenever her plumbing was in order. Periodically, puberty-stricken boys painted the nymph's crotch red, but the Ladies' League kept a supply of dull green paint on hand.

The Presbyterian Bench was near the Founders' Stone, on which were inscribed the eight family names of the ladies who occupied that bench each Sunday morning. That the Parmalee name came last was no accident. It was, in fact, the cause of the Parmalee-Cole feud.

The first seven Oriskany Forks families had begun to clear land in May of 1794. That July, Amelia Horton and Amadasah Cole decided that the names of the founding families should be carved on a stone in the new square. The decision had hardly been made when the Parmalees, who had been detained by illness, arrived in an ox-drawn wagon.

"Johnnys-lately-come," said the Coles and Hortons. "Their name shouldn't be on the stone."

The matter was decided by a secret ballot among the first seven families. A white bean in Amelia Horton's butterchurn meant "Yes, put the Parmalees on the stone," and a black bean meant "No." When the votes were cast, the bean-counter found

five white and two black beans in the churn. It was easy to
guess who those black beans belonged to.

The animosity between Parmalees and *Coles* might not
have been so intense, however, were it not for the fact that when
Hezekiah Cole chiseled his cousins' name on the stone it came
out wrong. Hezekiah smiled when informed of the error. "I
thought you spelled it 'Parma*lee*' Cousin Tom."

"We didn't," said Thomas Parma*ly*, "but we will." And thus
began a century of getting one up on the other.

After the marriage of Flora Cole and Frank Parmalee,
and especially after Jason Cole's death in 1909, things
simmered down. The Hortons, however, got stuck with
displaced Parmalee animosity for their suspected role in the
bean affair. It seemed to Harley that every time he heard the
story, the role of the Hortons got bigger and blacker. He had
no doubt that before long they'd be saying that only the
Hortons had opposed putting the Parmalees on that stone,
that there had been only one black bean, a Horton bean, and
that it had been a Horton who carved the Parmalee name
wrong.

At the library Harley tethered Polly in the shade, knocked at the
side door, and waited for Cyrus Hamlin. Cousin Cyrus had
been librarian since 1871 and was seldom to be found outside
that building. He enjoyed Harley's Sunday visits; Harley knew
how to treat a book.

Arthritic fingers fumbled with the lock, and the door
opened. "Step lively," said Cyrus. "Don't want to let the heat in."
But at that moment Harley caught a movement out of the corner
of his eye. Right in front of the library, a young girl was
watching him.

"Come on, Lil," someone called. "We'll be late."

"Coming, Cass." The girl's eyes met Harley's. She lifted a slender arm and impatiently flipped the heavy red hair from her neck.

"Lilith! Don't dawdle!"

"Yes, Papa."

The girl turned and hurried after her family; Harley shrugged and stepped into the library.

CHAPTER FOUR

THE BASCOMBS

AT SIX THAT morning Lil Bascomb had opened her eyes to find Cass already out of bed and naked by the open window, her long dark hair only half concealing her breasts.

Rubbing it in, that's what she was doing. "Where's your nightgown?"

"On the lawn, where I threw it. I wanted to be unfettered."

"Cassie!" Lil sat up. "Are you playing fairies?"

Cass's blue eyes widened and she flushed. "I didn't think. I just—I'm sorry, Lil. She moved to the dresser for a concealing garment.

Lil sighed at the fullness disappearing into her sister's petticoat. At fifteen, Cass was Coke-ad pretty, and shaped like the pictures the boys passed around at school. Lil, at sixteen, was a tall skinny collection of disjointed parts with no bosom worth the mentioning.

Cass was giggling now.

"What's the matter?"

"There is nothing more beautiful in God's green earth than the sight of a young, healthy body," said Cass.

"You sound just like her." Cass was good at things like that.

"Poor Aunt Alice, I wonder where she is now."

Cass plopped onto the bed. "Probably chasing a new husband around a woodpile somewhere."

Paul Bascomb's eight children, including one son, Curt, had been born over a twenty-year period. He was a wandering man, Paul Bascomb; but somehow, no matter where he moved, Aunt Alice moved with him, dragging her husband Harry along.

Paul's oldest girls, Jane and Laura, had been the first initiates to Aunt Alice's game of "fairies"; then Milly, Mary, and Susan; finally Lil and Cass.

The first few times it was just that Aunt Alice loved to watch them undress. "Beautiful, beautiful," she would say, "there is nothing more beautiful in God's green earth than the sight of a young, healthy body."

Then came the night when Aunt Alice shed her own clothes. "Come, my young bodies! We're to the woods!" And off she flew, her dark hair tumbling about her healthy shoulders, her nieces shivering and whimpering behind her. "We're fairies," Alice would cry, "dancing in our sylvan glade."

The girls tried hard to copy Aunt Alice's movements, casting embarrassed glances at Harry watching at the back door.

"Look at the moon. We're unfettered! Daughters of Artemis!"

Once Milly had complained to her mother. Emma told her she must have had a bad dream. Paul washed out Milly's mouth with soap, both for having and daring to repeat such a dirty dream, and no one ever complained again.

Cass and Lil had finally been delivered from Aunt Alice's games by an incident they never understood. They had spent the night at her home and were to be picked up by their father after breakfast. Aunt Alice, as usual, made pancakes.

Harry was in a bad mood.

"Alice," he said, "I gotta tell you something. Your pancakes stink." He picked up the pancakes, squeezed them into a ball, and dropped them, splat, into the syrup. Then he went out the back door, picked up a pail, and went into the chicken coop. Aunt Alice walked to the woodpile, picked up an ax, and went into the chicken coop, too.

There was a shout of terror. Harry shot from the coop and dashed for the woodpile. Aunt Alice was right behind him, whooping and swinging her ax. Around the woodpile they went, Harry only a few strides ahead of the flashing steel.

Lil and Cass began to scream, pleading with Aunt Alice to stop. But when she did, it was not because of Lil or Cass.

Paul leaped from his wagon. He seized the ax, and brother and sister faced each other, Paul trembling with fury, Alice with a wonderful fierceness on her face.

Alice laughed. "Blood will tell. Won't it, Paul?"

With a single blow Paul struck her to the ground. "Lilith! Cassandra! Into the wagon."

"It's in the blood, Paul." Alice sprawled where she had landed. "I've tried to fight it for your sake, but I won't anymore. She's won!" Her laughter followed the wagon down the road.

The very next day Alice left town with a hired man from the next farm, and neither Alice nor the woodpile incident was ever mentioned in the Bascomb home again.

"Do you think she's crazy?" Cass lay on the bed now, staring at the ceiling.

"I don't know."

"Wonder if it's catching. She said it was in the blood."

"But we don't know what was supposed to be in the blood."

"Being crazy, probably. And if it is," said Cass, "I'll catch it."

"Why?"

"Sometimes I just know things."

Lil sighed and turned away. She wished she had a room of her own. She closed her eyes and imagined how she would fix this room after Cass was married and she, herself, had a job. The quilt her mother had made thirty-five years before in a sod hut in Oklahoma would be covered by a pink satin bedspread. The sampler Emma had stitched when Paul was running a livery stable in Kansas would be replaced with an oil painting, the rag rug by a carpet. She'd have a mirrored dressing table and a closet full of lovely store-bought dresses—never another made by Emma.

In the succession of hand-me-downs, Lil had had one bit of luck. Bascomb girls were petite, five feet three at the most, with dark hair and porcelain skins—replicas, Paul said, of Emma when he'd married her.

Lil was cut from different cloth. Her hair was deep red, her eyes a gold-flecked brown. She had no tan but she always looked as if she did. At thirteen she should have inherited clothes from eighteen-year-old Susan; but at thirteen Lil had already been taller than Susan. Emma had tried adding flounces to Susan's dresses (which had been Mary's before they were Susan's), but it was soon evident that there was a hitch. Emma had planned each dress for small rib cages and full breasts, not a full rib cage and small breasts.

So Lil got new dresses. It didn't help.

She turned her head on the pillow and looked at Cass. Whether Cass wore hand-me-downs or new clothes, she looked the same—pretty. "I've got to stop this," Lil thought. "So I won't be pretty, I'll still be me. I'll make up for not being pretty by being special."

Special. She'd always felt her difference from her sisters, and her father's distance from her because of it. Oh, Paul Bascomb was a fair man. On the surface he treated his girls equally. But Lil caught him looking at her sometimes as though she carried plague.

"I wish I could practice," said Cass suddenly. "I'm going to *die* before we get to church!"

Cass was to sing her first solo with the Methodist choir that morning. "Mrs. Keats will make me look bad. When she plays the bridge, she hits wrong notes, and she goes too slow!"

"That's because she's a terrible organist," said Lil.

"No, it's because she hates me. I wish you could play for me. And if Mrs. Keats got sick and couldn't come to church, you'd *have* to."

Lil turned away, realizing suddenly what Cass was up to.

"Could you do it, Lil? Could you make her sick?"

"No! I don't know where you get this idea that I'm some sort of a witch."

But she did know.

So silly. Jealous of Cass even at age six, when she'd heard Mama telling Jane that they'd known Cass would be their last baby, and how disappointed Papa was that the last one hadn't been a boy. Lil had told Cass that Papa hated her for not being a boy, that he was going to give her away if she didn't watch her step.

Cass hardly ate for days after that. Lil worried. "I'll work a spell," she told her sister finally, "I'll make Papa love you."

She should have told Cass the truth, that it was *she* Papa didn't love. Instead, she'd whisper to Cass when jealousy moved her, "The spell is wearing off. I heard Papa say he was thinking of selling you to a man who buys little girls for slaves. Don't worry, I won't let him. I'll cast a new spell."

Something had stopped that cruelty about a year after its inception, but Lil couldn't remember what. Perhaps love of Cass. Perhaps guilt.

Cass, however, remained convinced of Lil's powers. No amount of explaining, no amount of confession would change her mind.

And things kept happening. Coincidences.

Mrs. Hopper's piano, for instance. That had begun back in Missouri the night of Cass's ninth birthday.

"Aunt Alice will be here at six," Emma had said. "You're going to her house for the night."

"Those two get all the luck," said Susan, and Mary and Milly laughed.

But once out of sight of the house, Alice headed the horses not toward her farm, but toward the town of Lebanon.

"This is just between your Ma and us three girls, you understand. If your Pa knew I was taking you to a traveling minstrel show, he'd have my hide for a hearth rug!"

They sat in the middle of the front row, before the first stage they had ever seen.

Halfway through the show, a voice said, "Mr. Interlocutor! How about a song from Miss Philimentha Lee?"

She had been sitting among the performers all the time, but as she rose and walked into the lights, Cass and Lil saw her for the first time. She was dressed in billows of pink. A picture hat framed her face, and a parasol shielded her from an arc-lamp sun.

"Your hair is the color of hers," Alice whispered to Lil. "Maybe you'll look like her when you grow up."

Never, thought Lil.

Philimentha Lee was not a soprano. Neither was she an alto. Her voice was rich and thick and warm.

She sang, it seemed, right to them. "Out of my lodge at eventide, among the sobbing pines. Footsteps echo by my side, my Indian Brave, Pale Moon.

"Speak to thy love, forsaken, a spirit mantle throw. Ere thou the great white moon awaken, and to the east thou swingest low.

"Then to the east I'll follow, across the deep lagoon. Swift as a flying arrow, to thine abode, Pale Moon."

After the show, Alice led them backstage to a small dressing room crowded with minstrel ladies and damp costumes.

Philimentha's was among them—torn and soiled about the hem, Lil noticed. Even Philimentha herself looked more worn than she had behind footlights. And old!

She saw them in her mirror as they entered, turned and looked at Alice. Then she smiled, "Give us a kiss, my dear. Are these your girls?"

"No, they're Paul's, my brother's. His youngest."

Philimentha lifted Cass onto her lap. "What's you name, dear...? Cat got your tongue?"

"Her name's Cassandra," said Lil. "We call her Cass."

Philimentha studied Lil. "And yours, my red-haired comrade?"

"Lilith."

Philimentha's smile faded. "Who named you that?"

"My father."

On Philimentha's lap, Cass was entranced. Philimentha fondled her hair and patted her shoulders. "Are you good to your little sister, Lilith?"

Lil reddened. "Sometimes," she said. The skin above Philimentha's bodice showed more and more wrinkles, the closer you got. And there was gray in her hair!

"You must always be good to Cassandra," Philimentha said, and her eyes held Lil's. "Little sisters need looking after. Especially when they are Cassandras." She set Cass down. "You'll have to excuse me, Alice. We're catching the 10:20. By the way, this will be my last tour. I'm undertaking a long project. I don't expect to outlive it." She wrote something on a slip of paper and handed it to Alice. "The address of my people in Pennsylvania. If you're ever in need, you'll be welcomed there." She kissed Alice, kissed Cass—and shook Lil's hand.

They walked toward the door. "Alice," said Philimentha. "Did you like 'Pale Moon'? I sang it for you."

"You sang the lyrics wrong," said Alice. "The moon sets in the west."

"I never did have a sense of direction," Philimentha smiled. "Good-bye, my dears."

Aunt Alice was preoccupied that night. She didn't even watch them undress.

"Lil," Cass said the minute their bedroom door was closed, "I've decided. I want to be a singer, just like that lady. Can you cast a spell and make it so I can sing and so Papa will let me?"

"Cass, I've told you. I'm not a witch."

"Please help me. I'll die if I can't be like that lady!"

And thus the conversation went; until finally, in the dark, snuggled deep in the bed, Lil sighed. "All right. But you'll have to practice every day."

To practice right, Lil decided, Cass needed a piano.

"We're too poor to have a piano," her mother said. "Anyway, the way your Pa likes to move around, it would be a nuisance."

"But your chifferobe's bigger than a piano, and we always take that when we move."

"A chifferobe's different."

"Why?"

"It just is. And don't you go asking your Papa about any piano."

"But if I ask nice—"

"Lil! Unless you want a tongue-lashing, don't even say the word 'piano' to your Pa. He's funny about pianos."

"Oh," said Lil. "Then *that's* why we can't have one."

"Even if we had a piano," Lil told Cass, "we couldn't use it. I've decided we should keep your singing a secret. Papa mustn't hear a single note until you're so good he can't say no."

So the first few weeks of Cass's career were *a capella* in the fields, Lil beating rhythm with a stick while Cass sang her scales.

Then, in the fall of 1920, they moved to Oriskany Forks.

Lil and Cass never understood exactly how it happened. There'd been a letter for Papa. Then there was a lot of discussion between Papa and Mama, Papa and Aunt Alice, Papa and Curt. That evening the five younger girls were told. "Curt's moving east. He's going to farm it there." Curt left the next day.

"Glad to be rid of him," said Paul. "Argues my every word!"

He stewed around for six and a half days. The rest of the family waited, silent.

The evening of the seventh day, they were packing trunks and selling furniture. "The young fool'll get into trouble if I don't keep an eye on him."

"Are we going to live on Curt's farm?" said Cass.

"No. I'll find a job."

"Gives up an inheritance, then goes looking for a job," muttered Emma.

Lil didn't know what her mother was talking about. She did know this was one time it wouldn't do her any good to ask.

Paul Bascomb got a job managing the Oriskany Forks cider mill. With the job came the house next door.

It wasn't much of a house; small, with only two bedrooms. But it had a shady porch and lawn, and it was in town with people instead of out with cows.

Every day after school, Cass and Lil went past the last house on Elm Street to practice at a spot on the banks of Oneida Creek. Cass got so she could hit F above high C as clear and sweet as the water in the creek. And it got so she needed a better accompaniment than a stick.

Then came the matter of Mrs. Hopper's piano. Walking home from school one day, they stopped as they always did, to say hello to that lonely old woman. As they walked away, Cass said, "Lil, why don't you make Mrs. Hopper buy a piano? We could stop and practice there every afternoon, and Papa would never know."

The next two nights, at Cass's urging, Lil closed her eyes, screwed up her face, and repeated over and over, "Let Mrs. Hopper get a piano."

A week later, Mrs. Hopper's sister died and left her a piano. Coincidence?

No, Cass insisted. Witchcraft.

Now, thought Lil, she's expecting me to make Mrs. Keats too sick to accompany her today. Well, she's in for a big disappointment.

She turned her back on Cass.

Of course, Mrs. Keats did mutilate that bridge. Lil's own playing was nothing but the chords Mrs. Hopper had taught her. But at least she kept time.

"Why don't you give Mrs. Keats pen-tod-in-the-runits," said Cass suddenly.

"No!" Lil turned. "Look, Cassie, I can't do it, and that's final."

Cass smiled, a conspiratorial smile. "OK, you can't." It was obvious that she didn't for one minute believe it.

CHAPTER FIVE

"LILITH!" PAUL BASCOMB turned and frowned at his daughter. "Don't dawdle!"

"Yes, Papa." Lil threw a last glance at the door of the library as she hurried after the others. It wouldn't do to make Papa mad, today of all days.

A new boy in town? He must be, for she'd never seen him before. Yet it seemed she knew him. From long ago, she said to herself, and her face puckered with concentration. But when?

"I hope your face doesn't freeze like that," said Cass. "You working at your spell on Mrs. Keats?"

Mr. Grogan was just closing his soda parlor to head for church as the Bascombs paraded by. He smiled. It was a smaller parade than it had been when they first moved to town, but it still caused a stir. First came Paul, stiff as his collar, with Emma on his arm wearing anything for which she'd found matching material to make a big enough dress; then the girls. There'd been five at first, but Milly, Mary, and Susan had got married off fast.

The Sunday appearance of unmarried Bascomb girls never changed; pastel cotton pinafores, white cotton hose, black patent leather shoes, and hair so long and heavy it seemed to pull their noses into the air. Old-fashioned, but somehow the boys couldn't stop looking at them.

Of course, the attention directed at poor Lil was usually teasing.

Mr. Grogan remembered the day in his soda parlor when Muriel Moore had called Lil a flat-chested, red-feathered duckling, to her face—so loud it set the boys in the next booth to snickering. Lil brought her Coke to the counter and sat there, trying not to cry as she sipped.

Mr. Grogan picked up a rag and wiped the counter, working along till he stood in front of her. Then he leaned over and spoke gently. "Lil, you're going to have the last laugh."

Her brown-gold eyes flickered to him, filled with tears, and returned to her Coke.

How could he tell her? Those eyes against the tan-looking skin were already something magic. The rest just hadn't fallen into place yet.

Her lips were perfect, if you measured from top to bottom; but they were too wide. Her cheekbones flared high, but they needed growing into. Her legs and neck were well-shaped, but so long they reminded him of a baby giraffe's.

Mr. Grogan, though, was a man with some vision. He knew what Lil was going to look like when her parts caught up to each other. "You listen to me, Lil. I've been around for sixty-five years, and I know. You're going to be the finest-looking woman this town has seen."

He'd never forgotten the shock in her eyes. She hadn't believed him. But when she left the store, there'd been an extra lift to her chin.

Now, as she and her family passed him, Lil nodded and smiled; and her chin raised that extra bit.

Lil and Cass entered the back door of the church and hurried toward the babble of voices in the cloakroom.

Violet Baxter and Binny Wesley, the leading sopranos of the Methodist choir by virtue of seniority, sat in their usual places on the only two chairs. Binny smiled at Cass. "Nervous, dear?"

The choir director rushed forward. "Have you girls seen Mrs. Keats this morning?"

Cass sucked in her breath. "Why, Mr. Webster?"

"Is that clock right? Who's got an Ingersoll?"

Lil felt sick. "I'm sure she'll be here, Mr. Webster."

"Of course she'll be here," said Violet Baxter. "Sit down, Phineas, you'll have a spell." She made no move to vacate her chair.

Cass followed Lil to the robe closet and jostled her shoulder. 'Thanks," she hissed.

"I didn't do anything," Lil hissed back.

"Well, either way, it looks like you'll have to accompany me." Cass was still giggling when Evelyn Keats swept into the room on a wave of cologne.

"Everything went wrong this morning, Phineas, just everything." Mrs. Keats whipped out her hatpins and tossed the mass of floppy velvet roses onto a table. "Charles woke up with the runs, and my zipper broke." She rummaged through the closet. "Where's my robe? Oh, here it is. Help me, Lil, I should have started the prelude already. Poor Cass, I'll bet you were frantic. Thank you, Lil. Where's my music? Thank you, Phineas. All right, here I go." She disappeared through the door to the choir loft, leaving behind her scent and a glaring Cass.

"I told you I didn't do anything," Lil whispered.

"You did so." Cass didn't lower her voice. "But you made Mr. Keats sick instead of Mrs. Keats!" From the church came the first strains of the prelude, with three wrong notes in as many measures. "And now she can't even play the prelude right!"

It was just after the second hymn, as Reverend Smith began the reading of the Scripture, that the choir became aware of a disturbance. Mrs. Keats was searching for something.

And this shall be the priests' due from the people, from them that offer a sacrifice whether it be ox or sheep, and they shall give unto the priests the shoulder and the two cheeks and the maw.

The choir lost track of the Reverend's words. Mrs. Keats pawed through her briefcase, shuffled the music on the organ, muttered something, then went back to her briefcase.

Binny Wesley leaned forward. "What's the matter?"

Mrs. Keats shook her head, slid off the bench out of sight of the congregation, and began to search the floor.

They shall have like portions to eat beside that which cometh on the sale of his patrimony.

Phineas Webster dropped to the floor and crawled up the aisle on his hands and knees. "What in heaven's name is going on, Evelyn?"

When thou art come into the land which the Lord thy God giveth thee, thou shalt not learn to do after the abominations of those nations.

Mrs. Keats was whispering urgently to Phineas.

There shall not be found among you any one that maketh his son or his daughter to pass through the fire...

"How can she sing without music?" said Phineas, not bothering to whisper.

Or that useth divination, or an observer of times, or an enchanter or a witch.

Lil turned to stare at the minister.

"I could have sworn I brought it," said Evelyn. "I was just practicing the bridge this morning!"

Or a charmer, or a consulter with familiar spirits, or a wizard or a necromancer.

Now Lil was on the floor among the altos, crawling toward Phineas and Evelyn. And crawling from the soprano section was Cass.

For all that do these things are an abomination unto the Lord: and because of these abominations the Lord thy God doth drive them out before thee.

"What's the matter, Mrs. Keats? You forget my music?"

The four knelt behind the organ, sheltered from Reverend Smith and the congregation.

"I'm so *sorry*, Cass! I was certain I put it in my brief-case."

"That's all right. It could have been worse, you could have gotten diarrhea. Lil can play for me. Right, Lil?"

But the prophet which shall presume to speak a word in My Name, which I have not commanded him to speak, or that shall speak in the name of other gods, even that prophet shall die.

Lil's skin felt ice-cold in the heat of the church. "Yes," she said. "I can play it."

❁ ❁ ❁

Lil sat staring at her bulletin. One more short prayer, one more response from the choir. Then it would be time.

What were the first notes?

She couldn't remember.

Oh, Lord, Lil prayed. Help us!

She waited, her fingers wiggling in her lap, for the Lord to remind her of the notes. Nothing came. She was being punished for setting a spell on Mrs. Keats.

But that wasn't fair! It would be Cass that was punished, not her. Poor Cass, waiting to show Papa, her whole future in the balance—she *couldn't* fail Cass! She had to do something!

Lil closed her eyes tight and prayed again—this time to Aunt Alice's Artemis. She began to feel dizzy.

Then Marion Bedford was poking her, and Cass was walking toward the piano.

Lil rose too. There seemed to be no floor beneath her feet. She felt nothing, not the wooden stool as she took her place at the piano, or the keyboard as she placed her hands upon it.

Then Cass was singing. *A capella.* No—there was a piano accompanying her. Lil looked down at the keyboard. Hands were moving, pressing down keys. How graceful they were. She watched in admiration, hardly aware of Cass's voice.

Then the hands stopped playing, and Lil looked up. Cass was walking away. Was it over?

Still giddy, Lil rose and followed. She took her seat and looked over at Cass.

Cass gave her a look so strange that Lil jumped.

She looked at Emma. Emma was smiling. Thank God!

Not so her husband. Emma's words came flooding back with the anger Lil saw there: Don't even say the word "piano" to your Pa!

"Our Scripture reading," said Reverend Smith as he began his sermon, the third in a series he hoped to eventually expand and publish, "was Deuteronomy, Chapter Eighteen. I'm sure its meaning was not lost upon any of you." He allowed his spectacled gaze to travel the faces of the congregation. "In it, the author, Moses, touched upon an ancient problem—sorcery, witchcraft, conference with the Devil."

Lil stiffened.

"Ah, but you say, those things don't happen anymore. Just as miracles don't happen anymore. Oh, ye of little faith! I say to you that manifestations of good and evil never have and never will cease to occur. Satan wages a constant battle with the forces of Heaven for control of men's minds! He secretly, and with stealth, creeps among us, ferreting out the weak ones as instruments of his unholy will.

"Who are those weak ones?

"I say to you, there are those among us born evil! There are those among us who, even without being aware of it, are constant heralds of the Prince of Darkness. So weak are their wills, so unthinking their deeds, yet so unsuspected are they by family and neighbors, that they are as passive receivers and transmitters for the words and deeds of the Devil."

Reverend Smith droned on. And on. I won't listen to him, thought Lil. I mustn't.

It wasn't true, not one word. He'd come off his rocker, the sermons he'd been preaching lately. She opened the bulletin. "A Modern Look at Old Problems Facing Christianity. Number Three. PAWNS OF SATAN." Last week it had been Jews, the week before it had been Catholics. What next?

"And should these weak souls catch some awareness of their condition, should they become intrigued by it, then they become practicing sorcerers—witches, actively importuning and receiving Satan's pleasures.

"And the weakness is inherited, my friends. It is passed from parent to child like a bothersome spleen or the color of the eyes. It is mankind's most dread and secret disease."

Lil glanced around the congregation. Not a head nodded, not an eye wandered.

"So I say to you, seek them out. Listen for the voices of evil in your midst as you listen for the voices of good."

Lil's eyes, sweeping the congregation, found Paul's. She gasped as she saw his look.

"They are there, perhaps on your street, perhaps *at your dinner table.*"

Papa knew! His eyes moved away, but he knew and he hated her for it.

"But when you find them, seek first not to destroy them as did our misguided predecessors."

How did he know? Had Cass told Papa? She wouldn't!

"For we are New Testament Christians. We are enlightened. Seek instead to rehabilitate these Pawns of Satan."

What was he doing, this horrid little man?

"Cause the voice of God to be sounded loudly and clearly in their ears. Cause the standard of the Prince of Light to be raised always, above the standard of the Prince of Darkness. "Let us pray."

The choir intoned the closing prayer. Reverend Smith closed his Bible and paced with dignity to the back of the church as Mrs. Keats struck up the recessional: "Onward, Christian Soldiers."

Mrs. Keats played it well. It was the one piece she knew by heart.

CHAPTER SIX

W HEN THE AMEN finally sounded and the door of the choir room closed, there was a moment's silence. Then a torrent of voices.

Cass pushed through to Lil's side. "How come you've been holding out on me? Where'd you learn all the fancy things you played?"

"What fancy things?"

"You mean you didn't use any new notes?"

"Not a one." Lil watched Cass turn and remove her choir robe. "Why, Cassie? What did I do?"

Cass grinned. "You figure it out—witch!"

The door to the choir loft opened and Mrs. Keats rushed in. "Cass, I'm sorry! Forgive me, dear, but you were marvelous, and Lil, good heavens, I didn't know you could play like that. Where do you take lessons?"

Lil hesitated. She couldn't tell her about Mrs. Hopper, it might get back to Papa. "From no one. I mean, I just kind of picked it up."

"Picked it up? I work all my life to play decently and you just 'pick it up.' Why don't you come over to the house some afternoon after school? You could show me how you did that variation in the bridge."

Lil flushed. "Well, to tell you the truth, Mrs. Keats"—Cassie was standing right behind Mrs. Keats, making faces—"I'm not really sure what I did. I mean, you know how it is. I just sort of make it up as I go along."

"Of course, I understand, dear. You don't want to give away your little treasures."

"Honestly, Mrs. Keats, I'd tell you if I could."

"Don't give it another thought. Phineas, can you ever forgive me? I played terribly, I know…" She made a great fuss as she took off her gown and pinned on the floppy roses, forcing the other members of the choir into assurances.

Lil propelled Cass toward the door.

"Cass." Mrs. Keats dogged their steps. "What did you mean behind the organ when you said I could have gotten—you know."

Cass glanced around and saw that the others, with the exception of Binny and Violet, were paying no attention. She ignored Lil's frantic tug. "Oh, well, you see, Lil's a witch. She put a curse on you so that you couldn't play for me today. You were supposed to get diarrhea, but you forgot your music instead."

No use trying to make excuses, thought Lil. She towed Cass through the door.

Mrs. Keats sniffed and turned to Binny. "That Cass is a real smart aleck. Did you hear what she said?"

"About Lil being a witch?" said Binny. "After that sermon, I thought it was kind of cute."

"Cassie, why'd you do that? People have been burned to death because other people thought they were witches!"

"Oh, silly, nobody was listening except those two old biddies, and they wouldn't think for a second I was telling the truth."

"You've never told Papa, have you?"

"Of course not!"

"Well, don't. And nobody else, ever again. Cross your heart and hope to die."

"You don't have to make me say that." Cass was quite serious now. "We both know you could put a curse on me if I crossed you."

Lil sighed. "Listen, you've got to tell me about how I played. All I know is, I couldn't remember the notes, and then it seemed as if my hands were playing by themselves."

"Then I guess that's what they were doing," said Cass.

"Cassie, you've got to believe me. I swear to God, I don't do *anything*. It's all coincidence."

"I believe you. At least, I believe you believe it. But how do you explain playing like that?"

"Was it really that good?"

"It was that good."

✿ ✿ ✿

Paul and Emma were passing time in the park with the Grogans. "Here they come," said Mr. Grogan. "Cass, that was just fine."

"What do you say?" prompted Paul.

"Thank you," said Cass.

"So pretty," said Emma. "Wasn't it, Paul?"

"Pretty is as pretty does."

"I think she's the best soloist anybody ever heard," said Lil, hoping to spur the group to more imaginative remarks.

The smile that lit Emma's face straightened with a look from Paul.

"Were my eyes doing tricks," he said, "or were you playing the piano, Lilith? I don't recall that you could play the piano before today."

"Well, no, I couldn't," said Lil. "But I could. I mean, there's a piano at school. I guess I've just got a natural gift."

"No such thing," said Paul.

"But, Paul," said Emma, "your Ma—"

"Emma!"

Emma flushed.

"It's time we was getting home."

"Ohh-h-h!"

The sigh came from Cass. It was soft, but not lost on Emma. "Why don't we let the girls stay and visit with their friends a while, Paul? I don't need help with dinner."

"Nonsense and compliments, that's all Cassandra would hear," said Paul.

"Just this once, Paul."

Paul frowned. He could tell from the tone of Emma's voice that she was ready to put up a fight. He didn't like being talked back to by a woman, but he could count the times Emma had done it on his fingers. "All right, but mind you two be home," he checked his timepiece, "at one o'clock." Taking his wife's arm, he moved away.

"Cassie!" Muriel Moore swooped down with Janet Martin in tow. "You were absolutely the most super-scrumptious thing I've ever heard!"

"Yeah, super-scumptious," said Janet.

Lil sighed. She wished Cass would find another set of best friends. Muriel, gorgeous, blond, and know-it-all; Janet, dark, fat, and dopey. When those three got together, the conversation was too stupid to bear, and the sight of Muriel and Cassie in tandem brought out all Lil's misgivings about herself. She walked ahead toward Grogan's, toying with the idea of getting a strawberry cone. Maybe if she ate a lot, she'd get bosoms.

She stopped. The boy from the library had just rounded Grogan's corner riding a gray horse.

"Who is he?"

Lil jumped at the sound of Cass's voice behind her.

"That, my dear, is Harley Westcott." Muriel poked Lil in the ribs. "Isn't he gorgeous?"

"He's the handsomest boy I ever saw," said Cass.

Lil ignored them. All they could see was his looks, and there was so much more—a mysterious intensity that fairly screamed at you.

"He's so rich, you can't believe it," said Muriel. "His father owns a big Holstein farm just past your brother Curt's place. Spring Farm. They say Westcott bulls are worth twenty thousand dollars apiece. At least, one of them broke a leg last winter and the insurance company paid them twenty thousand. And they get a thousand dollars every time their bulls make a baby bull."

"How do *you* know so much about him?" said Lil.

"My dad built their big new house," said Muriel. "I've been there lots of times."

Harley ambled along in front of Grogan's windows, hands in pockets, intent on the display of confections.

He's sensitive, thought Lil. He gets pleasure out of really *looking* at things.

"Why's he staring at the candy so long?" hissed Cass.

"Shh," said Lil.

Harley entered the store, in no more of a rush than he'd been while window shopping, and the girls fell silent, waiting for him to reappear. When he did, he was empty-handed.

"Where's his ice cream?" said Janet.

"With his money, he probably bought a soda," said Muriel. Janet was so stupid.

Harley rubbed his mare's nose, swung himself up, and guided her in a slow circle.

He was going to come right by them. Lil's mouth went dry. He'd recognize her and—

"Hi," said Cass. "What's your horse's name?"

Muriel and Janet gasped. Lil felt as if she'd turned to stone.

"Polly," said Harley. A sideways grin twisted his lips. "What's *your* horse's name?"

Cass seized the opportunity. "I haven't got a horse, but my name is Cassandra Lee Bascomb."

"I'm Harley Westcott." With this he seemed to have exhausted his chatter for the day. "See you," he muttered. Spurring Polly into a canter, he disappeared around Grogan's corner.

"Cass!" Muriel squeaked. "Gol-ly, I wish I had your nerve. I think he likes you! Did you see the way he looked at Cass, Lil?"

"Yes."

"Do you really think he liked me?" Cass said. "Maybe he was just being nice."

"Harley Westcott isn't nice. I mean he's nice, but he's so shy he never talks to anybody except his horse. Wouldn't it be exciting if you married him? Then you'd have tons of money and we'd visit you every afternoon and drink tea. La de da!" At Muriel's demonstration of her tea-sipping technique, Cass and Janet broke into laughter. "Lil, can't you stand still a second? Where are you going?"

Lil was halfway across the street. "To get a cone," she called over her shoulder.

"Hey, I'd like one," said Janet.

"So would I. He has banana this week."

Lil bit her lip. She was going to cry if they didn't leave her alone. How could one person feel something so powerful for another, and that other pass by and never even look? He'd looked at Cass. And Cass, who had never before shown interest in any boy, chose to be interested in this one. I hate her, thought Lil.

"What's the matter, Lil?" Cass slipped up beside her sister and took her hand. "Don't you feel well?"

Lil extricated her hand and dashed into Grogan's. Make her leave me alone, she prayed. Make her leave me alone or I'll do something terrible.

The soda parlor was alive with young people. Everyone was talking loudly, irreverently.

Where had he stood? Maybe where she was standing now. "Lil? What *is* it?"

Lil turned and looked into Cass's round blue eyes. "I'm going home. You stay a while."

But within a block, Cass caught up with her. "I'll bet I know what's wrong with you."

Lil gave Cass a sharp glance. "You do?"

"Sure. It was that sermon, coming after everything that happened."

"Oh."

"Reverend Smith has evidently never met a single witch in his whole life. If he had, he wouldn't run around saying nasty things about them."

Then Cass stopped short. The gray mare was tethered to the rail in front of Coopers', and lounging on the front stoop, reading, was Harley Westcott.

"Hi," said Cass. "Fancy running into you again."

Harley muttered an embarrassed response.

"You must be new in town," said Cass. "You live here?"

"No." Harley thought a moment, then put his book on the steps and stood up. "I live on a farm past the college."

"Is Polly your very own horse?"

"Yes."

He was coming closer, almost beside them now. Lil took a deep breath and wished she could wipe her palms on something. She couldn't help staring at him. Her brain ached, sending him messages.

"Hello."

With a little shock Lil realized he was speaking to her.

"Harley, this is my sister, Lil. She's a witch."

"Cassie!"

"I'm just kidding. Our silly old minister preached a sermon about witches this morning. So I've been teasing Lil and calling her a witch."

"What did he say?" asked Harley.

"Oh," Cass shrugged, "he said they're all around us, maybe even in our own families, and they're pawns of the devil, and we should watch out for them and try to convert them."

"To what?" said Harley.

"Methodists, I guess."

Harley snorted.

"What's wrong with that?" said Cass.

"It's stupid," said Harley.

"Well, what would you convert them to?"

"I don't think that's what he meant," said Lil softly. "I think he means Reverend Smith's concept of witchcraft is medieval."

Harley's eyes flickered to Lil's then away. "Yeah."

Cass looked from one to the other. "Why?"

"Well," said Harley, "he said witches were 'pawns of the devil.'"

"Yes."

"There you are. Consorting with the devil, killing Christian babies, stealing eucharists—all the usual church propaganda. See, according to the most accepted theory, 'witch' or 'sorcerer' was what priests of one religion called priests of another, and 'devil' meant 'little god.' So, when Christianity got the upper hand, the old witchcraft god became the 'devil,' and people who kept worshiping the gods Christians didn't believe in were called witches." Cass's face was expressionless. "Do you see?" said Harley.

"Oh, sure," said Cass.

"And besides," said Lil, "Reverend Smith's medieval because he believes there still *are* such things as witches." She waited, fingers crossed, hoping that Harley would back her up.

But he shook his head. "According to my—teacher, there are still people who worship the old god and goddess. He says they're just like any religious group, except for their secrecy. And then there are people who practice black magic, but they're not real witches."

"How does your teacher know so much about witches?" said Cass.

"Well," said Harley, "he feels that if you're going to understand the world, you have to understand its religions. He teaches everything as part of religion, like geometry and Latin and art and history. Everything kind of happened because of religion."

Cass shrugged. "You still haven't told me how your teacher knows about witches."

Harley frowned, wondering how he had failed to make everything clear. "Witchcraft was probably the first religion, don't you see?"

"There's a new book in the library you might like to read," said Lil. "It's called *Witch Cults of Western Europe.*"

"I know," said Harley, "but someone's had it out ever since Cyrus bought it."

Lil's face reddened. "I'm sorry, I wouldn't have renewed it if I'd known you were waiting."

"You've got it?" Harley looked at Lil with sudden interest. "Lilith Bascomb! You didn't tell me you had a witch book."

Lil shrugged. "You didn't ask me." It was because of Cass that she'd had to renew it—hiding it, reading in bits and snatches when Cass wasn't around.

Harley was trying to examine Lil without being obvious. Taller than he'd imagined when he saw her in front of the library. And her face was—well, you had to look at it twice. Funny he hadn't done that right off. "It's nice to know who has that book," he said.

"I'll bring it back tomorrow," said Lil.

"You don't have to."

"Oh, but I'm finished, and I've had it too long. I'll take it in after school and tell Mr. Hamlin to hold it for you."

"He can't. He'll have to give it to whoever asks first."

Cass was suddenly concerned. "But people might keep taking it out, and you'd never get it. Why don't we meet you at the library some afternoon this week?"

Harley shrugged. "I'm really not in any hurry."

Silence.

"What time is it?" said Lil.

Harley withdrew Jason Cole's gold pocket watch. "Five to one."

The girls exchanged glances. "We have to go," said Cass. "It's been nice passing time, Harley. Maybe we'll see you around."

The girls moved away.

"Hey, listen," said Harley.

Two faces turned. "What?"

"Actually—I *am* pretty anxious to read that book. What if I was at the library at three-thirty on Wednesday?"

CHAPTER SEVEN

"CASS?"

Cass stood in the bedroom, riffling through the book she'd found beneath Lil's pillow. No pictures. She tossed it onto the table. "Coming, Mama."

Emma was at the iron stove. "Pump me another pot of water, please, Lil. And whip those potatoes. Use plenty of butter. Cass, see if the pie isn't done."

This time of the year, Sunday pies were usually custard. Cass opened the oven. "Pumpkin! Oh, Mama!"

Emma laughed. "You and your Pa are a pair. You both think heaven's made of pumpkin pie. Is it done? Well, put it on the windowsill to cool." Emma tested the chicken. "I got more of your Pa's favorites, too. Creamed onions. A loaf of fresh bread packed full of raisins. Whipped cream for the pie—he'll be in a good mood after dinner." She gave them a sidelong glance. "I got my suspicions you two have something you want to speak to him about."

The two girls exchanged surprised looks. "How long have you known, Mama?"

"Land sakes, a mother can't see her girls come home late from school too many afternoons without getting curious."

"Does Papa know?" said Cass.

"If he did, you'd have no need to ask me that. Set the table now, will you?"

Emma watched the girls as they moved back and forth to the dining room. "Lil? Cass?" She stopped in the middle of dishing out the chicken and dumplings, and nodded them closer. "You got to be prepared that your Pa might say no. He doesn't hold with musical things, and he's a mighty spotty leopard."

Lil saw the look on Cass's face and took her hand. "Why, Mama?"

"That's just the way he is."

"Was his mother musical?" said Cass.

"What makes you think that?"

"Well, after church you said—"

"I don't know a thing about Paul's ma. We don't speak of her. And if I were you, I wouldn't mention anything about Cass going on any stage. I'd just ask your Pa if he didn't think it was a good idea for Cass to take singing lessons, seeing as how her voice is better than the average. You might point out that the ladies who sing at the big churches in Seneca make three dollars a—no, on second thought, I think the idea of taking money for singing the praises of the Lord—wait, that's it!" Emma's eyes sparkled.

"What is it, Mama?"

"Cass, you tell him the power of the Lord came over you this morning when you were singing, and you felt your calling to sing His praises as well as possible, so can you please take singing lessons." Emma went back to ladling up the dumplings. "That's about the only chance I can see. And even then, I don't know. Table all set?"

"Yes, Mama."

"Help me carry, Lil. Cass, tell your Pa we're almost ready."

"Mama..." The two of them said it together, moved by the impulse to thank Emma.

"Butter on the table, Lil? Fetch the gravy boat on your way back, Cass, and take that pie off the sill. Mrs. Parkinson's cat's been watching that window awful close on Sundays lately."

Meals in the Bascomb household were lengthy affairs. First, grace was said; the more eagerly awaited the food, the longer the grace as prepenance for gluttony.

When all were served, the food was eaten. Slowly. No mouthful descended a throat until it had been chewed twenty times. To break that rule meant a lonely fast in your room for the rest of the day. "If you can't show your food and your stomach the proper respect," Paul would say, "you don't deserve to use them."

It being forbidden to speak with food in your mouth, conversation had to be carried on between mouthfuls. The natural inclination was to devote the first few minutes exclusively to chewing and swallowing; but here again, an iron-clad rule intervened. "The art of conversing's one of the most important things a girl can learn. There'll be no long silences to the tune of chomping teeth at my table. I want to hear one voice talking about something sensible at all times."

After the meal every member of the family lay down for fifteen minutes. Then there would be the dishes to wash...

All things considered, Cass figured it would be four o'clock before she and Lil could approach Papa. She broke off a piece of raisin bread and thought of Harley Westcott.

"Cassandra? Would you oblige us with a little conversation, or did singing do you in?"

"No, Papa. I was just thinking how good the bread is."

"If you've a compliment for your Ma, say it, don't think it."

"It's delicious, Mama." Suddenly she wanted to shout. "I'm so lucky!" she said.

"There's no such thing as luck, Cassandra, only the Lord's blessing. Why do you feel blessed?"

Cass grinned. She could say, "Because I sang beautifully today, because I fell in love with a rich boy, and because I have my own personal witch." But she said, "Because I have a nice family."

Paul's face softened. "That's nice sentiment, Cassandra."

Having said it, he was quiet. A silent Paul at the table was a serious thing; the others grew silent, too, watching him.

He was a big man, Paul Bascomb, wide and strong despite his sixty years. He could still be mistaken for his son Curt until you got right up close. Then you saw the age difference; not so much lines as sternness in Paul's face.

"I've an announcement to make," he said finally. "I got my notice."

Emma looked blank. "What?"

"Mr. Scott's closing the mill, Emma. Seems cider's not a money-making thing anymore."

"Do you mean you've lost your job?" said Cass.

Paul's eyes flickered. "My job's been discontinued."

"What about the house?" said Emma.

"I can't manage the rent Scott will be wanting," said Paul. "We gotta be out of the house by Wednesday."

"Wednesday?" said Lil.

"*This* Wednesday?" said Cass. "But I have to go to the library Wednesday!"

"What will we do?" said Emma. "Oh, Paul, we're not going to leave Oriskany Forks, are we?"

They all waited for the answer.

I won't leave, Lil was thinking. Even if I have to run away and hide until they're gone.

Cass was praying: Don't let Papa make me go now.

Paul took a bite of chicken. Lil and Cass counted the movements of his jaw beneath his troubled eyes. "I had a talk with Curt," he said at last. "Guess I can't be stubborn any longer. Curt's got plenty of room in that house. He said we'd be no trouble at all."

"But we will!" said Emma. "Him and Helen are so shortly married. Couldn't—oh please, Paul—couldn't we take the other house?"

"No."

"But—"

"No, I said."

Emma sighed. "Well, maybe we're being hasty. Maybe you could find another job, and we could stay right here."

Paul frowned. "Fact is, Emma, I started asking around three weeks ago, when Mr. Scott gave me my notice. Not too many openings for a man my age, except janitor. I could get a job as janitor at the Town Hall, but that's not proud work, Emma. I've done proud work all my life. Now, you know how much I hate going to that place. But at least, farming it with Curt, I'll be able to hold my head up instead of emptying spittoons."

The juice seemed drained from the chicken. Lil chewed dutifully. Then, "How will we get to school?"

"It's only a six-mile round trip. The walking won't kill you. Me and Alice—" Paul stopped. "Six miles a day won't kill you."

Cass had been silent, thinking hard. Now she smiled. "I think it will be wonderful to live on a farm again—all that fresh air." She took a mouthful of mashed potatoes onto her fork and paused. "Don't the Westcotts live out near Curt?"

Paul frowned. "Who?"

"I think that was the name." Cass looked at Lil. "Muriel was telling us about them today. She says they're rich and have all kinds of prize stock."

"They live somewhere past Curt's road," said Paul. "I don't pay much attention to people like that."

Cass still held the potatoes, unwilling to put them in her mouth, for then she'd have to chew them twenty times. It always seemed silly to chew whipped potatoes. "What's wrong with the Westcotts?"

"It's easier for a camel to pass through the eye of a needle than for a rich man to enter the Kingdom of Heaven," said Paul.

"I don't understand," said Cass.

"I mean," Paul said with unaccustomed malice, "that Thomas Westcott and his family are so busy being rich they don't have time for God nor anybody. I mean, a camel will go through the eye of a needle before they'll get to Heaven."

"I read," said Lil, "that in Bible times there was a small low gate in the walls of cities, called a 'needle.' So you see, camels could get through, baby camels easy, and it's not impossible for a rich man to get into Heaven." She caught Paul's withering glance. "Or at least a *small* rich man."

"Where you been getting this literature?"

"In the library."

Paul shook his head and gave Emma a look. "Criminal to leave books like that where decent young girls can get their hands on them."

"It was a history book, Papa."

"Don't back-talk me, Lilith."

"I wasn't, I just—"

"Lilith!"

Lil quieted. One more word would send her to her room.

"From here on, you bring me any books you get from that library. I'm going to make sure you don't read no more trash."

"Yes, Papa."

"You too, Cassandra."

"Of course, Papa."

"Any library books in your room now?"

"Paul, don't spoil dessert."

"Quiet, Emma. Lilith?"

"Paul, I worked hard on this dessert," said Emma. "Can't the books wait?"

"This is important."

"So's my dessert."

Paul's eyes narrowed. "Why you got a special dessert?"

"Because of Cassie's first solo day. That's special. So's pumpkin pie."

"Pumpkin pie? Well, if that don't beat all." Paul's tongue swept his lips.

Lil looked at Emma as she followed her mother from the table—round, bustling, pleased as punch. How'd she know things like she did?

"I'm glad I made that pie," said Emma as she took the whipping cream from the icebox. "Your Pa was set to work himself into a spent-horse lather. Where'd you put the pie, Cass?

Silence.

"Cass?"

"I didn't take it off the sill."

Emma and Lil turned to where Cass was looking—at the empty windowsill.

The pie! From the lovingly hoarded pumpkin!

They converged on the sill. Three heads thrust through the window.

"Oh, Mama!"

"Oh-h-h!"

The pie had landed on its edge, splattering most of its contents over the lawn just below. Beside the splintered shell crouched Mrs. Parkinson's yellow tiger tomcat, purring as he lapped pumpkin from the pastry. He glanced up. "Me-ne-r-roow!"

Cass pushed Emma and Lil aside, leaped over the sill, and descended on him. "Shoo!" A violent toe caught him in the ribs. He howled and leaped back. "You hateful animal!" Her foot swung again. The cat spit and raked her ankle, then ran, bristling, for the safety of Mrs. Parkinson's back porch.

Unmindful of her bleeding ankle, Cass dropped down beside the pie. "Maybe we can save a piece for Papa!" Trembling hands tried to fit pieces of shell into a portion that still had some pumpkin clinging to it.

"No use, honey. That pie's done."

"No! I'm sure there's enough here!" Cass picked specks of grass and dirt from the piece in question. "See, Mama? There's enough. And with whipped cream on it he'll never even know!"

Lil climbed out and knelt, her arm around Cass. "It won't work, Cass. It's a dirty mess."

"You gotta eat a peck of dirt before you die, Papa always says that." But as she said it, she picked a dead fly from the pie. She stared at it, then flung it away, dissolving into tears. "I'm so sorry, Mama! It's all my fault!"

"It's all our faults, sweetheart." Emma could scarcely cover her disappointment. "We were none of us paying attention."

"Oh no! You told me, and I didn't do it, and now he'll hate me again. Lil!" She grabbed Lil's shoulders. "Help me! Work a spell! Please!"

"Shh-h-h, Cassie!"

"What's all the noise?" Paul was entering the kitchen.

"Lil! Help me!"

"All right, Cassie. I'm doing it." Lil began to say, over and over to herself: Make Papa love Cass. Don't let him be mad.

Paul leaned out and looked down. "Oh-h-h," he said, like he'd found his pet dog poisoned.

Cass scrambled to her feet, hiccuping now, the pie tin raised. "There's enough left to make you a piece, Papa. It didn't get too dirty."

Paul snatched the tin. "Who wasted this pie?"

"There was only one place where there was a fly," said Cass.

"It was an accident," said Emma. "Parkinson's cat."

"Well, what was it doing where the cat could waste it?"

"We forgot to take it off the sill," said Emma.

(Make Papa love her. Don't let him be mad.)

"Who forgot to take it off the sill?"

(Please, *whoever is listening to me*, make Papa love her, don't let him be mad.)

"I did! I did!" Cass was hysterical now, climbing back through the window. "Oh Papa, you wanted that pie so much. Don't hate me. I love you, Papa." She wrapped her arms about his waist. "Please don't give me away! I'll do anything to make up."

"What are you talking about?" said Paul. "Emma!" He felt Cass's brow. "See how hot she is."

"Too much excitement, poor child."

"Don't hate me, Papa!"

"Now, how could I hate you?" He placed comforting hands around Cass. "She ought to be in bed." As he said it, he swung Cass into his arms. He carried her to the bedroom, Emma and Lil behind him.

"Do you love me, Papa?"

"Yes."

"You won't give me away?"

"No. Take a nap for Papa now, That's my girl." He touched his trouser pocket and frowned. "Ow! I got such a pain here."

Cass sniffled, managed a smile, and reached into the pocket, withdrawing a chocolate-covered cream. Papa had been having chocolate-cream pains as long as the girls could remember. "That make it better?"

"Sure does," said Paul.

But as he spoke, he spotted *Witch Cults of Western Europe* on the bedside table.

For a moment he stared, his jaw working. "What are you doing with this thing, Lilith?"

Lil jumped. It had been *under* her pillow!

Paul hurled the book across the room. "Why are you bringing evil into this house?"

Suddenly Cass was screaming. She dived beneath the covers and started thrashing, shouting incoherence.

Paul patted the heaving quilt. "Cassandra. Baby!" But Cass would not be comforted. "She's either sick or possessed, Emma. How much is Barnes charging for house calls these days?"

"Three dollars, I think."

Cass's shrieks filled the room.

Paul sighed. "I guess you'd better run get him, Lil. You'd better run fast."

CHAPTER EIGHT

IT WAS 2:30 when Hitty and Harley turned back into the mapled drive of Spring Farm.

"Looks like rain," said Hitty. "Chess?"

"Maybe later."

"I'd think she'd be tuckered," said Hitty, knowing Harley meant to take Polly for a run. She eyed the mare. *I want to get Harley a good thoroughbred*, Tobin had said. He'd bought a jumper and never even told her. *Make a man out of him.* Which was a pack of foolishness. Harley was a boy and he'd grow to a man. Jumping fences would neither help nor hinder.

Hitty paused at the door of the house and watched as Harley cleared the orchard fence and raced away. She could almost feel the animal's muscles between her legs, the explosion of power, the wind rushing at her face.

Too bad her Papa hadn't owned a saddle horse. She would have been a fine horsewoman. She could have cleared any fence in the county.

Harley followed the cart path through the main pasture, which was bounded on the east and west by the woods, and to the north, where Harley was headed, by the densest and most forbidding part of those woods—the Crazy Lizzy Sixty.

The clouds were a leaden mass, and the air was heavy. Harley had the sensation of swimming. Any minute he'd hear the thunder. Tobin would never keep working in the rain, he'd head back. He wouldn't expect Harley to show up. Why had he told Tobin he'd come in the first place?

Polly and Harley moved steadily closer to the Crazy Lizzy.

To Harley's right, beneath the trees, the herd was forsaking clover for cover. They raised their heads, curious. A few of them feinted at Polly with nonexistent horns.

A hundred yards farther, he touched Polly's flank and they sailed over the board fence into the woods for the long-way-around trip to the shed. Polly's hooves on earth and debris grew louder as the heaviness of the day met the stillness of the forest, and, beyond the trees, Harley heard his omnipresent outrider, the echoing hooves.

He cut down a ravine to the brook. Cole's Creek it was called, for it rose from a spring at the northernmost edge of the woods—on the farm that had been Jason Cole's. Harley halted, allowing Polly to take some water; wondering, suddenly, whether Curt Bascomb was any relation to Lil and Cass Bascomb.

Harley often headed for Curt's farm, meadows cleared in the midst of the woods to the east of Spring Farm. He'd swing down by the house, stop for a moment with Curt's wife, Helen, if she happened to be out gardening or doing her chores; shyly accept a cinnamon bun if she happened to have just made a batch.

There came a pattering, like drops of water on leaves. Harley looked up, but the clouds still hoarded their rain. Just another of the woods' secret sounds.

He had always known about these woods. Even as a child, looking across sunny fields to their dark perimeters, he had known the woods for what they were: not separate trees and logs and bushes but one spirit, one malignant spirit. Yet again and again fascination drew him into them.

The Crazy Lizzy Sixty, which comprised the central portion, was so named for the simple reason that Thomas Westcott had purchased sixty acres, before the turn of the century, from a recluse called Crazy Lizzy. Eliza Stockbridge had lived at the very end of Curt Bascomb's road, a quarter of a mile inside the woods. Her place and Curt's were the only two houses on that road. Old man Stockbridge, so the story went, had built the house in the meadow about 1865, and brought his bride, Lizzy's sister, there from Pennsylvania. About a year later, at his wife's insistence, he built the strange round house in the woods. Mrs. Stockbridge painted weird things on the walls, and they moved in. In it their children were born.

Ten years later Mrs. Stockbridge disappeared—died, went away, no one ever knew for sure. Mr. Stockbridge gave out no information, but since he brought Lizzy home to care for her sister's children and had the Presbyterian parson marry them, folks assumed the first Mrs. Stockbridge *must* be dead.

Of course, there were rumors. The ladies of the farms surrounding the woods had been happy to be rid of Mrs. Stockbridge. According to Hitty, Harley's great-grandmother had displayed real venom whenever the first Mrs. Stockbridge was mentioned. The one thing Harley knew for sure was that she had been a beauty. The second Mrs. Stockbridge was not, and neighboring wives were pleased to see her come.

After Lizzy's arrival, the family moved back to the house in the meadow, leaving the other place and all the whispers about it to be reclaimed by the woods. The Stockbridges lived quietly for a while, until Lizzy started acting strange. To anyone who would listen she announced that she was afraid of living in the open meadows. One day she left her family behind, moved back to the round house in the woods, and went into hiding.

Then the inhabitants of the meadow house disappeared.

When their absence was noted, there was an investigation of sorts. But no bodies were ever found, and maybe, after all, they'd just gone away. Lizzy was no help. When anyone managed to coax her out from wherever she was hiding that day, she'd say she reckoned they'd been hexed away, then scurry off.

Lizzy's funny round house was empty now. Curt Bascomb hadn't been able to find one tenant who'd stay there longer than a month.

Maybe, Harley thought, it was the stories about the disappearance of the Stockbridges that spooked people out of the place. One version had it that Lizzy had been a witch, and some folks said she'd killed her family, cut each body into eleven pieces, and strewn them through the woods in some sort of hellish rite.

Of course, the way Lizzy met her end, just six years back, didn't help people to feel comfortable in the house. Apparently she had gone to the carriage house one day—for what reason no one could ever figure, since Lizzy had owned neither carriage nor horse for years. When she'd tried to open the door, the rusted hardware gave way, and the door fell upon her.

Had it not been for the two long, rusty nails sticking out of that door, Lizzy might have been able to drag herself out. But she'd been impaled beneath it for days when the Sears-Roebuck salesman found her body, and there were people who'd swear on the Bible they sometimes saw Lizzy walking at night and heard her phantom screams of agony.

Then again, maybe the reason people couldn't stay in that house was not because of any stories but because of the house itself, with its strange paintings, windowless second story, and self-willed doors. Or because of the feel of the clearing in which the house stood.

It seemed to be a natural clearing, a large, round indentation in the side of the hill where no trees would grow.

There was never a breeze in that clearing. Never.

Birds didn't sing in that clearing. Ever.

At least that's what tenants said.

Harley himself had never chanced to feel a breeze or hear a bird on any of his visits there, but he knew that didn't prove "never" and "ever." On the other hand, that clearing did seem to be the heart of this Titan Woods. He sometimes had the feeling that if he were to go there and put his ear to the ground, he'd hear a heartbeat.

A stick snapped.

No secret sound this time. At the crest of the ravine, obscured by the bushes, stood an albino deer! At least, it must be a deer. Harley grinned as it darted away. If it was a doe, it was trying to lure him away from its fawn. He guided Polly to the top of the ravine and slipped off, continuing on tiptoe, scanning the brush, pulling aside branches. The land sloped down as he progressed, and within a hundred feet Harley found himself at the edge of a pit.

It was circular, perhaps twenty feet wide and six feet deep, with natural walls. Not too far from Lizzy's house. Why hadn't he come across it before?

He climbed down into the pit. It was colder there, and he shivered. He moved toward the center and, as he did, began to scuff his feet. Strange texture to the floor. No softness. No resiliency. Surprisingly thin layer of fallen leaves.

He had the feeling that someone familiar stood behind him.

He turned. Not quickly, not even stopping his scuffing. He just turned. There was no one. He resumed his inspection of the floor.

The dirt was like that of an abandoned cow path, still so closely packed that it was incapable of growing vegetation. Yet there did seem to be a kind of life beneath his feet.

His scuffing was becoming rhythmic.

A sound like a scraping of hooves came from the rim, but Harley didn't bother to look up. He leaped high, dancing now, as naturally as he breathed, moving not to music but to the *feeling* of *this place*.

Then he stopped. He understood, suddenly, what this place was.

He turned—slowly, deliberately, searching for what he knew must be there; the almost imperceptible lines describing circles of up to eleven feet in diameter. Yes, there they were. He began to move on tiptoe away from those lines, stepping carefully, holding his breath, noticing for the first time the ash of fires at the edges, and an opening in the rock as to a tunnel. He scrambled hastily out of the pit.

Only a hundred feet back to Polly. There should have been a fawn. Every doe had a fawn at that time of the year.

Then he noticed a musky smell. He didn't turn. "Mr. Upjohn?"

A twig snapped.

"Mr. Upjohn? I know you're here."

If he turned around and looked toward the circle, he would see him there.

He did not turn. Without rushing, he mounted Polly and guided her forward. The creek burbled an unconcerned welcome as he gained its edge.

Now he looked back, And somehow he wasn't surprised. He'd think about it later, figure it out then.

For the albino was back in its thicket. He could see part of the white flank among the trees. He even imagined he saw eyes, peering through leaves, watching until he rode from sight.

CHAPTER NINE

HARLEY AND THE stream emerged into the clearing at right angles to the cart path. The storage shed near the first of the fields Tobin had cleared in the Crazy Lizzy housed the supplies for working those fields.

On a ladder against the shed stood Tobin, applying red-brown paint. "Didn't expect you," he said. "Account of the rain."

"I almost didn't come," said Harley. "But it seems to be holding back."

Rose was tethered to a sad old oak, unhooked from the wagon so she could pass the afternoon in comfort. Harley dismounted and tied Polly beside her. He slipped Polly a cube of sugar. Rose nickered. "You, too?" Rose's head pumped. "Let's see you take it nice." Rose accepted it daintily. "Well! Another one?" Rose's head pumped again, but Harley caught the gleam of mischief in her eyes. "No you don't!" He gave Polly the second cube instead, then turned, chuckling, ignoring Rose's conversation.

"That tree's in bad shape," said Tobin, not looking up. "Have to chop it down before it falls on the shed."

Harley glanced at the oak, almost fearing that the surrounding woods heard the threat to one of their number. "We shouldn't kill it before its time," he said. "Might be bad luck."

Tobin looked at the woods. "I've got a lot of bad luck coming, then." In clearing the land, Tobin had been responsible for the death of hundreds of trees. He was none the worse for it yet.

The shed was little more than half painted. Harley was glad he had come. Tobin would never have finished without him.

He walked to the base of the ladder, watching Tobin paint with sure, steady strokes, up and down, up and down, and then stop to force the wet bristles into a cranny.

"You didn't quite get it," Harley started to say, but Tobin's brush swooped back and jabbed into the hole. "Where's another brush?"

"You'll get it all over yourself," said Tobin. A knothole wouldn't cover; Tobin put the tip of his brush against it and swiveled.

"No, I won't."

"I'm almost done."

"I *like* to paint, Dad. Please let me help you."

"Almost finished," said Tobin.

A few moments later Tobin turned to see why Rose was nickering. Harley was climbing back onto Polly. "Where are you off to?"

"I promised Mother we'd play chess."

"Oh." Tobin nodded, then looked at his paintbrush. "Well, thanks for coming by," he said. "It was nice having a talk. We *should* talk once in a while."

The appeal embarrassed Harley, and his irritation increased. He started up the cart path.

"Isn't there something else?" Tobin persisted.

Harley stopped. "Something else what?"

"Something else you want to talk about."

Both fell silent; the father as uncomfortable as the son. Each gave the other stingy glances.

"No," said Harley. The Voice? Aunt Carrie? The Bascomb girls? The circle? There were really so many things, and Tobin had offered, and here he was turning him down. "There's really nothing."

"Oh," said Tobin; a little hurt, a little relieved. "Well, son..." Harley tried a grin, but it felt mushy on his face.

Tobin touched his cap and returned to his painting.

"You sure I can't help you, Dad?"

Tobin's brush slowed, then resumed its pace. "No," he said, sounding cheerful now. "Go on. Don't keep your mother waiting."

At the crest of the hill, Harley looked back. Only Rose watched after him, still hoping for a second cube of sugar.

Harley kept riding.

His throat felt tight. Overhead, the leaden clouds still held their moisture. Clouds couldn't get that black without raining. Sometime soon they'd have to let go.

The smell of something freshly baked filled the kitchen. Henrietta and the cook, Agnes, sat at the trestle table, a pile of potatoes and a pot between them.

"Mother upstairs?" said Harley as he entered.

"Far as I know," said Henrietta.

Harley stepped into the darkened hall as the first flash of the storm illuminated the staircase. He flipped the switch for the chandelier over the staircase. Nothing happened. "The line for the hall is out, Henrietta."

"You'll have to wait till your father gets home," she called back. "We're not crawling through those do-jiggies down-cellar electrocuting ourselves."

More lightning flashed and thunder sounded layer on layer. From the kitchen came squeals and the sound of the trestle table being dragged away from the windows. Still there was no rain.

Harley started up the stairs. The wind slapped branches against the window panes. Tobin must be on his way home. He'd drive the cattle down to the barn, if they hadn't already made tracks themselves. Dangerous, crossing the pasture with all the lightning.

At the head of the stairs Harley found that the second-floor lights, too, were dead. He groped his way to Hitty's door, knocked, and entered.

The room danced in candlelight. Hitty stood at the open French windows, with Fluffy in her arms. She wore a lavender peignoir, her silver hair loose. As the lightning flashed and thunder rumbled, the wind blew her hair like a pale flame. "Isn't the storm beautiful?" she cried. "Isn't it the most beautiful thing in the world?" She turned slightly, not really looking around. "Come look."

The trees in the orchard seemed to fling themselves hither and yon, as though impelled to free their roots and march on the house. The avenue of maples looked as if it would devour a man foolish enough to enter. And over it all shot the lightning in vivid staccato strokes.

It *was* beautiful. It was something else, too.

Along the northern horizon squatted the Crazy Lizzy. "Have you ever thought," said Harley, "that those woods are evil?"

Hitty gave no answer. Thinking she hadn't heard, Harley turned and was surprised to meet her eyes, luminous in the reflected light of the storm. Standing close, he realized that clinging to Hitty was the musky scent of Mr. Upjohn.

"What makes you think the woods are evil?" she said.

"They just look that way sometimes."

Her hand touched the down of his cheek. "I remember hearing people say the same thing when I was a child, Harley."

She must know he could smell it! "What perfume do you have on, Mother?"

"Lilac."

"It smells like the stuff Mr. Upjohn uses."

"Oh? That's right, I used some of that dusting powder he gave me for Christmas. I didn't realize it outdid my perfume."

Harley turned back to the storm. Mr. Upjohn had given Hitty a leather-bound *Shakespeare's Sonnets* for Christmas. "Do you want to play chess?"

"I'd rather just stand here."

"Then I'm going to the barn."

"What on earth for?"

Harley shrugged. He had to get away, or he'd say something awful. "I want to make sure Dad's gotten back all right."

Hitty laughed. "Lightning wouldn't dare strike Tobin."

And, indeed, it hadn't, for as Harley started down the staircase, the front door opened and Tobin swept through. He headed for the parlor, breathing hard and muttering. He fumbled with the light switch, swore, and started through the room. There was a thud and the shattering of china, followed by more epithets.

"What's the matter, Dad?"

Tobin got to his office and began to rummage through drawers.

Harley followed, bumping his knee on the overturned table and crunching over the remains of Hitty's Meissen group. There'd be hell to pay. "Dad?"

"Get the car out and wait for me."

"What—"

"Run, Harley!"

Harley ran. The Duryea was in the driveway, swaying in the wind and rattling like a tin lizzie when Tobin reached it. He got in the driver's side and thrust his shotgun at Harley.

"Why—"

"No time, Harley!"

The auto careened up the wagon road and headed across the main pasture—exposed, taller than anything else if lightning came looking for a target. Tobin seemed not to care. He leaned over the wheel, as though his own urgency could lend them speed.

"Now will you tell me where we're going?"

"Back to the storage shed."

"Why?"

"We got to put Rose out of her misery, son."

"Rose!" Harley had been holding the shotgun. Now his hand jerked back, and he stared at the weapon. "What happened?"

Tobin's knuckles were white as he held the wheel against the wind. "God damn old oak tree. I'd just hitched Rose, got up in the wagon. Lightning, I guess, or wind. That oak came down clean as a whistle, roots and all. Tried to gidderup, but I guess Rose was playing games. Foolish old girl saved my life. If she'd moved, I'd be under that tree right now."

"But she's not really hurt bad enough to shoot!"

Tobin shook his head. "You ain't seen her, Harley. I ran every step of the way home for that gun."

"We can save her! I'll nurse her, Dad. She won't be any bother to you!"

"She's broke, Harley!"

"But if we can get the tree off her—"

"It would take two teams and fifty men to get that tree off, son. I'm not being hard. She's squashed like a bug."

Rose. He mustn't cry. Sleek, black, practical-joking Rose. Tobin would call him a baby if he cried. He hadn't given her that second lump of sugar this morning, or this afternoon. He patted his pockets frantically. One lump! Her nose would be soft, and she'd take the sugar and look at him for more and he wouldn't have it.

She couldn't be hurt that bad. They'd do something. Tobin would do something. He mustn't cry.

The gate was already open where the cart path headed into the woods. In the trees that engulfed them, the wind howled like a creature with a bloodlust.

It *was* evil here. Please God, Harley prayed, be stronger. Don't let it get Rose!

But the black mare lay, as Tobin had said, squashed like a bug beneath the fallen oak. Her eyes were terrified, beginning to glaze. Foam oozed from her mouth and nostrils; organs from her belly. Her breaths came in agonized gasps.

Harley fell to his knees beside her. "Rose!"

Recognition struck the soft, hurt eyes. She tried to lift her head, but fresh foam bubbled out and she groaned.

"Stand away, son."

"No!" Harley shielded her. "Let me give her some sugar. Look, Rose. Take it!" He held the cube to the velvet muzzle, but she didn't respond. "Please take it. I'm sorry I didn't give you any more today. Please!"

"Stand away, Harley." The hand that touched Harley's shoulder trembled. "She's hurting too much to know sugar."

Harley pushed the sugar into the senseless mouth. He bent and kissed the mare, bestowed one last, lingering caress, then stood up.

"Turn away, son."

As Harley turned, his tears rushed out.

The shot reverberated through the woods—woods that went suddenly silent, wind and trees hushed, listening. The sound died, and only Harley's sobs could be heard.

Tobin's hand touched Harley's shoulder and turned him back to the car.

"Sorry," said Harley.

"For what?"

Crying."

"We lost a friend," said Tobin. "No shame us crying."

Harley looked up. He couldn't see through his own tears, but there was no need. The tears in Tobin's voice must certainly be in his eyes.

They climbed into the car, neither of them looking back. And as they turned toward home, the clouds opened and released their rain—as though propitiated by the blood sacrifice of a gentle black mare.

The rain that fell on Oriskany Forks that night was the kind that turns houses to homes.

In the Bascomb home the rain had a countertheme, as drips of varying size and frequency fell into pans. Emma's big copper kettle sat in the hall just outside the girls' door. The drip it captured had made a lovely plink at first, like an A-string plucked on a cello. Now the kettle was half-full and produced only a watery plop.

Lil lay on top of the covers, staring into the rain.

Cass lay with her back to Lil. She had been pretending to sleep since Dr. Barnes's departure hours before. *I gave her a light sedative. Should sleep the night through.* Funny, she didn't feel sleepy. She should just open her eyes and say, "I'm sorry, Lil. I was curious. I found the witch book and left it out when I came to the kitchen this afternoon. How was I to know Papa would see it?" Her nose itched. Why didn't she just scratch it? Even if Lil was angry, even if she was a witch, she wouldn't do anything to her own sister. Or would she?

Maybe she's working a spell on me right now. This afternoon—was it an accident? Maybe that cat is her familiar. Maybe she told it to waste that pie just to make Papa hate me!

No. She wouldn't do that. She loves me.

But a little later, Cass fell asleep and dreamed that Mrs. Parkinson's yellow tiger tomcat leaped onto the windowsill. It meowed and Lil raised up. "Scat," said Lil. "I don't want you now." The cat licked his lips and blinked his green eyes. He twitched his tail and defiantly made himself comfortable on the sill. "All right," said Lil, and settled back down. "You do the spell if you like. My power is gone." The cat meowed again. His green eyes fastened on Cass, and he began to purr. It wasn't a nice sound, but she didn't know how to make him stop. The cat sat there till dawn, watching her with his green eyes, purring the night away. It seemed, in Cass's dream, that she didn't get another wink of sleep.

CHAPTER TEN

"DEAR HARLEY," CASS wrote the next morning,

Don't think me forward, but—

She stopped. He'd think she was stupid for not just telephoning, and if he knew they didn't have a telephone, he'd know they were poor and think she was after his money. Cass sucked at the tip of her thumb, then went on.

it's just that I know of no other way to get a private message to you. I do hate telephones, don't you? One simply cannot speak one's mind, what with reletives and operaters hanging about. The thing is, Papa anounced at dinner yesterday that he is giving up his—

Cass started to write "job at the cidermill," then changed it.

manegerial position at the Oriskany Forks Cidermill. Our brother Curt has found that his farm is much too big for one man to handle, so Papa has agreed to move out there and give him a hand. It will save Curt the expense of a hired man, and it doesn't matter to Papa, he's put money by over the years. It will really be nice, all that fresh air and stuff. Farming is proud work, don't you think? I mean, a farmer need bend his head to no man.

Anyway, the point is, we're moving to Curt's on Wensday—the very day we promised to meet you at the library, and—

She stopped again, wondering how to explain the next.

through a misunderstanding, my father returned the witch book to the library this morning.

Cass stared at this last, nodded appreciation of her noncommittal wording.

I am so very sorry, and I do hope my letter enables you to reach the library before someone else gets the book.

I hope, too, that we haven't seen the last of you. Perhaps you know our brother, Curt Bascomb...

"You did *what?*" said Lil.

"Wrote him a letter. I couldn't let him make a wild goose chase to the library. What's so terrible about it?"

"It was forward, that's what. And unnecessary."

"Why was it unnecessary?"

Lil reddened. "Because I telephoned him."

"From where?"

"From Grogan's, on Monday."

"Well, talk about forward!"

"That's not forward, that's businesslike. Besides, I didn't talk to Harley, I gave the message to the maid."

"A real maid? Gosh." Cass looked off across the fields to the western edge of the forest, beyond which, they'd learned from Curt, lay Spring Farm. The Saturday afternoon was sunny and warm, smelling of newmown hay. They were crawling along the banks of the road above Curt's house in search of dandelion greens for supper. "I wonder when he'll come."

"Why should he?"

"Because I told him when he went out riding, he'd just better drop by and say hello or we'd think he was downright unneighborly."

That meant he could appear at any moment!

"What's the matter, Lil?"

Lil gestured to their cotton dresses; faded, and, on Lil, shapeless.

"Oh," Cass frowned. "If we knew when he was coming, we could put on our Sunday clothes."

"But there's no telling, and Mama wouldn't let us wear them all the time."

They were silent.

"Lil. Why don't you just make some new dresses appear?"

If only she could. "Cass, the things that have happened have all been through people's heads—you know, putting an idea in someone's mind, making them act or feel a certain way. I couldn't just make a thing appear."

"Try."

Lil shrugged. She shut her eyes. "What kind of dress do you want?"

"Cornflower blue. With big puffy sleeves and a skirt so full it'll flare right up to my waist when I twirl around. What kind are you going to get?"

"Pink."

"Redheads can't wear pink. Muriel said so."

Lil gritted her teeth. "Be quiet." She squeezed her eyes hard and pictured her dress beside Cass's. Pink. Crepe.

Sleeveless. Clinging. An inch above the knee! Her eyes opened in shock, then closed. Well, why not? She concentrated with all her might.

Cass waited, hardly breathing. A bee droned toward Lil. Cass swatted it away. She stared at the ground before them, wondering if that was where the dresses would materialize.

Lil's face was red with effort. At last she opened her eyes and shook her head. "See? I told you it wouldn't work."

Cass patted Lil's hand. "Keep practicing. You'll get so you can do it." She reached for another fistful of dandelion greens, then let out a whoop. "Flowers!"

"What about them?"

Cass began to crawl, snatching at dandelions and buttercups, daisies and bluebells. "We'll cover ourselves with flowers. We'll make crowns and necklaces and belts and even skirts. We'll be so beautiful, Harley will fall off his silly horse when he sees us!"

Lil began to scramble too. "What will we do when they wilt?"

"Make new ones." Cass jumped up and stood over Lil, framed against the sky. "Look out there, Lil!" The meadows danced with wildflowers. "There are enough dresses out there to last us even if Harley Westcott doesn't come till Doomsday." She stopped suddenly, staring at the place where the road plunged into the woods.

"What's the matter, Cassie?"

"I thought I saw something."

"Harley?"

"No, something white. An animal."

Lil scanned the trees. "I don't see anything."

Cass shrugged. "I wonder where the road goes."

"Curt said it doesn't go anywhere."

"All roads go somewhere, or they wouldn't go." Cass shrugged again and returned to her flowers. "Shall we be twins?" she asked. "Or shall we each create our own?"

Helen Bascomb knew the story of Crazy Lizzy Stockbridge. Everybody but Lil and Cass did know it. "You couldn't get me to live in those woods," folks would say. And Mr. Timmans, who'd once lived in meadow house, came by a couple times a week to check up. He'd accept Helen's cake, then look up the hill toward the woods. "Poor Lizzy," he'd say. "I paid my rent in food—used to leave it on her stoop. Never saw her 'cept the time she told me I could move in—and the time she asked me to file her will. You sure you never seen her ghost walking at night? Lots of us have."

"I'm positive. More cake?"

Helen was a sensible woman. Homely women had to make up for their looks, she'd always felt, especially if they went year after year childless. Being sensible was one of the ways Helen made up.

Yet her imagination had, on several occasions, gotten the best of her. She thought she'd seen someone, or something, walking into the trees at the edge of the meadow. And sometimes, at night, as she and Curt slept, she'd imagined a face at the window. She wasn't frightened so long as Curt was with her, or when she could look out and see him in the fields or around the barns. It was when he was out of sight that she thought about Crazy Lizzy. *Lizzy began to act strange, afraid of living in open meadows.* Helen's bespectacled eyes would scan the meadows.

The weatherworn house and the equally weatherworn barn on the other side of the road stood in the center of those meadows. They drifted gently away from the house and barn; rising here, falling there. On a bright summer's day, the meadows were lovely—green, wildflowered, perfumed. Yet at night...She and Curt often sat on the porch on summer evenings, listening to the maples and the crickets. Wasn't it strange that neither she nor Curt had ever suggested taking a walk?

Of course, Helen knew perfectly well that there was nothing on those meadows to drive a woman crazy.

The woods? That was a different matter. Those woods would scare any woman—unbroken, black, encircling the meadows as invading hordes might have encircled a doomed village; watching, awaiting a signal to sweep down and destroy.

But the woods did not sweep. They inched forward—by night. She and Curt had lived in the meadow house two years before she'd noticed the advancement, but now she checked it each morning. Their greatest activity was in spring and summer. During April and May alone, the woods had moved a total of ten feet. Progress slowed in the fall, and all but stopped in winter.

Helen had never even thought it worth mentioning to Curt. It was easy enough to see that if the trees maintained their current rate, both she and Curt and their prayed-for children would be long dead before the trees even got within falling distance of the house.

Still, the news that Curt's family would be moving in with them had been a relief. "I'll enjoy the company." She'd thrown her slight, shapeless frame into cleaning, preparing the old house for new voices, new footsteps.

"Will you look what's coming up the driveway?" Emma laughed, a soft, gentle sound.

Helen smiled and joined Emma at the kitchen window.

Cass wore a mantle of bluebells with violet polka dots and a crown of Queen Anne's lace. Lil wore a sheath of pink lady's slippers with hollyhock buttons. Her crown of buttercups was fashioned into ropes that tumbled with the bronze of her hair.

"Behold, the lilies of the field," said Helen, "coming home to lunch."

Flower dresses were, the lilies found, exceedingly fragile. No amount of sprinkling with water or care in wearing could extend the life of the garments beyond a day.

The days moved through June into the heat of July.

"I can't find any more blue flowers," said Cass.

"You *would* choose the hardest color."

"Well, if you'd done the spell right, you'd have gotten us real dresses and we wouldn't have to keep making them." Cass stood up and surveyed the meadows for the twentieth time that Saturday morning. "When is he coming? It's been six weeks now."

"I don't know," said Lil, "but if he comes this morning, you'll be caught in nothing but your crown."

"Let's go into the woods. There must be blue flowers there."

There had been no definite instructions from the elders, just pointed remarks that the woods were no place for young girls to play. Until now they had ventured only to the edge. "I don't suppose we should," said Lil.

"You're trying to keep me from seeing something," said Cass.

"What, for heaven's sake?"

"We can't get lost if we stay near the road. And anyway, we don't have to be afraid. I mean, what could there possibly be in those woods for a *witch* to be afraid of?"

Lil sighed. Cass would never be satisfied until they did it. "All right." She tied a rope of lady's slippers to her dandelion belt. "We'll go in a hundred feet or so."

"Cassie!"

Two figures on bicycles pedaled out of the yard and up the road toward them. Muriel and Janet.

Lil sat down and started a new plait. One of the best things about moving out of Oriskany Forks had been that they seldom got to see Muriel. Lil glanced at Muriel's dress. New, as usual. "Don't tell them why we're making our flower dresses," she said.

"Cass," Muriel said, "that three-mile ride might be the end of our beautiful friendship!" She dismounted gracefully and arranged herself upon the grassy bank. Plump and puffing, Janet caught her hem on a pedal and fell. Muriel sighed. "Did you hurt yourself again?"

"Heck, no." Janet looked at Lil, then at Cass. "Whatcha got the flowers on for?"

"We're making dresses out of flowers," said Cass.

"Because we've got nothing else to do." Lil shot Cass a look.

"Oh, come on," Cass said. "We can tell Muriel."

"What? What? Tell me!"

"Cass, I'm warning you," said Lil.

"Because of the lady," said Cass, sitting between Muriel and Janet. "She came to us about a week after we moved here. She said we should dress ourselves in flowers every day, or something awful would happen to us." She looked back over her shoulder. "Right, Lil?"

Lil made a face and nodded.

"Pooh," said Muriel, "I don't believe you."

"Honest," said Cass. She looked at Lil a moment, hesitated, then dug into her pocket. "The lady gave us this."

Muriel and Janet stared at the object. So did Lil. It was a circular medal, of a silverish color. On one side was a long stick of some sort with a snake entwining it. On the other side was a six-pointed star, enclosing the head of a dog.

"What did the lady look like?" said Muriel.

"Dead," said Cass. "Very dead."

Janet squeaked.

Muriel gasped. "A ghost?" She jumped to her feet. "Cassie, tell me. What did she look like?"

"Very pale," offered Lil.

"Don't tease. This is important!" said Muriel.

"Well," Cass closed her eyes and rolled the silverish medal between her fingers. "It was hard to see, it was so dark out there—"

"Where?" whispered Muriel.

"The outhouse."

"Oh, come on!" said Muriel.

Cass opened her eyes. "Listen, do you want to hear this, or not?" She closed her eyes again. The medal glinted between her fingers. "It was about midnight. I woke up and had to do number two. I lit a candle—but you know, sometimes the dark is worse with a candle. You feel like everything can see you, but you can't see anything. So I blew it out and woke Lil. There are two ways to go to the outhouse. The right way is down to the parlor, through the egg-weighing room, and into the carriage house. The fun way is through a little door in the rear bedroom to an open loft over the egg room. It has a ladder down into the carriage house and the outhouse is opposite. It's only a two-holer, and it gets hot with the door shut, so we left the door open. I was constipated, and we played 'I Packed My Grandmother's Trunk' to pass the time—"

"We'd gotten to L," said Lil.

"Yeah, to L," said Cass. "Then we heard the little door between the bedroom and the loft open, ever so slowly. 'Papa or Mama?' Lil said. 'No,' I said, 'they'd come through the egg room.' Then we saw *her*—walking toward us through the loft. She was kind of..."

"Luminescent," said Lil.

"That's it," said Cass. "Lil and I grabbed hold of each other. I remember wanting to scream, but we were sort of paralyzed. Then she came down the ladder—"

"Kind of bobbing and swaying," said Lil.

"And talking to us," said Cass. "She wasn't just wandering, like some ghosts. 'I'm your friend,' she said. 'I want to help you.' She came within ten feet of us. 'Dress yourselves in flowers, or evil will befall you,' she said. 'Wear flowers till I return.' Then she lifted her hand, and the door of the outhouse slowly closed."

"When we got the nerve to open it," said Lil, "she was gone."

"And where she'd stood," said Cass, "was this medal."

"But what did she look like?" asked Muriel.

"Oh." Cass winked at Lil and closed her eyes again. "She wasn't young. Her hair was the color of Lil's and long. She was tall and sort of beautiful. I mean, her face was... commanding."

Lil smiled. Cass was describing the lady from the minstrel show in Missouri.

"Blood was dripping on the ground behind her," Cass went on. "Like from wounds, and her fingers were bloody. She was painted all over with funny symbols, and she didn't have on any clothes."

"Cass!" said Muriel. "How did you know?"

"Know what?" said Cass.

"That they found Crazy Lizzy naked and painted."

Cass and Lil exchanged looks. "All right," said Lil, suddenly serious. "Who's Crazy Lizzy?"

"You honestly don't know?" said Muriel. "You're living right here on this farm, and you don't know?"

When Muriel finished telling them the story of the first and second Mrs. Stockbridges, she explained that her grandfather had been coroner at the time of Lizzy's death. He and Muriel's father and Sheriff Bailey, who came out to get Lizzy's body after the Sears-Roebuck salesman reported it, had been the only ones to see it. And until the night that

Muriel overheard them discussing it, they and the undertaker had been the only people who knew that Lizzy's body, beneath that door, was naked—and that she, or somebody, had painted strange symbols upon that naked body, with homemade dyes.

"The Sears-Roebuck salesman didn't notice?" said Lil.

Muriel shook her head. "Till you raised the door, all you could see was bloody hands sticking out. And it took the three of them to raise the door. Now, look." She lifted a stern finger. "You all have got to promise never to breathe this to a soul. Because if my Dad finds out I've told, I'll get a worse licking than the one I got the night I eavesdropped."

"Why must it be such a secret?" said Cass.

"Isn't it obvious?" said Muriel. "Crazy Lizzy was a witch."

They all stared at her.

Lil turned to Cass. "I can see where that *would* be dangerous. Start a witch scare and we'd end up burning each other on the village green."

"Exactly," said Muriel. "There'd always been stories about Lizzy being a witch. Her dying naked and painted would have cinched it. Daddy and Grampa and the Sheriff thought it would be better for folks not to know."

"Right! Because where there's one witch, there must be more," said Janet. "And why go burning them if they're not doing anyone any harm?"

Muriel stared at Janet a moment. "Cass, is that all Lizzy told you to do? Wear flowers?"

Cass and Lil exchanged glances. There was no going back. "Yes," said Lil. "That's all."

"Dress yourselves in flowers or evil will befall you," repeated Muriel. "Janet's right. There must be other witches around—and obviously not such innocent witches, if Lizzy is telling you how to protect yourselves from them."

"Shouldn't we be protected, too, Muriel?" asked Janet.

Muriel put her hand to her throat. "Maybe we should."

Lil and Cass waited in the shade of a bush while Muriel and Janet gathered flowers and constructed their armor. "Where'd that medal come from?" Lil whispered.

Cass turned and looked at her, a secret shade in the blue of her eyes. "It just came. It was—under my pillow one morning. I thought it was from you."

"Not me," said Lil. "Papa, maybe?"

"Probably," said Cass. "Say, how'd you know about Crazy Lizzy?"

"Cassandra Bascomb!" said Lil. "You're the one who knew about Crazy Lizzy."

"I thought you were putting it into my mind," said Cass. "It just came to me like I'd really seen her." She hesitated. "And, Lil, maybe I have. Night before last I was looking out the window and I was sure I saw something—like a person walking in the fields."

"It was your imagination," said Lil quickly. She, too, had glimpsed a figure more than once but she refused to believe it was anything more than a trick of the moonlight. She looked up the road. "At least now we know what's in there. I wonder why no one ever told us about the house."

"I don't know," said Cass. "But I can't wait to see it."

Lil sat up. "You can't possibly want to go up there now!"

"I need blue flowers."

"Cass, we're messing with—I don't know what. But I know we shouldn't mess with it."

"Nothing can happen," said Cass. "We're wearing flowers!" She jumped up and called to Muriel. "Let's go take a look at Crazy Lizzy's house."

"Cass, you're confused! We didn't really see Lizzy. We don't know she'll protect us."

Cass paid no mind to her sister's voice.

❀ ❀ ❀

They walked in a twilight filtered through the trees from the morning above. The birdcalls and secret noises underfoot seemed an extension of the silence.

But was it as silent as it seemed? The girls kept glancing back, feeling rather than hearing—something.

The road turned slightly, and the clearing was before them. It was overgrown with deep, fertile greens, as though all the small vegetation of the forest had crept into that clump of sun. In the center sat Crazy Lizzy's house.

It was small, octagonal actually. There was no porch to speak of, just a stoop. The bottom story contained perhaps a dozen regularly spaced windows. The top story appeared to have none. In the middle of the flat roof sat a widow's walk.

Muriel stepped from the shade of the trees and started across the clearing. Then she stopped and nodded with satisfaction. "There's never a breeze. Never. Birds don't sing. Ever."

Lil shrugged. "There just don't happen to be any birds around right now."

Muriel walked ahead of them toward the house, then stopped again. "Wasn't that door closed?"

All eyes traveled to the front door of the house. It stood slightly ajar.

"I'm not sure," said Cass.

"It's not open enough to have looked open from a distance," said Lil.

"Maybe it was the wind," said Cass.

"There isn't any breeze here, ever," said Muriel.

"Let's go home," said Janet.

"Janet's right," said Lil. "We should go home. Because this is stupid."

But Muriel stood rooted. "I wonder where the carriage house is."

Her tone infuriated Lil. It reminded her of the expression she'd seen on the faces of the Methodist congregation when Reverend Smith preached his witch sermon. "I'm sure you'd be disappointed," she told Muriel. "You said yourself there've been tenants here since Lizzy died. Some spoil-sport has surely wiped the blood off those spikes and hung the door back on its track. Or do you think Lizzy's ghost will appear and re-enact the whole thing for you?"

Muriel's eyes narrowed. "Why not, Lil? Is Lizzy's ghost your own personal property?"

"Certainly not," said Lil. "As a matter of fact, we've taken you right down the garden path. There *is* no ghost. That was all a story that Cass made up."

"So how come she described Lizzy perfectly, even to the paint?"

"Maybe she read it out of your mind," said Lil.

"Then there's no reason to be afraid of going into that house?"

"None whatsoever."

"Let's see you do it." Muriel's eyes looked just like a pig's. So damn self-satisfied.

"All right," said Lil. "I will."

"Lil, don't!" said Cass.

But Lil had already started. She knew there was no ghost, even if know-it-all Muriel didn't. Besides, she mentally warned anything listening, I'm supposed to be a witch. You'd better not cross me.

Then the door of Lizzy's house swung completely open. Cass and Janet squealed. And over their squeals, Lil heard—a bell. No. Not a bell. A voice like a bell. "Go back," it said.

Lil turned, deciding to do just that. Then, catching sight of Muriel's triumphant smile, she did an about-face and kept on going. No need to be frightened, it had been the wind that had opened the door. And the bell had to have been her imagination.

"Come back!" Cass called.

Only her imagination.

Through the open door she could see an empty wedge-shaped room—but so bright! What was it on the walls of that room?

They took shape as she mounted the stoop: daisies, daffodils, pansies, peonies, sunflowers, rioting with no plan or pattern over the walls.

She crossed the stoop and stepped through the door, pushing it all the way back, reached out and touched the wall to her left. The flowers were hand-painted! Lovingly, meticulously painted on a field of sweet-butter yellow, seeming as real as the flowers she wore.

But not just on the walls. On the ceiling, on the floor, on the window strippings and moldings. Swirling. Hypnotic in their beauty—and, suddenly, terrifying.

Lil stood there in the doorway, her hand resting on a clump of daffodils. It seemed—she jerked her hand away. It *seemed* as though those daffodils had moved. She stared at them, expecting to see a petal crushed or bent from her touch.

"Lil? Please come back!" It was Cass, calling.

Lil swung about—just slightly, not wanting to turn her back on that room. Cass was halfway across the clearing. "Stay there, Cassie. Don't come in here!"

She should get away now herself, just back out the door and down the steps, get away from this place and out of these woods.

But her eyes went to the doors on each inner wall of that pie-piece room, and questions that her mind could not find words for drew her toward the closest—first boldly, and then on tiptoe; for she had been discovered. She could see no one, but she knew eyes were watching her, and, as fear begged her to run, the questions in her mind found words.

Emma's words, packing trunks to move east: "...gives up an inheritance..."

This farm must have been Papa's! And with the inheritance, this house. But Papa hadn't wanted it. Because he knew whatever there was to know?

"It's in the blood!" Aunt Alice had said.

Madness? Witchcraft?

Papa must have inherited this place from Crazy Lizzy.

Stockbridge. Mama and Papa had never mentioned Stockbridge cousins.

"Crazy Lizzy was a witch," Muriel said.

And she, Lil, was a witch, Cass said.

"It's in the blood," Aunt Alice said.

Whatever thoughts had created this room with these ghastly flowers might still be alive, sleeping in her own mind. She had to know what this house was. She seized the rusted knob of that first door and pulled it to.

Springtime rushed her vision; a hundred shades of greens-to-be strained from velvet husks and layered buds. Lil turned from that wedge of spring back to the wedge of summer, not understanding how drawings so beautiful could fill her with such horror.

What if it wasn't the drawings? What if the malignancy that permeated this place flowed from the thing that was watching? She could feel it still. Did it have a voice like a bell?

A ghost? An inherent evil? Or just an innocent place remembering mortals who had brought it evil?

She walked quickly to the last door, knowing what she should find. Autumn. A cornucopia overflowing.

She opened the door, prepared; then stepped back.

It was only a kitchen—the rest of the circle, a half-moon. Windows marched in orderly fashion around the outer wall.

Sunlight filled it. But painted, decaying vegetation slimed every surface. The kitchen was a place of death.

Lil slammed the door and turned to flee.

Across the room the front door began to close. Lil stood rooted, sounds jammed in her throat. She could get through before the door completed its arc. Instead, she watched as the door moved slowly to its latch and clicked into place.

Alone with *it*! There was a horrible silence.

Then, "Don't be afraid, Lilith."

Lil gasped and looked upward. Nothing! A ceiling of flowers. "Who are you?"

"Lil!" It was Cass, trying to open the door. "Are you OK?"

"I'm a friend." A man's voice. "Take the others and go home. Don't come here again."

The door flew open and Cass burst through, her energy carrying her halfway to the middle of the room before she saw the flowers. As she gasped, Lil had her by the arm and was pulling her toward the door.

Cass stiffened. "What is it?"

Muriel and Janet were climbing the stoop. "Don't come in!" called Lil.

Muriel stopped, then came right on. "I don't take orders from you, Lil Bascomb!"

The door swung shut in her face.

Cass clawed Lil's arm, staring at the door. She began to giggle, high and strained.

"What's going on?" called Muriel.

Lil took Cass's hand and tried to pull her. Cass wouldn't move. Her giggles became laughter. "Stop it!" said Lil. She gave a nervous laugh herself and glanced at the ceiling. "We're going. Really we are!"

Cass looked up, hiccupped, and began to sag, still laughing.

"Lil! Cass! Open this door!"

"Come on, Cass!" Lil tried to lift her sister. But Cass sank until she sat on the floor, clutching her stomach.

The hysteria was communicable. Lil let it out.

"We're coming in at the count of three!" warned Muriel.

Lil sank to her knees, laughing.

"One!" said Muriel. "Two! Three!" And she flung the door open. At sight of her friends, Muriel put her hands on her hips. "I suppose you think you're very funny," she said. Then her eyes swept the room.

Janet had seen all she wanted to see. "Let's go."

"No," said Muriel. "I came up here to see this place and I'm going to see it." Janet dogged her heels, unwilling to be left alone as Muriel circled the room, staring at the flowers. "No wonder they called her Crazy Lizzy."

Then there came a sound so tiny that only Lil was aware of it—a scraping from overhead. Lil jumped to her feet, tutting at Cass. "We're going home!"

"Why are you in such a hurry to make us leave?" said Muriel. She marched to the kitchen door and opened it. "Ugh!" She slammed the door and turned on Lil. "Why didn't you warn me it was so ugly?" Then her eyes went to the front door.

It was closing again.

"Lil Bascomb!" said Muriel. "You stop that!"

"Me?"

"Yes, you! You're trying to scare us away. I don't know how you make the door close, but I don't think it's funny."

"For your information, I'm not making that door close. And also for your information, I want us to get out of here because when I was in here alone someone told me to get us out."

"What someone?"

"Not someone. Just a voice."

"Just a voice," mimicked Muriel. "Where'd it come from?"

"Up there."

"You know what you are, Lil? You're a filthy rotten liar!"

"Don't you talk to my sister like that!" said Cass.

"If she wasn't your sister, I'd tell her what I really think of her."

Lil studied Muriel's sticky-sweet face. She'd always wanted to hit Muriel. And now, she decided, she would. She started forward. "What do you really think of me, Muriel?"

"I think you're gawky, homely, jealous, and stupid. No boy is ever going to look at you. You're going to be an old maid!"

"That's not so!" said Cass.

"Stay out of this," said Muriel.

"Don't tell my sister when to talk," said Lil. She was now within striking distance.

"Nnayyahh!" Muriel stuck out her tongue.

Lil's open palm caught Muriel with her tongue still out. She saw Muriel's face distort, saw the pink tongue collide with the teeth and go red.

"My teeth!" Muriel screamed as she felt the blood. Then she lunged, clawing at Lil's face.

Lil ducked, but Muriel's nails raked the side of her neck. Lil kicked Muriel's shin. Muriel doubled over. Grabbing Lil around the waist, she sank her teeth into Lil's midriff. Lil screamed. Muriel bit harder. Lil dug her fingers into Muriel's yellow hair and twisted. Muriel squealed, unclamped her teeth, shoved her finger into Lil's nose and raked with the nail. "Ow-w-w!" Lil released Muriel's hair, grabbed the offending finger and bent it back, hard.

"I hate you," screamed Muriel.

Lil brought her knee up, caught Muriel in the chin and sent her sprawling.

Janet and Cass were on Lil immediately. They were all too busy to hear the hoofbeats outside. "Stop," cried Cass, "you'll kill each other!"

"I *want* to kill her!" Lil shook them off.

But Muriel had gained her feet as Lil wrestled with the others. She'd gotten a running start, and now she hit Lil broadside, smashing her elbow into Lil's stomach. Lil doubled over, gasping. Muriel hit the back of her neck. Lil tumbled to the floor, and Muriel fell on top of her, pummeling with clenched fists.

Lil couldn't see clearly. A roar filled her brain. People shouted. She was crying. But she was fighting back, striking Muriel with everything she had.

Her hands wrapped around Muriel's neck. She squeezed until, suddenly, she felt herself being lifted. Still she fought. She saw Cass and Janet dragging Muriel away from her. "Let me go!" Lil screamed. "I want to kill her!" But the arms held her like a straitjacket.

As those arms changed position for better leverage, the attached hands cupped Lil's breasts. Firm and excited by battle, her nipples sent a shock zinging downward. She stopped struggling.

Hastily the hands lowered to her waist.

As in a dream, Lil saw Muriel across the room with Cass and Janet. And as she smelled the odor of horse and leather, felt the buttons of his shirt, his face alongside her ear, his breath quick and warm—right at the crease of her buttocks something between his legs grew large and hard and pressed against that surprised part of Lil.

Every muscle below Lil's waist tightened. "Harley," she gasped, "let me go!"

His arms squeezed, held one second longer than they had to. Then she stood alone.

She turned. Their eyes met; she flushed and looked down. But what she looked at was the front of his trousers. Her eyes widened, and she glanced up ever so quickly to make sure that he hadn't caught her looking at that place. He had. They both flushed crimson and turned away from one another.

Cass broke the silence. "What a surprise to see you, Harley!"

"Guess it must be." Harley leaned against the doorjamb, trying to be nonchalant and still keep his back turned to all of them.

A buttercup hung in Lil's eye. She swatted it away and lifted the hair from her neck. Her hands came away bloody.

"I'll bet," said Muriel to Harley, "you thought Lil and I were fighting!"

"Something like that," said Harley.

"Heavens, no," said Cass. "See, this is our clubhouse. They were roughhousing. You know, playing."

Harley looked first at Muriel, then at Lil. "I'd hate to be the one that had to play with either of them."

It wasn't true. The memory of Lil struggling in his arms was stirring his imagination as it could never be stirred by his own lonely hands in his own bed. Lil looked like some wild creature, drenched in flowers and sweat, blood on her neck, those wonderful unhaltered nipples showing through her thin little dress. At that moment Harley Westcott wanted nothing more in the world than to cross the few feet of space between him and Lil and rip that dress off her and look at those hard little breasts, and bite those nipples till they bled, with her fighting and scratching and biting back.

Her sister kept chattering. Harley kept nodding and saying, "Yeah," and "Uh-huh." But his eyes kept looking for Lil's and hers for his.

Then Lil walked to the other side of the room, deliberately placing herself where he couldn't see her without turning. He glanced down at the still obvious tent in the left side of his jodhpurs.

"Do you think it's silly" said Cass.

Harley blushed.

"Our club dresses. The flowers."

"Oh," said Harley. "No."

Cass smiled and came to his side. "Were you coming to see us?

Harley looked away. He *had* been thinking of maybe, kind of, dropping by to say hello. But it wasn't the first time he had thought of it. Several times he'd got to the edge of the woods, looked down across the meadows, seen the two girls gathering their wildflowers. He'd turned and gone back home. Today would have been the same.

Then he'd seen them all heading for Lizzy's. It was all right for *him* to go snooping around that place, but *girls*, he felt, should not go there unprotected.

Their screams had justified his gallantry; the race to the rescue and the ensuing struggle with Lil had filled him with glorious self-admiration.

Now he felt ridiculous, leaning against the door, hiding his shrinking erection; Cass there at his elbow. He felt unmanned before the gaze of that small, persistent person.

"Why'd you take so long to come see us, Harley? It's been weeks!"

"Cass," said Lil, "don't be nosy."

"I'm just interested," said Cass. "You don't think I'm nosy, do you, Harley?"

The open blue eyes beneath a crown of Queen Anne's lace could not be wounded. "I guess not," he muttered.

"There, you see?" said Cass to Lil. She returned her attention to Harley. "Would you like to be a member of our club?"

"I'll let you be president instead of me," said Muriel.

"No thanks," said Harley.

"Great idea," said Cass. "Let's take a vote. All those in favor of Harley Westcott for president of the—"

"Stockbridge Sorcery Society," whispered Muriel.

"—Stockbridge Sorcery Society," said Cass, "signify by saying 'aye'!"

"Sorcery Society?" said Harley.

"Aye!" said Cass, Muriel, and Janet.

"Nay," said Lil. "Harley doesn't want to be president."

"It's an honor, and you're overruled," said Muriel. "But now Harley will have to pledge not to reveal any of the secrets of the Society on pain of death."

"Why do you call it the Stockbridge *Sorcery* Society?" Harley asked.

"Take the pledge," said Muriel.

"I pledge," he said. "Why *Sorcery?*"

The story, told in the flowered womb of Eliza Stockbridge's house, was more ghastly in its second telling. The atmosphere of the house and the clearing intensified. The five young people moved into a knot in the center of the room, and Muriel's voice dropped to a whisper.

Harley's eyes traveled to the ceiling as Muriel described Crazy Lizzy's painted body. He noticed Lil's doing the same, but his concentration on Muriel's words never wavered.

"How often do you come up here?" he asked when she'd finished.

"Oh, lots," said Cass.

"You never come at night, do you?"

"No," said Muriel. "But we've been thinking about it."

"Don't," said Harley.

"Who do you think you are?" said Muriel.

"Your president," said Harley. "And as president, I call this meeting adjourned."

"Now, wait a minute," said Muriel.

Harley walked to the door. "Come on. I'll see you all back to the Bascombs'."

Lil followed; the others hesitated, staring after him. "Cass, I don't know whether you'd want him for a husband or not," said Muriel.

"Or president," said Janet. "He can get awfully bossy!"

Cass shrugged. "We'd see who was boss if I married him. And as to his being president—well, there really isn't a club, so he only thinks he's president."

"But Muriel told him the secret about Lizzy," said Janet.

"Pooh," said Muriel. "I might as well have told it to these walls! Harley Westcott only talks to his horse."

Outside, Harley untethered Polly and called softly to Lil.

She turned, shy, but Harley's mind was miles from what had passed between them. "Don't any of you come up here again."

Lil started. "It was you!"

Harley frowned. "Me, what?"

"You that spoke to me when I was in the house alone. You said, 'Don't be afraid. I'm a friend. Take the others and go home and don't come here again.'"

"You just heard a voice? You didn't see anyone?"

"No."

"Where did it come from, Lil?"

"You mean it wasn't you? It came from the ceiling."

Harley turned and looked at the windowless second story.

Lil turned too. "I didn't realize," she said. "There aren't any windows, but there must be rooms up there. I didn't see a stairway. How do you get up?"

"I don't know," said Harley. "I've never been able to find a way—Lord! It's been staring me in the face all the time, but I never saw the connection until I heard Muriel's story."

Inside the house, Muriel watched Harley and Lil from the window. "Cass," she said, "if you want Harley for a husband, you better watch out. I think Lil's trying to take him away from you."

Cass came to Muriel's side. "Don't be silly," she said, but as she saw Harley and Lil, her blue eyes clouded.

"You see," said Harley, unaware of the attention, "now that I know Lizzy was involved in some kind of witchcraft or black magic cult..." He looked at Lil. "Don't you get it? You read

Witch Cults of Western Europe. The house is round—possibly designed to have the upstairs one large round room!"

Lil sucked in her breath. "A witches' circle! And upstairs must be Autumn. There's Spring and Summer and Winter downstairs, but no Autumn."

"A few weeks ago I found a witches' circle in the woods, not a quarter of a mile from here. But I never connected witches with this place until today." The other girls were single-filing down the front steps. "Walk ahead with me," he whispered, and they started side by side down the road through the woods. "It's possible that a coven might still be using this place. That's why you girls shouldn't come up here."

"The voice I heard!"

Harley nodded. "There must have been someone up in that room all the time we were there. I heard noises. Didn't you?"

"Yes." She hesitated. "I heard another voice, too, Harley. As I was crossing the clearing to go in. It said, 'Go back.' But I thought it was my imagination because—well—it wasn't like a voice. It was like a bell."

Harley stopped. "A bell?"

The others overtook them. They walked on, not talking, ears closed to Cass's chatter. Behind them the clearing grew silent once more—and the door of Crazy Lizzy's house slowly closed.

CHAPTER ELEVEN

"WHERE HAVE YOU been, young man?"

Harley was tethering Polly by the kitchen door. "No place special."

Henrietta sighed. "Just out dreaming. And forgetting. Your Gramma and Grampa Parmalee have been here an hour already, and your Aunt Carrie ought to be coming along any minute."

"Aunt Carrie?" Harley frowned. Of course. Today was the day. "But I thought Grampa was sick."

Frank Parmalee's health had been failing for six years, but the attacks of the last ten days had been something else again. Doc Barnes was at a loss to explain them. Sudden nausea, accompanied by pains and a choking sensation in the throat.

"According to your mother," said Henrietta, "he's feeling better. Hasn't had an attack yesterday or yet today."

"I wonder what he had?"

"Why don't you go in the parlor and ask him?" She seized his arm and towed him across the kitchen, into the foyer, and through the door of the parlor.

"Here's our boy!" said Frank Parmalee.

Hitty's foot was tapping. "Where have you been?"

"Now, Hitty," said Frank, "don't scold. Can't blame a boy for wanting to be outside instead of in the parlor with the poor, sick old folks who love him. Right, Harley?"

Harley shrugged. Trying not to show shock at Frank's deterioration, he went to kiss Flora.

"I swear, you look more like my Daddy every day," she said. "That would be your great-grandfather Jason Cole, Harley."

"Yes, Ma'am. You've mentioned that before."

This would ordinarily have been Frank's cue to start cursing, but today Thomas's tongue was quicker. The elder Westcott hunched in his chair, irritable at the prospect of spending the day without access to the bottle in Hitty's settee. "Doesn't look at all like Jason. Harley takes after the Westcotts. Look at that forehead!"

"Fiddle-faddle!" said Flora. "What's a forehead?"

"It's where you keep your brains, Flora. Can't keep 'em in your mouth, 'less you're part squirrel. But then, I don't expect you're up on matters like that."

"Father Westcott. Please!" said Hitty.

Thomas chortled. "Come to think of it, old Jason didn't have much of a forehead, and he weren't much of a talker. Squirrel blood showing up, I expect. Got his mouth all clogged with brains."

Frank guffawed.

"Frank Parmalee!" Flora fluttered her fan. "Just because you and Daddy didn't see eye to eye, that's no reason to laugh when someone maligns his dead soul!"

"Who's maligning?" Frank grinned. "My fault your father didn't have a forehead?"

"All right," said Flora, "if you're going to talk about my family, I might say a thing or two about yours. Hitty, did you know your Grandmother Parmalee was a kleptomaniac?"

Tobin appeared in the door. "I thought," he said, "the Parmalees and Coles had stopped feuding."

"Not so long as one or the other has breath," said Frank.

"How are you, Mrs. Parmalee? Sorry I'm late. One of the hayloaders broke down, and I had to see to it. My men have ten acres to get in today."

"Hell of a rainy year," said Frank. "Ruined more hay than it's grown. You haven't put any stuff in wet, have you?"

"I hope not," said Tobin. Wet hay in the mow, Harley knew, meant moldering pockets of heat—and the danger of fire.

Frank chortled. "You know that Polack that moved in at Jason's old place? He's been putting in hay so wet you can see the water running off of it. Gonna have a barn-burning, sure as you're born. Should stick to being tenants, instead of trying to run a place of their own. Or better yet they should stay in Poland! Can't be much of a place, though, the way they're all flocking over here."

Harley stared out the window and willed the voices of the adults to go away. To Frank and Tobin, hay was one of the most important facts of existence. To Harley, hay was a smell. He wished there was a way to bottle it. If he pressed grass between two big stones, would he get a liquid? And would the smell of hay be in the liquid? If it was, he'd make a fortune.

Take an awful lot of hay, though; he'd have to charge a hundred dollars a bottle. But he'd get so rich that soon he'd be able to buy himself a private country just to grow hay. France? Germany? Too much history, too many monuments. He'd need a country nobody wanted.

Of course. Poland!

A few thousand Poles—if any were willing to stay in Poland—tending the fields and pressing the perfume and serving him in his mansion, somewhere in the endless, rolling plains. He'd sit in his mansion, at his concert grand, and play Chopin.

Lil would be with him. She'd sit in the same room, on a settee of burgundy velvet just like Hitty's. She'd wear flowers in her hair and she would be naked, for he would never allow her to wear clothes. And every so often the breeze would bring him a whiff of New Mown Hay and he would rise from the piano, go to her, and they would make love there on the burgundy velvet settee.

And later he'd buy Russia.

"Harley, I'm talking to you," said Hitty.

"Sorry."

"I asked if you've seen Carrie's new husband."

"How could I?"

"I thought you might have ridden by her house."

"Not lately," said Harley. Lately he'd been riding over Bascombs' way.

"Carrie finally caught herself a man," Hitty had announced a week before. Harley had felt an unaccountable loss at those words. "Nobody even knows what he looks like, but she's condescended to bring him over to meet us all on Saturday."

"Carrie finally caught herself a man" had struck Harley as an unfair and inaccurate description of Carrie's marriage. Carrie was a beautiful and singular woman. The fact that her singularity made everyone, including Harley, nervous in no way nullified the fact that she was singular. "A man has finally caught Carrie," is the way Harley would have described the match.

Harley had not even known of Carrie's existence until he was ten; for in 1907, a week after Hitty and Tobin were married, Carrie ran away from home. "Crazy jealous because I'd taken her beau," Hitty liked to boast. "Couldn't bear to see Tobin and me so happy."

Harley knew all the details. Carrie had left at night, hitched Frank's horse by herself, loaded all her belongings, and driven to Seneca. She arrived at Union Station at about six A.M., talked the stationmaster into buying the horse and buggy for the price of a one-way ticket to New York City plus fifteen dollars, and boarded the Express when it came through at seven A.M. That was the last the family saw or heard of Carrie for thirteen years.

Except at Christmas, when a card would arrive addressed to Flora, postmarked Lancaster, Pennsylvania. "Merry Christmas, Mother," it would say. "Your daughter, Carrie."

Each Christmas season found Flora watching the mail. Frank, too, would ask each day, "Well? Did it come?" But on the day that Flora finally answered "Yes," Frank would turn his back and refuse even to look at it. "At least we know she's still alive," he'd grumble.

Then, one afternoon in the summer of 1920, a Ford motorcar stopped in front of the Parmalee home and a slim, stylishly dressed woman got out. "Hello, Mother," she said when Flora opened the door. "Have you missed me?"

Flora fainted a total of five times that afternoon, a record even for Flora.

To this day no one knew exactly what Carrie had done in those thirteen years, how she had lived, or whom she had known.

"I suppose," said Frank that first afternoon, "you need money."

"No, Father. Don't worry about my funds. They're sufficient."

"Well, if you think you're going to live with us—"

"I've taken a room at the DeWitt Clinton," said Carrie. "And I intend to buy a home."

So she bought that strange cottage on the edge of the woods and hung upon her gatepost the family's one clue to the thirteen dark years. It was a small, neatly lettered sign: *Caroline Parmalee, MS.D.*

"Doc Barnes says there's no such thing as an MS.D.," Frank told Flora. "Now what do you suppose she's up to?"

No one knew. The shingle now had hung there for six

years. No clients had ever been seen to enter or leave the house. Carrie was a hermit, except for those occasions when she got in her Ford and disappeared for days or weeks.

The family had learned of her marriage through a one-sentence postcard, "Dear Mother, I am married. Your daughter, Carrie." The invitation for today's meeting and its acceptance had also been accomplished through the mail. Of the whole family, Harley with his rides past her house was the one who had seen Carrie most often.

The wheels of a car crunched gravel in the driveway.

"They're here!" Hitty made for the window. "That must be him getting out of the car. He's a big man. He's—" she stopped. "He can't be." She looked again. "He is!" She turned to face them.

"What is it?" said Flora and she, too, looked out.

Tobin sprinted across the parlor and caught Flora as she fainted.

"Carry her to the drawing room," said Hitty. "They mustn't see her this way."

But Tobin was staring out the window, and Frank, Thomas, and Harley crowded in beside him.

"Stand back!" said Hitty. "Give her air. Tobin! She's not a sack of potatoes. You're letting her rat fall out!"

"What the devil has Carrie got there?" roared Frank.

"Control yourself," said Hitty. "You're ill."

Flora moaned and opened her eyes.

"Looks to me," said Thomas, "like the fella's *black*. "

Flora fainted again.

"He's not black," said Harley. "I think he's Hindu."

"Why's he got the towel on his head?" said Thomas.

"Mehitable! Don't let them in!" said Frank.

"I think we ought to be polite," said Tobin.

A gleam appeared in Hitty's eyes. "Of course we'll let them in. I want to know all about my handsome brother-in-law."

"You're not going to let that black man in," said Frank.

"He's not black," said Harley. "He's a Sikh."

"I *will* let them in!" said Hitty. "And you're going to behave yourself, Papa."

The door knocker sounded, slow and heavy.

"Harley." Hitty shoved him toward the door. "Open it. But don't let the servants see him yet. Take them into the drawing room—"

"I won't meet him!" shouted Frank.

"Tell them—oh, tell them anything. Henrietta! Wait! Harley will answer. Play the piano for them, Harley." The knocker sounded again. "Go. And close the door."

But even thick oak could not muffle Frank's voice. It wouldn't do, Harley decided. He couldn't let them in.

Yet he wanted to. His heart pounded at the thought of actually speaking to Carrie.

The knocker sounded again; patient, measured.

"Well? You going to answer that or not?" Henrietta said.

"Yes," said Harley. "Go back to the kitchen. And don't come out till Mother says it's all right."

Henrietta disappeared into the kitchen.

Again the knocker. Deliberate.

And, still, the shouts from the parlor.

Harley walked slowly to the door, trying to formulate a suitably grand greeting, his first utterance to Carrie. Then he turned. "No peeking."

The kitchen door slammed. "I'll disown her!" Frank was shouting.

The measured thuds of the knocker came again, right in Harley's face.

"Welcome," he would say, and he'd try to look Carrie in the eye. Then he would say "Welcome" to the Sikh, and he'd try to look *him* in the eye. He braced himself and opened the door.

The greeting froze on his tongue. Nor, after the first glance, could he bring his eyes to theirs.

The Sikh was large, yet he had no superfluous flesh. The skin of his clean-shaven face was but a thin, dry covering for his skull. He wore a high-collared jacket of black and silver brocade and a spotless white turban. In the center of the turban was an enormous red stone.

Carrie wore a stylishly short frock of black silk. She, too, had a turban hat, of braided black and white silk. Her dark, bobbed hair was brought forward, sleek against her cheeks. Her eyes were calm, fastened on Harley, and she made no move to speak or introduce her husband.

They all just stood there, Harley trying to remember what he'd meant to say. "Hello" didn't seem special enough. For no good reason his eyes sought the stone on the Sikh's turban. "Is that a real ruby?"

The Sikh's lips parted in a lifeless smile. "Yes. It is." His voice was clipped, light and hard.

Harley offered his hand. "I'm Harley Westcott," he said. "I guess you're my new uncle."

The lifeless smile did not quicken. "I believe that is correct. I am Satyendra Singh." The Sikh's hand gripped Harley's. It was cool—strong and cool, and charged with energy.

As Harley finally met the Sikh's gaze, he found the life that was missing in the smile. Dark, cruel humor danced in those eyes. "What shall I call you?" Harley said.

"Satyendra will do. Not Uncle Satyendra, if you please, for that would be unrhythmic."

Harley nodded and shrugged, discomfited by the man's rudeness. "Satyendra," he repeated. He looked to Carrie. "Won't you come into the drawing room?"

"Why the drawing room?" Carrie's voice, oiled and polished, sounded at last. "My family seems to be in the parlor."

Harley avoided Satyendra's eyes. "When you drove up, everyone looked out the window—"

"And Mother fainted and Father is livid with rage," said Carrie.

Harley nodded and shrugged. "So Mother told me to take you into the drawing room till she gets them both talked around."

"You mean," said Carrie, "that Hitty is actually taking my part?"

She seemed pleased by the thought. Harley hurried to further her pleasure. "Sure she is. She *wants* to meet Satyendra."

He had never seen Carrie smile, but now her mouth twisted upward. "I'm sure she does." She took Satyendra's arm. "Shall we grant Hitty's wish, my dear?"

"But of course, my dear."

Carrie's free hand moved to Harley's shoulder. She shoved him aside like a chair, and she and Satyendra started through the foyer.

For a moment Harley was merely surprised. Then indignation swept him. "Say, who do you think you're shoving around?" He raced ahead to the parlor door. "You're not going in there!"

"Why not?" said Carrie.

"Because!" She was treating him like a kid! "You can't go in because I say you can't."

"Stand aside, you ill-mannered brat!"

Harley caught his breath. He wanted to shout at her. Or hit her. Instead, he drew himself up and, with stony determination, continued to guard the parlor door.

Carrie's eyes were slits. "What a strange child. Blushing boy one moment, *Chun Di* the next."

"I'm a man!" It was the first time Harley had thought it, much less said it. "And I'm not a *Chun Di*. Wouldn't I look stupid crouching in front of some Buddhist temple trying to impersonate a doglike cat?" He waited for Carrie's surprise.

"No more stupid than you are right now, trying to impress me with your intelligence."

"Me?" Harley felt the telltale flush creep over his face as he searched for something nasty to say. "You're the one who used an obscure phrase to impress me with *your* superior intelligence."

"You admit, then, that I do have superior intelligence?" said Carrie.

"No." Harley frowned. She twisted everything he said. "I admit that you're older and you've had time to learn more than I have. But you've certainly never learned any manners."

"How careless he is," said Carrie to Satyendra, "with the love and goodwill of his aunt."

"Aunt?" Harley looked at Satyendra. "She exhumed that title." Then to Carrie, "Love and goodwill?" To Satyendra, "She didn't have to find graves for those two. They never existed. She has a tricky imagination." He was getting the round-smooth-stone-exhilarating-down-a-hill feeling. Why should he care if he hurt her? She didn't care about him. "Why should I worry about your goodwill, Carrie?"

"Perhaps for reasons you cannot fathom."

"Bullshit!" Harley said it to shock Carrie. She didn't flinch. "Don't talk to me about love," he went on. He felt his face burning. "You know what I think?" Again he aimed for Carrie's heart. "I think you hate my guts."

"That's true," said Carrie.

Harley's mouth opened and he just stared at her. He'd expected her to deny it, to reassure him. "Why?" His eyes stung, and he clenched his teeth. "I'll tell you why," he said. "You think I don't know? You hate me because I'm the son of the sister who stole the man you love!"

At that moment Harley realized why Carrie's gaze was so unsettling. Things happened in her eyes. Pain happened in them, ever so briefly, at his words. But she literally didn't bat an eyelash. He tried to remember if he'd seen her blink even once since he'd opened the door. She must have blinked! She hadn't.

Suddenly, Carrie smiled. "Tell me, Harley." Harley straight-ened. Carrie had never used his name before. "Since you won't allow us to enter the parlor, what shall we three do to amuse ourselves while my sister persuades my father to feign toleration for my husband?"

She didn't seem angry now. That quickly, and that easily, Harley seemed to have won. And the way she said "we three" made him feel—accepted. "Well, Mother told me to play the piano for you."

"Must you?"

"No," said Harley. He cast about for an idea. "I could show you the house."

"Excellent," said Carrie. "I've never seen the upstairs."

"The upstairs?" He'd had in mind the downstairs.

"Of course, if it is too much trouble..." said Carrie.

"Why no," said Harley, "I guess..." The argument still raged in the parlor; he'd been sent to keep the visitors occupied; and though asking to see the upstairs was strange, he had to do something. He shrugged. "Come on."

The moment he started up the staircase, he wanted to turn and say, "Forget it!"

He could feel their eyes: Satyendra's, cruel and amused; Carrie's, unblinking.

And he could feel—

Danger. What he'd felt when he opened the front door. What he'd felt the day he and Hitty passed Carrie on the road. What he'd felt the times he'd ridden by Carrie's house and locked eyes with her.

The feeling had always been vague and incomplete.

The feeling this time was neither. It was as though Carrie, alone, had not been enough, had needed Satyendra to join the circle. Carrie's hatred was now a vital force, and it flowed into Harley's mind as though she screamed it at him.

Could she actually hate enough to harm her own family?

Who would she harm? How would she do it? She and Satyendra weren't about to knife him in some upstairs chamber or machine-gun the family in the parlor.

Subtle, calculated, like themselves; that's how the harm would come, he decided.

He should stop, make them go back down. But he couldn't. He'd won the battle of the parlor door. As forcefully as he sensed their malice, Harley sensed a sign of weakness now might bring them to his throat.

And what if he was wrong? What if the encounter at Lizzy's was making his mind play tricks?

The pink marble staircase led to the gallery, which described a square and overlooked the staircase and foyer. Its railings were of polished oak, as were the doors of the family's bedrooms opening off it. At the head of the stairs, a passage led to unused guest rooms over the servants' quarters. Harley gestured grandly as he reached the last step. "What shall it be first?"

"I'd like to see your bedroom," said Carrie.

"Fine," said Harley. "Dad and Grampa and I have the west side." He led the way around the gallery. "Mother likes the morning sun, so she has the east. She has a suite really— bedroom, sitting alcove, sewing room..." Carrie's eyes were studying Hitty's doors. "Well, here we are." He opened his door and stood aside for them.

After a preliminary glance, Carrie went directly to Harley's bookcases. Satyendra's movements were less certain. He hesitated, drifted toward the desk, then changed course; looked at the bed, looked at the balcony, and turned.

"You can tell a lot about a person by examining his books," said Carrie.

"What can you tell about me?" asked Harley.

Satyendra had stopped and was running his fingers over the laughing Buddha on a table by the bathroom.

"I can tell," said Carrie, "that you are a serious young man. Studious. Perhaps intelligent. Time will tell."

Satyendra's hands made no suspicious moves, and Carrie's rested easily at her sides.

"You love history," Carrie went on. "You are interested in the occult and you have a passing knowledge of world religion and mysticism. You most likely have a vivid imagination. Yes." She turned, and to Harley's surprise, she was smiling—openly, genuinely. "You most likely have a *very* vivid imagination."

The sudden warmth and the feeling that his mind was being read made Harley flush and turn away. Satyendra must have stepped into the bathroom at that moment—when Harley turned back, he was gone.

It took only seconds for Harley to reach the door and shove it open. Satyendra stood by the toilet, a package of toilet paper in his hands, shaking his head at the neatly stacked tissue. "I never cease to be amazed," he said, "at Western superfluity." He put the toilet paper down and went back to the bedroom.

Harley checked the bathroom; nothing amiss. Except that his hairbrush, always neatly placed on a small tray, was halfway off the tray. "If you don't mind," he said to both of them, "I'd rather not have you wandering where I can't see you."

Carrie hadn't moved, but her smile was gone. "Do you think we're thieves?" she said.

"I have a vivid imagination," said Harley. "Humor me. Shall we see Dad's room next?"

Carrie shrugged and preceded the other two onto the gallery.

"What a shame you are Mehitable's son," said Satyendra as he passed Harley. "I think my wife could have liked you."

"Charming," said Carrie. Harley glanced about Tobin's room, wondering what was charming about maple furniture, a rag rug, and photographs of bulls. "Magnificent creatures," said Carrie. "Are they vicious?"

Harley wished Satyendra would stay put instead of wandering around, fingering things.

"King's the only one we can handle without a bullstaff," he said.

"We?" said Carrie. "You mean your father and his men. *You* couldn't handle those animals."

"I can too! As a matter of fact, Dad doesn't trust them to the hired men."

"And he trusts them to you?"

"I can do anything I want with King," said Harley. "We're friends. I go right in beside him and scratch his back."

Carrie smiled. "But not the others."

"I can handle them, too. If you like later I'll take you out and—"

At that moment, Harley realized that Satyendra was gone. He rushed to Tobin's bathroom. "What the heck is it with you and bathrooms?"

The Sikh stood at Tobin's sink, Tobin's hairbrush in his hands. "As my wife learns of people from their books, so do I from their bathrooms. Besides," he said with no hint of humor, "I find Western plumbing an endless source of fascination and delight."

"We have a guest bathroom downstairs," said Harley. "Please take your fascination and delight there or in your own house."

"Alas." Satyendra replaced the brush and came out wearing his lifeless smile. "We have only, in our home, what is called here an outhouse. But I shall be pleased to inspect your downstairs guest bathroom."

"I must see Hitty's apartment first," said Carrie.

"Of course." Harley bristled. That was twice she'd played decoy for Satyendra, and she wouldn't get away with it again. As he led them around the gallery to Hitty's door, he tried to think up a way to avoid entering. If he was not imagining things—if Carrie and her toilet-prowling Sikh did, in fact, plan some sort of revenge—Hitty must be the prime target of that revenge. Downstairs the parlor door was still closed. Perhaps it would open in the nick of time.

It didn't. He would just have to keep the two of them together. He opened the door. "Voilà!" he said. All was as usual in the room: the lavender satin bed, neatly made; French furniture, well-placed and polished; Hitty's dressing table, cut crystal bottles, cosmetic pots; the scent of lilac overpowered by Upjohn's musk, which had replaced lilac as Hitty's favorite perfume; the chessmen poised for battle; French windows open, a breeze stirring lacy curtains; Genevieve sunning her blue self on the balustrade.

All as usual.

And yet, as though repelled by some invisible barrier, Carrie and Satyendra stopped stock still in the doorway. "I've changed my mind," said Carrie. "I don't care to see Hitty's room." She and Satyendra walked quickly to the stairs and descended.

"Good afternoon, Miss Carrie."

It was Henrietta's voice. Harley closed Hitty's door and hurried down the stairs, making faces at his old nurse. "I thought I said—"

But Henrietta crossed her arms and, examining Satyendra from the corners of her eyes, assumed the belligerent air that Harley knew meant business. "Cook's soufflé is set for one o'clock dinner. It's almost that now."

"Then we'll have to do without the soufflé," said Harley.

"Then you'll do without Cook," said Henrietta. "She says if you aren't at the table in five minutes, she's leaving."

Harley frowned at the parlor door. Agnes had departed twice before over matters such as these. Pursued by Hitty in the Stevens-Duryea all the way to Union Station in Seneca, she'd been persuaded to return. Each time, Agnes swore it would be the last time.

Now, Harley vacillated between distaste at the thought of life without Agnes' cooking, and fear of what would happen if he opened the parlor door.

Carrie solved the dilemma. Before he could stop her, she had opened that parlor door and stuck her head in. "Good afternoon, all! Hitty, your cook is threatening to quit unless we're at table in five minutes. When you've finished your debate, you'll find us there." She closed the door. "Come," she said, and placed a companionable arm over Harley's shoulder. "Let's rescue the soufflé."

The dining room, pale pink and strawberry, was made airy by banks of small-paned, floor-to-ceiling windows and the avenue of maples beyond. At the far end was Hitty's hothouse, where flowers grew the year round. The table had leaves to seat forty, but today it was charmingly set for eight.

Colleen pushed a serving cart with a soup tureen in from the kitchen; Henrietta followed, wielding a copper ladle. The two set to serving soup, trying to keep their eyes off Satyendra.

Carrie circled the table, reading place cards. "Here we are, my dear, 'Carrie' and 'The Groom.'" She sat down and took up her napkin. "Since I am hostess in the absence of my sister, I say 'begin' for the sake of the soufflé." She tasted the soup. "Excellent vichyssoise. No, we mustn't chance losing the cook."

Footsteps sounded in the drawing room and Thomas appeared. "Never seen such goings-on in my life." He came directly to Satyendra. "Hello, there." He stuck out his hand. "I'm Thomas Westcott. Glad to meet you. What's your name?"

"Satyendra Singh."

"I think that takes more exercise than my tongue's used to," said Thomas. "Mind if I call you Sam?"

"Not at all," said Satyendra.

Thomas nodded at Carrie. "Miss Carrie. Nice to see you. Now where's that daughter-in-law of mine want me to put my carcass? Here I am, right between the newlyweds." He sat down, seized his napkin, consumed a spoonful of soup, and turned back to Satyendra. "You black, Sam?"

"If you mean of the negroid race," said Satyendra, "no."

Thomas nodded. "That's what Harley said. Said you were a Hindo or something. You sure look black to me. Get a lot of sun out your way, I expect."

"Quite a bit."

Harley frowned into his soup. Satyendra was acting almost human. He was not offended by Thomas. He seemed, rather, to be amused by the old man. And Carrie, too, was smiling at Thomas. She winked at Harley.

Where were his villains?

"I've never seen you smile before today," he said to Carrie.

"You never saw me happy before today."

Maybe that was it. Maybe there'd never been any threat or mystery in Carrie, just bitterness and loneliness.

"Sorry, Carrie." Tobin entered with Flora, pale and thin-lipped, on his arm.

Hitty was right behind; pretending to lean on Frank's arm as she actually dragged him in. "We had the most dreadful accident just before you drove up, Carrie. Mother was eating peppermint candy and she swallowed the wrong way. She went into a fit of coughing, just like convulsions—thrashed about, knocked things over—then, of course, she fainted. We could hardly allow your husband to meet her in that condition."

When the family had been seated—with a rapid reshuffling to place Frank at the other end of the table from Satyendra—Hitty took her seat and lifted her napkin. "You may serve the soup, Colleen."

"It's served, Mum."

"My stars!" Hitty laughed. "Had it been a snake, it would have bitten me." As she leaned toward Satyendra, Harley saw him stiffen. "You must have that saying in your country, too, Mr. Singh."

"I don't believe we do," said Satyendra.

"But you have so many snakes. All those cobras."

"Really? I've never seen one. But, then, I was sheltered. What you might call a palace child." He glanced at Carrie. "Tell me, Mehitable, what is that perfume you wear?"

"It had no label."

"It is unusual. Where did you get it?"

"I don't remember. You were a *palace* child?"

"Oh, yes. My maternal grand-uncle was the Maharaja of Patiala. I was raised in his palace."

There was a moment of respectful silence at the table.

"Who'd of ever thought I'd be sitting next to a prince and calling him Sam," said Thomas.

"I'm sorry to disappoint you, my friend. I am not a prince, merely a poor relation on whom an esteemed uncle took pity."

"Well," said Thomas, "we got poor relations in America, too. But not so many esteemed uncles. He did all right by you, I see."

All eyes went to the ruby on Satyendra's turban.

"He was most generous."

"What do you do?" said Frank Parmalee. "Just sit around and count your rubies?"

"No," said Satyendra. "That would grow tedious, as I have only one ruby to count. I am a doctor."

Frank snorted. "Of what? You another one of these MS.D.'s?"

Satyendra seemed about to answer, then he stared at Frank's face instead. A frown wrinkled his brow, and he looked away.

"What's the matter?" said Frank.

"Nothing, sir." He smiled at Hitty. "This is excellent soup. My compliments to the cook. And forgive me for pursuing the subject, but I remain intrigued by your perfume. Are you sure you cannot remember where you obtained it?"

Harley stopped with his spoon midway to his mouth, suddenly convinced it was Upjohn's musk that had kept them out of Hitty's room. Without really understanding why he did it, he poked Hitty under the tablecloth. Her small hand closed around his as he heard her say, "Now that I think about it, I believe I got it from a Sears-Roebuck salesman."

"Do you remember his name?"

"Let's see—Arbuckle! Angus Arbuckle...Henrietta, you may serve the next course."

"Damn good soup," said Frank. "Cold, though."

Satyendra turned again and gave Frank a long, worried look.

"What's the matter?" said Frank. "I got a fly on my nose?"

Satyendra started, as though he hadn't expected Frank to notice the scrutiny. "Forgive my rudeness, Mr. Parmalee. It is simply that, as a doctor, I am aware of certain symptoms. You have been extremely ill, have you not?"

"Doesn't take a doctor to see that."

"I was not commenting of the fact of illness. It is the form of illness which intrigues me."

"And you know the form of my illness?"

"I do."

Frank stared at him. "I don't believe you."

"Doc Barnes said he'd never seen anything like it," said Flora.

"I'm sure that is true," said Satyendra.

"It's rare, then?" said Hitty.

"In your country, yes," said Satyendra. "It is common in mine."

Frank's voice hardened. "That might be so, Mr. Whatever-your-name-is, but for one thing I don't believe either you or Carrie are doctors. For another, I'd sooner be treated by a horse doctor than by either one of you."

"I, too," said Carrie, "would sooner you were treated by a horse doctor than by either one of us." She said it so quietly and with such a lack of malice that it might almost have been a jest.

Hitty laughed. "Some people claim Dr. Barnes is a horse doctor." Then, as if that remark had settled everything, she said, "Carrie! Where ever did you and Satyendra meet?"

"Wait a minute." Frank held up a hand. His eyes flicked from Carrie to Satyendra. "Maybe I've been unfair. We got a brilliant doctor here. An MS.D.! And he's so smart he knows just from looking, what's wrong with me. Go ahead, Mr. MS.D.! Tell me what's the matter!"

"You might not like it," said Carrie.

"I think," said Frank, "I'll be able to stand the shock."

That, it occurred to Harley, was not necessarily true. Frank Parmalee still thought he was the man he'd been before six years of bad health and ten days of acute illness. He wasn't. And he'd already had one bad shock today.

"You have, of course," Satyendra was saying, "been suffering from nausea, sharp pains in the abdomen, difficulty in breathing much like strangulation."

"Who'd you hear that from?" said Frank.

"And you have been having another difficulty, which delicacy forbids me to mention."

"What's that?" Flora demanded.

Frank's face reddened. "Nothing." He turned to Satyendra. "How come you know all this? You bring some kind of Asian epidemic to Oriskany Forks with you?"

"I said it was common in my country," said Satyendra. "I did not say it was endemic. And it is not contagious. But perhaps, after all, I am wrong. Let us enjoy our meal and forget my presumption. Mehitable, the soufflé is superb."

Frank frowned at his spinach soufflé and at his roast chicken. He tried to eat, then slammed his fork to the table. "God damn it! You're a doctor. If you know what I got, it's your duty to cure me."

Satyendra sat quietly for a moment, then summoned Colleen and whispered something to her. She curtsied and ran from the room. Satyendra returned to his meal.

Frank watched him for several exasperating mouthfuls. "What the hell was that all about?"

"I sent the young lady to the automobile for my bag," said Satyendra. "I have something that will help you." He fixed Frank with his dark eyes. "It will help. It will not cure. There is no cure for your affliction."

The color drained from Frank's face. "What do you mean, no cure?"

"Fiddle-faddle," said Flora. "It's indigestion."

"Hush, Mama," said Hitty. "Satyendra, what is this disease?" Satyendra sighed.

"It has no name, really. Africans call it *tandritanitani*. In my country we call it Curse-Death. Mr. Parmalee, is there a curse on you or your family?"

Frank's eyes darted to Carrie's. "You told him," he said.

"Don't be silly," said Flora. "You know the gossip about Papa's curse isn't so!"

"You weren't there," said Frank. "I was."

Hitty shook her head. "No, Satyendra, you've got to be wrong. A curse won't kill a good person and Papa is good. He's never harmed anyone in his life."

But he has, thought Harley. She's right at his elbow, coiled and ready to strike. Doesn't anyone else realize?

He searched the faces around him for an ally—Thomas, old and innocent; Flora, telling herself Frank had indigestion;

Tobin, staring out the window and thinking about things he would rather be doing; even Hitty—having for some reason known enough to protect Upjohn, now displaying no hint of awareness.

Only Frank, avoiding Carrie's gaze, felt the danger which Harley knew suddenly to be a reality.

It was up to Harley to sound the alarm, to cry "danger" and save his grandfather. It would be as good as murder if he didn't.

Colleen returned with Satyendra's bag.

Harley kept trying to figure things out.

Upjohn was a witch. That had been Harley's major premise since the day he'd discovered the circle in the forest with Upjohn's scent so near, and then had recognized that scent so strong around Hitty.

But, now, as Harley pondered his premise, it no longer led him to assume that his mother was involved in witchcraft, or worse yet, was Upjohn's lover. Now, it seemed obvious that Upjohn was a witch and had given a witch perfume to Hitty. Maybe for protection from Carrie and Satyendra. Maybe he knew them, and if that was so...

Satyendra was taking a small black bottle from his bag, handing it to Frank. "Empty this into your water and drink it," he said.

...Then Carrie and Satyendra were witches, too! Six years ago, Carrie had come home. Six years ago, Frank's health had begun to fail. And the violent attacks of the past ten days coincided with the arrival of Satyendra Singh in Oriskany Forks.

Harley leaned forward. "I wouldn't drink that stuff, Grampa Parmalee."

"I wouldn't either," said Thomas. "Looks just like blackstrap molasses."

Frank put the cork back into the bottle. "I'm not gonna drink it."

He took up a chicken breast. "Curse-Death! Never heard such foolishness in my life."

"Of course, it's foolishness," said Flora. "My father wouldn't have put a curse on you."

"Why not, Mother?" said Carrie. "Grampa Cole had good reason to hate Father—Gramma Cole *died* of shame when she found out you were pregnant and had to marry him."

Frank choked on his chicken.

"Mama died of pneumonia!" said Flora. "And I wasn't in the family way, you were premature!" Frank was still choking. "Take some water, Frank." Frank tried to drink, but fresh choking seized him and the water spewed over the table.

"Give him a piece of bread," said Hitty.

Tobin stuffed a bit of roll into Frank's mouth.

It, too, got lodged in Frank's throat.

"I fear it is Curse-Death," said Satyendra.

Frank's eyes widened. He clutched at his throat.

"He's having one of his attacks," Flora said calmly.

Satyendra took the black bottle and moved quickly to Frank's side. "Please, sir, drink it!"

Frank backed away from Satyendra. The choking worsened.

"Please, Daddy, drink it for me!" Hitty seized the bottle from Satyendra. She held it to her father's lips and poured. Frank swallowed.

Then a look of horror crossed his face. He slumped to the floor, gasping, arms clutching frantically, pulling Hitty with him.

"Somebody better do something," said Thomas, and he ran from the room.

"Papa!" Hitty pounded Frank's back. "Satyendra, you're a doctor!"

"There is nothing I can do," said Satyendra.

Frank's head jerked up. Eyes popping, breath wheezing, he stared at Satyendra.

"He looks like a beached fish," said Carrie.

"Here!" It was Thomas, out of breath, having run for his precious whiskey.

"He doesn't drink," said Flora.

"This is tonic." Thomas gave Frank a slug. Frank gurgled. The whiskey bubbled out of his mouth and down his chin.

"Why, I've never seen it so bad," said Flora. "He's turning blue."

"He's dying!" said Hitty.

"It's the Curse-Death," said Satyendra.

"It's not!" cried Hitty. "It's chicken and bread stuck in his throat! Do something, *some*body!"

Tobin seized Frank's legs. "Harley. Give me a hand." They hoisted Frank till he hung upside down. "Shake him," said Tobin. "Pound his back, Hitty."

They shook and pounded; Frank flopped and gagged. Then the gagging stopped. "I think we did it," said Tobin. But when they lowered him, Frank was still. His mouth was slack and his eyes stared, unseeing, at the ceiling. Only a rattle in his gullet signaled life.

"He will be dead in a minute," said Satyendra.

"No!" Hitty plunged her fingers into her father's gaping mouth.

Harley knelt quickly. "Let me try." It was no use. "It'd take a doctor, Ma."

"To do what?"

"To cut the chicken out."

Hitty stared, wild-eyed, at her son. Then she jumped to her feet and ran into the kitchen. Her cries were muffled by the door. "Don't give up! I'm coming, I'll help you!"

She burst back into the dining room with a short, sharp paring knife in her hand.

"Hitty!" Tobin tried to head her off.

"Out of my way!" Hitty sliced the air viciously, and Tobin leaped back.

"Why's she got the knife?" said Flora.

"Ma! You can't! You don't know how!"

Hitty dropped to Frank's side, and pulled his limp torso onto her lap. Frank's head fell back over her legs, presenting a naked stretch of throat. Hitty stared a split second. Then, with a cry, she sliced open her father's Adam's apple and plunged her fingers into the bloody slit.

Flora screamed and fainted.

Harley turned away, sick and dizzy, thinking that Hitty was ruining her Karastan rug.

"A tube," said Hitty. "Quickly."

Harley swallowed his nausea and raced for the kitchen.

"Hurry!" screamed Hitty.

Harley found an eyedropper. He ripped off the top and ran back to his mother.

Hitty pushed the short glass tube into the wound. "Help me! Over the chair! On his stomach! The blood is blocking his air!"

They pushed Frank into what struck Harley as a guillotine position—on his knees, chest on the seat of the chair, head hanging.

"Hold his head level," said Hitty, and she began to pump his back, down and up, down and up, her breath escaping in sobs. "Please, Daddy. Breathe. Breathe!"

Harley stood back, crying—not for the grandfather who had been least favorite, but for Hitty. Soft, pampered Hitty.

Carrie and her Sikh stood side by side, their faces expressionless.

"Breathe!" cried Hitty. "Breathe!"

Then Frank did breathe—if you could call the sounds which began to suck and whistle through the medicine dropper in his throat "breath."

CHAPTER TWELVE

IT TOOK BURT Barnes, Jr., only seven minutes to reach Spring Farm. He had been the first citizen of Oriskany Forks to drive a motorcar, and the only speed limit he ever observed was the nature of the emergency.

"Hurry!" Henrietta had said on the phone.. "Mr. Parmalee choked on a piece of chicken and Hitty cut his neck open!"

That was a pedal-to-the-floor emergency.

It seemed to Harley that the summer day had grown cold. Everyone but Hitty was gathered in the library, and Tobin had lit the logs. No one spoke. An hour passed. A nurse arrived, officious in white.

Hitty passed the room on errands several times. Tobin rose whenever her footsteps sounded and watched her from the door of the library. Then he'd return to his chair and stare into the fire. He looked, Harley thought, like a man who had lost something but couldn't remember what.

At last Hitty came into the library, still wearing her blood-stained lavender gown. She walked to the fireplace. "That's good," she said. "I didn't realize I was so cold." She seemed taller, straighter, so much more commanding than Harley remembered.

Then he understood what Tobin had lost.

"Can't I do something for you?" said Tobin.

"No. We can only wait," said Hitty. "He's unconscious."

"Will Doc be moving him to the hospital?"

"He doesn't think he could stand the trip." She turned to Thomas. "Father Westcott, did I see you with a bottle of whiskey a while ago?"

"Tonic," said Thomas. "You saw me with tonic."

Hitty gave him a tired smile. "That's a shame. I was hoping it was whiskey. I know Agnes has some rum flavoring for baking and I thought we might all do with a hot toddy."

Thomas stared at Hitty. A trap if he'd ever heard one.

"I remember," Hitty said wistfully, "whenever I was very sick with a cold, Papa used to make me a hot toddy."

Flora gasped.

"It always made things so much better," said Hitty. "Do you remember, Carrie?"

Carrie was silent a moment. Then, "Yes. He brought me a toddy once."

Hitty turned toward the fire. "He used to sit me on his lap while I drank it. Did he do that with you?"

"Yes."

"And then," said Hitty, "he'd tuck me in. He'd put that old yellow violin under his chin and play till I was fast asleep. Remember the tune, Carrie?" Hitty began to hum.

Harley sat forward. Of course Carrie remembered. She hummed that melody every time she worked in her garden. At what did she work? At what would a witch work? Herbs, root—*poisons?*

Harley jumped to his feet. "I think I know where there's whiskey, Mother. I'll get it." He raced to the dining room.

But not in search of whiskey.

The black bottle. Harley had seen it fall from his mother's hand as Frank pulled her to the floor. He searched the blood-soaked rug, under the table. The black bottle was nowhere to be found.

Then he remembered. Satyendra had stayed in the dining room when they carried Frank out. To retrieve the bottle?

"Harley!" Thomas checked the room for spying ears. "I hid the whiskey in the centerpiece."

"Grampa, did you see who picked up Satyendra's medicine bottle?"

Thomas produced the bottle. "Me. Like I thought—black-strap molasses."

"Did you taste it?"

"Didn't have to. I got a smeller."

"Smelling's not enough," said Harley. "I'm taking it to Dr. Barnes. Tell Mom I found some whiskey, I'll give it to Agnes."

"But how we gonna explain finding whiskey?"

Harley grinned. "I'll say I got it from Upjohn."

Harley stood in the doorway of the small room in the servants' wing, trying not to look at Frank.

"You get out of here," said Henrietta.

"I've got to talk to Dr. Barnes privately. It may be important."

Barnes smiled. "Step into the hall a moment, ladies."

Ignoring Henrietta's expression, Harley shut the door behind her and the nurse. "Doctor, what actually happened to Grampa?"

"I wish I knew." Barnes stared down at Frank's drawn face. "Apparently he commenced choking to death and Hitty performed an emergency tracheotomy." He shook his head. "She's no hand with a knife, though, I could hardly sew him up. I think he had a seizure of some sort. I don't know whether he choked because he was having a seizure or had a seizure because he was so scared of choking. He's a stubborn man to be living still."

"It's Mother who's stubborn," said Harley. "She would have followed him to hell and had a tug-of-war with the devil. I think it's her sap that's keeping him alive. Does that make sense?"

Barnes nodded. "I've seen stranger things. Is that the vitally important information you had to give me?"

"No." Harley paused a moment. "You just said you've seen stranger things than one person's will keeping another person alive. Have you ever seen one person's will kill another person?"

"What are you getting at?"

"I think," said Harley, "that my Aunt Carrie has been working some sort of black magic on my grandfather ever since she got back six years ago."

"Oh, Harley!"

"I think," said Harley, very fast, "that his attacks of the last two weeks have been brought on by the culminating ceremonies in that magic. I think that Carrie and Satyendra came here today to give him the coup de grace, and they would have if Mother's will hadn't turned out to be stronger than theirs."

Barnes just stared at him. "Satyendra," he said finally. "The dark chap in the turban. What makes you think he and your aunt are responsible for what's happened to Frank?"

"It's all too involved to explain now, but at the dinner table Satyendra said he was a doctor—"

"Why the hell didn't *he* do something for Frank?"

"He did. He gave Grampa this medicine." Harley produced the bottle. "And that's when Grampa *really* started to choke. I think it should be analyzed."

Barnes took the bottle and sniffed. "You say Frank drank this?"

"Yes."

Barnes ran his finger around the rim and touched the finger to his tongue. He coughed. "Blackstrap molasses."

"It can't be. Molasses isn't poison."

"When my Dad used to make me swallow a tablespoon of it every night, I sure as hell thought it was," said Barnes.

"Well, maybe it is—in combination with certain other ingredients. What if there was something else in that bottle? Something you couldn't taste or smell?"

"Let me get this straight," said Barnes. "Are you claiming your Aunt Carrie tried to do Frank in with black magic, or are you claiming she used poison?"

"Both."

"That doesn't make sense. Why fool with black magic if you've got poison?"

"I don't know. Maybe the combination produces results that can't be recognized as murder. Look, you don't have to believe me. Just get that bottle analyzed. How much will it cost? I'll pay for it."

"Hold on, I didn't say I wouldn't have it analyzed. If it contained anything to affect Frank's condition, I should know about it, and on that count you were right to bring it to me. But son..." Barnes laid both hands on Harley's shoulders and looked him in the eye. "Don't ask me to *believe* any of this junk!"

It didn't matter to Harley whether Barnes believed him or not. It only mattered that a curious Henrietta was dispatched to find Sailor, who left, black bottle in hand, for St. Luke's in Seneca.

"Now get back in with your folks," said Barnes. "I'll be calling the hospital in a few minutes to let them know Sailor's on his way. Make sure no one goes listening in on my conversation. Because if there's nothing but molasses in that bottle, it'd be mighty embarrassing explaining to your aunt."

Harley trotted down the hall to Upjohn's door. When it opened to Harley's knock, the musk scent issued forth. "Harley. Is there a problem?"

Harley had imagined that, in the privacy of his own quarters, Upjohn would at least take off his tie. "Did you just get in?"

"No. What is the trouble?"

"My Aunt Carrie is here." Search as he might, Harley could find nothing more than polite interest in Upjohn's eyes. "She has a new husband with her. His name is Satyendra Singh."

Upjohn's eyebrows lifted. "Your aunt has married a Sikh?"

Harley pounced. "How'd *you* know he's a Sikh?"

"My boy, I'm disappointed. Singh is a Sikh name. We discussed it at length in our studies of Far Eastern cultures."

"Oh." Harley studied the floor a moment. "OK, Mr. Upjohn, I won't beat around the bush. I'm on to the whole thing."

"What thing?"

"Witchcraft. You protecting Mother."

"What?"

"Look, I don't have time. I've got to get into the library and make sure no one listens on the extension while Doc Barnes calls the hospital."

"What is he doing here?" Upjohn could not have missed the bustle in this normally quiet hall. "I thought you said you'd been in all afternoon."

"I didn't say that at all. I merely said I had not just gotten in. Is someone ill?"

"Grampa Parmalee. He almost choked to death, and Mom cut his neck open—"

"Good Lord!"

"But I'm sure it was Carrie and Satyendra who caused it. We're having the medicine analyzed, because I think it's poison."

"What medicine?"

"Mr. Upjohn, I *told* you—I'm on to everything! Look, we'll talk later. I just thought you should be warned about Carrie and Satyendra so you could keep out of sight. Mother told them a Sears-Roebuck salesman sold her the perfume, so they don't suspect you or even know you're here. That stuff's powerful, too. When they started to go into Mother's room—"

"When who started to go into your mother's room?" said Upjohn.

"Carrie and Satyendra. It's too long a story. Don't worry, I kept them in sight all the time. Except twice—once when Satyendra sneaked into my bathroom, and once when he sneaked into Dad's. He was fooling around with our hairbrushes."

Down the hall Frank's door opened. Burt Barnes stepped into the hall, then turned to give a last-minute instruction to the nurse.

Harley squeezed Upjohn's arm. "Stay out of sight. We'll talk later."

He made a rapid head count as he entered the library. Everyone was there, including Agnes. A copper bowl containing toddy sat over a brazier on a serving cart before the fire, its contents already lowered.

"Harley!" Hitty took his hand. "Thank you for finding the whiskey, dear. Agnes, pour some toddy for Harley."

"Hitty!" said Flora, "what can you be thinking of with that child?"

"Harley has had as hard a day as the rest of us," said Hitty. She gave Agnes her own mug for a refill. "And, in case none of you has taken a look lately, Harley is no longer a child. He's a young man."

Harley lifted his chin as he took a sip of the toddy.

"Before you know it, he'll be a grown man and then..." Hitty reached out and touched Harley's face. "Enjoy every moment, Harley. We're old so soon, and life is so short." She began to cry.

Tobin jumped up, seeing his chance. "Don't, Hitty." He took her in his arms. "Stop crying, love. You've had too much toddy. No more for Mrs. Westcott, Agnes."

Hitty pulled away. "Fiddlesticks! I've not had too much."

"Hell, no," said Thomas. "She's doing just fine."

"Why do people do that?" said Hitty as she took her refilled mug.

"Do what?" said Tobin.

"What you just did. Tell me not to cry. Rob me of my sadness."

"I was only trying to help."

"I know you were, but you weren't! My father almost died a few hours ago. He may still die. I'm sad. I look at my son and see he's almost a man. I grow sadder. I start to cry. I'm going to have a wonderful cry. Then you rush in and stop me. Now I'm frustrated! I'll have to have at least two more toddies before I can feel that sad again."

"I'm sorry," said Tobin, but he smiled. There was a pout in Hitty's voice. Tobin, Harley realized, was reacting to her tone, not to what she said.

"I wanted to cry! We *all* want to cry sometimes—or scream. Or hit someone. But we can't. We're supposed to hold it all in." She spun around. "Carrie! I'll help you." She dropped to her knees before Carrie's chair. "Hit me! Go ahead! You want to so badly. Then I'll hit you, and we'll both feel better."

"I don't want to hit you."

"Yes, you do. You hate me. Let's drag it into the open!"

"If you do, I'll faint," warned Flora.

"Satyendra," said Carrie, "I think we'd better go."

"No!" Hitty held her. "Let's fight! Slap and pull hair and scream. If we get it out, we'll feel better. Maybe we can be sisters again."

"We were never sisters," said Carrie.

"Oh, but we were, at first! Remember how we used to make snowmen? And the games we played when we walked to school?"

"Shut up," said Carrie.

"And how you asked the teacher if you could sit beside me so—"

"Leave me alone!" Carrie sent Hitty sprawling onto the floor. Then she rose. "I'll hit you, all right, sister, dear. But not as you'll expect me to—and never *when* you ex—"

Upjohn stood in the door of the library.

Carrie stared.

Satyendra got to his feet.

How, Harley wondered, could he ever have thought of Upjohn as old and stuffy? Lounging against the doorjamb, smelling of musk, elegantly dressed, he looked more than a match—no. There was no way to compare him to Carrie and her Sikh. They were only—people. While he...

But that was silly.

Upjohn straightened and walked gracefully into the room. "Mrs. Westcott," he said, "I've just heard of your father's accident. I am so sorry. We must all turn our thoughts to his recovery." He took Hitty's hand in his. "If we do that, I can assure you he *will* recover. There is nothing stronger on this earth than minds in concert."

"Yes. Yes!" Hitty returned his grip. "I believe you. Thank you, Mr. Upjohn. Please stay, and have some toddy. This is my sister, Carrie, and her husband, Mr. Singh—our dear Mr. Upjohn, Harley's tutor."

"How do you do," said Upjohn.

"How do you do." It seemed to Harley that Carrie and Satyendra shrank from Upjohn.

There was something wrong—dreadfully wrong—if Upjohn had chosen to reveal himself and his scent. Harley wished he hadn't drunk the toddy. He should be razor-sharp to help Upjohn if Upjohn needed him.

"I seem to have interrupted something," said Upjohn. "Do go on. I'll help myself, Agnes." Upjohn looked around. "May I fill a cup for someone else?"

Thomas held forth his mug.

"And warm mine up," said Hitty.

Carrie sat back in her chair. Satyendra settled onto a stool by her knee.

There was a moment's silence.

Then Carrie said, "How long have you been Harley's tutor, Mr. Upjohn?"

"Nearly ten years," said Upjohn. "Harley, would you please give this to your Grandfather Westcott?"

Harley rose and crossed to Upjohn. The floor seemed spongy and farther away than usual. And it seemed that Upjohn held the steaming mug at a strange angle—out over the serving cart, so that Harley would have to stretch to get it.

And then he was falling—toward the serving cart, toward the punch bowl and brazier—because Upjohn's hand was on his back, pushing!

Things crashed and splintered and shattered. Satyendra yelled.

"Is he hurt?"

"Get those coals off the rug!"

"Agnes, get some grease," said Hitty.

"Ice?"

Harley sprawled in the rubble, watching the faces overhead.

Satyendra was moaning—struggling, with Upjohn's help, from his coat.

Then he stopped and stared at Upjohn, who was moving toward the door of the library, the jacket on his arm. "Where are you going?" said Satyendra.

"To clean your jacket," said Upjohn.

"No!" Satyendra went after his jacket.

"But, my dear fellow!" Upjohn refused to release it. "You have no idea how liquor can stain fine fabric."

"Think nothing of it." Satyendra pulled on the jacket, and it stretched between the two of them.

"I insist!" said Upjohn. He gave the garment a twist, gained possession, and made for the door.

Harley leaped to his feet and grabbed the Sikh's arm. "Gosh, Satyendra! I'm so sorry I hurt you!" Upjohn disappeared into the foyer. Satyendra tried to follow, but Harley held on to the naked arm.

Carrie started after Upjohn.

"Grampa! Stop her!"

Thomas caught Carrie's arm. "Let Upjohn clean that jacket, Miss Carrie. You'd better take care of Sam, here."

"Let me go, you old fool."

Thomas chortled and held fast. "No fool like an old fool!"

The Sikh's eyes met Harley's. Then he turned on Harley's confused parents. "What an insufferably clumsy and crude cub you have whelped!"

Tobin frowned. "You mean Harley?"

"Yes," said Satyendra, and the "s" hissed.

"When you get to know him, you'll love him," said Hitty. "Here." She took two chunks of ice from Agnes and poised to touch them to Satyendra's bare chest.

Satyendra dodged. "Good heavens, Madam!"

"Shall I wrap them in a towel?" said Hitty.

Carrie sighed and wrapped some ice in a napkin. "Sit down," she told her husband. "It looks as though we can do nothing but nurse your wounds."

Upjohn returned to the library a few minutes later. "Here you are, old man. Still damp, but I have removed all the offending matter."

Satyendra accepted the jacket. "I'm sure you have." He rose. "Come, Caroline."

"I'll send word the minute there's a change in Daddy's condition," said Hitty.

"Don't bother," said Carrie. When she reached the foyer, she turned: "Until he is dead."

The door opened after one knock. "Come in," said Upjohn.

The glow from the fireplace burnished the books and leather and polished wood.

"Sit down." Upjohn indicated an armchair near the fire.

"I'll sit here if you don't mind." Harley chose the edge of a comb-back Windsor close to the door.

Upjohn took the armchair. "I was having a brandy." He held forth his snifter in toast. "I won't offer you any. You become unsteady under the influence of alcohol."

"You pushed me! You know you did."

"Perhaps. And perhaps it was a fortunate accident."

"Why'd you have to get Satyendra's jacket?"

Upjohn smiled and drew from his pocket two wisps of hair.

Harley frowned. "From our hairbrushes. But why?"

"They believe that to work a spell, they must possess articles from the victim's person."

"Then I was right. That medicine may have tested out as blackstrap molasses, but they *are* witches!"

"Not witches. Have I been that poor a teacher? They're practitioners of black magic."

Harley shivered.

Upjohn rose. "On second thought, I think I *shall* give you a spot of brandy." He poured a small amount from the decanter on the mantle and handed it over. "I think in this case the benefits will outweigh the disadvantages. Warm it in your hands, Harley, then sniff the bouquet. Sip it with the smallest possible sips."

The idea of drinking brandy offered by a witch unsettled Harley, but the importance of the occasion appealed to him. So he sat back, cupped the snifter, sloshed the liquid, and sniffed as directed. He took the smallest possible sip. As the warmth traveled to his stomach, he took a few more sips, not so small. Upjohn began to look less like a witch upon a throne and more like a tutor in an armchair.

"I'm sorry," Harley said. "I know I shouldn't have been scared to come in here but—"

"You think I am a witch."

"Well, aren't you? You know all about witches!"

"That should come as no surprise." Upjohn sighed. "You disappoint me, Harley. Despite all our discussions, you persist in confusing witchcraft with black magic."

"You knew about Carrie and Satyendra! *I* wouldn't have known about them unless I'd known about *you*. See, this afternoon when they started to go into Mother's room they stopped dead and left. I didn't understand why until I saw how they reacted to Mother when she came into the dining room. It was that!" He gestured at the scent in the air. "Ever since the afternoon I found the witches' circle in the woods and you were there—"

"I?"

"I smelled you. Anyway, I put two and two together. Then I came home and Mother was wearing the stuff, too, and I got the crazy idea that you'd indoctrinated her into witchcraft. But this afternoon I realized that wasn't it—you'd given her that stuff to protect her. So I thought, protect her from what?"

"Carrie and Satyendra."

"Because you knew they were—whatever you want to call them—and you could only know what they were if you were the same thing." Harley folded his arms triumphantly.

Upjohn smiled. "It was a nice piece of reasoning, and one that led you to a good deal of fact. But I am not and never have been a witch. Or a practitioner of black magic."

"I don't believe you."

"I never lie, Harley."

"Then what are you?"

"Just a friend, armed with a good deal of knowledge and possessed of eyes and ears."

"Well, I've got eyes, too! Carrie and Satyendra knew you. When you appeared in the door of the library today, they both reacted!"

"Yes, they knew me—even though they had never seen me before in their lives." Upjohn's brow furrowed. "I would rather not have presented myself. Now they are sure of what they only sensed before."

"What's that?"

Upjohn smiled. "Resistance. Would you like more brandy?"

"Do you think I should?"

"No. But I'll give you some anyway."

Harley watched him pour. "Does Grampa know you've got brandy?"

"If your grandfather knew, there would be none left. It is not easy to obtain, so I'm afraid I am jealous in dispensing it. It makes this room less lonely."

"I shouldn't be drinking it, then."

"No, my boy. You are special."

"Me?"

Upjohn's face was somber. "I am quite alone in the world, Harley. I always have been, and I always will be. When one is alone, selected people come to mean a great deal." He paused. "You, and any you will ever hold dear, need never fear me—whatever you believe of me. Consider me your faithful guarddog."

Harley shifted position. "I never thought of you as a guarddog."

"But I am. And I have been for many years."

Harley studied the shadowy face. "You've known about Carrie all along?"

"Yes."

"And how have you—guarded us?"

"You once asked me, Harley, if things could be born evil. Evil cannot be evil unless there is an opposite and equal force. It is that force which I have attempted to muster."

"But why didn't you just tell us about Carrie so we could all help you muster it?"

"Because not all minds are strong enough to know the facts and remain impervious. Your Grandfather Parmalee, for instance. I tried to talk to him on several occasions. It was no use. He believed that Carrie was destined to kill him—and in the end, his own fear accomplished Carrie's goal and brought on his attacks. No. Only those minds strong enough to have faith in their own force should know of the danger. I hope the knowledge has not come too soon for *you*, Harley. I have tried these many years to make your mind strong, to show you the way to a truth of your own."

"Has the knowledge come too soon for Mother?"

"Your mother knows nothing of this."

"But she's wearing that stuff! And this afternoon she protected you. She told Satyendra she'd gotten it from a Sears-Roebuck salesman named Angus Arbuckle."

Upjohn laughed. "She'd be boiled in oil before she'd give away her secret. Especially to her sister."

"What secret?"

Upjohn cleared his throat. "I told her that the scent is an elixir of youth."

"And she believed you? Why?"

"Because she wants to believe it. And when I told her that I am actually centuries old, preserved by means of my dreadful perfume..."

"You said a while ago that you never lied!"

Upjohn took a sip of brandy. "I didn't lie to her. If she believes the perfume will keep her young, it will."

"But you lied about your age."

Upjohn smiled.

"Will it really protect her from Carrie and Satyendra?"

"Yes. Because they believe its presence counteracts their own power. They also believe that direct contact with the powder could kill them."

"But how could it do that? What is it made of?"

"The ingredients are in the woods. Let us just say that their combination is, to Carrie and Satyendra, the odor of the other force."

The log was burning low. Upjohn rose and turned it. The flames licked high once more, and sent strange shadows dancing over his face.

"You *were* lying to Mother about being centuries old—" said Harley.

"Do I look centuries old?"

"No."

Upjohn shrugged. "Have you met the two young ladies who moved in next door?"

Harley leaned forward. "As a matter of fact, I wanted to talk to you about them. You know that abandoned house in the woods? It was used for witchcraft once, wasn't it? Is it still?"

"No."

Harley sat back. "Isn't it even haunted?"

"Not that I know of."

"Oh. Well, then, I guess there's no danger in their using it as their clubhouse."

"Danger can take other forms, Harley. I suggest that you discourage them from frequenting the house or the woods. Lilith, especially, should never go there alone."

"How did you know her name?"

"I chanced upon her brother one day during a walk. She seems to be an exceptional young creature, don't you think?"

Harley flushed. "Yes. But why shouldn't she go there alone?"

"Simply because I say so. Is that good enough for the time being?"

"I guess." Harley thought a moment. "Mr. Upjohn, you said they should stay out of the house and the *woods*. I've always had a feeling about them. I've always felt that the whole place is one—entity—and that it's evil. That it reaches out to everything around it, trying to spread itself, trying to take over. Is that crazy?"

"Imaginative."

"You've always said imagination is the threshold of perception."

"Yes, I have," Upjohn smiled. "And I never lie."

CHAPTER THIRTEEN

CASS LAY EXHAUSTED on her bed. It seemed she hadn't slept for days. There was just so much to think about.

For one thing, there was her singing career. But there was also Harley Westcott. She didn't much see how she could have her career and still have Harley Westcott.

On the other hand, since Papa didn't have enough money to buy chocolate-covered creams more than once a month lately, she didn't see how she could have the singing lessons she needed for the career.

"Don't give up," Lil kept saying. "So what if he does say no when we finally ask him? As soon as you're eighteen, you can leave home and do whatever you want. You'll be good enough without lessons."

Cass regarded this suggestion with more than a little suspicion. She still wasn't positive that Lil didn't hate her. Allowing herself to be talked into leaving home if Papa didn't approve might be playing right into Lil's hands.

Worse than that, allowing herself to be talked into leaving home would leave Lil with Harley Westcott all to herself. For

Muriel was right; Lil *was* trying to take Harley away from her. Every time Harley came calling, Lil hogged his attention. She'd get him going about some stupid old book and act like he was the greatest thing in the world, just because he said he'd decided to leave home after college and become a struggling writer in Paris, France. Cass couldn't see why Harley should be interested in leaving home. If he didn't make his Dad disown him, he'd inherit bulls that got $1,000 for every baby! Cass certainly wouldn't want to go running off if *she* stood to inherit those bulls. She'd pay for singing lessons, finance her own traveling minstrel...Harley should stay home and be a farmer. Then, after he got those bulls, he could be a writer, and she could be a singer, and they'd travel together, writing and singing.

All things considered, Cass had about decided she would have to marry Harley Westcott. She'd even figured out a way to keep Papa from hating her for it.

But what would Lil do when she found she'd lost Harley? How did you protect yourself against a witch?

She wouldn't want to hurt me. She's my sister. Somehow those words no longer carried their magic.

Cass reached up to the windowsill and took the silvery medal from its hiding place. It had been meant for Lil. They'd been picking flowers for their dresses one day near the woods. Lil had placed her sweater on a rock at the edge, but her back had been turned when the white animal darted out. Only Cass had glimpsed it, going back into the trees, just before she noticed the medal on Lil's sweater.

Why would a white monster give Lil a gift?

Cass turned the medal over in her fingers. It had to be a charm, a protection. From one witch to another. And if the protection was good for a witch, it should be good for a nonwitch against witches.

She took a string and passed it through the hole in the medal. She would wear it always, hidden beneath her clothes.

Especially now that she was going to take Harley Westcott away from Lil.

It had taken a lot of planning, a lot of acting, and a lot of lying. But finally, on a sunny Sunday early in December, Cass was alone, running up the road toward the woods—toward Lizzy's house.

"I really think I ought to stay," Emma had said.

"Oh no, Mama. Please go. I'd feel terrible if you missed the dinner just to sit here while I sleep!"

She'd known what to do the minute she learned that the Ladies' Thursday Evening Bible Class was planning a covered-dish luncheon after church that Sunday. "It's such a worthy cause," Cass had told Curt. "Please, just this once, you and Helen plan to go to church with us. We'll all have dinner there, and it will be a wonderful day off for Mama and Helen."

On Thursday night she'd begun to feign symptoms of a cold. Friday afternoon, she fainted in gym class and was driven home by the nurse. All day Saturday she stayed in bed, allowing herself to be greased, fed bowls of consommé, and fussed over as she "improved."

Then, Sunday morning, she'd crossed her fingers beneath the covers until the family climbed into the wagon, and the sounds of its wheels faded away down the road.

Now Cass emerged from the trees into the clearing and heaved a sigh of relief. "Hi!"

Harley rose from the stump on which he'd been sitting.

"I'm so glad you got my letter!" said Cass.

Harley shrugged. "You said it was a matter of life and death. Besides, I couldn't let you come up here alone." He waited for Cass to pour forth her problem.

But Cass poured forth nothing. "Do you like my dress?" she asked.

Harley eyed the starched blue pinafore. "Sure."

"I'm glad." She walked toward him, slowly.

Harley could not understand why he wanted to move away. His heels were already against the stump, and he would have to back around it.

There was no way, Cass was thinking, except to come straight out with it. But she couldn't just say, "Marry me." That would sound like an order. "Marry me, please," would sound like begging. She stopped before Harley and looked into his eyes with all the emotion she could muster, the way Lillian Gish always did. "I love you," she said.

Harley backed around the stump.

Cass followed, reaching for his hands. "Do you love me?"

"No! I mean, I like you. You're very nice."

"What do you like best about me?"

Harley turned his head so he wouldn't have to look at her. "I don't know."

"You must know! My eyes?"

Harley shook his head.

"My hair, then? My skin?"

"Something like that."

Cass wrinkled her brow. "What do you like about my skin?"

"It's soft," said Harley.

"Isn't every girl's?"

"Well, yes. But yours looks like it would be nice to…"

"To what?"

"To—kiss," said Harley.

Cass blushed. She was still holding Harley's hands, and suddenly, in the silence, that touch assumed gigantic proportions in both their minds. Cass almost dropped his hands, but decided against it. "Then you do love me," she said. "You want to kiss me, don't you?"

"Well, yes."

They stood, face to face but with heads averted, until Cass whispered, "I've never kissed anyone. I mean, a boy. Have you?"

"Kissed a girl? No."

"Is it a sin, do you think?"

"No."

"Then go ahead."

Harley swallowed and looked at her. "Could you kind of—close your eyes?"

"Sure." Her lashes descended and she pushed her lips out.

Harley disentangled his hands and placed them around Cass's shoulders. As he moved closer, he felt the tips of her breasts against his chest.

Cass stiffened. "I don't think—"

Harley plunged forward, pressing his lips onto hers.

It didn't feel like he'd thought it would so far as the lips went; Cass held them hard and puckered, with no feeling but fear. Her body was another thing. The stiffer she tried to hold it, the softer the soft parts felt. His hands crept from her back toward the front.

Cass, trying to say no, succeeded only in opening her mouth, and Harley slid his tongue inside. She squealed and began to struggle, but Harley held her tight and searched with his tongue. "Frenching," Sailor called it. It was better than it sounded.

Cass wrenched free and backed away, wiping her mouth. "That's not the way you're supposed to do it!"

"It is so!" said Harley.

"It is not," cried Cass. "That's awful!"

She shuddered. "Aaaargh."

"I'm sorry."

"You ought to be," said Cass. She dissolved into tears.

Harley watched her helplessly. "Oh, hell," he said and went to Polly.

Cass's sobs stopped. "Where are you going?"

"Home."

"Don't. I—I want you to kiss me again."

Harley had dreamed about that first kiss so often—possibly he'd make the girl swoon. Instead, he'd made her sick. "Let's forget it," he said.

"No, please!" Cass grabbed his arm and pulled.

"Come on, Cass, let go. I don't want to play your silly game!"

"It's not a game!"

But Harley swung onto Polly's back.

"Harley! You can do anything you want!"

"What?"

"Don't go. I'll let you. I love you."

Harley stared down at her. "Anything?" he said.

She nodded. "I *love* you."

No one had ever said that to him. "And you really want me to—"

His heart began to pound. This was it! It was going to happen! What would he do? How would he begin? Slowly he dismounted. "I love you, too," he said.

As he reached for Cass, Harley thought he heard his name called. A voice like a bell; distressed, warning.

He put both arms around her and stuck his tongue back in her mouth.

Cass became aware of the eyes watching her much later. She thought at first it was her imagination, her own shame playing tricks.

But the sense of being watched was overwhelming.

Then she saw it, sitting right at the edge of the trees. A big, yellow tiger tomcat. She cried out and pressed her head against Harley's shoulder.

"What's the matter?" said Harley.

"That cat!" said Cass.

"I don't see any cat. It must have been your imagination."

It hadn't been. The cat had vanished from Cass's sight, but she could still feel its green eyes—watching!

The following day, Cass went to school—but during the three-mile walk she marched ahead of Lil, refusing to speak to her even once.

At lunch hour, Cass left the school by the back door, crossed the athletic field, and cut through a vacant lot to Elm Street. She hardly looked at the cider mill as she approached, or at the house that had been her home for so long. She went straight to Mrs. Parkinson's door.

Mrs. Parkinson was unused to callers. "Cass Bascomb! What ever do you want?"

"I just wanted to ask you about your cat," said Cass.

"You mean Bobby?"

"Do you still have him?"

"Why, no. The day after you folks moved out—"

"I knew it!" said Cass. "My sister has him, Mrs. Parkinson. I don't know where she keeps him, but she's got him. She uses him as her familiar. I saw him just yesterday."

"But that's impossible. Bobby is dead."

"He's what?"

Mrs. Parkinson was explaining, something about Meiklejohn's delivery wagon the day after they moved out. Cass backed down the steps as the old woman talked. "You're lying," she said.

"Mind your manners, Cass. Why should I lie?"

"You must be a witch, too. Just like my sister. You gave Bobby to Lil, and you're lying to protect her!"

Mrs. Parkinson started forward.

"Don't you come near me." Cass scooped up a rock.

Mrs. Parkinson retreated. "Your father will hear of this," she shouted as she closed the door.

Cass didn't return to school.

How many supposed friends, besides Mrs. Parkinson, were really witches? How many of them were in league with Lil against her? Their familiar had surely told them what she'd done with Harley. She had to do what she'd been planning—now, today—before Mrs. Parkinson had time to get to Papa and turn him against her.

Reverend Smith was working on his Sunday sermon. The working out of sermons was always a great trial to him. He found it necessary to pray a great deal, and Amanda never disturbed him at these times.

So it was with amazement that he heard her knock. "I'm sorry, Philip, but an emergency has arisen. The youngest Bascomb girl is here."

"Can't it wait?"

"She's distraught, Philip. One of your sheep is distraught."

"Of course." Philip flushed, as he always did when Amanda showed him the error of his ways.

He rose from his desk as Cass entered. "My dear girl, what is the trouble? Bring her some tea, Amanda. Sit down, Cassandra. Have you a handkerchief? Here, I believe this one is clean."

Cass wept for an appropriate length of time and then drank a little tea. "I'm sorry," she said. "But I've been so frightened. And I'm so happy to be here where you can protect me."

"From what, dear girl?"

Cass shivered and fastened her blue eyes on the Reverend. "I'm afraid to tell you—I'm afraid you'll think I've taken leave of my senses."

"No one is going to think that," said Amanda. "You're a lovely, intelligent little girl. You go right ahead and tell us."

"Well," Cass folded her hands, "there are really two problems. The first is my visions. They've been coming ever since I can remember."

"And what do these visions consist of?"

"I've always been afraid to tell, for fear people would think I was crazy or lying."

"We're not going to think that, my dear."

"Well," Cass tilted her head and stared at the ceiling, "they're awe-inspiring. I tremble for minutes after he's gone."

"After *who* has gone?"

"The man who comes. At least, I think he's a man. He has golden hair and dresses in long white robes and has wings."

Reverend Smith gasped. "An angel? You see an angel?"

"Oh, no sir! It couldn't be. I'm unworthy!"

"But you're describing an angel."

"I know it sounds like it, but it must be something else. Who am I that an angel should come to me?"

The first thought in the Reverend's mind had been that Cass *was* crazy, or lying. But now as he looked into those eyes and saw the humility with which she rejected the idea that she might be one of God's chosen...Was it possible?

All his life he had hoped that he himself might be blessed with a visitation. Second best to having a personal visitation would be finding a young virgin so touched!

"My child, others before you have considered themselves unworthy. But God knows no class, no station. He knows only hearts. Now, tell me about your angel. When does he come, and how often? Amanda, bring more tea. Start at the beginning, Cassandra."

Cass began. She'd had her visitor at least a dozen times. He came on a ray of golden light at night, as she said her prayers, and though no one else in the house ever seemed to hear, he was always accompanied by a chorus of voices. "They sing very loud," said Cass. "Sometimes they're so loud I can't hear him talk."

She went on to the angel's seemingly innocuous prophecies—the move east to Oriskany Forks, the move to Curt's farm.

"But you came in here frightened," the Reverend finally said.

"Well, I was coming to see you today anyway, because he appeared last night and told me to. But on the way I stopped to see Mrs. Parkinson because of something the angel told me, and she tried to bewitch me."

"Mrs. Parkinson on Elm Street?" Reverend Smith touched his forehead. "Let's take one thing at a time. Why did your angel instruct you to come and see *me?*"

"For help. He said you're a great man."

"He did?"

"Oh yes," said Cass, and she buttressed that statement with the grandest thing her imagination could seize: "You're going to publish a book."

"My book is going to be published?" Reverend Smith rushed to his desk and withdrew a manuscript. "This one, Cassandra? Did he mention the title?"

Cass looked in surprise at the manuscript thrust before her. *A Modern Look at Old Problems Facing Christianity: A Series of Sermons by Philip Smith, D.D.*

"Is that the only book you've written? I guess that must be the one, then. He said he's read it."

Reverend Smith carried the manuscript gently to his desk. Then a frown touched his brow. "But why tell you, Cassandra? Why didn't he just come to me?"

"He says it's easier to talk to children," said Cass.

Reverend Smith stared a moment, then slapped a palm to his forehead. "Of course! To be born again we must be as little children. Oh, Amanda! How far we've stumbled from the path! This beautiful child has been sent to lead us back! What did he like best, Cassandra? Which sermon did he think has the most import?"

Cass looked again at the manuscript. She had no idea what it contained. Then she remembered the church bulletins every Sunday. The Jews, the Catholics—"The witches," she said. "That was the most important, and that was why he sent me to you."

"Aaaaahh." One long, pleased sigh. "Mrs. Parkinson. The angel himself advised you that Mrs. Parkinson is a witch and advised you to come to me for aid?"

"Yes."

"But you were overzealous in your concern for Mrs. Parkinson's soul and went to her directly instead of coming to me? I commend your intent, Cassandra, but in the future you must do exactly as the angel directs."

"I will," said Cass. "I promise."

Amanda poured another cup of tea, and Cass described her experience with Mrs. Parkinson. "She had always seemed so nice. And when I knocked on her door, she seemed pleased and invited me in. But the moment I was in, she slammed the door behind me and said 'Now! Now I have you in my clutches!'"

"What did you do?" said Reverend Smith.

"I told her I knew all about her, but she couldn't harm me because I was under the protection of heaven. She got furious! She said she wasn't afraid of heaven. 'I spit on heaven!' she shouted. And she did spit, right on her living-room rug."

"Disgusting," said Amanda.

"Well, it was pretty silly. She'll only have to clean it up."

"Did you see anything incriminating?" said Reverend Smith. "Any proof of her activity?"

"Only the dead baby," said Cass.

A dreadful silence. Cass wondered if she had, at last, over-strained their credulity.

"Are you sure it was a real dead baby?" said Amanda.

"Yes," said Cass. "It was very shriveled, but it was real."

Reverend Smith and his wife exchanged glances.

"The Benson child?" whispered Amanda.

Reverend Smith shook his head. "Too shriveled."

"Not if she drained the blood out of it," said Cass.

"Of course!" Amanda sprang to her feet. "But it wouldn't have been the Benson child." She rushed to the bookshelves and withdrew a volume. "Montague Summers speaks of it quite specifically. Philip, don't you recall? In most of the documented cases of witchcraft, *live* children are used for their ceremonies!" She handed the book to her husband.

"He's a Papist," said Reverend Smith.

"He's a very sensible man," said Amanda. She riffled the pages. "I underlined the passages, they were so horrifying. Here, read it. You see? It seems much more likely that Mrs. Parkinson acquired a *live* child by some means and drained the blood from it."

"I think," said Reverend Smith, "that it is highly unlikely, my dear. We have had no missing children in this community that I recall."

"It is just possible, my dear, that the child was from some other community."

Cass sat watching them. They had quite forgotten her. She fell to her knees and raised her eyes toward the ceiling.

Reverend and Mrs. Smith bowed their heads and waited patiently. "I just had to thank Him," Cass said, returning to her seat. "I realized suddenly why Mrs. Parkinson said, 'Now I have you in my clutches!' She meant me to be a human sacrifice."

"What did she do? And how did the Lord deliver you?" asked Reverend Smith.

"The dead baby," said Cass. "The witch held it out to me, and one little hand touched my face. I couldn't control my legs, and everything started getting black. I fell down, and she laughed and left the room—probably to get her knife. Then I saw it—it was like a ray of light come down from heaven, and it pointed straight to an open window. I crawled through, and the minute I was out, the strength came back to my legs and I ran. I heard her calling, 'I'll get you anyway! You know too much!'"

"Is Mrs. Parkinson the only witch that the angel told you of?" asked Reverend Smith.

Cass lowered her head. She didn't want to get anyone into trouble, only to protect herself. "There are others," she said, "but the angel didn't name them. He said he would tell me if it ever became necessary."

"Fine." The Reverend nodded, in immediate agreement with the angel's reasoning, whatever it might be. "Now, let me make order of this. Why did he send you to me? What does he wish us to do?"

"He wants you to keep an eye on things," and Cass. "He wants you to keep a notebook on Mrs. Parkinson and any other suspicious people. And you should be on special lookout for a yellow tiger tomcat."

"A familiar?" said Amanda. "Good heavens, Philip, I saw a yellow tom in our yard just today."

"Write it down immediately, Amanda. Is that all the angel told you, Cassandra?"

"Well, there's one other thing," said Cass. "The angel said—" She lowered her eyes. "I can hardly believe it. I'm to become the mother of a very special baby."

"Am I to understand, Cassandra, that you are in the family way?"

"No!" Cass started. "Did I make it sound like that? The angel means in the *future* I will become the mother of a very special baby."

Reverend Smith sank onto the couch beside Cass and took her hand. "When will this come to pass, Cassandra?"

"As soon as you can talk Papa into it."

"I don't understand."

"The angel says I'm supposed to marry Harley Westcott."

"Aren't the Westcotts—"

"Presbyterians," said Amanda.

"And obscene in the flaunting of their wealth," said Reverend Smith.

Cass smiled. "God knows no class, no station. He knows only hearts."

The Reverend reddened.

"And that's why He chose the Westcotts. Their hearts are good, but they've strayed. I'm to lead them back to the fold. The angel said, 'The meek shall marry the mighty—and the mighty shall become meekened and righteous—and the new meek and righteous and the old meek and righteous will bear fruit, and that fruit will be blessed as it was spoken of old.'" Cass hoped the speech had sounded as impressive to the Reverend as it had to her.

"Unspeakably lovely." Amanda wiped a tear from her eyes.

"Unspeakably," said Reverend Smith.

CHAPTER FOURTEEN

THE HENS CLUCKED warnings to each other and fixed their unblinking eyes on Paul Bascomb.

The menace in Paul's eyes equaled the chickens'. His hands twitched with anticipation. He loved to gather eggs, had loved it since he was a boy. Those mean little females always looked set to rip you apart. Once in a while one of them did, and that was what made egg-gathering a kind of sport.

You'd come close, looking as bad at her as she was looking at you. Your hand would sneak toward that soft, warm breast. She'd press down; you'd press up. Then your fingers would touch the shell, and you'd get a thrill like you'd found a hidden treasure. You'd pull the egg out, careful and quick, all the time not knowing if she was going to come at you with that beak and draw blood. Then you'd give her a parting look and pass on.

Paul came to the last hen in the row, a red biddy so old her meat wouldn't be fit for a dog. His hand was bandaged where she'd ripped into him the day before.

He paused, squinting at the hen, then placed his pail on the floor and extended his right hand as usual.

The hen tensed, ready.

Paul's other hand shot out and grabbed her neck. The hen squawked and started to struggle. Paul reached beneath her and found an empty nest. "What's this? You stopped laying?" He lifted the cheating chicken by the neck and peered beneath her. A claw nicked his wrist.

Paul watched a drop of blood ooze from the scratch, then he threw the chicken across the coop.

She met the wall with a thud, hit the dirt, and began to flop, her head hanging limp.

"God!" said Paul. He hadn't meant to do that. He looked about the coop, as though something other than hens had witnessed his act. He approached the chicken, who was no longer flopping. Now she simply quivered, her beak working soundlessly. Her filmed eyes stared up at him.

"I didn't mean it, Chickie." He reached to stroke her, but tears blurred his vision—and suddenly her red feathers resembled the flowing red hair of a woman. Paul gasped and recoiled. "You!"

The chicken gave a last twitch. The brown lids closed.

"No!" Paul shook her. "Don't go!" But no amount of importuning could bring the hen back. He could only gather her into his arms, rock her, and stroke her, supporting the broken neck in the crook of his arm.

He sat that way for some time.

The sun was strong on the December landscape, but stark, and the wind that had come up before noon was getting stiffer by the moment.

The farm was pretty in summer, with the two granddaddy maples in the front yard, and all the hills rolling in wildflowers. But in late fall and winter, when the buildings stood gaunt against the side of the hill, depression set in.

Depression had been setting in with Paul since the last of the flame-red leaves had fallen. He'd known it would come, had dreaded that coming as he had dreaded it every autumn of his boyhood. He wished now he had taken the job as janitor. He wished he had done anything rather than return to this place and the memories he'd spent a lifetime running from.

His eyes followed the road up the hill to the woods. He still hadn't gone up *there*.

Paul shivered. He had been standing stock still in front of the chicken coop, holding the hen close; wasting time and letting the wind chill him.

He walked a few steps and stopped again, wondering how he'd explain the hen's death. He was stroking the ruffled feathers when the crunch of footsteps sounded from behind.

"What's the matter, Pa?" Curt stopped beside him, his face red in the cold, stamping and blowing on his big rough hands. "What happened to the hen?"

"She's dead. Found her when I went in to get the eggs."

Curt reached over and touched the chicken. The head fell to the side. "Her neck's broke!"

There was no way for a chicken to break her own neck in a closed coop. "Well, to tell you the truth, I found her dying when I went in. Old age. I wrung her neck to put her out of her misery."

Curt nodded. "Good. Couldn't eat her if we didn't know what she died of. Take her in and give her to Helen." He glanced at the sky. "Pond's freezing over. Bet we'll have snow before nightfall." He started for the barn, then turned. "The Jersey's about to calf. Come on out when you're finished."

Paul opened the door to the woodshed, grateful to be out of the cold. He was greeted by the smell of fresh-split wood, and as he stepped into the kitchen it mingled with the scent of Helen's bread-baking.

She was nearly Paul's idea of a wife, that Helen. Good cooking, good housekeeping, dependable company. If only— Helen ought to fatten herself up. A scrawny thing like that, no wonder she wouldn't quicken.

"What's the matter with the hen?" Helen finished crimping a pie and pumped water to wash the flour from her hands.

"Dead," said Paul. "Old age, I guess. Died while I was getting the eggs." That, after all, was the truth.

Emma sat churning butter by the window. "She's like to be stringy meat. Reckon she's good enough for stew, Helen?"

"Or soup. I'll take her, Pa."

A final comforting pat, and Paul released the hen. The broken neck flopped sideways. "Getting mighty cold out, said Paul.

"Sounds that way from the wind," said Helen. She poured scalding water from the kettle on the stove and plunged the bird into it. Paul winced. Helen took the bird out of the water, patted it with a towel, and began to pluck the feathers with short, sharp yanks.

"I been thinking," said Paul. "Maybe I ought to take the buggy down and get the girls. It's a long, cold walk and Cassandra just out of bed."

"Good idea," said Emma.

The pile of red feathers mounted, and, with it, Paul's agitation. "Nothing you can use those feathers for?"

"We got all the pillows and mattresses we need," said Emma.

"Well, shouldn't we dry these out and save them till we need more?" Paul bent and retrieved one large, red feather. "Such an awful pretty color." He dried the feather on his coat. "My mother's hair was just this color."

Both women stopped work, Emma in shock and Helen with a quizzical look that melted to a smile. "You know, Pa, I do believe that's the first time I ever heard you speak of your mother." At the churn Emma's expression signaled danger, but Helen was looking at Paul. "Guess I know now where Lil gets her coloring. Takes after her Gramma Bascomb."

Paul frowned. "No," he said. "She will not."

"Was she pretty? Tell me about her."

Emma held her breath, waiting for the rebuff that would bewilder and hurt Helen.

It didn't come. Paul just looked down at his feather. "Nothing to tell," he said. "I don't remember much, except that long red hair of hers. And the way she'd play the piano. And the way she'd sing." He put the feather in his pocket. "I guess she was beautiful. At least I thought she was. I don't remember. She died when I was a boy."

"I'm sorry," said Helen.

"Don't be," said Paul.

Then the sound of carriage wheels reached their ears.

Paul looked out the window; the two in the carriage didn't belong together. If Cassandra had been sent home sick again, why would the parson be bringing her? On the other hand, if the parson had decided to pay a visit and give the girls a lift home, he'd have brought them both.

Helen and Emma headed for the parlor with dustcloth and broom.

"Is she sick?" Paul asked as Reverend Smith handed Cass through the front door.

"She is filled with the Lord. If that be sickness, Paul, then Hallelujah! May we two men have a private talk?"

By the time the Reverend reached the parlor, the dust rag and the broom had been tossed into Helen's bedroom, the coal stove had been lit, and inroads were being made into the cold and damp of that seldom-used place.

"You'd better go and tell Curt I won't be coming to help him," Paul whispered to Helen as she left.

Helen closed the door and went to the kitchen for her coat. Cass was sitting at the table in the dining room, her eyes fixed on the parlor door. Emma was standing by the window, watching Cass.

Helen shrugged and went out, shivering as the wind hit her. She'd no idea it was that cold.

Poor Lil, walking all the way home by herself.

She'd speak to Curt. Surely it wouldn't be too much trouble for him to hitch up the team and go get her.

"The meek shall marry the mighty," Reverend Smith's voice sounded as if he were quoting scripture, "and the mighty shall become meekened and righteous, and the new meek and righteous and the old meek and righteous will bear fruit and that fruit will be blessed as it was spoken of old."

"Dad—blast it!" Paul struck the table between them. "I know who you're talking about—that fool Westcott kid comes around here on a horse! Well, the answer is no!"

"Paul. You can't go against heaven. It's blasphemy."

"No, it's not! A match with a Westcott isn't heaven's way. They're bad people!"

"But that is exactly the point, Paul. Cass has been chosen to save their souls. She'll bring them back to God."

"God wouldn't want them."

"Paul! God loves *all* his children."

"There's no way for a rich man to be God-fearing."

"But don't you see? 'The meek shall marry the mighty—and the mighty shall become meekened.' Your daughter intends to make them distribute their wealth to the poor."

"Reverend, I'm telling you, I won't allow it. I know that heaven never told Cassandra to marry a Westcott."

"You just told me yourself, she would never lie."

Paul searched for a way to explain this misunderstanding. "Don't you see, Reverend? She's dreamed all this. She's gotten sweet on that darn fool kid and convinced herself her dream was real."

"Paul, she doesn't even *like* Harley. That was one of the factors that brought her running to me in tears. That and the fact that she knew the marriage would displease you and Lilith."

"What's Lilith got to do with this?"

"Lilith is the one who wants to marry Harley Westcott."

Paul felt suddenly ill. Lilith and Harley Westcott—evil joined to evil, passing on the curse to yet another generation. *That* was hell's match. And heaven was trying to prevent it.

A calm came over Paul. "How does it go again, Reverend? What the angel said?"

Reverend Smith repeated the message.

"'Blessed fruit,'" said Paul. "That'd be a boy, of course." Tears stung his eyes. "You know, Reverend, I got eight children, just one a boy. And out of eight grandchildren, just one boy again." He blew his nose. "I'd surely like to see the Westcotts low and meekened."

"You have but to give your consent to this match."

There was a long pause. Then, "If you're really convinced of this whole thing..."

"I am. For one very sound reason. The angel revealed something else to Cassandra last night. He sent her to me because I am the one man in the village conversant with the problem."

"What problem?"

"Witchcraft!"

A cry escaped Paul's lips.

"Don't be frightened! The angel is going to protect us. He will name the witches as the need arises."

"Has he—named any yet?"

"One. Mrs. Parkinson."

Paul heaved a sigh of relief.

"And Mrs. Parkinson's cat is a familiar."

A queer look came over Paul's face. "That's the cat wasted my pumpkin pie. Knocked it right off the windowsill."

"I'm sorry to hear that," said the Reverend.

Paul's mind was racing back over the events of that last Sunday afternoon on Elm Street. The pie, the cat eating it. Cassandra going after the cat. Her fit—

No fit. Cassandra had been bewitched!

"Poor baby!" Paul ran to the door and threw it open. "Cassandra? Come here, darling!"

Cass came, her head lowered. Paul folded her in his arms. "My sweet little girl."

"You don't hate me, Papa?"

"Of course I don't hate you. What could my baby ever do that would make me hate her?"

"Even if I have to marry the Westcott boy like the angel said?"

"Not even then."

Cass sighed and cuddled closer. "It won't be so bad, Papa. The angel said after I bring Harley to God, I'll fall in love with him."

Over Cass's shoulder, Paul saw Emma standing in the door. "Curt just sent word by Helen," she said. "The Jersey heifer's calfing and he's got his hands full. If anyone's to go after Lil, it'll have to be you. But it's late already. And it's starting to snow, Paul."

Lil had waited at the meeting spot in front of the school, stamping in circles to keep warm, for just ten minutes after classes. There was no need to wait any longer. Cass hated school. She was always first out of class, first to the meeting spot. If she wasn't there, it meant just one thing.

Cold and frightened, hoping the worst of the snow would hold off, Lil trotted toward home. They should never have let Cass come to school this morning. She'd been sick, that's why she'd acted so funny. She must have been taken home before noon, or Lil herself would have been excused from classes.

Pneumonia? It couldn't be anything that bad. It would have been, though, if Cass had had to share this trip. Running through the cold, Lil was grateful that Cass, at least, was safe in a warm bed.

She passed the Coopers' and Mrs. Hopper's, the library, then Oneida Creek at the village limit. Two and a half more miles to go. If she could keep running, it would go faster. And she'd stay warm.

As she ran, she kept glancing over her shoulder, hoping to see some conveyance coming, someone to give her a ride. The Bowen boys sometimes walked with them and when their mother came for them in the buggy she'd give Lil and Cass a ride to their house just past the college. She'd probably come for the boys early today, seeing the snow about to start.

It was coming down faster now, in large, moist globs. The road was wet and treacherous, and Lil had no boots. The wind was wet, too. It crept under Lil's dress, up her sleeves, and down her neck as though she wore no clothes.

She managed to keep running until she was halfway up College Hill. Then she slowed, her breath coming in gasps, a stitch in her side.

Not a carriage, not a car, not a person. Everyone seemed to have vacated the world and left her alone, struggling up the icing hill, listening to the rasp of her own breath.

Nobody cared about her. Least of all Papa! Cass was home, the Bowens' mother had come for them, but nobody would come for her. Nobody would even drive by to give her a lift.

Suddenly she was crying. She tried to run again, slipped, and fell, scraping her knees. Her books scattered into the wet, and her papers blew into the wind. She rose and dashed in circles, sobbing, slipping, trying to salvage her things. Finally, blinded by tears, a sodden mass in her arms, she resumed her trudge up the hill in the swirling snow.

"Hey!"

A young man stood on the porch of a house.

"Hey!" he called again. "You need help?"

Lil just stood in the slush and stared at the boy, crying.

He bounded off the porch to her side. "Come on inside, for gosh sakes. Wherever you're going, you won't get there this way." He took her by the shoulders and steered her toward that forbidden port, a fraternity house. At that moment Lil didn't care what Papa would say. The boy's hands on her shoulders were so comforting. She just wanted to be warm!

Paul drove all the way to the school, the parson's carriage right in front of him. "You didn't see her, did you, Reverend?"

"Not a hair," said Reverend Smith.

Paul looked at the deserted school. "She must have gotten a ride home is all I can think."

"Then you'd better start back yourself, Paul. I don't think this snow is going to let up."

Paul started back, studying the roadsides for Lil's tracks, but the snow was already too deep.

Dread crept into his heart.

He was warmly dressed and bundled with quilts he had brought to wrap around Lilith. Still, the wagon in which he rode was open, and the cold went right to his bones.

How cold must she be out there with just a thin coat! Had she worn a scarf? Mittens? He knew she had no boots.

What if she had stumbled and fallen and was freezing to death—him driving right past. His heart pounded as his eyes investigated each mound beside the road.

More likely she'd got a ride, he kept telling himself, or maybe went into someone's house. He'd head on home. And if she wasn't there, he'd start back, house by house, mound by mound.

As he came out of the woods and into the meadows surrounding the farm, Paul looked ahead and saw a Ford motorcar in the drive. His heart leaped.

Then he frowned. Who that they knew had a Ford motorcar and would give Lilith a ride? He spurred the team onward.

Curt came out of the house as he pulled up. "I'll take the horses, Pa. You must be froze."

"Who's in there?"

"A boy. He just brought Lil home."

"Lilith went riding with a boy in a motorcar? Who is he?"

"Now, Pa, he's a nice kid, and it was unusual circumstances."

"Who is he?"

Curt gestured. "A boy from Franklin College," he said. Paul stormed into the kitchen.

"Papa! I'm so sorry. If I'd known you were coming after me—you didn't get chilled, did you, Papa?"

"Howdydo, sir, my name is John Stanley, and I really do apologize for pulling your daughter off the street, but she'd fallen and cut herself and she was chilled through and crying and quite a mess."

Paul waited until they both ran out of words. "Did either of you imagine," he said quietly, "that I would let my daughter walk three miles in a snowstorm?"

Lil hung her head.

"Begging your pardon, sir," said John, "she'd gone almost a mile and a half as it was, and she was really in distress. I am sorry that you had a fruitless ride, but I am not sorry I came to your daughter's assistance."

Paul fastened the boy with cold blue eyes. "You're a college fellow, aren't you?"

"Yes, sir. I'm a sophomore and Phi U."

"That's real nice," said Paul. "Now let's be straight between the two of us. I thank you for helping my daughter, but I'll also thank you to leave now and never see her again."

"Paul!" said Emma.

"Papa! How could you!"

"I'll have no sass!"

"Sir, I assure you, I had no intentions—"

"Good!" said Paul. "You still got your coat on, you can leave."

There was a long embarrassed moment, then Helen said, "I can't tell you how rude you're being, Pa." Paul started. He'd never heard anything but gentle words from Helen. She touched the young man's shoulder. "Please accept our apologies, John. We're grateful to you for bringing Lil home. Have some coffee, won't you?"

"No thanks, Mrs. Bascomb. But thank you." He backed toward the door. "Bye, Miss Bascomb. Ma'am. Sir." And he was gone.

Paul hardly waited for the door to close. "What do you mean, telling that boy he'd be welcome here? I'll thank you not to interfere with the management of my daughters."

"And I'll thank you not to tell me who I can have in my house!" said Helen.

"It's not yours. It's mine."

"You deeded it to Curt! If you want a house of your own, there's one up there in the woods, empty and waiting!" Helen turned and disappeared into her bedroom.

Lil bit her lip and looked at Emma. "Where's Cass?" she said, trying to sound normal.

"In bed," said Emma.

"Did the nurse bring her home?"

"The Pastor."

"Why?"

"Lilith?"

"Yes, Papa."

"How many times have I told you I never wanted to see you taking up with a college boy?"

"But, Papa, I wasn't."

"Don't tell me that what I just saw with my own eyes wasn't so!"

"But, Papa—"

"Did you or did you not go into a fraternity house?"

"Yes, I did! But—"

"Did you not go riding in a motorcar with a college boy?"

"You make it sound dirty, Papa!"

"It was dirty. And sinful!"

"It wasn't!"

"Don't sass me, Lilith! It's a devil of a job keeping you straight. You lean toward evil too easy, girl, it's in your blood. If I didn't love you, I'd just let you go, but I got to keep you straight. Now get out to the woodshed and take your bloomers down."

"Paul!"

"Quiet, Emma." Paul removed his coat.

"Papa, I'm too big to spank!"

"Get to the woodshed."

"Paul, she's *sixteen*! You can't make her do that!"

"I can and I will. And it'll hurt me worse than it'll hurt her."

As Paul started after Lil, she dodged behind the kitchen table.

"Mama!"

"Don't you interfere, Emma." Paul rolled up his sleeves. "I hadn't really made up my mind about this thing, Lilith. Always remember that. But now your own bad acting's made me decide."

"I don't know what you're talking about, Papa."

"You were setting your cap for Harley Westcott, weren't you? Well, weren't you?"

"No!"

"Don't lie, Lilith."

"I'm not lying! I like Harley, but—"

"But what?"

Lil stared at her father. "Well, look at me, Pa!" She burst into tears. "I'm ugly. He'd never marry me!"

"Don't you go saying you're ugly," snapped Paul.

Emma moved to her daughter's side. "Not a boy alive wouldn't be proud to have you, honey. You're going to be a fine-looking woman." She folded Lil to her chest. "You set your cap for anybody you want. Pay no attention to your Pa."

Paul's face contorted. "What's gotten into you, Emma?"

"What's gotten into *you*?"

"I won't have this! She's even infected you with her bad acting!"

"You're talking crazy, Paul. She hasn't done a thing. And why are you torturing her about being sweet on Harley Westcott?"

"Because *Cassandra* is going to marry Harley Westcott!"

Lil felt the pain even before she understood. She wouldn't have been able to point to any spot and say, "Here. It hurts here." It was everywhere, pressing down on her shoulders and out from her head. She stood, just heavy, unable to move.

But Emma flew at Paul. "What do you mean Cass is going to marry Harley Westcott? Has he come asking for her hand?"

"Not yet," said Paul, "but it will be arranged."

"What call you got to go meddling? I don't think Harley *wants* to marry Cass!"

"It's heaven's meddling, Emma. An angel of the Lord has appeared to Cassandra."

Lil looked up. What crazy story had Cass told? Lil could see her, leading Papa and the Parson down the garden path, the way she'd led Muriel and Janet on about the ghost. It must have been funny. Lil wished she'd been there. And suddenly she was laughing.

"Stop it!" said Paul.

She couldn't.

Paul seized her arm. "Stop it! That's the devil laughing. Just like Alice. And just like *her*!" Then he was yanking Lil, pulling, pushing her through the kitchen door and into the woodshed. "I'll beat it out of you!"

"Paul! No!" Emma followed, trying with all her strength to stop him.

"Leave me be!" shouted Paul. He slapped Emma with the back of his hand.

Emma gasped and backed away.

Paul paid her no further heed. "Take your bloomers down, Lilith."

Numb, Lil loosened the string of her drawers and let them drop.

"Bend over."

"You can't beat it out of her." Emma had no tears. She stood with incredible presence there in the woodshed, scorning to touch the place that was swelling beneath her eye. "You can't beat it out of her because the evil's not in her. It's in you. It won't die until *you* do."

"Get out!" said Paul.

Emma nodded. "I'll get out. But not because you say so. My daughter's a woman of dignity. I won't watch her be shamed by an inferior." She left.

Lil waited, thinking perhaps now he wouldn't. Then her dress was flung violently upward over her backside and cold air rushed between her legs. And Papa was looking at her, all naked, and she knew he could see *that spot*! She cried out.

The first blows fell, with all the strength of Paul's anger. Lil didn't feel them. She only felt Papa's eyes on her nakedness.

And then the door of the woodshed opened and Curt was standing there. And *he* could see her, too. "What the hell—"

Lil screamed and began to fight. She tumbled to the floor

and covered herself, sobbing, scrambling upward, and then she was running, holding up her bloomers, shielding her face in shame, through the kitchen and dining room, up the stairs to her room. She snatched a blanket from the bed and crawled underneath the bed, up to where it met the wall.

Her room was near the woodshed door. Curt must still be standing in the door, for she could hear his voice, "You fool! You damned insensitive fool!"

And curled in a ball beneath the bed, through the tears and the pain, Lil's mind sought for a way to avenge her shame.

The Bascombs woke to a new world. Half a foot of clean white snow had fallen during the night.

Lil sensed, the moment she opened her eyes, how clean and new everything was. Not just the world, but her. She dressed and lay down on the floor by the hole where the stovepipe from the dining room came through. She heard Emma and Helen moving about the kitchen, taking food to the dining room with none of the usual conversation. She heard the family come, silent, to the table. Then Emma called, "Breakfast, Lil," and Papa said, "What's this on my plate?" Lil rose and looked at herself in the mirror. Unhurried, she left the room.

Paul picked up the note attached to a sack tied with a pink ribbon; *From Lilith to Papa. Please don't wait till I get here to open it.* Paul smiled, surprised at a gift from Lil, pleased that yesterday's unpleasantness was forgotten. "Pretty ribbon," he said, and untied it carefully.

There was an uneasy silence at the table. On the landing overhead they could hear Lil's footsteps starting down the stairs.

Paul put the bag on his lap, opened it, and looked inside.

Then he brought his hands to his face; put them over his eyes.

Lil reached the doorway.

And they all knew immediately what was in the bag.

"Do you like my gift, Papa?"

Paul didn't look up. His hands, shaking, still covered his eyes..

Lil smiled. "You can keep it forever, but it will never bother me again." Her red hair, now standing out every which way, was shorn to within two inches of her head.

"Lil!" said Cass. "How could you?"

Lil smiled again. "It was easy," she said. "I used scissors."

CHAPTER FIFTEEN

HARLEY WESTCOTT WOULD not have considered himself a plum; certainly not one ripe for picking. He considered himself a man in love.

Daily he waited for a summons from his lady. Nightly he remembered her body. A week passed; then another.

He hadn't seen much of that body—she had refused to remove her clothes—but he'd felt it. And he felt it over and over, thrashing in his bed, assaulting his pillow.

It wouldn't be right for him to go see her, and he could understand how the time could go by with no word from Cass. She believed all that religion stuff. She was probably beating herself for being "sinful."

Harley spent most of his days in the library with Upjohn, his energy tumbling into verbiage. He rambled on about every subject in the world, except Cass. Upjohn wouldn't understand about Cass.

Upjohn, for his part, was strangely silent.

"What's the matter?" Harley finally asked him. "You haven't said two words all morning."

"You haven't given me a chance. What's the matter with *you*?"

"I've got something on my mind, that's all."

"Is the something named Bascomb, Harley?"

"How did you know?" A flush crept over Harley's face. "You've been spying on me!"

"Merely observing. May I offer a word of advice?"

"No!" Harley rushed out of the library.

Upjohn went up to the room in Hitty's suite where Frank had lain these months, and where, despite the fact that Frank had a nurse, Hitty sat in almost constant attendance.

It had been a month after the accident, with Frank still in a coma, that Hitty went to Mr. Upjohn. "I was wondering, would the elixir you gave me help Papa get well?"

"I'm afraid not, though a dab now and again might make him more comfortable."

"Then what about 'minds in concert'? Remember? You said that day in the library that there is nothing stronger in the world. Do you suppose you could teach me how to do it?"

Ignoring the nurse, they had taken seats beside Frank's bed; facing one another, they had held hands and concentrated. On the third day, Frank came out of the coma. He was unable to move, but his eyes followed Hitty about the room, and, occasionally, unintelligible sounds issued from his lips.

Hitty made the nurse join in. "The more minds, the better— right Mr. Upjohn? Now the idea is this, Whitcomb. We join our energies into a single beam and send it to Papa. We tell him to trust in himself and trust in us."

After another week Frank moved one arm. Hitty's spirits soared; even the nurse began to wonder.

Harley remained in his room during the third week of waiting, refusing to come downstairs. The fourth week he returned to his lessons, but Upjohn made no attempt to teach or talk. He merely read to himself, allowing Harley to write or stare out the window or wander about the room as he pleased. Only when Harley stopped pacing and turned as though ready to speak, would Upjohn look up.

Harley's face would redden, and he would turn back to the window. Upjohn would reluctantly return to his book.

On the first morning of the fifth week, Colleen brought the letter to the library. Harley read it, stuffed it into his pocket, and headed for the foyer. "I'm going someplace," he said. "It's nothing that concerns you, so don't follow me!"

As Upjohn watched him dash up the stairs, the letter so hurriedly stuffed into Harley's pocket fell.

> *Dear Harley,*
> *I'm desparate. If you love me come at once. Do you have a sliegh? If so, bring it. Tell Papa and Mama you've come to take me sliegh-riding. That will get us away from the house so we can talk.*
>
> > *I love you.*
> > *Cassandra Lee Bascomb*
>
> *P.S. Make sure you bring a sliegh that only seats two. Otherwise they might make us take Lil for a chaparone.*

When Harley clattered back down, bundled up for the wintry ride, he saw the letter on the stair and scooped it up. Mr. Upjohn sat on the bottom step, his back turned.

"Did you read it?"

"Yes."

"You didn't have the right."

Upjohn looked up. "Maybe not, Harley, but I had the duty."

"Are you going to try to stop me?"

"If that letter had been signed 'Lilith Bascomb,' I wouldn't want to."

"I'm not in love with Lil."

"That is your misfortune. By the way, how do you spell 'sleigh'?"

Harley frowned. "So what if Cass doesn't spell so good?"

"Exactly," said Upjohn. "Think about it."

The road to the Bascombs' seemed interminable. What difference did it make whether Cass could spell? It was obvious that Upjohn had never had sex.

As Harley left the sleigh by the Bascomb woodshed, a movement in the second-floor window caught his eye. Glancing up, he saw two hands on the curtains and a face peeking between. Lil.

The curtains quickly closed.

Lil was probably a good speller. He didn't know why the thought occurred to him, but with it came the impulse to jump back into the sleigh and go home.

Too late. Cass stood in the door of the woodshed; the sight of her flooded Harley with new impatience.

Cass had passed on to her father another message from the angel. Harley Westcott would come soon, gliding up a road of white to ask for her hand.

So when Paul caught sight of Harley's sleigh, he sighed and said, "Here he comes. Gliding." And when Harley asked to take Cass riding, Paul agreed. "But have her back here in thirty minutes."

After all, a girl couldn't get her honor threatened in a two-seater sleigh in the dead cold of winter with only half an hour to kill.

"Haw, Violet!" Violet took off in the mistaken assumption that she was heading for home. "Haw!" Harley urged her around the first bend of the road and halted to crush Cass in a passionate kiss.

But once his hands get busy, Cass held him at bay. "We've got to talk," she said.

"About what?"

"Us."

Something in her tone quelled Harley's urge to touch her. "What about us?"

Cass looked up, fixing him with her gaze. "Will you marry me, Harley?"

Harley stared at her.

"Will you?"

"Do you have to know today?"

"Yes."

"Why?"

"I just have to, that's all."

"I can't decide to get married just like that!"

"Don't you want me?"

"Yes, but—"

"Then marry me."

"No! Look here, Cass, if I ever decide I want to marry you, I'll do the asking!"

"Can't you decide right now?" said Cass.

"No."

Cass sighed. "I was hoping you could." She folded her arms and stared at Violet's rump.

They sat that way for nearly a minute, while Harley tried to figure out how he could touch her without promising to marry her.

Then he saw Cass's round blue eyes fill with tears. They rolled down onto her out-thrust lower lip. Harley squirmed in his seat until he could stand it no longer. "I'm sorry!" he said. "I'm really sorry. Please stop crying."

"I can't." The output of tears increased.

"Cass!" Harley gestured helplessly. "We've got all the time in the world!"

"Maybe *you* have," said Cass. "*I* haven't."

"What do you mean?"

"Never mind,'" said Cass.

An awful possibility presented itself. "Tell me what you mean."

"I won't," said Cass. "It would have been different if you'd said yes when I asked you to marry me. But I'm not going to push myself on anyone who doesn't want me. I've got pride, you know. So take me home. And don't worry, I won't bother you anymore. And I won't shame your family. I'll run away tonight and—"

"But we only did it once!" Harley cried, his face crimson. "Are you sure?"

"I don't know what you're talking about," said Cass. "Take me home."

"I'm not taking you back till you tell me!"

"Then I'll walk." Cass started to get out of the sleigh.

Harley pulled her back—roughly. Cass squeaked. "I'm sorry," he said. His roughness reminded him of Lil, and the way she'd felt struggling in his arms that afternoon in Lizzy's house. Remembering, Harley kissed Cass. "I love you," he said.

"Do you really?" Cass's lips, warm and open, formed the words beneath his eager lips.

"Yes!" He kissed her again. "I've thought about you every minute. You've driven me crazy at night!" Then a thought so wonderful took possession of Harley that he stopped kissing her. "That won't happen anymore, will it?"

"What won't?" said Cass.

"Alone, in my bed. I'll have *you*!" It was as though the sun had risen to reveal not the lonely landscape he was accustomed to but an enchanted world of flowers and streams, and naked Casses playing tag through the woods. "How soon should we be married?"

Cass blushed. "Are you asking me to marry you?"

"I'm asking."

"It better be just as soon as possible," said Cass.

Harley glanced down at her abdomen. He wasn't sure about these things, but they might still be able to claim the baby was premature.

He shifted uncomfortably. "What's your Dad going to say when we ask him?"

"Oh, we can't ask him," said Cass.

"How do we do it then?"

"We keep going right now. We go into town have Reverend Smith marry us. This afternoon."

Harley stared. "We're underage! He won't do it."

"I've already talked to him. He was the only person I could go to. He said we had to get married right away, today." She embraced him. "Oh, Harley, it will be so wonderful. We'll be together forever and ever." She hopped out of the sleigh, ran to the trees and returned with a suitcase.

Harley swallowed. "Where'll we go afterward?"

"Your house, of course."

"Are you crazy?" Hitty and Tobin had never even *heard* of Cass Bascomb. "I think we should talk to our parents first."

"They'd just say no. Oh, Harley!" She threw her arms around him again. "I'm frightened. Marry me this afternoon! Then, after we're married, they can't undo it. Please!"

It would be dark by the time they could drive to town, get married, then drive back. Maybe he could sneak her up to his room—

"Harley?"

"Hm-m-m?"

She still clung to him, and now *she* was touching *him.* "Tonight I'll even take my clothes off."

At nine o'clock the next morning, the Westcott household was preoccupied with preparations for Hitty's New Year's Eve Ball. A hundred names were on the guest list. The drawing room and foyer had been cleared of furniture, and a five-piece orchestra would be coming in from Seneca. The dining room was dotted with twenty-five small round tables; the ceiling was hung with hundreds of balloons. In the kitchen, Agnes, Henrietta, and Colleen stirred and measured, baked and simmered, preparing the genuine French dishes Hitty had selected. Hitty herself was making centerpieces of pine cones and ribbon and poinsettias from her greenhouse when the door knocker sounded.

"Drat!" said Hitty and went to answer it. She didn't recognize the man who stood there, hat in hand, smiling. He was quick to assist her. "Reverend Smith, Mrs. Westcott. Methodist congregation."

"You've come to the wrong place. We're Presbyterian."

He smiled again. "I know that, Mrs. Westcott. Might I come in anyway?"

"We're in a bit of an uproar. Perhaps the library."

Reverend Smith missed nothing as he followed Hitty through the foyer. "Having a party, I see. You have a lovely home."

"Yes." Hitty was thinking of the nineteen centerpieces still to be done, the hundred napkins to be folded like swans, the fresh candles to be placed, her own self to dress, and Frank to prepare. "The music and dancing will do Daddy more good than all the medicine in the world," Hitty had contended. Now, she was of no mind to small-talk. "Is it a contribution you want, Reverend?"

"Mercy, no," he said. "I've come about your son."

"Oh, well, you wouldn't want him, either. He's practically agnostic."

"Yes, I know. Have you seen him this morning?"

"No. He's in bed with a cold."

Reverend Smith could not suppress a smile.

"It's not funny," said Hitty. "He told the maid it's a very bad cold."

Reverend Smith spread his palms. "Mrs. Westcott, I really don't know where to begin."

"Perhaps near the end," said Hitty. "I don't have much time."

He shrugged. "Mrs. Westcott, I married your son last night."

Hitty stared. "*You* married Harley?"

Reverend Smith flushed. "I mean, I officiated at his wedding."

"My goodness!" What a time to have to think about such a thing.

"She's one of my flock," the Reverend was saying. "Mrs. Westcott, I know this must come as a shock, but—"

"Is she my size?"

"I beg your pardon?"

"What will she wear?"

Hitty swept up the staircase and was halfway around the gallery to Harley's door before Reverend Smith reached the hall. "What's her name?" she called back.

"Cassandra," said Reverend Smith. "I beg you not to be harsh, Mrs. Westcott. You haven't heard—"

"Harley? Cassandra? Are you dressed?"

"Come in, Mother."

They were sitting at Harley's desk, playing Parcheesi. They had obviously been waiting for some time.

Hitty's gaze swept Cass from head to toe. "Oh, dear. I'm afraid you're too small."

Harley smiled nervously. "Shall we throw her back?"

"Back where? Where did she come from?"

"I'm Cassandra Lee Bascomb, ma'am. I live—I lived on the next farm."

"You mean there are more of you?"

"Beg pardon?"

"Well, they'll have to be invited, too. How many are there, Harley?"

"Five."

"Another whole table!" said Hitty.

"What's she talking about?" said Cass.

"Stand up," said Hitty. She took Cass's hands and raised her. "You're not really that much smaller—" A hope lit Hitty's face. "Did you bring a party dress of your own?"

"I've got my Sunday pinafore."

"For heaven's sake, you can't wear that," said Hitty. "Oh well, don't worry. Come along. You'll have to make swans while I find you a dress. Harley, ride over and invite her people. Tell them it's formal. Do they have formal clothes, Cassandra?"

"I don't think so."

"Take their measurements, Harley."

Reverend Smith was waiting at the top of the stairs when Hitty started back down. "Oh, you're still here," she said.

The Reverend stiffened. "Yes, Mrs. Westcott, I am. And I must say I am amazed at this whole performance. Aren't you even surprised that your son is married?"

"Very. But my son is a level-headed boy. Either he is in love with this pretty child, and/or he has got her in the family way." The Reverend gasped. "In which case an early marriage is best for all. Now I hope you'll excuse us, because we have a great deal to do."

A few moments later Hitty snapped her fingers and rushed to the window. "Too late," she said. "I should have asked that man to stay. He could have helped us make swans."

For the second day in a row, Harley stopped the sleigh by the door of the Bascomb woodshed and glanced at the upstairs window. She wasn't there. He was ushered into the dining room where the family sat in conversation. Lil was not there either.

The Bascombs shook Harley's hand with varying degrees of enthusiasm. Emma, Helen, and Curt would have been pleased—Cass could not have made a better match—had it not been for Lil. But Emma and Helen bore Harley no grudge. It wasn't his fault. They tried to smile.

Curt could find no smile. Since the day of her spanking he'd been heartsick for Lil and bristling with hostility toward Paul. *Damn*, Lil had been magnificent when she cut her hair! That was the kind of sister to have. As for Cass—well, if Harley had been stupid enough to take her, he deserved her.

Paul was the most expansive. He clapped Harley on the shoulder.

"The ways of the Lord are strange, aren't they, son?" He chuckled. "I imagine your folks weren't too pleased."

"My mother didn't seem to mind," said Harley. "In fact, that's why I came. She wants you to come to her party tonight."

"What kind of a party?" said Emma.

"Well—it's formal."

Paul laughed. "Son, you go back and tell your Ma the Bascombs are simple, God-fearing folks. We got no clothes for affairs like that. When you're doing the Lord's work, you don't have need for such trappings." Besides, the point of the marriage was to save the Westcotts, not to lead the Bascombs to perdition.

Emma shook her head. "They're our in-laws now, Paul. If we turn them down, it would be an insult."

"Ma's right," said Curt. A twinkle materialized in his eyes. "Would Sunday-best suits do for me and Pa, Harley?"

"Sure."

"And Helen here's got her wedding gown—"

"Heavens, Curt, that's too fancy!"

"The ladies'll be dressed real fancy," said Curt. "Won't they, Harley?" He rubbed his hands together. "What'll we fix you up in, Ma?"

"I got some blue satin yard goods in the trunk. I guess if I got to work right away, I could whip something up." Emma frowned and glanced toward the ceiling. "Lil's got nothing, though."

"Don't you worry about Lil," said Curt, moving toward a wooden cabinet on the wall.

"What do you think you're doing?" Paul demanded.

Curt glanced at Helen. "None of your damn business," he told Paul.

Helen smiled and went to help him count the egg money.

"Curt, I don't know what you're talking about. I can't go to the party. I look awful! Besides," Lil's voice lowered to a whisper, "I can't face Harley!"

"Yes, you can," said Curt. He took her in his arms. "You and me are going into town, and when you walk into that party tonight, Harley Westcott's going to know he left his brains at home when he went sleigh-riding yesterday."

"What the hell are these?" Paul had seemed content enough with the high-necked, long-sleeved, white ruffled dress that lay in the "*It* Shop" box. His consternation was with the other items therein. "High-heeled shoes, Pa," said Curt. "And silk stockings."

"She's not gonna wear 'em," said Paul.

"She is, too. She's sixteen years old."

"You talk like sixteen is grown up!"

"Her sister's fifteen and a married lady. God only knows how the Westcotts will have *her* dolled up tonight. What have you got against Lil, Pa?"

Paul reddened. "All right, she can wear the consarned things." He looked around. "Where is Lil?"

"She got out at the county road. Said she wanted to take a walk."

Lil had, in fact, left her brother at the curve just before the house. Now, after ascending the ladder to the loft opposite the outhouse and tiptoeing through the back bedroom, she was locking the door of her own room.

"Why's she taking a walk?" said Paul.

"How should I know?" said Curt. He closed the "*It* Shop" box and took it upstairs. Four taps, and the door opened. Curt handed the box in, then went back down. "Come on, Pa. Let's get an early start on the chores. Helen, you'd better heat plenty of water, because I'm going to want a bath tonight, too. Son-of-a-gun! It's been a long time since I've been to a party."

As the family dressed that evening, all knocks at Lil's door brought replies of, "Soon! I'll be ready soon."

Helen, who had carried bathwater up to Lil, hid her elation carefully. She clucked and shook her head at Curt when he came in from chores. Emma caught the look, but asked no questions.

Curt pulled the sleigh up to the woodshed door.

"Don't know why these girls take so long," said Paul.

"Get loaded," said Curt. And when all were tucked beneath the lap robes, he went for Lil.

She emerged from her room in an ankle-length coat, with a scarf concealing her hair, and another covering her face. "Think you'll be warm enough?" asked Curt.

Tobin stopped at the head of the stairs and tugged at his collar. The hall below was warm in the light of candles. Bouquets of flowers dotted the tables. Around the concert grand in the drawing room, the orchestra was tuning up. Tobin sighed and descended. He hated parties.

Hitty was in the drawing room with Harley, Thomas, and Mr. Upjohn. That tutor seemed to be included in everything lately. And Frank was there, dressed in a tuxedo, his nurse beside his chair. He seemed, at first glance, lifeless. Then Tobin saw his eyes following the movements of the violinist. Tobin nodded hello, then threw a puzzled look at the young girl beside his son. He cleared his throat and waited for someone to make the introduction. Hitty was alternately fussing with Frank and watching the window for guests.

Harley spoke up. "Dad—I want you to meet Cass."

Tobin took the girl's hand. She must be an early arrival. "Nice to meet you. Are you new around here?"

"Oh, good heavens!" Hitty wheeled and stared at Tobin. "You don't know! I'm sorry, dear. I meant to send you word, but we all got so busy—"

"Send what word?" said Tobin.

"If you'd only come in for lunch…" Hitty placed her hands on Cass's shoulders. "She's ours! Isn't she lovely?"

Tobin smiled. "Where'd we buy her?"

"Oh, silly!" said Hitty. "We *married* her! That is, Harley did."

Tobin kept on smiling. Hitty's words were ridiculous. "Harley's too young to get married."

"*We* know that, sir," said Upjohn, "but I'm afraid that Harley did not. The young lady is, in fact, your daughter-in-law. She and Harley were married last night."

The only words that came to Tobin's mind could not be uttered in front of Hitty.

Cass put her arms about Tobin, and kissed his cheek. "Don't be cross," she said. "I'll be a good wife and a good daughter. Let's be friends right away."

Tobin flushed. "Well, of course, we'll be friends. It's just—a shock."

"Of course it is." Cass hugged him again. "Harley, why didn't you tell me your father was so handsome?"

Tobin wished Cass would let go of his arm. She wore one of Hitty's dresses, tiers of lavender chiffon. Her hair was Hitty's handiwork, too, upswept and demure. In fact, she had a style that reminded Tobin of Hitty. But he didn't like her. He glanced at Harley. He looked dazed. If Tobin made a scene—no, he couldn't ruin Hitty's party. He'd get Harley aside later and find out what had happened. He'd get him out of this thing. Sixteen years old, no parental permission—any judge would annul it in a second!

But what if the girl was pregnant? A wife, maybe a child at sixteen? There would be the end of Harley's fine dreams. He'd have nothing to do but what Tobin had always wanted and hoped he would do—stay right here and be a farmer. Especially if Tobin made him support her, and refused to pay his college expenses.

Tobin lowered his eyes. That would be a shameful way to win.

"Now when Mama comes," Hitty was saying, "we'll just introduce Cassandra as Cassandra. I'll sit Mama down later and tell her the whole thing, so she won't wrinkle her gown when she faints."

CHAPTER SIXTEEN

FLORA WAS THE first to arrive, fetched by Sailor in the Stevens-Duryea.

She had been content, since Frank's attack, to leave her husband and his nursing to Hitty. Now, she grimaced when she saw him. "Feeling better, dear?"

Frank's eyes flickered.

"That's fine," she said and turned away.

Other guests were soon filing into the drawing room. The orchestra struck up a waltz, and Colleen and Henrietta began to circulate with canapés. Upjohn led Flora off to inspect the dining room, while Hitty, Tobin, Harley, and Cass formed a reception line.

"Gillespie, Odelia! Cynthia, Jeremy! So glad you could come. You know Tobin, and Harley, and Harley's wife, Cassandra."

"I don't recall hearing that Harley had married," said Gillespie Hamlin after two puff pastries.

"But, Gillespie, you couldn't have," said Cynthia Cole. "Only Hitty's very closest friends knew anything."

"Exactly," said Gillespie's wife. "I knew about it weeks ago."

"Give me *all* the details," said Cynthia. "I want to know if it's the same story Hitty gave *me*."

By the time sixty guests had gathered, a dozen versions were circulating.

One had it that Tobin was in poor health and, wanting to secure his succession, had married Harley to the daughter of a fellow Holstein-man from Wisconsin.

According to another, secrecy had been maintained because the bride was a cousin—close to the point of incest. Of course, most of the guests were cousins, and since not one of them knew Cassandra, that story rapidly lost credibility.

Everyone did allow, though, that she looked familiar.

"Who do we know with a girl named Cassandra?"

The question was answered at the entrance of the Bascomb family.

Although the assembled were nearly all Presbyterian Founding Families, no one could forget the Bascombs' Sunday parade past the bench.

A sign of recognition. Heads wagged. Eyes traced Cass's abdomen.

"Not showing yet."

"Poor Hitty. She's being so brave!"

"Well, you know they do say that Frank and Flora—"

Feeling as though a fairy godmother had done something to a family of pumpkins, the Bascombs handed their wraps to a butler and, led by Paul, approached the receiving line.

"You must be Cassandra's people!" cried Hitty. "We're so pleased you could come. Here we've been next-door neighbors, and we've never even met! How do you like her?" She hugged Cassandra and spun her around. "Isn't she beautiful?"

"Fool woman acts like Cass is some sort of doll," Paul muttered to Emma. But he had expected Cass to be garishly dressed and shamelessly painted. He cast about for something else to get indignant about. Turning to introduce the rest of his family, he found it.

Lil stood beside Curt—tall, slender, and defiant. Her shining red bob swept toward her cheeks in soft beauty-parlored puffs. Lip color had been applied with suddenly sensuous results. Her mascara-lashed gold eyes shone. And was that *rouge* on her cheeks?

There was more. Lil was not wearing the high-necked ruffled dress Paul had seen. Her pink dress hung by the grace of two shoestring straps and descended in simple, clinging lines to the top of her thighs. From there a hundred crepe streamers swirled downward and ended at her *knees!* Below that, silk-stockinged legs took an unashamed journey to prettily arched feet in high-heeled pink satin pumps.

No one said anything for a moment. Emma smiled, Cass stared, Harley flushed.

Paul mustered a smile. "We figured now that Lil's baby sister is a married lady, Lil ought to have a grown-up party dress."

At the other end of the room, Thomas Westcott stopped dead and stared at Lil. He poked Gillespie Hamlin. "Who's those people just come in?"

Gillespie clucked. "You oughta get out more, Thomas. Them's the Bascombs, your new in-laws that moved in that old Stockbridge place." "

And who's the red-headed girl with them?"

"A daughter, I guess."

"Thought I was dreaming." Thomas' voice dropped to a whisper. "Don't you know who she looks like?"

"Can't say as I do."

"That's right," said Thomas. "You'd be too young." He started toward the reception line. He circled, studying each face, then halted behind Paul. "I know the lady in blue ain't *Alice*

Stockbridge, so you got to be *Paul* Stockbridge. How are you, Paul?" Thomas grinned and offered his hand. "It's good to see you. Hell, we all thought you was dead forty-five years ago, done in by your crazy Aunt Lizzy!"

For the first time that evening, Lil's and Harley's eyes met. Paul said nothing.

"Don't you know me?" said Thomas. "Thomas Westcott!"

Paul took his hand. "I'm pleased to make your acquaintance, Thomas. But you have me confused with someone else. My name is Bascomb, Paul Bascomb."

Thomas wavered a moment, then grinned. "Bascomb, is it?" He glanced at Lil. "This your daughter?"

"Yes," said Paul.

"Well, you got to forgive me, Mr. *Bascomb*. It was a natural mistake, seeing as how you're living in the old Stockbridge place, and seeing as how your daughter's a dead ringer for Paul Stockbridge's mother." Thomas' eyes twinkled. He turned to Lil. "Your name wouldn't be Philimentha, would it?"

Lil's startled glance met Cass's, then she lowered her eyes, knowing, without seeing it, the expression on 'Paul's face. "No," she said. "My name is Lilith."

"That," said another voice, "is inapt." Upjohn had joined the group quietly. "You do not look as though you would devour small children."

Lil saw the understanding eyes of this stranger and smiled. "I only eat children on the first and third Thursdays of the month."

"I don't understand a bit of this," said Hitty. Other guests were arriving and needed greeting. "This is Harley's tutor, Mr. Upjohn. Father Westcott, Mr. Upjohn, will you take charge of the Bascombs?"

"Glad to," said Thomas. "Come see our swans."

Lil didn't move for a moment. She had wanted to savor the way she looked, Papa's shock, Cass's envy, the grand house, her first party—and Harley's furtive glances.

But now, suddenly, she was a Stockbridge, with a crazy aunt and a grandmother she had met in a dressing room in Missouri. She resented finding it out just at that moment.

There was a touch on her bare arm, and Upjohn's face moved close. A shiver traced her spine.

He offered his arm. "May I escort you to the punch table?"

"Thank you." She couldn't help looking at Harley as they passed, hoping to meet his eyes again, hoping to find jealousy there.

But Harley's eyes were evasive. She caught instead Cass's eyes, unsure where the sisters stood, for they had hardly spoken in a month. Impulsively Lil winked, and a smile lit Cass's face.

"So you are Harley's sister-in-law," Upjohn was saying. Strange to hear herself called that.

"I guess I am."

"You are not at all like your sister. Tell me, how would you spell chaperone?"

"C-h-a-p-e-r-o-n-e. Why?"

Upjohn shrugged. He leaned closer. "You're causing quite a stir, you know."

Lil did know. She could feel the eyes, hear the whispers. She took a better grip on Upjohn's arm, refusing to wobble on her high heels. She had waited too long—to be pretty; to be a woman.

"How old are you?"

Lil was shocked to find her thoughts read. "Seventeen in April."

"How old is Cassandra?"

"Fifteen."

"How did she do it?" said Upjohn with simple candor.

"She lied a lot," Lil said with equal candor. "She told Papa and Reverend Smith that an angel of the Lord appeared to her in visions and commanded her to marry Harley—to 'bring the mighty low and meekened,' and to give birth to some sort of Messiah."

"Extraordinary."

"She's quite an actress."

"My amazement is not so much at Cassandra's performance as at the credence of your father and your Reverend."

As they entered the candlelit dining room, Lil drew a soft breath.

"You seem to belong in this room," whispered Upjohn.

Lil smiled. She did match the pink and strawberry room— and the red poinsettias! "Where did they get the flowers in the middle of winter?"

"I'll show you." Upjohn ladled her some punch and smiled at Paul. "May I give your daughter a tour of the greenhouse?"

Paul was still sparring with Thomas. "Have her back in ten minutes," he said, automatically setting a limit.

The greenhouse was pungent, the party far away. Lil admired a row of carnations and tried to be offhand. "Maybe you can tell *me* something. How did Cass ever talk Harley into getting married?"

"I'm afraid Harley's taste has not developed apace of his appetites," said Upjohn. "I blame myself. I should have tied him to a chair. I knew of the—affair he was having with your sister."

"He never acted as if—I mean, when he came to see us…"

Upjohn corrected her. "He came to see *you*."

Lil nodded. "At least, I was beginning to think so." The muscles in her throat tightened. She walked deeper into the greenhouse. If she had to cry, she'd rather do it there with Upjohn than in front of the guests in the dining room.

"Harley *was* coming to see you, Lilith. But he fell prey to the oldest female trick in the world."

Lil forgot the lump in her throat. Was that what he'd meant by "affair"? Had Cass— "Cass would *never* do that!"

Upjohn smiled. "I admire your loyalty, Lilith. Especially when you are the aggrieved party. It is the truth."

Lil walked along a row of mums, swatting at the blossoms. Then she turned, with light voice and lifted chin. "Tell me about the original Lilith."

"I thought you knew about her."

"Only what Papa says. That she was the first wife of Adam, and that she was evil."

Upjohn tucked a white mum into his buttonhole. "We first hear of her among the Babylonians and Assyrians, but I'm sure she's older. She was thought to exert power over children. Jewish mythology adopted her and expanded the theory, saying that she *devoured* children. I suppose she is the basis for some of our superstitions about witches."

"Then you're wrong. I *am* aptly named."

Upjohn raised an eyebrow.

"My sister thinks I'm a witch."

"Are you?"

Lil studied him thoughtfully. Harley had told her so much about him, she felt she knew him. But even without that—there was something in his eyes, his touch, the way he said "Lilith." It didn't seem strange at all to be standing here in the Westcott greenhouse telling him her secrets. "I don't know if I'm a witch. I never used to think I was, but things have happened to make me wonder. Like piano-playing. That wasn't coincidence."

"You play the piano?"

"Not really. But one day I accompanied my sister when our organist forgot her music, and played very well."

"Might I suggest that you reserve supernatural explanations until you have exhausted all the natural ways in which this phenomenon might have come about?"

"You mean like self-hypnosis?"

"Or untapped powers of recall."

"Or reincarnation?"

"I said we should reserve the supernatural explanations."

Lil smiled. "You're very nice. I like you."

Upjohn—whose gaze, Lil sensed, was always direct— looked down at the floor.

"I'm sorry," Lil said quickly.

"Not at all," said Upjohn. "It is merely that I have grown away from the habit of receiving affection."

"But Harley thinks the world of you!"

"Harley, my dear, is afraid of me. Which is exactly as I mean it to be, for there are still certain things I hope to teach him. When I cease to teach him, there will be time to discover our mutual affection."

"That day isn't long off, is it?—When you stop teaching him?"

"He'll be my student for one more year."

In the dim light Lil studied Upjohn. She was not good at guessing the ages of adults, especially men, but it did not seem to her that he could be much past forty. What was in his eyes? Now the twinkle that had sent a chill down her back when first he took her arm, now a look of incredible sadness—and age. Lil was suddenly overcome by the knowledge that he must be lonely. "What will you do," she said gently, "when they don't need you anymore?"

"I will leave," said Upjohn.

Lil touched a plant, gathering courage. "I've got to tell you," she said, "I don't understand why you're here. Or why you want to stay." She looked up. "I envy Harley's being near you all these years. But you could have been having a wonderful career in some exciting place instead of spending all this time teaching one boy halfway between Oriskany Forks and Chuckery Corners and a hundred miles from nowhere."

"Maybe, Lilith, I have all the time in the world, and a hundred miles from nowhere can be the center of the universe. I am where I am needed."

He had not spoken in rebuke, but Lil felt ashamed. "I didn't mean...It's just—"

"You think there are more important things elsewhere. Harley feels the same. And maybe there are."

"Have you a family? A home?"

"No."

"Where were you born?"

"Lilith, my dear," he put a hand to her shoulder, and again she felt the pleasant chill, "please don't ask about me. Not because I mind the questions, but because I would be forced to lie."

Lil smiled. "I wouldn't want you to do that. But can I tell you something?"

"What?"

She looked down and untangled two pink streamers. "I'm glad you won't be going for a while."

His hand moved from her shoulder to touch her hair.

But Lil and Upjohn were no longer alone in the greenhouse. Three women had entered, exclaiming over the carnations.

Upjohn dropped his hand. "Do you dance?"

"No," said Lil.

"It's time you learned."

Tobin pushed his way through the crowd to Paul and Emma Bascomb. "May I sit down?"

Paul moved over on the bench.

Tobin watched the dancing for a moment. "Enjoying yourselves?"

"Just fine," said Paul.

"Thought maybe you'd be wanting to have a little talk. About the kids, of course."

"Make a nice couple, don't they?"

"Well, yes," said Tobin. "But they're too young!"

"Emma, here, was only sixteen when I married her. And the mother of Our Lord was even younger."

"That may be fine for a girl, Mr. Bascomb, but Harley hasn't even finished his schooling. He can't support a wife."

"I expect they'll get on somehow."

Tobin stared at him. "You sound as if you approve of this marriage."

"Always have. Right from the beginning."

"You mean you knew about it beforehand? I didn't know one thing about it till ten minutes before you walked in tonight!"

Now it was Paul's turn to stare. "Where you *been* all day?"

"Working!" Tobin jumped to his feet. "Is she pregnant?"

Paul, too, got to his feet. "She is not, sir, and I resent your inferment!"

"Well, fine," said Tobin. "If she's not pregnant, I got to tell you, I'm going to get it annulled."

"You won't be able to get it annulled. Heaven ordained this marriage."

"Heaven, my foot!"

"Don't go tempting the wrath of God, Tobin Westcott! Listen to me. I'm older than you are, and I'm telling you the truth. An angel of the Lord came to Cassandra in visions and told her she was to marry your son. How do you think this thing all came about so smooth you didn't even know about it? It was heaven, Tobin. Heaven greased the tracks for those two, and there's no going backwards on heaven's tracks."

"Could you produce this angel in a court of law?"

Paul raised an accusing finger. "That's blasphemy!"

Tobin would have answered, but at that moment the front door opened. "Good Lord!" He hurried to Hitty's side. "Carrie and her husband just came in," he told her.

Hitty's mouth fell open. "I didn't invite them." She peered into the foyer. "Oh dear, go tell Agnes we'll need two more places somehow."

Across the room, Toynbee Upjohn raised his eyes from the pink and red dancer in his arms. Without missing a step, he reversed and waltzed Lil into the dining room. There he stopped, keeping her out of sight, and looking back toward the foyer.

"What's the matter?"

"I'm trying to decide," said Upjohn. He took Lil by the hand and led her into the kitchen.

"Get out of here," said Agnes. Tobin followed them through the door. "And what in Scott's name would *you* be wanting?"

"Mrs. Westcott's sister has arrived. We'll need two more places."

"We ain't got two more places," said Agnes. "They'll have to sit on the floor. Where you taking that girl, Mr. Upjohn?"

Upjohn was halfway through the pantry door. "On a tour of your magnificent pantry, my dear Agnes."

"You keep out of my pantry!" But it was too late. They were gone. And now Tobin was heading for the pantry, too. "What are *you* up to?"

Tobin didn't answer. It didn't look proper for Upjohn to be taking a young girl into the back part of the house, and he meant to tell him so.

But as the door shut behind him, Tobin found himself alone in the semi-darkness. "Upjohn?" There was no answer. He entered the servants' section, and knocked on Upjohn's door. "Upjohn?" Silence. Tobin hesitated, looked about, and opened the door. Only the scent of musk.

Feeling foolish, Tobin went back to the pantry and, rather than raise Agnes' dander once more, entered the foyer by way of the door beneath the staircase. A wall of warm air enveloped him. He tugged at his collar and scanned the dancers for Lil and Upjohn. Then he jumped. Something was moving in the alcove under the stairs. "Who's there?"

"Me."

Tobin took a candle from a nearby sconce and held it to the darkness. "What the hell are you doing?"

"Hiding," said Lil.

"From what?"

"I don't know. Ask Mr. Upjohn. He went back to the party."

Tobin sighed. The whole Bascomb clan was mad.

Then a scream came from the parlor—and another, and another. Tobin whirled, unable to comprehend the word being screamed.

Charlie Comstock skidded into the foyer. "Tobin! Your barn's on fire!"

Smoke enveloped the men as they rushed into the barn. Tobin ran to open the pasture door, and they all began to loose the herd.

But terror rendered the cattle, stupid at best, only more stupid, and variously stubborn or vicious.

"Haw!"

"Move, you idiot!"

"Watch her! Watch out!"

Milling, charging, defecating, bawling, the cattle defied their rescuers. One was finally expelled into the night. She turned and rushed back in.

"Get feed bags! Cover their heads!"

Smoke poured down the hay chutes. Seeing was through tears; breathing was coughing.

Men rushed to the calf shed and formed human barricades to drive the calves out one by one.

The champions were still in their stalls. And the bulls.

"Dad!" Harley found Tobin wrestling a feed bag over Laura Beets's head. "I'll find Sailor. We'll get the high-testers and the bulls."

"Keep away from those bulls, Harley. I'll get 'em if I can."

"*We*'ll get them, Dad. Don't worry!" Harley dashed away, dodging crazed cattle.

The heat in the barn rose, as though fanned by bellows. And for the first time the men could hear the crackling over their heads. The haymow must be an inferno. Its floor would collapse on their heads before long. "Get 'em moving, boys. Get 'em moving."

Harley fought his way along the barn, choking, unable to see. "Sailor!"

"I'm here."

"Get the high-testers. Take them out the front, one by one!"

"May I be of service?"

Harley spun around. The face of Satyendra Singh swam in the smoke. Harley hesitated only a moment. "Yes. Help Sailor with the high-testers. And after you get them out, Sailor, come help me with the bulls."

"Right," said Sailor. "Come on, fella, let's get cracking."

A board fell from the ceiling, showering sparks.

Inside the bull shed, separated from the barn, the smoke wasn't yet thick. Its occupants were, nonetheless, thoroughly alarmed—and vicious. Harley thought fast. He couldn't take them through the barn with that bedlam: someone would be killed. Besides, he could never get them all out that way with the roof set to go. But if he let them into their runs, they'd be trapped too close to the burning barn. The gates would have to be opened, and the bulls let loose into the pasture. There'd be fights and pregnant cows and hell in rounding them up, but it couldn't be helped.

As he turned to reopen the door to the barn, it was thrown back.

Upjohn stood there, gasping in the heat. "Sailor said you were here. Let me help!"

"Go outside and open the gates at the end of the bull runs. Start with the one farthest from the house. Then get the hell out of the way."

"Yes. But be careful!"

"I can handle them."

"I'm not thinking of the bulls. I'll be back as soon as the gates are open." He disappeared into the smoke.

Harley closed the door, grabbed a gaffing pole, and climbed onto the partition that separated the stalls of Wellsland Sir Korndyke and Aaggie Cornucopia Johanna Lad. He shinnied along the topmost two-by-four, then reached out with his pole and jiggled the slide bolt on the door of Sir Wellie's pen. Sir Wellie charged the pole. Harley yanked it back, turned, and slid back the bolt in Johanna Lad's pen. He put the butt of his pole against the door and pushed it on its track a few inches. "Are you ready, Mr. Upjohn?"

"Go ahead!"

Harley shoved both doors open. The bulls just stood there, making belligerent chuffing sounds. "Go!" They wouldn't move.

"Come on, boy! Come get me!" It was Upjohn, down at the opened gates, trying to entice the bulls in his direction.

Harley grinned, shinnied back, and gave each bull a whack on the rump. It did nothing to improve their tempers, but it moved them toward their doors. "They're coming, Mr. Upjohn!" A few more gaffs saw them outside. Harley dropped into Wellie's pen and closed the door, checked to see that Johanna Lad was not re-entering, and closed the second door. Outside, Upjohn was on top of the fence, inching toward the next gate.

The two of them worked their way down the row of stalls and runs, until only Duke Pietertje Butter Boy Korndyke and King were left. King displayed none of his usual friendliness.

"Don't worry, fellow." Harley climbed onto the dividing wall, swaying in the heat. The fire was getting awfully close!

He unlocked Butter Boy's door, gaffed that unwilling ton of muscle into the night, and closed the door behind him. Then he unlocked King's door and tried to slide it open. It wouldn't slide. Harley took a firmer grip on the pole and tried again. Nothing.

Frozen! It was the pen closest to the silos. The snow must have drifted there.

He dropped into Butter Boy's pen and cracked the door. "Mr. Upjohn? See if you can open the stall nearest the silo. It's stuck!"

The only answer was a resounding crash as Butter Boy charged Harley's voice behind the door.

"Mr. Upjohn!" Harley waited, coughing in the thickening smoke. Upjohn must be on his way back. He wheeled, cursing to himself. He'd have to find a run vacated by its tenant and lead King out there. He opened the door in the next pen, then closed it just in time to stop the charge of Sir Johanna Aaggie Fayne. He started for the next one.

Then Harley halted in his tracks, realizing what he had seen as he closed that door. He ran back and opened it a crack— the gates were closed. The bulls were still in their runs!

"Mr. Upjohn?"

A fit of coughing seized him. No time to think. He and King had to get out. Hump Hollow! He'd lead King out there.

He ran to the hook where the bullstaff was kept. It was gone. He groped on the floor. "*Damn* it!" King was bellowing, circling his pen; beyond handling without the bullstaff.

He heard shouts and a crash. The floor of the haymow was caving into the barn. Where was Sailor? He'd promised to help. And Upjohn? Harley stumbled to the door which led to the barn, tried to open it, to shout for help if anyone could get to him. It wouldn't open. It had been locked.

"Help!"

He would be dead in a minute if he didn't get out. But he couldn't leave King.

He moved toward the bull, dizzy and sobbing now.

How the hell I ever got such a sissy son, I'll never know.

That bull's worth ten of you.

He opened King's door. They'd go out together or not at all.

Then Harley felt a blow and fell, rolling sideways instinctively. King completed his charge as though Harley were still there. He smashed into the opposite wall, staggered and shook his head—and found Harley beside him, twisting his ring. He bellowed. It had been years since anyone had twisted his ring. Growling and gurgling, he allowed himself to be led down the aisle to Hump Hollow.

When they got there, Harley swayed, leaning on King for support. The door had been padlocked. Dazed, he reversed direction and headed for the door to the truck-loading chute at the silo end.

Another padlock.

Harley lost balance, fell, and landed, still clinging to King's ring, upon a small coil of rope.

Flames were licking down from the ceiling as he struggled to his feet. He found an end of rope, threw it over King's great neck, tied it as best he could, then passed the other end through the padlock and held on tight. He released King's nose ring and smacked the bull in the face. "Haw!" With a mighty lift of his head, King snapped the padlock off clean.

Clinging to the rope, Harley dived for the ring, caught it, and twisted. Dragging the bull he reached the door somehow and pushed it open.

The loading chute ascended to the height of a truck bed—too far for King to jump without breaking a leg. And on each side of the ramp was a board fence. Harley shook one of the slats. "Help!" he shouted into the smoke. "Help me get this fence down!"

For a long time it seemed no one heard. Then there were men in the smoke, shouting and ripping at the fence.

And suddenly Harley could lend no hand. He shoved

King's ring at the closest body. "Take him. Get the others out of their runs," he said as he succumbed to the smoke.

It felt as though snow was falling over him and into him. He was being carried—Curt at his shoulders, Paul Bascomb and Grampa Westcott at each leg—and Cass was fussing about. Harley looked at Curt and Paul, their clothes dirtied and smoke-blackened. What a shame, he thought. The Bascombs didn't have many good clothes.

Then he remembered what had happened. He began to struggle. "Who's got King? Who's got the bulls?"

"Take it easy. Gillespie's got King." Thomas spread his coat, and they lowered Harley onto it.

Unconscious on the ground beside Harley was Upjohn. "What happened to *him*?"

Hitty was attempting to revive Upjohn with handfuls of snow to the forehead. "Your father was trying to get to the bull shed when the ceiling started to go, and there was poor Mr. Upjohn on the floor. Tobin dragged him out, then raced around to try to get into the shed through the runs."

Harley struggled to rise. "I've got to go help him. The bulls are in the runs!"

Thomas pushed him back down. "Some of the men ran around to tell him you were out. He's got plenty of help."

"Poor Tobin," said Hitty. "I've never seen him so upset. Mr. Upjohn kept mumbling, 'Harley! I'm coming!' And Tobin turned just white! He said, 'My God, Harley's in that shed!' and he took off like a deer." She smoothed Harley's hair.

Harley was embarrassed. Stood more to reason that Tobin had been worried about his bulls. But an unaccustomed warmth filled him, and he looked toward the corner of the burning barn, hoping that all the bulls *were* safe—for Tobin's sake.

"Are you cold?" said Cass.

"No." He wished she'd stop fussing over him.

Upjohn moaned and opened his eyes. He stared at Hitty a moment, and sat up like a shot. Then he saw Harley. "Thank God you're safe! Forgive me, Harley. I tried to get back to you."

"What happened?"

"I don't know. Something hit me on the head. A timber, I'd guess. That's the last I remember."

"Did you try to open the door into the bull shed?"

"I didn't get that far."

Harley lowered his voice so Cass couldn't hear. "It was locked. From the barn side."

Upjohn stared at him.

"Did you open the gates to all the runs?"

"Of course, Harley."

"Someone closed them again. And the doors to Hump Hollow and the loading chute had been padlocked."

Upjohn's face was expressionless. "It's a miracle you got out," he said.

They both got to their feet and began to scan the crowd. "Have you seen your sister and her husband?" Upjohn asked Hitty.

"They were around a few minutes ago, watching the fire over by the bull shed. I don't see them now."

Tobin came into view, followed by his helpers. They gave the burning barn a wide berth, and Tobin motioned at the crowd of spectators. "Better move back, all of you. It'll collapse any minute."

The crowd obeyed, save those crouched on the roofs of the outbuildings with pails of water ready for stray sparks. The barn was a mere etching of white-hot beams now. Tobin stood looking for a moment, then went to Harley.

"Are all the bulls safe?" said Harley.

Tobin nodded and scuffed the snow. "It was hot enough so they were glad to move when we opened the gates." He kept scuffing and studied the small mound he was constructing. "You did a fine job, son. I'm mighty glad you're safe."

If he only knew how close! Harley looked over for Upjohn. He wasn't there. "Where'd Mr. Upjohn go?"

"To the house for a coat," said Cass.

A sound like a skyrocket split the night. A patch of silo wall disintegrated, and multicolored fire corkscrewed out.

"I wonder what's in ensilage to make it burn so pretty," said Hitty.

Harley turned and headed for the house.

When Upjohn entered, the house seemed deserted, until he glanced into the library. The hired help crowded around the window, including—

Upjohn ran to the drawing room. Frank sat slumped in his chair. Upjohn touched the old man's shoulder, and Frank's eyes opened.

"Nurse!"

Whitcomb came running. "What is it, sir? Has something happened?"

"Luckily, no!" Upjohn hadn't meant to snap. "I just don't feel he should be left alone."

"I just left him a moment ago to take a peek at the fire."

Upjohn glanced up and saw Harley in the doorway. "Have you seen anyone come into the house, Miss Whitcomb?"

"Come in and go out, sir. One couple. Couldn't miss the man, that fellow with the turban."

"What did they do?"

"Came to the door here and looked at Mr. Parmalee. Then they went upstairs."

"You should have stopped them!" said Harley.

"Well, they weren't up there but a few minutes."

Upjohn sighed. "Go back and watch the fire."

The nurse left. "There's nothing we can do," said Upjohn. "Whatever they wanted, they got."

"Not quite," said Harley.

Upjohn frowned. "Think, Harley. Are you sure the door back into the barn was locked? Might it have been stuck? Or jammed by fallen debris?"

"I hadn't thought of that."

"And the padlocks?"

"Well, there were always padlocks there, but they were hardly ever locked."

"Where were the keys kept?"

Harley's jaw dropped. "On a nail beside each door. I was so scared I forgot! I'll bet they were there."

"I want to think they were," said Upjohn. "And I want to think it was suction from the fire that closed the gates. And that I was hit over the head by a falling beam." He sighed. "Let's find Sailor. He was working with Satyendra."

Upjohn trotted into the foyer. Then, inexplicably, he ran to the alcove beneath the stairs. "Lilith, are you there?"

"I wouldn't be if I had any sense!"

It was as much of a mystery to Harley as it was to Lil, and Upjohn refused to clear that mystery. "I had my reasons. You'll just have to trust me."

"I *do*," said Lil. "That's why I stayed under the stairs. But I think you should tell me why you put me there! Is it because I look like my grandmother? Did you know her? Who wasn't supposed to see me? Is it because I'm a witch, like my Aunt Lizzy?"

"What's going on here?"

It was Cass in the doorway.

"Just talking about the fire," said Lil.

"Yeah," said Harley, "just talking about the fire."

And, for the moment, he and Upjohn forgot about finding Sailor.

Supper was finally served, overdone and overstirred, at the twenty-five little tables with pink tablecloths, flowers, swans, and candles, to fifty still fairly elegant ladies and fifty dirt-smeared men.

As wakes often are, it was a merry affair.

Most of the guests did not go home that night. The men went right back out to help with temporary lean-tos, to round up cattle, to sort the jumble of machinery that had been drafted from the burning barn, and to begin clearing the rubble when it had cooled enough.

In the house the ladies napped, gossiped, and carried coffee and fresh kerosene to the men—Tobin's powerhouse had gone with the rest of the barn.

Even the members of the orchestra stayed, on their own time. They put on coats and played on the front porch, where they could be heard by those indoors and out, until the dawn.

It was an especially satisfying night for Paul Bascomb. The meekening had begun.

And it had begun more thoroughly than most people knew.

For Tobin had carried no insurance on his barn. "Only on the stock," Paul heard him admit to Gillespie.

Just before dawn the men working among the ruins near the door to the bull shed found the body. It was burned beyond recognition, but they all knew who it was. All night Harley and Upjohn had been asking, "Has anybody seen Sailor?"

It saddened Paul Bascomb to think that a man had lost his life in the meekening of the Westcotts. "The ways of the Lord are strange," he reminded himself, "His wonders to perform."

CHAPTER SEVENTEEN

BY THE BEGINNING of March, the barn had been rebuilt, a hired man named Chuck had taken Sailor's place as overseer, and finances were on an almost even keel with the help of a $7,000 bank loan. The new barn was, of course, less of a showpiece than the first. Tobin was not quite sure how it happened, but the bank loan was all he'd had to spend.

Impossible that Hitty could have spent all he'd made over the years, Tobin thought. Where had it gone? Back into the farm; into the house; into the servants' salaries; into feeding all those people, the hired hands, his father, Hitty's father, the nurse, and now—it was almost the first he'd thought of it—Harley's wife!

Oh, he'd seen the girl at the supper table, but he hadn't really thought about her. He'd hardly thought about anybody these months since the burning.

But now he realized the time had long since passed when it was possible to press for an annulment. Harley had a wife, and it was about time he and his son had a talk about her.

He summoned Harley to his office late that evening. "Well, son, how you planning to support this wife of yours?"

"Well, I'd thought—"

"That you could pick up a wife like a kewpie doll, bring her home, and expect your Dad to foot the bill?"

"Well, sir," Harley paused. "I kind of *had* to bring her home."

Tobin stared at his son. "Her father told me she wasn't pregnant."

"I don't think he knows about it," said Harley.

"Well, then." Sure, Harley had accounted himself well at the fire. But a baby—that would be living, squalling proof of his son's manliness. "Well. That's different."

After this talk Harley had a time figuring out why the news that Cass was pregnant should have made Tobin drop the subject of Harley's supporting Cass.

Responsibility. That had to be it. While daily watching his wife's small, gently rounded stomach, Harley, for the first time in his life, thought about responsibility.

The way Tobin must figure it, if Harley had just fallen for Cass and decided to marry her, never thinking of the future—well, then, he'd have to support her himself. But if he'd accidentally gotten her pregnant—well, you couldn't punish someone for an act of God, and Harley had done the honorable thing.

The trouble was, four months after he'd married Cass, her small and gently rounded stomach was still just that. Perhaps the trouble was a gap in his own knowledge. At five months, Harley told himself. It must be at five months that women began to swell.

But one morning during the fifth month he finally said, "You're not pregnant, are you, Cass?" Cass was lying beside him, a sheet covering her nakedness after lovemaking. She turned her head away. "You lied to me, didn't you?" he said.

"No!" She turned back, and her eyes were bright with tears. "I lost it!"

"When?"

"A month ago. I was afraid to tell you. I thought you'd hate me."

There was nothing to do but believe her. He turned away. "I don't hate you."

But even now, still sweaty from having her body, he wished he wasn't married to her.

Lil came now, every weekday, and Upjohn had a class of three instead of a class of one. It had been Upjohn's suggestion—it was silly for Cass to go to the village school with a tutor right in the house, and silly for Cass's sister to make the six-mile round trip alone each day.

It would be harder to see Lil from now on, though—knowing there had been no reason to marry Cass.

Harley began to think about Tobin. And about responsibility. He got up and went to the barn.

"Cass isn't going to have a baby. She says she lost it."

Tobin kept on stripping a cow's bag, spurting fat streams of cream into a pail.

"I'll get a job," said Harley. "I'll support her."

Tobin stopped. "No need. If you'd be willing to work here in the barn, I could let one of the hands go. It would be a help." He'd almost said "please." But he couldn't. Finances weren't that bad; no call to alarm anyone else.

Harley shook his head. "If I start being a farmer, I'll never get away from it."

Tobin looked up. "Why *should* you? What's the matter with being a farmer? And what the hell else you gonna do?" Then, sharpest of all, "What the hell you think you *can* do?"

"I can play the piano!" said Harley.

"At weddings? Two bucks every Saturday."

"After I finish Franklin, I'll be a teacher. Maybe even a writer."

"Where you gonna get the money for Franklin, Mr. Married-Man?"

When Harley finally answered him, his voice was low. "I assumed you'd be sending me."

Tobin nodded. "That's right, I will. All you got to do is go to work for me."

"No," said Harley. He started to leave the barn, then turned back. "Dad? If I *can* earn money another way, and I give it to you for board and room, will that count? I mean, would you still put me through college?"

Tobin seemed about to say no, but then he nodded. "All right. If you pay me twenty-eight dollars a month—that's about what it costs to keep you two. I should charge you more, really, your accommodations are deluxe—but seeing as how you're my son…"

How, Harley wondered, could he possibly earn twenty-eight dollars a month? "When do I have to start paying?"

"Well—what day is this? May twenty-third. Let's say I start charging you as of the fifteenth of June, and collect on the following fifteenth. That'll give you some time. And when you find you can't get no job that will pay you that much, come talk to me. My offer might still be open."

"I'll get a job," said Harley.

Tobin watched him stalk away. A smile—half smug, half admiring—played about his lips. "Good luck, son," he said softly, and went back to his work.

"What do you mean, you have to pay your father board and room?"

"Just what I said. We can't live here free, Cass. We're grown. We've got to take responsibility."

"Your father's rich!"

"He's Tobin and he's rich. I'm Harley and I'm not." Harley went back to scratching on a pad of paper.

"What are you doing?"

"Writing a short story."

"At a time like this?"

"I'll send it in and maybe get some money!"

"Don't shout at me, Harley Westcott!"

"I wasn't shouting."

The room subsided into silence, broken only by the jabbing of Harley's pen on the paper.

Cass walked to the window and looked out for a minute, went to the bathroom and fixed her hair, came back and flopped on the bed. "I'm bored."

"Go see Hitty. She'll find something for you to do."

"I don't like your Mom."

Harley looked up. "What do you mean, you don't like her? What's she done to you?"

"Nothing, yet. But she will. All her smiles and showing me off and 'isn't she sweets' don't fool me. She hates me."

"You're crazy."

Cass smiled. "Maybe. My Aunt Lizzy was crazy, and a witch. I inherited being crazy, and Lil inherited being a witch."

"Look, you shouldn't go around saying Lil's a witch. You could get her into trouble!"

"Pooh."

Harley sighed and returned to his writing.

"Harley? Why don't we ever see your Aunt Carrie?"

"We don't get on with her, that's why."

"Maybe I'∂ get on with her."

"You stay away from Carrie! You hear?"

"But I get so lonely, Harley."

"Well, invite Muriel up or something."

"OK. Do you suppose I could take singing lessons, too?"

"Sure. Talk to Mr. Upjohn. He can teach singing."

"But I don't *like* Mr. Upjohn."

Harley threw down his pen. "Who *do* you like?"

"Lots of people. Harley, couldn't I go into Seneca to a voice teacher?"

"Where am I supposed to get the money? I don't have the first idea how I'm going to come up with twenty-eight dollars a month!"

"What if I went to work, too?"

It hadn't even occurred to Harley. "What could you do?"

"I can sing. We could do an act together."

Harley stared at her. "Why not?"

The Winters' Theatrical and General Employment Agency was a one-man operation over an Italian restaurant in Seneca. Oscar Winters sat at a desk with three telephones, none of which was ringing. He didn't even say, "Can I help you," when Harley and Cass walked in. He just looked them over.

Harley cleared his throat. "Mr. Winters, my name is Harley Westcott. This is my wife, Cass. I play piano. And she sings…" Harley hesitated. He'd never heard Cass's voice-she might be awful. "I mean, primarily. But we—I'll do anything you've got."

"What I've got ain't much right now."

"Oh, it doesn't have to be today," said Cass. "Just so it adds up to thirty-eight dollars a month."

"Why *thirty*-eight?" muttered Harley.

"My lessons."

"That's a lot of money," said Winters. He looked them over. Harley held his breath. "Okay, you say you play and sing—well, play and sing."

With trembling hands, Cass and Harley examined the sheet music on Oscar Winters' piano—all current hits that neither of them knew. Finally Cass seized a sheet. "Can you play this?" she whispered. "Pale Moon."

And with the first note from Cass's throat, Harley forgot to be nervous. No church choir voice that! Tears stung his eyes.

When the song ended, Harley turned confidently to Winters.

Winters nodded. "Tell you what—you take that pile of music home with you and practice. We'll start you out in places where you can do your 'Pale Moon.' But if want to make your thirty-eight a month, you gotta learn some zippier stuff."

"In the land of San Domingo, lived a girl named O-By-Jingo—yah dah, yahdedah de dah dah, oompah, oompah, oompah, oompah. From the fields and from the marshes, came the young and old by garshes, yah dah—"

Hitty appeared in the door of the drawing room. "What in the name of heaven is *that*!"

"It's popular music, Mrs. Westcott," said Cass.

"Popular with whom?"

"Lots of people."

"I don't believe I know any of them," said Hitty, and left.

But several minutes later the chair lift Hitty had recently had installed on the stairway began to hum. Hitty descended with Frank in his chair and wheeled him into the drawing room. "You don't mind if Papa listens, do you?"

"Of course not," said Harley.

Cass poked him. "We charge fifty cents an hour."

"For doing what?" said Hitty.

"You're asking us to perform and to play nursemaid. That's fifty cents an hour. Per person."

"Oh." Hitty thought it over. "Well, I suppose you children do have to have pocket money."

"That was awful," said Harley the moment Hitty left.

"More awful than charging your own son room and board? Listen, if we practice an hour a day, it will add up to—" Cass muttered a moment. "Fourteen a month—that's half of the twenty-eight dollars. And if we practiced two hours a day, we'd earn twenty-eight dollars a month. Wouldn't that be funny? Your mother would pay us, and we'd turn around and give it to your father, so *he'd* be paying for our room and board...Why are you looking at me like that?"

"We're just lucky my mother's mind doesn't work like yours."

"Why?"

"Because if it did, she'd charge us fifty cents an hour to rent the piano."

The first month, the bulk of the twenty-eight dollars came from Hitty. "You're not stopping already," she would say when they called her to take Frank back to his room. "It makes Papa so happy. Play more. I'll pay."

The next month was not so easy. The need to practice lessened. They had to fake rehearsals to collect their fifty cents.

They did have one stroke of luck. The regular soloist of Seneca's Calvary Presbyterian drowned in the Pacific Ocean while visiting her daughter in California; Oscar Winters arranged for Cass to take her place. But she couldn't possibly work for the offered three dollars a week, Cass told them. She'd need five dollars a week, and fifty cents carfare. Calvary Presbyterian countered with four dollars and carfare. Cass graciously accepted.

Harley found this humiliating. Not that Cass ever rubbed it in. But that summer he got only one job on his own—five nights of work replacing the sick pianist with "Marsdon Dillenbeck and his Gypsy Revelers."

Fortunately, Tobin was reasonable those months when they fell short of twenty-eight dollars. "Pay me next month," he'd say.

Then, in August, Harley again found himself pondering the word "responsibility" and worrying about the future. Cass's small and gently rounded stomach began to protrude.

"Please, let it be a boy," Cass prayed over and over. "Let it be a boy so Papa will love me."

CHAPTER EIGHTEEN

THEY NAMED HER Emily. Cass turned her head to the pillow and cried when they handed the baby to her.

Paul wondered how a girl-baby could be marked by God for any special role.

Tobin, too, was put out that his first grandchild hadn't been a boy.

Hitty had only one response. "Just keep her away from me. Can't stand to hear a baby fussing!"

And Harley? In the months after Emily's birth, he'd go often to the small iron crib that had cradled Thomas, Tobin, then himself—and just stand, staring down.

My daughter. Over and over he would repeat those words to himself, waiting for them to mean the sweet things that, even at seventeen, they should mean. Once in a while, when a gas pain twisted Emily's face into a smile, or when her tiny fists opened and lifted as though reaching for him, a tenderness would seize him. He would lean forward; his hands would move toward her, then halt. He would turn and walk away.

Why? She wasn't to blame for anything; she didn't even look like Cass. As a matter of fact...

She was a long baby; she'd probably be as tall as Lil. And there were occasional red glints in the nondescript brown of her hair.

As the months wore on, even the embryonic personality began to remind him of Lil.

And Harley *did* begin to feel those sweet things he had so earnestly sought. The strength of his emotion sometimes frightened him.

He began to avoid Emily.

The baby had but four staunch friends—Emma; Helen, who all but suffocated Emily at every opportunity; Upjohn; and Lil.

Through the efforts of these last two, Emily won admittance to the schoolroom, where she would sleep, play with her toes, chew on toys, and watch.

"A good baby," Upjohn said.

"I think she's just dumb," Cass said.

Upjohn sighed. What would he do the following year with Harley off to college, Lil up to heaven knew what, and only Cass in the classroom?

One evening in late June, Upjohn was summoned to Tobin's office. "Mr. Upjohn, I know you'll be wanting to get yourself a new position in the fall. I thought we might write up some letters of recommendation."

"That's kind of you," said Upjohn, "but I wasn't intending to leave. I'll help Harley with his college work, and tutor Cassandra, and Emily when she's old enough. I'll help you with your bookwork, write letters—"

"Whoa!" Tobin held up a hand. Then he lowered it and looked at it for a long moment. "Mr. Upjohn, I'm sorry. I'd like you to stay. But the truth is, I—the barn-burning hit hard. Then there's the way things are now. The price of milk keeps dropping, and no one's paying the breeding prices. I've had to let go of a couple of the hired men. I can't afford you, Mr. Upjohn."

"But you can. My room and meals, that's all I ask. Since the room costs you nothing, and I eat like a bird, you'll have my services most reasonably."

"I can't let you do that."

"But of course you can. You're a businessman, sir. What I'm offering is profitable for you and comfortable for me. Now if you'll show me what correspondence needs to be done, I'll get to it first thing in the morning."

As was his custom, Upjohn went to Frank's room that night and concentrated with Hitty until nearly eleven. The target for the week was Frank's malfunctioning bladder.

At last Upjohn rose. "Good night, my dear. Get some sleep. You look exhausted."

Hitty smiled. "I will."

But she sat beside Frank's bed until well after midnight. She'd grown proficient at meditating, and could direct her thought in the concentrated beam that Upjohn described. Sometimes it seemed she could feel the tip of that beam probing about the soft innards of her father, searching out his sickness and eating it away. She was sitting quietly, meditating and probing, when the tip of her beam touched something else. She stood up with a start.

There was something cold hovering over Frank. "My God! It's come for him! Whitcomb!"

The nurse sat up on her cot.

"Death has come for Papa. Hurry! No, don't touch it! It may kill you, too!"

"Touch what, Mrs. Westcott?"

Hitty crept forward and waved her hand over her father. "But it was there a minute ago!"

"What was?"

"Cold! A cold thing. I thought it was Death."

Whitcomb put Hitty to bed. It was a wonder, the nurse thought, that Hitty hadn't given way long before this.

Polly and Harley started down the west side of College Hill. The sun was lowering in the August sky. Hillocks rolled from the base of the slope to the woods, where Harley could pick out the Crazy Lizzy Sixty; see the Bascomb meadows. He might ride and say hello to the Bascombs; maybe see Lil.

A few minutes later he did see her, walking just ahead. He swung down. "Hi. Where you been?"

"Down to Schyler Normal School to enroll."

"I didn't know you wanted to be a teacher."

"I just want to keep studying."

"Why don't you apply to the State University? Maybe you could get a scholarship."

Lil shook her head. "That wouldn't help. I'd have to come up with room-and-board and books—and, besides, Papa would have a conniption if I lived away from home." She glanced at Harley. The truth was, leaving home would mean leaving him. "You know how Papa is about 'college men.'"

They walked on in silence, Harley leading Polly. He didn't look at Lil, but he knew she was wearing pink again, and he knew her hair was so clean that flyaway strands caught the sun and made a halo.

"How's the baby?" she said. "And Cass?"

"They're fine. Cass and Janet and Muriel are out berry-picking this afternoon."

Lil wanted to say, "Are you happy, Harley?" But she didn't.

She was afraid he'd say no. "Have you gotten word on any of your stories yet?"

"Uh-huh. 'Thank you for submitting your manuscript, however, we are not buying stories of this type at the present time.'"

"Don't you dare get discouraged. You name me five famous writers who haven't had a drawer full of rejection slips."

"Homer. Virgil. Shakespeare..."

They laughed, and their eyes met. The laughter trailed off, and they walked on in silence.

"I'm really going to miss the lessons with you and Mr. Upjohn," said Lil at last. "He's not going away, is he?"

"No, he's helping Dad with the office. Funny guy. You'd think he'd want to move on."

"He said he'd stay until you didn't need him anymore."

"What did he mean by that?"

"I haven't the faintest idea. What do you know about him, Harley?"

"Not a thing."

"I think he must have been born around here. He knows everything about everybody. Harley, what's the story on your Aunt Carrie? And why does she want to make friends with me?"

"How? When?"

"Like a few minutes ago, she drove by and offered me a ride. She does that often."

"Lil. Don't ever get in her car. I can't tell you the reason, but don't."

"Is it the same reason Upjohn hid me in the closet the night of the party? And doesn't it have something to do with the fact that I look like my grandmother?"

Carrie and the first Mrs. Stockbridge? What possible connection could there be?

"Upjohn must have talked to you about it, Harley. I think he *knew* my grandmother—"

"He couldn't have. She disappeared in 1875 or so."

"She was still alive in 1920. Cass and I met her. She must have been seventy or so, and she's surely dead by now, but Harley, there's no other explanation for what Upjohn did that night. He was trying to protect me from your aunt, because I look like my grandmother. And it's part of the protection not to tell me why Carrie is dangerous to me. Why?"

Harley shrugged. He had never been able to figure out Upjohn's reasoning himself. There was all this gabble of Cass's about Lil being a witch. If Lil found out Carrie was a practitioner of black magic—but what could the grandmother have to do with it? Could Philimentha, too, have been a practitioner of black magic? And, somehow, a friend of Carrie's?

That would explain why Upjohn had hidden Lil. Why Carrie was coming after her now. They both thought Lil might have inherited her grandmother's evil. Upjohn was afraid Carrie would teach Lil black magic! "You've got to stay away from Carrie. I don't know why, but Upjohn does, and I know you've got to trust him."

Lil flung up her hands. "Aren't these things for me to decide? I mean isn't it my life? My father hates me because I look like his mother. I'm on trial and nobody will tell me what the charges are. It's unconstitutional!" Her eyes narrowed. "Give Upjohn a message for me, will you? Tell him I'll give him a month. If he hasn't come to me by then and explained everything, I'll go to Carrie for my information."

"You can't!"

"Oh, no?"

From back down the road, they heard a siren. They'd reached Bascombs' road. They stepped out of the way and watched as Sheriff Bailey's car streaked by.

In 1919 the sheriff had single-handedly captured the twentieth-most-wanted criminal in the nation. He had never recovered from it. Now Harley and Lil watched him, hunched with self-importance over the wheel, hardly giving them a glance as he passed.

"Wonder what's up?" said Harley.

Half a mile down the road, Sheriff Bailey's car swung into the mapled drive of Spring Farm.

Cass and Janet sat in Hitty's parlor, watching Sheriff Bailey pace.

"You sure it was eleven o'clock you girls was supposed to meet?"

"Yes," said Cass for the tenth time. "I was a little late, and Janet didn't get there till eleven-thirty."

Janet burst into tears.

"Can't for the life of me see why you'd be meeting in a godforsaken place like Lizzy's."

"The berries are good up there," said Cass.

"It's not a place young girls should be."

The sheriff, Cass thought, cut a ridiculous figure—especially when he was angry. He was short and shaped like an egg, with the big part on top. He wore a brightly polished star and an oversized Stetson.

"You sure neither of you saw anything? Heard anything?"

Cass could sense the pain beneath his anger. Muriel's father was his best friend, and he himself was Muriel's godfather.

"Think—Cass, Janet? *Anything!*"

"I should have been with her," wailed Janet.

But Muriel, wanting to get an early start, had been too impatient to wait while Janet finished her chores.

If you weren't such a poke, you would have been finished an hour ago! And Muriel had ridden off: *You'll just have to catch up.*

Cyrus Hamlin had seen her pedal past the library. "Fresh as a daffodil," he'd told Sheriff Bailey. "Little dotted scarf on her yellow hair…"

Cyrus seemed to be the last person to have seen Muriel. Cass and Janet had waited at Lizzy's until after one, then cut through the woods to Spring Farm and a telephone. Since then the sheriff, his deputy, and Muriel's parents had been questioning house-to-house on College Road, searching the fields and the side roads.

The posse grew with each call. The woods around Crazy Lizzy's even now rang with their cries: "Muriel! Muriel Moore!"

Which was why it seemed mighty strange to Sheriff Bailey that Harley Westcott and Lil Bascomb could walk into the parlor and ask, "What happened?" He'd seen them standing back there at Bascombs' road and assumed that they, too, were searching.

"You mean to say," said the sheriff before either of them could react to the news, "that you didn't run across anyone looking for Muriel?"

Lil started to answer, then cocked her head. "Are we suspects?"

The sheriff cleared his throat. "Just seems strange, that's all. By the way, *have* either of you seen Muriel today?"

The search went on into the darkness and through the night. The next day the troopers were notified, and the search for Muriel Moore went statewide. Hardly a citizen of Oriskany Forks and environs remained stationary. Harley was out for three days and nights on Polly, riding in circles, watching, calling. But by the end of the week everyone knew there was just no use looking anymore.

It was assumed that Muriel was dead. And that someone— one of them—had murdered her. A man, naturally. Soon every man in town was changing the subject when Muriel's name came up. Who knew what slip of the tongue might cast suspicion on a fellow?

The women were not so easily discouraged from speculation. After all, there was a killer loose. At that very moment, he might be stalking one of them or their daughters.

The witchcraft business started that Sunday after Muriel's disappearance, when Reverend Smith treated his congregation to another sermon on the subject. This time, however, he did not limit himself to vague warnings. Without naming names, he came right out and said that Muriel Moore had been murdered by witches, as a blood sacrifice to the devil. By sundown everyone in town, including Catholics, had heard about the growing cult of black magic in their midst.

Sheriff Bailey paid a call at the Methodist parsonage that night, and remained closeted with the Reverend for over an hour. Then he drove to Spring Farm, where he spent a similar amount of time with Cass Westcott. The following day he appeared at the town library and asked Cyrus Hamlin for the names of all those who had borrowed books on witchcraft. He could be seen, for weeks afterward, cruising past Mrs. Parkinson's house on Elm Street.

The year went to autumn, and then to winter. People stopped talking about Muriel. Gradually everyone except her family and friends stopped thinking about her. After all, thinking about Muriel Moore was what Albert Bailey got paid for.

CHAPTER NINETEEN

COLLEGE WASN'T EASY. The work load was heavier than Harley had foreseen, and the textbooks were costlier. Tobin was paying only the tuition: "The extras are on you." And Harley's bedroom, once his sanctuary, became a prison. For one thing, Emily sat on the floor and stared at him when he studied.

"Well, let her," said Cass. "What's so terrible about that?"

"I can't concentrate."

"But she loves you. It's the only way she can get you to pay her any mind."

At moments like that, tears came to Harley's eyes. Emily would see the tears and crawl to him; hugging his leg or patting his knee. His hands would tremble, wanting to touch her, unable to do so.

And then there was Cass. She never sat still; she cleaned and cleaned, even when there was nothing to clean, she puttered and sang to herself. And she had a habit of looking over his shoulder. "What're you doing? History? I hate history. Anthropology? What's that?"

Finally Harley set up a study in his closet, with a bolt on the inside of the door.

"I think it's awful," said Cass. "If you were a decent husband, you'd *want* to be with us."

She was right. He wasn't a decent husband—or father. Only when locked in his closet, studying, could he forget it.

Lil's study conditions were hardly better. In addition to her courses at Schyler, she was taking correspondence courses that cost more than she'd expected. And with trolley fare, lunches— a hundred little things—

She earned the money with a part-time job at Robert Sawyer's law office.

At first Lil's day began at five. She rose, dressed, made a quick breakfast, and walked the three miles to Oriskany Forks. Then she caught the seven o'clock trolley and studied on the way to Schyler. She had classes from eight until two, then caught the 2:15 trolley past the school, studied some more, and was at her desk in Sawyer's at 3:15. She worked until eight, walked the three miles back home, ate a warmed-over dinner, and studied until her mind would no longer function.

Curt let that schedule continue for only a week. After that he did the chores alone. Paul drove Lil to the trolley, and at eight o'clock each night arrived at Sawyer's to take her home.

That was the only real unpleasantness. Riding with Papa.

"Anti-intellectual," her psychology teacher at Schyler had labeled Paul when she described his behavior. It was somehow comforting to remember that label when Papa's harangues on a woman's place and on Lil's "highfalutin" vocabulary grew trying.

There were so many things she understood better since Upjohn had taken her into the library at Spring Farm one

Saturday afternoon. "Harley tells me that you and I must have a talk," he said. And he told her about Carrie and then about her grandmother, Philimentha.

Lil hadn't been able to suppress a smile. "A witch."

"Only when very young. She went on to black magic. Witchcraft is nothing more than the worship of the life cycle of the moon goddess Artemis and her horned consort."

"But isn't he the devil?"

"Yes," said Upjohn. "And no. Poor fellow, he went along minding his own business for millennia, playing second fiddle to Artemis and doing all the work. He made sure there was game for her worshipers and plenty of worshipers born to hunt the game. He had agriculture foisted upon him, and had to see to the natal problems of pigs. And then along come Christianity, bristling with rivalry and spreading nasty rumors about his 'evil.'"

Lil smiled.

"It's not funny," said Upjohn.

"I know. So many people have been persecuted." She thought a moment. "And actually went bad because of it, I'll bet. Being the church's idea of a witch would be very attractive to people who..."

You lean toward evil too easy, girl! It's in your blood!

"Like my grandmother." Lil's voice was strained. "She became a *church* witch. But she was only whistling in the wind. Because if what you say is so, there is no devil. No evil. She had no power to back her up." She turned to Upjohn, silently begging him to say she was right.

Upjohn's eyes were gentle, and troubled. "You wanted to hear the truth, Lilith. Truth cannot be found without examining all possibilities. There might be other forms of evil people like Philimentha can unleash. Something worse than any humanoid creature like a devil or even the Titans could ever be. A negative charge to the universe itself, just there, waiting, with no susceptibility to reason or death or anything—except encouragement."

"So that's why you were afraid to tell me. You thought I was the kind of person who would encourage it—just because I look like my grandmother!" She turned away, fighting tears. The day she had nearly strangled Muriel; Philimentha calling her a red-haired comrade on the very eve of her departure for the "east"—to help her friend, Carrie, destroy the Westcotts.

She felt Upjohn's hands on her shoulders. "Forgive me for not acting on what I knew to be so the first time I saw you," he said. "Forgive me for taking the time to be absolutely sure." He turned her and smiled with gentle humor. "Have I completely destroyed your faith in me? Or will you believe what I will promise you now."

She tried to look up, but couldn't. "I'll always believe you," she said.

"Then the promise is this. If the negative force is there, it will wait forever before it draws encouragement from you."

His hands remained lightly on her shoulders and a sense of peace flowed through her. She opened her eyes.

She had promised him once that she would never ask him a question about himself. She kept her promise now.

"Does Harley know all this?"

"Yes," said Upjohn. "I would have been hard put to turn his curiosity once he knew you had been told."

"But Cass. Please don't tell her, because if she knew—"

"If she knew," said Upjohn, "she would begin to lay at your door any number of strange and foul deeds."

Which, Lil now realized, Papa had been doing all these years.

Emily was sick with colds that winter. Cass took it in her stride, but it bothered Harley. Not that the child cried or made herself a pest. She was, in fact, quieter than usual.

"It's nothing to worry about," said Cass. "Doc Barnes says it's going around."

But Emily remained listless for months.

"She's been sick for too long," Harley finally said. "What if she died? I'd never forgive myself. Or you."

Cass called in a doctor from Seneca for another opinion.

"I wouldn't worry," he said. "I don't know exactly what it is, but there's a lot of this stuff going around."

"You see?" Cass told Harley when he came home.

Harley looked over at Emily. He walked to her side and reached down to cover her better, then he drew back. "Cass! You've got her in a draft!

They moved the crib to another spot.

"It's this drafty old house," said Cass. "No matter where I put Emily one minute, I come back the next minute and it's freezing; all around her crib."

"You mean," said Harley, "there's a draft in here that follows Emily around?"

"Where are you going?"

Harley was halfway out the door. "No place." And he was gone.

Suddenly, Cass felt quite alone. She turned and looked at Emily. "A draft that follows her around." That was exactly the way to describe what had been happening. But drafts couldn't follow people. Unless—

She circled the crib. The cold hadn't reached Emily yet, but it was on its way, like a blinded monster, creeping and searching. Cass put herself between the cold and the crib, her arms spread. How could she protect her baby?

Her hands went to her throat and to the medal hanging there. She pulled it off and started to put it on Emily, then she stopped. Giving the medal to Emily would leave *her* without protection.

She went to the desk, got a long length of string, and threaded it through the notch on the medal. Then she plucked

Emily from the crib, climbed into bed, and pulled the covers to their chins. She draped the string around herself and her baby, placing the medal between them, beneath the coverlet. "You can't get us now, Lil."

She had nearly dozed off when Harley returned. "Cass?"

She looked up. Upjohn stood behind him.

"Mr. Upjohn would like to come in and see Emily. Is it OK?"

Cass smiled. "Sure.

Upjohn came to the bed and made a show of chortling to Emily. Then he began to wander about. "My, you've done a nice job of feminizing the room, Cassandra."

Cass watched him with glittering eyes. Then, "Mr. Upjohn? What you're looking for should be right over the crib by now. It was almost there when I took Emily out. The cold spot, I mean."

Upjohn moved to the crib. "I do believe there *is* a cold spot here." He shook his head and clucked, testing the dimensions of the thing. "You oughtn't to leave Emily in a draft like this."

"As you see," said Cass, "she is not *in* the draft. She's here, and well protected." She raised the coverlet and held up the medal.

Upjohn froze. "Where did you get that?"

Cass decided it could do no harm to tell half the truth. "A white animal came out of the woods one day and left it on my sweater."

Harley laughed. Then his face straightened. "I saw a white animal in the woods one day."

"A unicorn, I suppose?" said Upjohn.

Harley smiled again. "Actually, I thought it was an albino deer. But now that I think of it," he said, returning Upjohn's teasing, "it probably *was* Grampa's unicorn."

"What does a unicorn look like?" said Cass.

"Some say a horse, some a deer, some a goat," said Upjohn, "but all agree it has a long straight horn in the middle of its forehead."

Cass nodded. "That's what I saw, a unicorn. It gave me this medal to protect me from harm, and tomorrow I'm going to Kramer's Jewelers and have one just like it made for Emily."

"You won't be able to do that," said Upjohn. "You're wearing a talisman of Mercury, made of fixed quicksilver. It must be composed on a Wednesday, beneath a moon passing through the first ten degrees of Gemini or Scorpio, and consecrated with the smoke of benzoin, macis, storax, lilies, narcissus, fumitory, and marjolane—in a brand-new clay pot. I doubt that Mr. Kramer is set up for such manufacture."

"How do you know all that?" said Cass. Upjohn held up his fob.

Cass gasped. She must have seen it there at his waist a thousand times, without ever really looking at it. "Where did *you* get one?"

Upjohn smiled. "A unicorn came out of the woods one day and left it on my sweater."

He was making fun of her—belittling her medal, striking at her support. "You're lying," she said. "And I don't have to do all those things with the moon and the lilies. I'll have it copied in silver!"

"Try it and see. If you believe in it strongly enough, maybe it will work."

"What's it supposed to do?" said Harley.

Upjohn looked at Cass. "What do you think, my dear?"

Cass looked him right in the eye. She didn't care if he *did* tell Lil.

"It protects me from witches."

"Is that right?" Harley asked Upjohn.

"Not exactly. It has a long list of properties. It supposedly brings fertility. If you bury it under your house, the superstitious say, it will bring prosperity. If you wear it about the neck, it will protect from madness…"

Cass looked at him sharply.

"Not to mention poisoning, murder—ah, here is where the witchcraft might come in—it protects from treasonous activities on the part of enemies." Then he smiled. "One thing it will not do is protect you from drafts."

"You said it protects from murder," said Cass. "A draft can kill you."

Upjohn didn't respond. "I must be going now," he said and started for the door. "Oh!" He returned. "I brought Emily a present." He took from his pocket tied with a ribbon. "A good-luck charm."

Cass opened the package, then threw it down, wrinkling her nose. "It's that awful stuff you wear. You don't expect me to put that on my baby, do you?"

Upjohn shrugged. "You may do as you wish. Of course, if you want to protect Emily, you can give her your Mercury medal. But that would leave you without the protection you seem to consider so essential." And he left.

All that day and night, Cass kept Emily with her, the Mercury medal draped around both of them.

The next morning was Sunday. Cass took longer than usual getting dressed to go to Calvary Church and made several false starts out the door. She finally went to her dresser, got out Upjohn's packet, and dabbed a bit of the powder onto Emily's forehead.

When they returned home, the room was warm and snug; Henrietta reported no drafts. From then on Cass always kept a dab of powder on the baby.

By her first birthday, Emily was healthy and pink, even pudgy. Agnes made a wonderful cake, topped with a confectionery bluebird of happiness holding one candle in its beak. All the Bascombs were there, along with the Cole cousins and the

Parmalees, and when Cass carried Emily into the dining room, everyone ooh-ed and aah-ed.

Except Hitty, who gasped and turned to Mr. Upjohn. "That baby is wearing *my* elixir," she whispered.

"Mehitable! You surely don't begrudge your granddaughter. It's never too early to start staying young."

Tobin sent Chuck in to tell Hitty not to expect him for Emily's party. "Don't mention the trouble," he said. "I don't want to worry Hitty." Then he went back to the calf shed.

Carl Chalmers, the vet, worked quickly and silently. He didn't even look at Tobin. He came to the last of the forty-nine calves, a pretty little thing with a white blaze from its crown to its speckled pink nose.

He stepped out, finally, still not looking at Tobin, and poured disinfectant on his hands. "You say nobody noticed these calves were sick till this morning? Doesn't make sense. Should have been all kinds of warnings."

"What have they got, Carl?"

Chalmers looked at Tobin now, and said it. "Pneumonia. Every last one of them."

They hung the windows with feed bags and blankets; they rounded up all the portable heaters in the neighborhood. The shed warmed up considerably, but nothing seemed to drive the drafts from the stalls. Tobin rigged tents of burlap over the sickest calves, and Chuck went to Seneca for the massive amounts of medicine that would be needed.

When Harley heard that Tobin would not be in for dinner, he went out to the barn. "What's the trouble?"

The men doing the chores pointed to the calf shed. Harley pushed aside the blanket hanging over the door of the shed and whistled at the temperature. Everyone was working in shirt-sleeves, perspiring freely. "What is it?" he asked Tobin.

"Pneumonia."

Harley slipped off his coat. "What do you want me to do?"

They worked through the night, operating vaporizers, keeping the restless youngsters covered, keeping them clean and comfortable.

Just before dawn, the first calf died.

It was Pontiac Lass's heifer. She'd been trying so hard to breathe; her sides heaving, frightened eyes pleading for help. All they could do was pet her. Then her sides stopped heaving, and she was dead.

Tobin stood up and turned away.

Harley's eyes filled with tears. He kept patting her. "We're sorry," he told her. "We're so sorry."

By noon the following day, they were all dead.

Funny, Tobin thought. When the barn burned, he'd been carrying insurance on the stock. Now, after the fire, he'd scraped together the premiums for the barn—but he hadn't been able to manage a policy on the stock. Funny the way things worked.

He would have liked to bury his calves on his own land, but all was frozen beneath the snow.

And he did need money.

He called the glue factory. Two men in dirty aprons arrived in a van truck, backed it up to the calf shed door, and dragged the calves out. They dragged them by one leg, the calves' pink tongues hanging, blue eyes staring. Then one of the men stepped up to Tobin. "Dollar apiece and I count forty-nine."

Tobin turned away. "Harley?"

Harley thrust out his hand.

The man counted out forty-nine bills, then saluted. "Call us again if you need any help."

And, whistling, he got into his truck and drove away.

They spent the rest of the day disinfecting walls and tools, burning straw and dung while Dr. Chalmers medicated the rest of the stock. "It'll be a miracle if it hasn't spread to the main barn," Chalmers told Tobin when they'd finished.

"Seems to me I should have a miracle coming." Tobin passed his hand over his eyes. Harley went to him and touched his forehead. "What do you want?" said Tobin.

"You have a fever. Go to the house and get in bed."

"I got work to do here."

"I'll do it," said Harley.

Tobin gave a short, tired laugh.

"Go on, Gov'ner," said Chuck. "We run on any problems, we'll call you."

And, to everyone's surprise, Tobin went.

As he climbed into his bed, it occurred to him to wonder how old he was. He hadn't thought about it in so long that he had to figure—he'd been born in 1886, which would make him forty-three come September. That wasn't old. Besides, age was how you felt about things. He'd always been busy, interested—eternal.

Not today.

He pulled the blanket up around him and put a pillow over his head. Hitty came in, frightened to see him ill. "Just get some more blankets," he told her. "It's so damn cold."

Tobin wasn't really ill after the first few days; he simply didn't get out of bed. He had them hang a quilt over his window so that his room stayed black, and, piled with coverlets and pillows, he slept.

He'd wake sometimes, decide to get up, then find when he tried that no part of his body would respond.

"So what if he *has* been sleeping for three days?" said Barnes when Hitty called him for the fourth time.

"Don't you think I ought to wake him? He'll starve!"

"Leave the man be. He's taking a vacation!"

When Tobin finally did rouse himself, he called for Harley. "Do we have any stock left?"

Harley grinned. "A few head."

"No more dead?"

"No more."

Tobin sighed. "Well, I guess we got to count our blessings." He dressed and went back to the barn.

CHAPTER TWENTY

TOBIN'S CREDIT AT Hepper National Bank was better than most that summer of 1929, but Dan Hepper was turning him down. "You already got one good-size loan, Tobin. You don't want to take on another."

"I do, Dan. You don't understand about them calves."

"You can't tell me losing one year's crop of calves is going to ruin you. Let a couple of hired hands go. Sell a bull or two."

"I'll have to."

"You ought to thank God you can. There's a lot of farmers around ain't got hands to let go of, nor bulls to sell. You know how many farms I'm ready to foreclose on? Friends of ours, who went near half-a-year without paying a penny on their mortgages."

"And you're going to foreclose? On friends?"

Tobin went home, took out his books, and refigured his income for the rest of the year.

Then he refigured his expenses. At the insurance figure he paused. Things came in threes, Hitty always said. The barn, the calves—no! He'd had his bad luck. He struck out the insurance figure, added up the two columns, and compared the totals. As he had done the day before, he tossed his pencil onto the desk and stared at the wall.

After a moment he bent back over the records and set his jaw. He supposed he *could* let two more hired men go. He scanned the other salaries. Colleen. He could certainly do without her. And Agnes. And Henrietta. And Frank's nurse.

But then Hitty would start asking questions. He remembered only too well what she'd said to Carrie that moonlit night on the Parmalee lawn. *"Papa's right. He'll support me in real comfort."*

He'd have to work things out by himself.

Stevens Brothers had been wanting to buy Butter Boy, but King didn't have many breeding years left, and Butter Boy was the second-most-requested bull. Without Butter Boy, Tobin's breeding business soon wouldn't be worth a damn. Still…

Butter Boy was sold for eight thousand. It wasn't half of what he was worth, but Stevens Brothers was feeling the pinch, too.

Tobin felt relieved as he drove home. He would let two more hired men go and get Hitty to tighten up on household expenses—without alarming her, of course. And with the eight thousand on top, they'd make it just fine through the year. Then next year, when things were going better, he'd buy Butter Boy back. Dan Hepper was right. There'd been no need to borrow from the bank.

In September Harley started his sophomore year at Franklin. And Lil went back to Schyler.

"I've decided to be a lawyer," she announced one afternoon.

Harley laughed.

"Mr. Sawyer said I could apprentice with him. What's so funny about that?"

"I don't know," said Harley. "I just never thought of you as a lawyer."

"Oh, she's real good at asking questions," said Cass.

They lay on the grass beneath the maples in Curt's front yard, digesting the fried chicken and potato salad of the annual Bascomb reunion and enjoying the Indian summer weather. In the kitchen, Helen and Emma and the older Bascomb girls chattered over the dishes; out by the mulberry bush Curt and the other husbands pitched horseshoes; and in an upstairs bedroom Jane's and Laura's teen-aged girls exchanged secrets.

Around Paul, in a porch rocker, gathered the youngest children. "The King of the Wind lives in the top of that one," Paul said, pointing to the tallest maple. "And the Queen lives in the top of the other. There's always a breeze beneath them maples. And you know what the breeze is? The breath of the King and Queen, whispering to each other. They never stop, and nobody knows what secrets they tell."

Cass rolled over and put her head in the small of Harley's back. "Lil," she said, "when are you going to tell Papa about being a lawyer?"

"Never, if I can help it," said Lil. "He's still sore about Schyler and the correspondence courses."

"Well, what does he expect you to do?" said Harley.

"The only thing a girl *can* do, as far as he's concerned. Get married."

"Haven't you met anybody at all?" said Cass.

"Cassie, you're as bad as Papa!"

"I just can't see why you want to go to all the trouble of being a lawyer. And how're you going to get the money for all the courses you'll have to take?"

"I'll work for it."

They were all silent a moment.

Then Cass said, "I think you're crazy, that's all."

Lil laughed. "*You're* the crazy one, remember? I'm the witch."

The late afternoon sun faded into twilight. Harley had never been particularly comfortable around Paul Bascomb, but for some reason today had been different. There had been a detached, dreamlike quality to the afternoon and, as darkness fell and the crickets began to chirp, the farmhouse became a cocoon in the night, safely removed from the encircling woods.

Harley wished he could stay there, suspended in time, with the crickets, the laughter of the children tumbling on the lawn, the murmur of the adults, the whispers of the King and Queen of the Wind.

But soon he found himself handing the sleeping Emily up to Cass in the front seat of the Stevens-Duryea, and they were driving down the rutted road, Bascomb voices following. "Good night!" "Take care of yourselves!"

The headlights seemed not even to strike a match in the darkness. Harley glanced back at the house, its windows glowing with lamplight. "What's the matter?" said Cass.

"I don't know," said Harley. "It was nice today. I didn't want it to end. I felt—" She wouldn't understand.

"I thought I was the only one who felt it." Cass moved closer and laid her head on his shoulder. "Like it was the end of something—something nice that you wanted to hold on to. Because the moment you let go, it would never come back."

Surprised, he looked down and kissed her dark hair. "That's silly." He glanced into the rear-view mirror again, then realized that Cass was looking up at him. "What's the matter?"

"Nothing." She smiled. "I just love you."

He looked away. "I love you, too."

"No, you don't."

He put his arm around her.

Cass snuggled closer and stroked Emily's hair. They rode the rest of the way home in silence.

One Friday in late October, Harley returned home from the morning class to find that something had indeed ended.

He went to the kitchen, hoping to find a fresh batch of cookies. The radio was on, but the familiar radio voices were not. "How come you got the news on?" he said.

"We haven't," said Agnes. "They've interrupted our program."

"I've a mind to write them a letter," said Henrietta. She pointed to the cookie crock. Oatmeal, still warm. As Harley went to the icebox for milk, what the broadcaster was saying began to sink in.

The news had been full of the stockmarket that week; Tobin had said Dan Hepper felt that J. P. Morgan was going to keep everything together, there was no need to be alarmed. Now, however, the broadcaster was talking about "incredible losses in the first hour of trading," using words like "crash," "panic," "suicides."

"They get no sympathy from me," muttered Agnes. "Fools and their money are soon parted."

"They should of bought nice safe government bonds," said Henrietta.

Harley stared at both of them. "But this might be serious," he said. "Don't you realize?"

"Pooh," said Henrietta. "President Hoover will straighten everything out."

Harley went to the barn. Tobin had said he owned a few shares of stock. If he didn't know what was happening, he ought to.

A battered Ford, familiar by now, was parked in front of the barn. The vet from the state. He'd been around for a couple of weeks, doing tuberculin tests on the cattle. Just routine.

But as he entered the barn, Harley saw a strange tableau. Tobin, his head bowed, was standing before the stall of Pontiac Lass. The hired men stood together some distance away, staring at the ground. And standing apart from everyone else was the vet from the state. He looked up at the sound of Harley's steps, his face twitched, and he looked away.

Harley heard a tortured sound—a sob. From Tobin! Whatever it was, someone should comfort Tobin. Harley started forward, then stopped. How did you comfort a crying father?

He turned to the man from the state. "What's happened?"

"You Mr. Westcott's son?"

Harley nodded.

"I had to give your Dad some bad news. The herd tested tuberculin."

"What does that mean?" Harley's voice would hardly come.

The vet wiped his brow with a rumpled handkerchief and looked at Tobin's bowed back. Tobin gave no sign of listening. He unlatched the Lass's stall and went in to stroke her.

The vet turned back to Harley. "They've all got to be destroyed."

The words fell like a wall of electrified water.

The man from the state kept apologizing, mopping his brow, and twitching. "It's the law. There's no other way. The infection's too far gone—got to stop it from spreading—can't even keep them in quarantine and use them for breeding. If there was another way—but the law's very strict. Gotta be destroyed—" The vet's face brightened. "Just the cows, though. Your bulls tested negative. You'll be able to start another herd."

"Go away," said Harley. He looked at Chuck and softened his tone. "You guys, too. Go on outside for a while."

Harley stepped into the stall with Tobin and Pontiac Lass. The Lass turned, curious, ruminating on a cud of alfalfa. Her eyes were cobalt blue. Harley scratched her crown. They liked that, the cattle. They liked to be scratched in that place they could never reach.

Harley looked at Tobin.

Should he reach out and touch Tobin's shoulder? Maybe just pat him and say something like, "Don't cry, Dad."

No. He remembered his mother turning on Tobin that day in the library. *Why do people do that? Tell me not to cry. Rob me of my sadness!*

Tobin hadn't understood Hitty that day, but he'd understood Harley the day they had to shoot Rose. *We lost a friend. No shame us crying.*

"Dad." He wanted to touch Tobin's hand. "I know how you feel."

"No, you don't." It was not mean, the way Tobin said it, just a statement of fact. "I hope you never have to know." He wiped his eyes, gave the Lass a pat, sighed, and stood back, staring at the straw. "I guess we'd better get to it."

"Not yet!"

"If I give myself time to think, I'll shoot that vet instead of my girls. That slaughterhouse isn't going to get them, nor the glue factory either. Those machines—they grind them alive!" Tobin's voice broke, and he covered his face. "They're prize cattle, and they're going to be *buried*. Decent, and whole."

Harley tried again to reach out. He couldn't.

"Get the men," said Tobin. "It's time for the milking."

As Harley and the men started the chores, Tobin went into the house to phone for a steam shovel and bulldozer from the quarry.

They did all the usual things—cleared droppings as they fell, fluffed the straw beneath each animal. But no one talked. And when a cow kicked, no one cursed.

Harley went down the lines, giving each animal all the grain she would eat. Then he got the currycomb and began to groom them. He didn't really look at them; he couldn't keep the tears back when he did. And he tried not to look at that worm of a veterinarian—Folger, he'd said his name was.

"What's he hanging around for?" muttered Chuck.

Harley kept currying. "Says he's got to oversee the extermination. He has to do postmortems."

Tobin returned, carrying his shotgun and boxes of shells.

Folger approached him nervously. "Mr. Westcott, I can spare you this. Let me call for some vans. We'll cart them away and do it ourselves."

"No." Tobin walked down the rows of cattle, brushing flies from rumps, picking specks of dirt from tails. "You curried the high-testers yet?" he asked Harley.

"No."

Tobin got a comb and went to the Lass's stall.

Thomas wandered in. He stopped to watch Tobin, then came to Harley.

"Dad tell you?"

"Agnes. She heard him on the phone."

Minutes later, Upjohn appeared—wearing old pants and a worn white shirt!

Harley stopped currying suddenly.

Frank's sickness, his own marriage, the fire, the calves, and now the herd. It was Carrie and Satyendra! Upjohn's "other force" was no match for evil.

Upjohn came directly to him. "I know what you must be thinking, Harley. But how can we attribute *this* to them?" He touched his temple as though he had a headache. "If we knew nothing about them, we'd simply accept it as an act of nature."

"No, we wouldn't," said Harley. "Nature just doesn't get perverse that many times with one family. It's them. And they *did* try to kill me the night of the fire!" He curried faster. "Even the calves—that was Carrie, too. There were cold spots we couldn't get rid of, no matter what we did, just like the ones in the house—" Harley stopped and stared.

Mehitable Parmalee Westcott, who had never been closer to the cows than the lilacs in the courtyard, stood in the doorway, wearing a pair of Tobin's coveralls.

Tobin was just coming out of a stall.

Hitty ran to him before he had a chance to speak, threw her arms around him, and held him. Tobin did not resist. His body sagged against hers. And for some time they just stood that way.

The chores were finished and the machinery washed when the steam shovel from the quarry clattered into the yard. Tobin had decided on an unused area between the barnyard and the orchard. The machine thrust its square metal jaw into the earth.

"Never seen one of these contraptions," said Thomas.

They watched with a sort of sick fascination. The pit grew.

A bulldozer moved down the avenue of maples and pulled up beside the pit. The operator sat back and rolled himself a cigarette.

"Fifty-eight head sure take a lot of burying," said Thomas.

A limbo held them. The cows were still alive. Nothing had changed.

But then the pit was finished.

"Should be plenty big," said the steam-shovel operator. "I'll wait around. If you need more space—"

"No," said Tobin. "That'll be fine."

So the steam shovel rumbled away and left them looking at the pit. The young man on the bulldozer shifted position and rolled himself another cigarette.

All of them began to move aimlessly.

Then, in the barn, a cow bellowed.

Tobin's anger exploded. "No, God damn it! You can't ask a man to destroy perfectly healthy, productive animals!"

The vet twitched.

Nobody said a word.

But Tobin glared from one to the next as though they were shouting arguments. "Tuberculosis, my foot! You don't see *us* getting sick from that milk, do you?" He wheeled on the young man aboard the bulldozer. "Fill it up."

The young man crushed his cigarette and looked at the vet. "I think I'd better wait a while."

"I'm telling you to fill that hole."

"I never do what I'm told, friend, only what I think." He shrugged. "I think you better wheel them bossies out here and get it over with."

Hitty stepped forward. "You, sir, are a totally insensitive man! How dare you speak to my husband like that? You have no idea how he feels."

"You're wrong, ma'am. I do." The young man's face was gentle. "Same thing happened to my old man a few years back, and he was as much of a fool as your husband. Tried to hold off the men from the state with a shotgun. Got two years in jail and probation for attempted homicide, and his herd got hauled off anyway."

Tobin stared at the young man. He was tanned and muscled; his hair sandy, his eyes a sharp blue.

A motorcar turned into the driveway. Cass, Harley remembered suddenly, bringing Lil to visit on one of her rare afternoons off from Sawyer's.

Tobin paid no attention to the newcomers. "I'm not planning to shoot at state men. I'll keep my herd up in the woods."

"I wish you could," said Folger. "I'd have to report you, and they'd come get them."

Tobin ignored him. "You just fill up that hole."

The young man shrugged. "Pretty chilly today, we'll get a snow pretty soon. How you gonna keep them cattle warm out there this winter?"

"We'll build a shed."

"I hear you milk your herd four times a day, Mr. Westcott." Tobin turned away. "You must be a hell of a rich man to hire hands to milk a herd that often when you can't even use their milk!"

Cass and Lil stood beside Harley now, staring at the hole and at the people gathered around, trying to understand. Harley told them.

The young man's eyes found Lil. "Hello," he said.

Lil looked up in surprise, thinking perhaps he was someone she should recognize. He wasn't. She turned away.

"Well!" He slapped a wheel of his bulldozer. "I'd better start shoving if you want that hole filled in." He switched on the engine.

"Wait," said Tobin. The noise of the engine stopped. "You!" Tobin pointed at Lil. "You're training to be a lawyer. I got any legal recourse in this thing?"

Lil's mouth opened. "I don't know. I've only just started."

"I'll call Sawyer." Tobin started toward the house.

"He's not there," said Lil. "He's gone to New York for some kind of meeting."

"Then I'll call a lawyer in Seneca."

"You're wasting your time." The young man on the bulldozer was rolling another cigarette. "You got no choice, Mr. Westcott. If they're that bad tuberculin—"

"*If.*" It was Cass. "Who says they *are*, Father Westcott?"

Folger cringed. "I'm only doing my job."

"Tobin," said Upjohn. "What do we know about this man? Except that he says he's from the state and he says your cows are tuberculin."

"With all you've got at stake," said Cass, "I'd think you'd want more than the word of one stranger."

"Call my office," said Folger. "They'll tell you."

Tobin took from his pocket the state order, signed by a commissioner and impressed with the seal. He handed it to Upjohn. "Look official to you?"

"Yes," said Upjohn. "But if there's the slightest chance..."

Tobin leveled a finger at Folger. "You stay here."

And he was off.

It took Mabel Wheelman five minutes to put Tobin through to the local Ag office. "We're expanding our service, Mr. Westcott. You've got be patient."

At last, Henry Cummings was on the line. "You didn't know, Henry?" Tobin's face brightened. "Well then maybe it's a mistake! Oh. Well, what department *do* I call? Calvin Jones, 4524? The man who signed this order's named McCullock. You don't—Well, I'll try this Jones."

It took Mabel only two minutes to get 4524 in Seneca.

"Mr. Jones? Henry Cummings in the New Devon office said you'd be able to help me. My herd's been declared tuberculin. *Dairy* herd. Cows! Oh. Well, Henry said...Who is Charles Fallon?"

Mabel was slower on the next connection. "It's just terrible, Mr. Westcott! All your lovely cows!"

"Goddamn nosy old maid," Tobin muttered.

Mr. Fallon was sympathetic; however, eradication was not his department. "That's the office of Farm Advisors...Yes, Mr. McCullock is with that office. Good luck, sir."

Tobin was finally connected with the office of Commissioner McCullock. "The Commissioner isn't in, may I be of assistance? Yes, I know. We're all so dreadfully sorry, Mr. Westcott." The secretary's voice was oiled and polished. "Dr. Folger tells us you have a fine herd. Well of course he's the veterinarian we sent. He took a great deal of care, sir. He tested them twice, hoping he'd made a mistake, but the results are conclusive. The Commissioner has already signed a voucher for maximum indemnity, one hundred and fifty dollars a head. No, I know it isn't, but I'm sure you have insurance...You don't? What a shame! Oh, just a moment, Mr. Westcott, the Commissioner just came in."

There wasn't much more Commissioner McCullock could add. Mabel was sniffling as the conversation ended. "Shall I try anyone else for you, Mr. Westcott?"

Tobin sat with his head in his hands. "No." He replaced the receiver and rose. "Stay inside, Hitty—and you girls, too."

"You, too, sir." It was the young man from the bulldozer. "You shouldn't have to see it. Me'n your hired men can do the job."

But Tobin did not stay in the house. Each gunshot would have been unbearable—which one had it been? Had she been frightened? Had they put the bullet squarely between the eyes, or was she suffering?

No. He had to see that each cow was led quietly from the barn, with no more fuss than if she was being led out to have

Strommeyer take her picture; that she was petted and soothed for a few moments, told "Thank you," and bade farewell. That she was allowed, in death, to sink to her knees with dignity befitting her pedigree.

He would take the gun himself and make sure that the blast killed instantly.

It didn't work that way.

The first animal brought out was Locust Leaf Aaggie Veeman. The pit and the ramp frightened her. She braced herself, forcing them to pull and shove. "Gently!" Tobin kept saying. "Don't upset her." But Locust began to kick and to butt. Before they got her under control, she had sent them all sprawling and led them several times around the pit.

At last she was backed into a position along the wall in the far corner.

Tobin tried to soothe her with words and touch, but her eyes rolled and her head jerked away from his caresses. As Chuck handed the shotgun to Tobin, she began once more to dance and kick.

Tobin backed away a few steps and leveled the gun at Locust's head. The tip of the barrel moved, trying to follow her. "Hold her steady." Tears and perspiration stung his eyes.

Then suddenly Locust stood still, staring straight at the barrel of the gun. Tobin gasped. A hot flush sped through him and he tried to squeeze the trigger. Another moment of hesitation and he squeezed.

But that moment had been too long. Locust moved, and the blast missed the merciful spot between the eyes and went into the eye itself. Locust fell, screaming and thrashing. Blinded by tears, Tobin tried to reload. He felt the weapon wrenched from his hands. The young man from the bulldozer changed the shell and fired. Locust's body convulsed once more, then was quiet.

The hired men stood back, trying not to look.

No one spoke.

"There must be a better way," Harley said finally. He couldn't leave Tobin, but he couldn't take fifty-seven more.

"Maybe if we lead them out with bags over their heads," said Chuck.

"You'd have to take the bag off at the last," said another man, "or you'd miss the spot for sure."

"Maybe like a blindfold just over the eyes."

"They'll smell the blood, though. The blood'll set them dancing." No one made a move to get the next cow. "Dr. Folger?" Upjohn stood at the side of the pit. "Don't you have a hypodermic syringe?"

Tobin looked up hopefully.

"Yes, but—" The vet got red. "The fluid is so very expensive. The department would never pay for it, and I personally just can't afford—"

"What if I supplied the fluid?" said Upjohn. "Would you do the injections without charge?"

"Of course," said Folger. A desperately sad expression passed over his face. "It's the least I can do."

No one questioned Upjohn when he brought Folger the jar of liquid and stepped back, mopping unaccustomed perspiration from his brow. Chuck got some lime from the barn and poured it on Locust's still-oozing wounds. "Maybe the next one won't smell the blood," he said.

And she didn't. Hemelle Topsy Ormsby Tobe followed Chuck lazily, cud working, bag swinging. She hesitated with only momentary curiosity at the ramp, then descended and allowed herself to be positioned beside Locust Leaf Aaggie Veeman. She examined her fallen sister with unalarmed eyes, then swung her head and scanned the men as though searching for the camera.

Tobin patted her and scratched her crown. He talked to her, saying foolish things that no one found foolish. Then he held her head, and Folger put the needle into a vein in her neck.

It was beautiful. One moment Topsy was standing, responding to Tobin's scratching fingers; the next, she was sinking, as Tobin had hoped, with stateliness befitting her pedigree. Just at the end, as her head settled onto the dirt and her eyes closed, she sighed, much like a person settling into bed after a long day's work.

Tobin turned to Upjohn. "Thank you," he said. He glanced at the liquid into which Folger was again dipping his needle. "That's good—whatever it is."

Perspiration still rolled from Upjohn's forehead, despite the cool of the day. "An old folk formula," he murmured. The answer satisfied Tobin. What did it matter? So long as it worked.

Which it did, every time. Some of the cows came less peacefully than Topsy, and some required more gentling. But they all went just as Topsy had.

And before the men quite knew it, they had worked their way through fifty-seven head-six and a half neat rows. The young man on the bulldozer rolled himself a cigarette as his moment approached. The fifty-eighth cow was led out.

Pontiac Lass.

Tobin turned away.

Chuck and Thomas brought the Lass down the ramp and backed her into position. Then they fell silent, looking uneasily at Tobin.

"Dad?"

Tobin didn't answer. He kept his back turned.

"Don't you want to pet her?"

Tobin shook his head.

The men closed in silently. A last scratch, a last word in the ear.

Folger lifted his needle. Harley took her head. He didn't

look at her. And, for Tobin's sake, he didn't cry. He just kept scratching and whispering to the Lass till he felt her sinking. He knelt with her, soothing and petting all the way.

When it was over, Tobin turned. The Lass's eyes had not closed. They gazed up at him, even in death expecting kindness and clover. Tobin knelt and closed them. He picked a speck of dust from her nose, then took a currycomb from his back pocket and began to groom her.

Chuck bent down, "Gov-ner. Maybe you hadn't better."

Harley took Chuck's arm. "Leave him."

"I got to do my postmortems," whispered Folger.

"Go ahead," said Harley. "Start on the other side."

The hired men withdrew. Tobin kept currying the Lass, currying away his own teardrops. Thomas and Harley moved among the rows, arranging tails, moving heads to more natural positions. Folger busied himself with his scalpels. The young man waited beside his bulldozer.

And Upjohn paced the rim of the pit, staring fixedly at nothing in particular.

The next day—after the young man with the bulldozer had neatly covered the slaughtered herd, after all the hired men but Chuck had taken their severance pay and trudged away down the avenue of maples, after Tobin had again gone to his bed and ordered the windows covered with blankets—Satyendra Singh was found dead.

An accident, Sheriff Bailey said. The man had obviously been drinking; everybody knew how these foreigners drank. And, it wasn't the first time a car had lost control on that curve by Carrie's house. Someday the county would have to get around to doing something about that curve.

CHAPTER TWENTY-ONE

TOBIN REMAINED IN his room longer than a week this time. When he came out, it was not to go to the barn.

Tobin wandered; through the house, around the yard. Time and again he'd go to that spot between the barnyard and the orchard. He'd stand there a while, scuffing at the mounded earth, then wander away. Soon he'd be back again, scuffing and staring.

At first the family let him alone, but then Upjohn began to accompany him. Day after day, they roamed the grounds— Tobin silent, Upjohn talking. Hitty was pleased. "He's telling Tobin all about minds in concert," she told Harley.

The day before Thanksgiving a check for $8,700 arrived in the mail. "Fifty-eight head of cattle at $150.00 per head."

And on the same day an early snow fell. It melted during the morning, but by afternoon the ground was frozen. The snow began to accumulate in troughs that the wind could not reach. The grave of Tobin's herd mottled and became impossible to scuff.

As though that barrier had closed a final door, Tobin squared his shoulders and turned his back on the grave. He and Upjohn returned to the house and sat down in the library in front of the fireplace. Hitty brought her needlework and hot drinks, and Thomas brought his reading spectacles and a newspaper.

They were still sitting there when Harley returned from school.

"Now we're all here, I'd like to have a talk," said Tobin. "Harley, maybe you'd better have your wife come down."

Harley went for Cass. "This is it," he told her as they entered the library.

Tobin stood leaning against the back of a chair. "Harley, maybe if I was a better father, I wouldn't be saying this, but—"

"It's all right, Dad. I know. My tuition."

Tobin turned away. Funny. He'd expected Upjohn to argue for Harley's college. "No, Tobin. Do what is right for yourself. *Your* self-respect will become Harley's." Still…

Tobin glanced around the library. He and Upjohn had thought of selling furnishings—Upjohn had made inquiries. Nobody to buy. He'd be giving the stuff away.

Of course, he'd be able to rent out the old red house now that there weren't enough hired men to need a bunkhouse, and after he sold the Stevens-Duryea and bought an old truck, there'd surely be a bit left over.

He cleared his throat. "If you can get enough together to pay the second semester yourself, Harley, I won't ask you and Cass for room and board."

"Maybe I could," said Harley. "How much do we have saved, Cass?"

"Nothing."

"Yes, we do," said Harley. He started for the door. "Where's the bank book?"

"All right! We've got forty dollars in the bank."

"How much in Emily's piggy bank?"

"Nine dollars and eighty cents."

"Fifty dollars," said Harley. "Plus two months not having to pay the twenty-eight—"

"I won't let you spend it!" cried Cass.

"Why not?"

Cass stared at him, her mouth working, then she began to cry.

An awful feeling crept into Harley's stomach. "Cass?" They'd been so careful. "You're not!"

"What's the matter with her?" said Tobin.

"I think she's in the family way again," Hitty whispered.

"I'm so sorry," Cass kept saying.

"It's not your fault." Harley's voice was flat. "There's always next fall. Or maybe some correspondence courses like Lil takes."

Hitty sat Cass down and poured her a rum-flavored drink. "You don't hate me?"

"Of course we don't," they all assured her.

"I was afraid to tell. It's such a bad time."

"It's never a bad time for a baby," said Tobin. He'd heard someone say that once.

Hitty picked up her embroidery. "Were you going to talk about anything besides Harley's college, Tobin?"

Tobin began to pace. He'd planned exactly how he'd say it, but that girl had thrown him off his stride. "I guess you all know we're going to have to economize." He glanced at Hitty. She didn't look up from her embroidery. Well, she hadn't understood. "I could buy a herd of grade cows, be just a farmer. But I've decided to use the check from the state to buy ten top heifers instead."

"Good," said Hitty. "People expect your cows to be the best."

She was in a dreamworld! "Hitty—we're going to have to let the servants go."

Hitty looked up now. "Well, not until December first. I only gave them their notice on November fifteenth."

"You what?"

"Of course, Henrietta won't be leaving. And I don't blame her. We're all she's got."

"But Hitty, we can't pay her!"

"Oh, that's all right," said Hitty. "She's staying for board and room."

"I won't have her giving us charity."

"Does Mr. Upjohn give us charity?" Tobin reddened.

"Your wife has a point," said Upjohn. "Henrietta has been here longer than I have. She's family, sir."

"And I'll need her even more now!" Hitty went to the door of the library. "Henrietta? Bring it in!" She turned. "We've been waiting for you to feel good enough so we could show you, Tobin. You *do* feel good, don't you?"

"I feel fine."

The noise from the foyer sounded like a chair being dragged, and Henrietta appeared in the doorway, lugging a large painted board. It bore scriptlike purple letters, surrounded by pink and yellow flowers. *Spring Farm Guest Home—Room and Board $1 per night.*

"I've already got an ad in the *Courier*," said Hitty.

"No," said Tobin.

"Isn't a dollar a night enough?" said Hitty.

"You're talking about a boardinghouse!"

"No, darling," said Hitty. "A tourist haven."

"And who's supposed to run it?"

"Me, of course," said Hitty. "Dad and Henrietta will help me."

Tobin looked at his father's sheepish grin and at Henrietta's.

"Now, Hitty," he said, "you don't want strangers running around your house."

"I do, too! It's a great big house. We've got five empty bedrooms."

"Well, they're going to stay that way."

Hitty raised her eyebrows. "That's bad business, Tobin. A good businessman takes full advantage of his assets when things get tight." She sighed and shook her head. "And I always thought you were such a good businessman."

Tobin's face was apoplectic. "I don't know why you suddenly consider yourself an expert on business. You've never done anything but spend the money I make and curl your hair twice a day."

"Is there anything wrong with that?"

"Yes, if you must know! There is something wrong with it."

"I happen to agree with you, and I'm going to change my ways. I take it I have your permission."

Tobin swayed. "No!" he said. "Look"—he tried to soften his tone—"I think you're wonderful to want to help me. If you said to me, 'Tobin, I'm going to crochet rugs and sell them,' or something like that, it would be fine. But you're not *fit* to run a boardinghouse."

"Are you casting aspersions on my character?"

"Of course not! You're delicate, that's all."

"Fiddlesticks. I'm strong as a horse. You just never bothered to notice. Heaven's sakes, Tobin, we'll be lucky if we get one guest a night. That's *one* extra set of sheets, *one* extra place at table." She paused. "But it would be seven extra dollars a week."

"No," said Tobin, "and that's final."

❀ ❀ ❀

Hitty's first boarder appeared at the door, *Courier* in hand, several days later. It was the sandy-haired bulldozer driver. "Remember me?"

"Oh dear, yes," said Hitty. "I don't know whether we can take you. Every time Tobin looks at you, he'll be reminded." Then she shrugged. "We'll change your sheets once a week. And you'll have to eat whatever the family's eating—no special menus. A dollar a day."

"Will a month in advance be enough?"

"Thirty dollars! Don't you want to see—?" He started counting the bills into her hand. "Oh my!" said Hitty. But at twenty dollars the young man stopped counting.

"You don't let *cats* in the house, do you?"

"Well, there's Fluffy."

The young man shuddered, and glanced around.

"She's not here now. I'll keep her out if you don't like cats."

The young man grunted. "It's just when they get near me," he said, and he counted the remaining bills into Hitty's hand.

"Wait and see," Tobin said. "She's like a kid with a new toy. She'll drop the whole thing after she's ironed a few sheets and cooked a few meals."

But Hitty sang as she worked, and strange new dishes began to appear on the table. "Chile con carne. Nick says he likes it, so I thought I'd give it a try."

His last name was Clunycourt. Nicholas Clunycourt. "We all have our crosses," he'd said. "If you're my friends, you'll forget you ever heard my last name." Everyone complied.

Except Harley. He hadn't liked him that first day and he never would. Sometimes the man irritated him so much that Harley entertained a thought he knew to be both childish and cruel—putting a cat in Clunycourt's bedroom. "You know why he answered Mother's ad?" he told Cass. "He figured it was the best way to get to know Lil."

"What's wrong with that?"

"He didn't even finish high school. He's not in the same class with Lil."

"Oh?" said Cass. "Who *would* be in the same class, Harley?"

"I just don't think she should get involved with Clunycourt," Harley said. "She'll meet lots of guys. She's got plenty of time."

❀ ❀ ❀

Which was how Lil felt about it. She wanted to be around, in case...

The fantasies were dreadful. Yet they wouldn't stop coming. She'd find herself imagining Cass dead of pneumonia, or vanished like Muriel, or killed in an auto crash.

She'd tried to get over Harley. She'd gone out with so many boys, she'd forgotten some of their faces already.

There'd been nothing wrong with any of them; all polite, intelligent men from Franklin, or the faculty at Schyler. She'd been careful to date college men—they got Papa's goat so well.

Especially John Stanley. John, who had rescued Lil from the snowstorm so long ago. She'd liked John, had even thought of saying yes when he asked her to marry him. He would have taken her to his home on Long Island. Away from Harley.

She hadn't gone.

Now there was Nick. And she didn't really *like* Nick.

It wasn't that Nick was coarse. It was just that he was too—blunt. Every time she dated him, she swore it was the last time. Then, there he'd be again, waiting outside Sawyer's, or class; or descending, unannounced, on weekends—always with a bouquet of roses. "Ready to marry me, Bascomb?"

"Nick, I've told you a dozen times. I don't love you."

"Well, you can have the roses anyway. Come on. I'll take you to dinner."

And she'd go.

But it wasn't the dinner she went for.

Afterward, on some dark road, Lil would forget that she didn't like Nick. There would be only a split second of stiffening as he reached out, so sure of himself, as though she was an instrument: he meant to play.

His lips would close over hers, and his hands *would* play her. Her body would fill with yearning, and she'd cling to him.

"I'm going to rape you some night, Bascomb!" His lips would move, rough, over her face and her throat; his teeth would bite, his fingers would press until she knew she'd be bruised. And yet she felt the tenderness.

"You won't." He'd never take until she gave.

"Want to bet? You're gonna lose. I can't be good much longer. I want in you, Bascomb."

"That's a nice young man," said Paul. "Spending a lot of money on roses. He asked you to marry him?"

"Yes. But I'm not in love with him."

"You better decide you're in love with *someone* pretty soon. You're getting a reputation, Miss! All the running you do with those college fellows."

"I don't care if I get a reputation."

Paul looked hurt. "Your Ma and I care."

So did Lil. But what was she supposed to do? Stop studying and get married to suit the neighbors?

And then she'd think about going away. Transferring to the University. Having a life of her own—

Not seeing Harley. She knew she'd never go.

Tobin had tried to rent the small red house. He ran ads and posted signs for miles around, but people just weren't moving— staying put like rabbits.

"Let's take the red house," said Cass one night.

Harley, working on a short story, barely looked up. "We can't afford it."

"You don't love me," said Cass.

She always used that. "I *do*."

Cass shook her head. "If you loved me, you'd want to be alone with me sometimes."

"We're alone here every night."

"We are not!" Cass slammed a pillow to the floor. In the crib Emily stirred. "See?" said Cass. "Three years of whispering, afraid Emily will wake up or your family will hear us. I want a home where we can be real married people—not two kids playing house in a bedroom!"

"Well, how about the attic? There's three or four rooms up there we could make into an apartment—"

"No!" Cass stamped her foot. "You haven't been listening, Harley." Her pregnancy had gotten obvious just the last week, in a becoming sort of way. She looked—succulent. Harley smiled.

"Why are you laughing at me?"

"I'm not." He took her hands and pulled her to him. "I'm just thinking how cute you look."

Cass jerked away. "I'll teach you to take me seriously, Harley Westcott! I'm taking Emily and moving out tomorrow!"

Harley scanned her face. She was serious. "Where would you go?"

"I'll go to Crazy Lizzy's house. Curt won't charge me."

"Come on, Cass. There's no electricity, or running water, or heat. I won't let you go there!"

"How are you going to stop me?" said Cass.

Harley stared at her. He was never going to finish college! "I'll rent the red house."

Cass made him take her up there that very minute. She scurried ahead, swinging the lantern and tossing clods of snow back at him. "Hurry!"

Harley laughed and returned the snow, making her giggle and skitter from the path with little shrieks. It made a beautiful sound, clear on the night air. He found himself hurrying despite himself.

Till, at the door, Cass stopped. "Carry me over the threshold, Harley."

For a reason he did not understand, tears came to Harley's eyes. He lifted her into his arms, a dark-haired kewpie doll with frostbitten cheeks and eyes as misty as his own, and he kissed her as he swung her over the threshold, relishing the chill of her skin and the warmth of her lips. Then he put her down. "You're heavy." She wasn't, but he needed something to say.

"That's because, please God, it's a big fat boy, this time." She held Harley fast. "I love you, Harley." With a hand on his lips, she stopped his reply. "Don't. I know you won't mean it. Let me tell you. I love you, and I'm going to make you happy. Let's forget the last three years, let's pretend we got married today. We'll start fresh. And I'll *make* you love me."

"OK." Harley turned away. He wanted to say "But I do love you," because, at that moment, he did. He wanted to grab her and hold her and never let go. "'Well, this is our house," he said.

Considering their few possessions, there was more than enough assistance the day they moved. But by the end of the day, they also had more than enough possessions.

Flora's attic gave up a table and chairs, two chests of drawers, and a hand-carved Victorian bed of heroic proportions; Hitty's yielded mirrors, chairs, a sofa, a bed for Emily, and a spinet piano.

Emma and Helen brought linens made of the printed cotton that the farm cooperative bagged its cattle feed in.

Curt contributed staples, and Paul gave them his father's Bible.

Lil brought a horseshoe and nailed it over the kitchen door.

Upjohn brought pots of herbs tagged with cooking suggestions.

And Thomas gave them a picture of the house as it had looked in 1890, with Thomas himself in the front yard holding a team of Percherons, and a four-year-old Tobin peering from behind his mother's skirts. Thomas offered it shyly, and Cass fussed as though he'd given her a diamond ring.

Everything pleased Cass that day. People laughed, cleaned, and carried; drank cocoa from the pot on the stove. Emily played with her first doll—a present from Nick, like the two dozen red roses. "I got nothing else to spend my money on," he said when Cass tried to thank him. Then he looked long at Lil and left the room.

By four in the afternoon the cold, empty house had been transformed into a warm, overstuffed home, and Cass had miraculously cleaned, dusted, and polished everything in the place. The Bascombs departed, for it was getting on to chore time, and Tobin went to see about his own stock.

Tobin apologized to Harley as he left. "I'm the only one didn't have anything for you. I just got no imagination." Oh, there'd been pictures—of the old herd, the old barn—but he couldn't imagine Harley wanting those. "Tell you what, son. You got a month's free rent."

By five, everyone was gone except Lil and Nick. "You two have to stay for supper," Cass said. "I'm going to make our first meal in our new home!"

"First since we got married," said Harley. "I don't even know if she can boil water."

Cass went to the icebox. "No meat. I could make biscuits, but that's no supper. How about pancakes? I could make an *apple* pancake. Harley, get me three nice apples from the sack Curt put down cellar."

A daughter of Emma Bascomb could not fail in the kitchen. Though Harley had to make an emergency sprint to the big house for some baking powder, the resulting pancake filled the griddle, high and light, topped by chewy, honey-glazed apples. With Curt's maple syrup, a fresh pot of coffee, and Nick's roses, it graced the old oak table like a banquet. And in the candlelight (for, with all the donations, they had not one lamp), Cass glowed.

Harley felt like a king. They'd made the right move, no matter how they'd have to scrimp. Tonight he could even look at Lil without regret.

Again and again he leaned over and kissed his wife.

As soon as Nick and Lil were gone, Harley and Cass retired to the darkness of their Victorian bed.

"I'm so happy," said Cass.

"I am, too." Harley began to kiss her.

"Not tonight," she said when he freed her lips. "I'm tired."

"OK." He understood. She'd been at it since sunup—and in her condition.

In another minute she was asleep in his arms.

Harley lay staring into the darkness. He was a man now, with a home and responsibilities, and his own college expense to manage. They'd need twenty-five a month for the house, then probably another ten or so for food, a couple of dollars for electricity, and coal—he'd have to see what that would cost. There'd be doctor bills with the new baby, and clothes and things. And a little bit more for some correspondence courses.

All of which meant he needed a job of his own that would pay at least fifty a month. He couldn't count on Cass. In a few weeks she'd be too big—have to take leave of absence from Calvary.

If only one of his stories would sell! It would sure help out.

Cass was getting heavy on his arm. He eased himself out from under her, and she rolled away in her sleep.

Somehow, the happiness of the day rolled away with her. He wouldn't be in this fix if he weren't married. If she hadn't tricked him into it—

No. If *he* hadn't been so stupid!

He thought of Lil. She'd been so quiet all day. He only saw her smile once, when she hung the horseshoe. He wondered what she was doing at that moment. She couldn't still be with Nick—unless they were necking.

Hell, no! She wouldn't let that gorilla touch her.

Riding away from her sister's home that night, Lil hardly knew that Nick was in the car with her. It didn't seem real. It didn't seem possible.

But that was just it. It *was* real, even though it wasn't possible.

Harley and Cass being married had always been so easy to imagine away. Even Emily, for some reason, had added no permanence in Lil's imagination. Lil had never actually seen them living together as a family, with Harley and Cass kissing and touching as they had tonight. He hadn't been able to keep his hands off her!

But the pain of it had cleared her vision. They were married. And, for the first time, she knew what that meant: he'd never be hers. There was not even any longer the comforting thought that Harley was a captive. He'd actually been happy tonight; any fool could see that.

When Nick pulled over at the last bend before the meadow and Curt's, Lil was glad the time had arrived, eager to forget.

But Nick rolled a cigarette. "That was nice today. They'll be OK, those two. Westcott's got some growing up to do, but he'll toughen now he's on his own."

It would do no good to explain to Nick about things like sensitivity. "I like him as he is," was all she said.

"Oh?" Nick tossed away the cigarette and reached for her. "That your type? The pantywaist?"

Lil frowned. "Maybe your idea of a man and my idea of a man are two different things."

Nick was silent in the darkness beside her. Then, quietly, "Does that mean I'm not your idea of a man?"

"Oh, no!" Lil turned quickly and touched his face.

"Kiss me."

Lil jerked away. She refused to be treated like a slut. *He* was supposed to do the kissing.

Nick started the car.

"What are you doing?"

"Taking you home."

"But…" Lil's face reddened. She lifted her chin. "That's fine with me."

Nick shrugged. The car rolled forward.

Tears of anger and mortification welled into Lil's eyes. "You bastard!"

Nick stopped the car. "That's not good enough, Bascomb. You thought we were going to neck, didn't you? And you wanted it so bad you could taste it."

"No!"

"But *I'm* supposed to make all the moves. That way you don't have to commit yourself, right? I get so worked up I could chew this steering wheel into confetti! Then just before *you* get to the boiling point, you yelp, 'Take me home, Nick!" And I gotta dump you off at your door with your Christian virtue intact, then drive back down here and take care of myself."

Lil gasped. "That's a terrible thing to say!"

"You bet your britches it's terrible. Well, I'm not gonna do it again. Put up or shut up, Bascomb. You're not getting kiss one until you tell me you want me."

Lil closed her eyes. She *didn't* like Nick. Not one bit.

"If I take you home now," he said, suddenly gentle, "there'll never be another night."

There it was, put right to her. And there were his eyes—so blue, so sure of themselves. "That's not fair, Nick!"

"Why not?" The eyes wouldn't let her go. "I love you, Lil. Why isn't it fair to make you say you love me?"

"Because I *don't*."

"You want me, don't you?"

"Yes! But—"

"Well bless your fickle little tongue." Nick kissed her—a long kiss that took the breath from her, demanding and receiving a response. But the moment she did respond, he pushed her away. "I'm only giving samples tonight, lady. You want the real thing, you gotta come up with hard cash."

"You bastard!" said Lil.

Nick grinned. "Which puts us back where we started."

"That's right!" said Lil. "Take me home."

The smile left Nick's face. "I meant it when I said you wouldn't be seeing me again. You want it that way?"

"I do," said Lil.

Nick released her and started the motor.

He's bluffing, thought Lil. He'll stop before he gets to the meadow and make another try. Then I'll get out and *walk* home.

But Nick kept driving. Soon his headlights would be visible from the house.

From the corners of her eyes, Lil watched him, searching for the glint of humor. There was none. "Stop!" she said.

Nick kept driving.

"Please!" She took his arm, but he shook her loose. "I'm sorry!"

Why was she saying all that? She didn't even like him. Only his arms, his kisses, the way he made her feel small and snug and soft. But that wasn't love. That was sex!

And what would she do without it?

Without Nick.

The car turned into the driveway. Nick left the motor running. "So long," he said. Lil didn't move. He waited, staring at the wheel. "I'm not going to kiss you good-bye, if that's what you're waiting for." Still Lil didn't move. "Go on, get out."

"No." Lil took a deep breath. "You can have your way."

She felt his hand on her shoulder and she closed her eyes. Then a feeling of incredible relief flooded her. She pressed toward the hand; pressed until her head was against his chest. She couldn't look up. "Take me back down the road," she whispered. "You can do whatever you want with me."

"You're sure you mean that? You won't back out, no matter what I want to do?"

"I'm sure."

Nick threw the car into reverse.

Lil felt alone and unbalanced. Nick put his arm around her. It was strong and steady. She leaned closer and shut her eyes again. The car seemed to be taking forever to reach the spot.

She felt Nick's arm, tightening and loosening with his own thoughts. He kissed her hair. "Scared?"

Lil nodded.

"I am, too," he said. "I've never gotten married before."

There was no doubt she had heard him correctly. And now she noticed the sound beneath the wheels of the car—they were off the dirt road, running on macadam.

To a Justice of the Peace.

Silly way to propose. But then, he'd tried the conventional ways so often.

You won't back out, no matter what I want to do?

No! she wouldn't be trapped by such a trick!

But then he'd take her home. She'd go into the house, and he'd never call again. If he said he wouldn't, he wouldn't.

It would settle everything for good, if she married him. She knew now she'd never have Harley. And she'd never love again.

What was there in marriage if not love? Maybe only what she felt when Nick took her into his arms. Heaven knew it was something enough that at this moment she felt she'd never be able to get along without it.

Lil straightened up. She had to smile, seeing that Nick was indeed nervous. "I suppose you have a ring?"

"They said they'd fix it if it was the wrong size."

Lil laughed.

Nick cleared his throat and glanced at her. "There's something I never mentioned. I know your Dad's real strong about these things—"

"What?"

"I'm a Catholic. Do you mind?"

Lil laughed again. So Papa wanted her to get married. Well, she'd just do that little thing. "Not at all," she said. "I think it's sheer poetry."

The next morning the world seemed filtered through gauze. Lil knew she wore a smug smile, but she couldn't raise the ambition to remove it.

They had entered the Westcott house unseen the night before. Now, as she and Nick descended the stairs, on their way to break the news to Paul, they passed Hitty on her way up.

"Good morning." Hitty smiled and was almost past them before she stopped and looked at Lil. Her smile was gone. "You Bascomb girls have a way of getting into my upstairs rooms without my knowing it. I do hope you're wearing a wedding band." Lil held up her finger. Hitty sighed. "I suppose this means you'll be moving out, Nicholas."

At that moment the front door opened.

"Morning, Harl!" said Nick. "Want to kiss the bride?"

Lil wasn't sure from Harley's expression what he was thinking. She thought she saw pain, and she found herself hoping she was right. They went downstairs. "Mrs. Nicholas Clunycourt, Harley. How does it sound?"

"Go ahead," said Nick. "Kiss her. It's good luck."

Harley touched his lips to Lil's cheek.

As he did, Lil caught a movement in the library. It was Upjohn, standing before the bookcases, his back turned.

"Mr. Upjohn?" She said it before the message of his back quite penetrated. She saw him set his shoulders, and wished she hadn't called out. Upjohn must be disappointed at her choice. *You deserve the best*, he'd told her once.

Now Upjohn turned and came forward, smiling. "My congratulations," he said and kissed her cheek. Not once did he meet her eyes.

Paul Bascomb had been waiting up all night—worried, furious, then jubilant.

"She's married, Emma!" After all, his daughter would not have stayed out all night with a man for any other purpose. "That's a nice young man she's got there. Stong. He'll keep her in line."

But after Nick and Lil left, it seemed to Paul that there would be no salvation for Lil. The Good Lord knew he'd *tried*, from the moment of her birth, to shield her.

Paul sat and rocked. "When they're bad, they're bad. No way you can save them."

"Paul! It's not the end of the world," said Emma. "Catholic's Christian, ain't it? We're all climbing to heaven, just by different paths."

"You don't understand," Paul said. "It's a symptom of her evil, taking an idol-worshiper to husband. It's coming, Emma. The devil'll be taking her soul. Any day now. Watch and see. We'd best start forgetting we ever had a daughter named Lilith."

CHAPTER TWENTY-TWO

EACH NEW MONTH of 1930 seemed to find more people looking for work, with fewer jobs available and wages going down. Harley took anything he could get—whatever the work, whatever the pay.

By the end of April the robe and the railing could no longer conceal Cass's pregnancy from the congregation. The end of her salary meant the end of her singing lessons. And with that came bitterness, and a strangeness that ended the idyll in their new home and left Harley bewildered.

"I'm sorry, Cass. You know I'd let you take lessons if I could. But we can't afford luxuries anymore."

"My lessons aren't luxuries. I need them!"

"Why? You're good enough already. Everyone says you're the best soloist Calvary ever had."

"So that's it," said Cass. "Calvary for the rest of my life. You're trying to keep me from ever going on the stage!"

"You never told me you wanted to go on the stage."

"You're against me. You're jealous of my talent. You've planned this whole thing so I can never *be* anybody."

Harley stared at her. "'That's crazy, Cass! You've got a better head on your shoulders than I have! Why are you talking so crazy?"

"Because I *am* crazy. Crazy Cassie!"

"Stop it. Look, if you want your lessons so bad, you can have them—but we'll have to move back into the big house. We can't afford this house and your lessons, too."

"We could if you earned decent money. If you worked harder."

"You must be kidding!"

"Look at Nick. He's got a nice steady job and he earns good money. You don't see him making Lil stop *her* lessons."

"Damn it, Cass, I wish you'd quit throwing Nick in my face! I tried the quarry, they're not hiring. Nick's just lucky, that's all. See how much he'd earn if he got laid off."

"Oh, he'd make out. He's talented. He does carpentry, electric work. He paints—he can do anything."

"Sure he can. He's another da Vinci! I'm beginning to hate that guy's guts."

"Why? I think he's very nice."

"Because—" Harley waved his hands in the air. Nothing made sense in this conversation anyway. "He hates cats."

"That's what I like best about him," said Cass. "Anybody who hates cats *has* to be nice."

The last week in May, Cass packed a small valise. This time, Dr. Barnes felt, the hospital was in order. "Looks like a mighty big baby there."

"That's because, please God, it's a boy," said Cass. "Michael."

During the last weeks she was too big to do much of anything. After breakfast each day, without clearing off the dishes, she took to the sofa to think and pray. She couldn't fail

Papa this time—but God must know, after all, how she'd lied and cheated to get Harley. Was he planning to punish her still further—with yet another girl?

In a way, she'd already been punished. The Lord had taken all the Westcotts' money; the mighty *had* been meekened.

Funny about that meekening. Papa just took it for granted. After all, wasn't it exactly what the angel had promised?

Perhaps there *had* been an angel guiding her, for the greater glory of heaven, through the labyrinth of plans that brought about her marriage. In that case she had only done the Lord's will.

The idea appealed to her. The more she examined it, the more she became convinced that it was so. Which meant there was no need to pray for a boy. It was time for *that* part of the prophecy to be fulfilled.

What she should concentrate on now was "bringing the Westcotts to God," as she had promised Papa, the Reverend, and God she would do.

Not having the faintest notion how to go about it, she centered her prayers on pleas for guidance.

And, in those last few days before the birth, she grew increasingly critical of Harley and of Emily.

The nurse came to the nursery window, her eyes smiling above her mask, and raised a small white bundle.

Harley smiled. He'd thought all babies were red and ugly. He'd also thought babies were born with blue eyes—closed. Not *his* baby. Her eyes were green. And they were looking at him. "Can she see me?" he mouthed through the window.

The nurse's eyes crinkled, and she shook her head.

The nurse was obviously wrong. That baby not only saw him, she knew who he was! He made a waggling movement with his fingers. "She *does* see me!" Wasn't that something? Just born, and see how she kept looking at him—already trusting her Daddy.

His palms got clammy.

Not a very smart baby. Trusting *him*.

Harley turned to go.

"Mr. Westcott!" The nurse stopped him, the baby still in her arms, in the door of the nursery. She checked the hall in both directions and gave him a wink. "It's against the rules, Mr. Westcott, but she's *such* a wonderful baby. Would you like to hold her?"

No! He didn't want her trusting eyes any closer. But then he was reaching, his arms adjusting to support the tiny bundle. Something near a sob fluttered through his chest.

And suddenly he felt strong.

A few minutes later, Harley crossed the hospital lobby, heading for Cass's ward.

In a gift shop with the customary display of stuffed toys and candies, an arrangement of artificial cornflowers caught his attention. They were the color of Cass's eyes. Nice. He looked at the price tag.

A dollar.

He dug into his pocket. Seventy-five, a dollar, a dollar fifty and six. If he bought those flowers, he'd only have fifty-six cents till he picked up another job.

But he *would* pick up another job!

Cass was awake in a twilight of ether, Harley held the flowers behind his back as he kissed her. "Hi. I've just seen the baby. She's beautiful. Like her mommy."

Cass looked at him. Her face had no color, but her eyes were bright. "She's not ours. You've got to get the police! Our baby was a boy—I heard Doc Barnes tell the nurse. But then they held up this girl. You've got to get my Michael back for me, Harley. You've got to find out what Doc Barnes did with him!"

Harley bent and kissed her again. "I'll speak to him the minute I leave you."

"Not to the doctor, he's on Lil's side! The police."

"OK." It seemed the only way to quiet her.

"You don't suppose they've killed Michael? They do, you know! They use newborn babies for blood sacrifices."

Harley made no attempt to understand. In a few hours, when she'd slept off the ether, she'd be clear again.

"What's that?" Cass pointed around him. "Behind your back."

Harley produced the flowers, hoping for a smile.

But Cass's eyes filled with tears. "See? *Blue* flowers. For a boy."

"No, honey! It's just—they match your eyes, and it's your favorite color."

Cass turned her head to the pillow. "Find my baby! I can't face Papa till I have a boy."

Harley sighed and set the flowers on the bedside table. "I'll see you later," he said.

Cass didn't seem to hear him.

"What is it this time?" Tobin came into the courtyard at the sound of the truck motor.

Harley hesitated. It would make him less of a man in Tobin's eyes. But who cared? "A girl!" he called.

"Figures." Tobin returned to the barn.

"Daddy, look!" Emily danced toward him, her chubby face aglow. She wore a faded red dress, too long; a sweater, too big; and a hood, pink and tasseled, fastened beneath her chin with a safety pin. Hand-me-downs, all.

He waited, impatient as she maneuvered the cobblestones with a brisk side-to-side toddle. She reached him, laughing, and grabbed his leg. "Daddy, look what I made!" A mud pie.

"That's wonderful." Her nose was running. "Don't you have a hanky?"

She dug into her pocket, withdrew a handkerchief and wiped her nose, smearing herself with mud. All the while she watched him. Harley realized she was waiting to hear about the baby.

"Well!" He tried to find the jovial tone he'd heard others use with children. "Mommy went to the hospital last night and, just like the doctor promised, she found a baby under the bed."

"A boy?"

"A girl."

Emily drew in her breath. "Mommy mad?"

Harley squatted, thinking that she might fall over backward from looking up at him so hard. "There was a mixup, you see. Mommy meant to find a boy, but found a girl instead. She's pretty. You'll like her."

Emily leaned forward and kissed him. He pulled away. "Go back and make more mud pies."

"Where you going?"

"I'm going to take Polly for a run." He wanted to get out, by himself, to think and plan.

"Take me?"

"No. Go back and play."

But as Harley cantered Polly up the wagon road a few minutes later, he heard a small voice calling. He turned.

Emily was following—stumbling, catching herself in the effort to get over the rutted road. "Go back, Emily, I can't take you."

Emily's legs lost the battle suddenly. She fell, face down, in a rut. She lifted her head, and her face crumpled into tears. "Daddy!"

Harley winced. Where had he heard a cry just like that? *Daddy!* Tobin, disappearing over the hill in a wagon. *Go back, Harley. I got no time for you now.*

Was that how easy it was to be like him?

Suddenly he was urging Polly to Emily's side. She stood now, and she reached for him. He swung her up; placed her on the saddle facing him. Her eyes widened and her hands grasped at his arm. Then she began to laugh.

Harley laughed back. He brushed the dirt from her face and from her dress. Then he spun her around and sat her in front of him.

They cantered up the hill and past the family graveyard. Harley glanced at Sailor's grave as they went by, then down at Emily's pink, tasseled bonnet. He smiled and hugged her.

For once in his life, he *knew* he had done something right.

CHAPTER TWENTY-THREE

O N AN AFTERNOON in the spring of the following year, Cass stood at her sink taking conciliatory swipes at the breakfast dishes and pondering her problems. In a wicker basket on the floor beside her was Michael. Asleep, thank goodness. For every good thing Cass could remember about Emily as a baby, she could think of two bad things for Michael.

"She doesn't have a very feminine temperament," Hitty was fond of saying.

Hitty was stupid, Cass thought. Masculine and feminine had nothing to do with it. Michael was just a bad child. You only had to look at her eyes—green, like a cat's!

Cass had insisted on using the name she'd picked for a boy. Her baby had been a boy, and she'd get him back one day, she was sure of it.

But, as she'd thought about it lately, she'd realized that God would never let her have the real Michael back until she kept her part of the bargain. She had to bring the Westcotts to

God. As a punishment for not doing so before, God had made her task even harder. He'd saddled her with this Michael—an evil child.

Cass had been going every week to Reverend Smith's house; they prayed for guidance and discussed possible methods of bringing the Westcotts to God.

The direct approach had not worked. Harley only grew angry when he was approached. He would do a lot of blaspheming, then get morose and go for a ride on Polly. Tobin wouldn't even listen to her. And Thomas just laughed whenever she cornered him.

Hitty was the worst of the bunch. She actually condoned the attitudes of her menfolk. "You'll tire yourself out, Cassandra. The Lord will gather His sheep when He's ready."

Cass had tried leaving literature lying around, and Bibles opened to appropriate pages. She had tried setting an example, praying often and conspicuously. Nothing worked.

But something *had* to work. She had to get her boy back for Papa.

Papa had been very sweet about the whole thing. "You brought about the meekening of the Westcotts, daughter, just as the angel promised," he'd said. "Heaven must have good reason to keep us waiting for the special child."

But Cass knew he hated her for failing him. Lil wasn't protecting her anymore—Lil might even be doing spells to make him hate her all the more!

Then the idea struck her.

Carrie's house was dreary there in the shadows of the woods, and Cass began to think that it was wrong of her to come calling so unexpectedly. Carrie probably wouldn't even remember her, they'd been introduced so briefly the night the barn burned. And Carrie might still be in mourning. It had been less than two years since her husband—

Of course! That was the reason for the dreariness—this was a house of mourning. She *should* go inside. No one from the Westcott family had ever paid the proper condolences. Hitty and Tobin had come twice, but no one had answered their knock.

There had been no funeral. Gossip said that Carrie had had her husband cremated at a place in Seneca and carried his ashes home in a Nabisco tin. Cass shivered—she probably had the ashes sitting around in there someplace.

But then, ashes weren't like a skeleton or a coffin. She had never heard of a ghost rising out of a Nabisco tin. Feeling braver, she went to the door and knocked.

The door swung open to reveal a pitch-black hall. For a moment it seemed that no one was there. Then she heard a voice. "What do you want?"

Cass blinked and strained to see the shadowy figure. "I'm Cass, Aunt Carrie. I don't know if you remember me, but—"

"Harley's wife."

"Oh, I'm so glad. I didn't want to come bursting in on you if—"

"What do you want?"

Cass hesitated. "Aunt Carrie, are you God-fearing?

There was a movement in the dark face. Aunt Carrie was smiling. "You might say I fear God."

"Well, I need advice," said Cass. "God has charged me with the souls of my husband and my in-laws. I've got to figure out how too save them. Can you help?"

"I might be able to," said Carrie. "Come in, Cassandra. I was just making a pot of tea."

There was only one light spot in Carrie's house, the kitchen at the end of the hall. Cass peeked into the living room as she passed. All she could make out was books—stacks and piles, thousands of books—and a strange odor. Probably all those books moldering.

The odor and the books were in the kitchen, too, though there seemed to be a greater attempt at order there. It was much like any other kitchen—not pretty; there weren't even any curtains at the windows, just dark green roller shades, but functional. There were hundreds of herbs and things lined up in glass jars; big kettles, a large round table, an old wood-burning stove, and a chopping block.

"You must do a lot of cooking."

"Hardly any." Carrie followed Cass's eyes to the bottles and kettles. "I make home remedies for a living. Will you take tea?"

The tea smelled funny, but Cass sipped it politely. "I was sorry to hear about your husband, Aunt Carrie."

"I miss him," said Carrie, "even though he's still with me in spirit."

Cass nodded and looked up at the jars, wondering if Carrie's husband might be with them in more than spirit.

"Tell me what you want me to help you with, my dear."

"Aunt Carrie, will you be truthful with me?"

"I'm always truthful."

"Why don't you associate with my in-laws?"

"Because I hate them," said Carrie.

Cass's eyes widened. "You mean you don't *like* them. You're not supposed to hate people."

"What we are supposed to do and what we actually do are often two different things."

Cass sighed. "I guess you can't help me, then. You're not a good Christian."

"Are you?"

"Yes! At least, I'm trying to be."

"And you don't hate anybody?"

"No! Especially any of my sisters. They're nice."

Carrie smiled. "All of them?"

Cass nodded. "Especially Lil. She did things for me. She made Papa love me. He didn't, until Lil *made* him."

"And how did she accomplish this?"

"She worked spells. She's a witch! She won't admit it, but she is."

"It must be handy to have a sister who's a witch."

"Well, she doesn't do things for me so much anymore."

"Why not?"

"I don't think she likes me since I took Harley away from her."

Carrie was silent, looking at Cass. "That wasn't a nice thing to do." There was a hint of amusement in her voice. "After all, if one does something nasty to a witch, that witch might do something nasty back."

"She wouldn't!" said Cass. "She loves me! At least, I'm sure she doesn't *hate* me."

"Well, if you're sure…after all, you know better."

Cass sat silent, looking into her tea. "Do you think she *would* do anything terrible?" she asked finally.

Carrie smiled. "I know what I'd do to a sister who stole my beau. Now tell me about your in-laws' souls."

❀ ❀ ❀

It was dark when Cass left Carrie's house. She felt relieved. Things were going to work out.

"Go ahead. See your Reverend Smith once a week and pray if you like. But when you come to me, we'll try something different. Maybe I'm old-fashioned, but I'm a great believer in the ancient remedies—charms and such."

"Won't we pray at all?"

"Oh, we'll say prayers of a sort. But whatever you do, Cassandra, don't tell anyone you're coming here. It would spoil the whole thing."

Of course Cass wouldn't tell. Carrie was her secret weapon.

During the next week she collected what Carrie needed for her charms—hairs from the heads of Harley, Tobin, Hitty, Frank, Emily, and Michael—and even from Upjohn. "Oh, yes, my dear, for you know Mr. Upjohn is an evil man, and he has a great deal of influence with your in-laws. Even he must be brought to God, or our whole campaign will be for naught."

And hair from the head of Lil.

After the crash it had seemed that things were as bad as they could get. But each month of 1931 brought an obvious worsening. People stopped saying, "It's bound to get better." Now they said, "Do you think it ever will?"

For the Westcotts that year the godsend was Hitty and her tourist haven. Even though most people did not have enough money to buy food or clothes, a few did seem to find money to get away from it all. Nearly every week, someone driving by saw the sign and stopped for the night. And though Nick and Lil had moved to a house in the village, Hitty had other boarders occasionally—schoolteachers mostly.

And Tobin was grateful for what came in. He hadn't had a call for the services of his bulls in over a year. He had not been able to rent any of his land, or even to sell any. His only income was the milk check from his slowly growing herd and Harley's rent for the red house.

When tax time rolled around, it was Hitty's cookie jar that came to the rescue. And those months that Tobin was short on his loan payments for the barn, the cookie jar again made the difference.

Hitty never said a word—she just went and got the money when he asked if she might happen to have that much. Usually she did.

Harley, too, had a wife with a cookie jar. But the sixteen dollars she earned each month at Calvary did not dent the expenses of two growing children. With increasing frequency Harley found himself borrowing from the few dollars he had saved for college courses.

There were plenty of band jobs that year—the same desire to escape which brought Hitty her tourists brought people out at night to dance and drink boot. But the jobs didn't pay what they used to. He and Cass together brought home less than three dollars for an evening's work; when Harley played a band date alone, he came home with only one dollar.

And so he kept scrounging for manual work.

He could count on picking up potatoes in Paris Hill each fall. But everyone else counted on picking up potatoes—a seemingly infinite number of workers for a finite number of potatoes. The man working the fastest earned the most at ten cents per hundred pounds, and once Harley took his place in the fields, his hands scooped like power shovels into the freshly turned row.

Each year at the potato harvest there were a few women— older women mostly, their hands and backs strong from years of hard work.

Then there was the mystery woman. She was younger than the others, and obviously unaccustomed to heavy weights, but she worked like a small tornado. She would fill her bag just a third of the way, gallop to the scale and back again, making up in speed what she lost in trips. Harley had noticed her at a dozen plantings and harvests of one kind or another, but she always wore a sunbonnet with a veil covering her face. She kept to herself at work and rest, and she never talked.

One day Harley chanced to glance up from his potatoes. The mystery woman was working half a field away. Just as he looked, she stood and stretched her tired muscles. The movement hit Harley as so familiar that he stopped his work and stared. The woman stooped back down and went on with her picking.

Harley rose and walked to her side. "Mother?" he said incredulously.

Hitty stopped work for a moment and sighed. "You're not going to tell your father, are you, Harley? We do need the money so badly."

He didn't tell Tobin. It was no time for pride, or for sadness, as old images tumbled. More and more, in the fall and winter of '31, they did all need the money so badly. The town raised the taxes on the farm, and the price of milk dropped even further. Tobin was sick a lot, and Harley had to handle the chores, giving up time in which he could have been earning a few dollars. And he wasn't able to get together enough money for even one correspondence course. In the spring, he told himself. He'd have it by spring.

Frank sank back into a coma that winter. For all the concert of minds between Hitty and Upjohn, he showed no sign of recovery.

Both the girls got whooping cough. It hit Michael the worst, sapping her strength and stealing the imps from her eyes. For months, into spring, she was sluggish and not herself.

"I don't know why you're so worried," Cass told Harley. "Michael is perfectly well. She's a much nicer child than she used to be."

Harley could only stare at her. "She doesn't even smile anymore! I'm calling Doc Barnes."

"We can't afford the doctor again. Besides, *I'm* nursing Michael."

"With what?"

"It's a home remedy, centuries old and very dependable."

"Let me see it."

When Cass showed it to him, Harley blanched. The stuff looked like cooked oatmeal, but was black and smelled like dead fish. "Where did you get this?"

"From Mr. Upjohn."

"Oh. Well."

What he really should make Cass stop, he decided, was her Bible reading. Each day she'd sit the two children on the sofa and read aloud for hours.

"Honest, Lil, she's driving me crazy. Is there any legal way I can make her stop reading the Bible to the kids?"

Lil laughed. "I can just imagine the judge's reaction. 'Am I to take it that you object to giving your children a Christian upbringing? Your wife tells me, Mr. Westcott, that you are not a churchgoing man. I suggest, Mr. Westcott, that you return home, fall on your knees, and give thanks for such a wife.'"

Lil should know. She'd taken her bar and become Mr. Sawyer's junior law partner.

The Bible readings continued. And so did Michael's illness. Finally Harley took the medicine to Upjohn. "What *is* this stuff you've got Cass giving Michael?"

Upjohn recoiled. "Keep it away from me! Take it out and bury it when you leave here!"

"What is it?"

"Poison."

"How do you know?" An incredible amount of perspiration was coming from Upjohn's forehead. "What's the matter with you?"

"Put it outside the door, Harley. I'll be all right."

Harley did as he was bidden, and Upjohn sank into his chair, mopping his brow.

"You allergic to it or something?"

"Yes."

"Where the hell do you suppose Cass got it?"

Upjohn seemed drained. His voice was barely a whisper. "Don't you know?"

Twice a week Cass had been leaving home "to go pray with the Reverend." It didn't take much investigation to find that she saw Reverend Smith only on Mondays. On Fridays—

"She evidently goes to Carrie," said Upjohn. "How long has she been praying with the Reverend twice a week?"

Harley thought back. "Since last spring."

"A year," said Upjohn. "What more could Carrie have asked?"

CHAPTER TWENTY-FOUR

DEAR CARRIE,

Please forgive the writing in this letter, but its the middle of the night, and I'm writing by light of a candle I hid away yesterday afternoon. I'm terrified Harley will wake and catch me, but I've got to get in touch with you.

I'm a prisiner, Carrie! That's why I haven't been to see you in so many weeks. I can't go any place alone in the truck anymore. I'm even forbiden to go see Reverand Smith, and they watch me all the time. Harley. Even Emily! (They've turned Emily completely against me, and she has a yellow tiger kitten that I'm sure is Mrs. Parkinson's cat!) Or Mr. Upjohn or Hitty or Lil. Even my mother! Lil brings her over a couple of mornings a week and she watches me all day.

They took Michael's medacine away from me. Harley said He'd break my arms if he ever caught me using it again. He claimed it was poison! And, oh, Carrie! It just tears me apart to watch Michael returning to her evil ways.

Yesterday she spilled her cereal on the floor and I could just see Satan in her eyes.

Harley hides my Bible. I can only read to the girls on Sunday now.

You've been so right about Lil, Carrie. I know that now. She hates me. She is doing witchcraft against me. She's bewitched everybody. I'm sure they mean to kill me! And I don't know who to turn to except you or the Reverand. Could you meet me in the hall on the way to the choirloft at Calvary some Sunday with more of Michael's medacine? That's one place they wouldn't think of to follow me. Or if you could come at night, I might be able to sneek out of the house after Harley is asleep.

But don't write. I'm sure they'd stop any letter. There is a rock just to the left of the Westcotts' mailbox. Leave a note under it. I'll check it every time I get a chance, even if I have to sneek up there at night.

Please don't fail me. I'm still reciting all the magic things you told me to say.

> *Love,*
> *Cassandra Lee*

P.S. They haven't found the charm under Gramppa Parmalee's bed yet. I hit it up in the springs real good, but he gets lower every day. Doc Barnes thinks he is going to die.

And I'm sure Mr. Upjohn hasn't found the red stuff. I smeared it on a bed slat right under his pillow.

I haven't used Mr. Upjohn's powder on Emily since you told me what it was. How evil that Mr. Upjohn is! (And the red stuff hasn't helped him a bit!) Hitty still wears the powder though. No wonder I can't reach her with God's message!

Dear Reverand Smith,

I have not been to see you these many weeks because I am prisiner in my own home. My husband has threatened

me with physcal violence, he has forbiden me to see you, and
he has taken my Bible away so that I may no longer read to
my dear children.

I thought God had deserted me, Reverand, and then the
Angel appeared to me again. He revealed four more witches
to me, and oh, how sad it is to tell you how close to my
heart it strikes. For the four are my own sister, Lilith, my
husband, Harley, Harley's tutor, Mr. Upjohn, and my
mother-in-law, Mehitable Westcott. The Angel says that
these four by their terribel, Satanic rites have turned my
mother against me, and my two dear children, so young
and impresionable, are being sucked into the Devil's
clutches. And they are working on my Papa. And that they
are planning to kill me!

I beg you not to tell my Papa about this, as the truth
about Lil would hurt him so. And if he's one of them now, he
might tell on me. Please help me. I'm afraid for my very life.

Awaiting your wise counsel, (Leave a note for me under
the mat of the 10th step leading to the choirloft at Calvary).
Cassandra Lee Westcott.

Cass sealed both letters and pinned them to the inside of
her dress. The next morning she asked for and was granted the
use of the truck. To her relief only Thomas was sent along to
chaperone. He was the easiest of them all. He always went to
Grogan's to buy rum-flavored candy, which left Cass just
enough time to run to the post office and get back to the grocery
store before Thomas.

The following day, Reverend Smith hitched up his buggy
and drove at a rapid trot to the Bascomb farm.

The family was finishing lunch as he pulled in. Helen and
Emma ran for broom and duster.

They didn't even have time to get to the parlor. Reverend
Smith leaped from his buggy and ran to the front door, not

waiting for Helen to answer before he opened it himself. "Paul! I've got to speak with you!"

Emma hung about the parlor door after it closed, not even pretending to dust.

Curt scowled at Helen. "Cass must be up to something again." He joined his mother at the door.

Reverend Smith paced as Paul read Cass's letter; it seemed that he would never finish the page. Then the Reverend realized that he *had* finished and was only staring at the words. He placed a comforting hand upon Paul's shoulder. "I know it's a shock, my son."

Paul folded the letter; carefully placed it in the envelope. "But no surprise, Reverend."

"You mean…you've known all along that Lil is a witch?"

"Not that she was." Paul handed over the letter, not meeting the Reverend's eyes. "Just that she would be."

The Reverend controlled his elation. "You have a family history of this sort of thing?"

Paul looked out at the maples. "You wouldn't remember the people built this place, Archie and Philimentha Stockbridge. They were my Ma and Pa. And Crazy Lizzy was my aunt."

"Then according to the story, your mother—"

"Disappeared? Truth was, my Pa sent her packing. He'd had enough."

"Of what?"

Paul was silent, then he sighed. "My Ma was a witch, Reverend. There was a whole pack of them—at least one person from every family that lived around these woods. There was a Cole—Hitty's grandfather Jason, that must be how Hitty comes by it—"

"And was there a Westcott?"

Paul took out his handkerchief and pretended that the moisture which appeared in his eyes was caused by specks of dust. "Thomas Westcott's father, John. He and my Ma—they were more than just friends, Reverend. It was *him* turned her bad! And that goat-faced Thomas had the nerve to tease me and Alice about our Ma deserting us. I should have told him. I always regretted I didn't tell Thomas about his own father."

"You did the Christian thing," said Reverend Smith.

"Sometimes the Christian thing ain't the *satisfying* thing." Paul rose in agitation. "After he sent my Ma away, Pa decided Alice and me needed a mother. So he got Aunt Lizzy to marry him."

"How did he get the divorce from your mother?"

"He didn't. He and Aunt Lizzy told the minister my Ma had gone home to see her people, got sick and died there. I guess that's one of the things drove Aunt Lizzy daft—being so guilty about living in sin and all. Well, Pa hated that house in the woods, so we moved down here to the meadow when Aunt Lizzy came. But then she got it into her head that my Ma was going to come back to get even with her, or put a hex on her or something. Packed her things and moved to the woods house—said that was the last place my Ma or her evil would ever think to look for her. Then my Pa got took, too. He developed this notion that it was because he hadn't loved our real Ma enough that she went bad—now that he loved her enough, the next time he met her she'd just naturally forsake her evil ways and come back. So one day he just deeded the place to Aunt Lizzy, packed me and Alice into the buggy, and away we all went, looking for her—even caught up to her a couple of times."

"Did she come back?"

"Hell, no! And I was so ashamed to be her son that after Pa died, I started calling myself Bascomb. Alice, too, though Alice is ornery, and she never would come right out and condemn Ma. Anyway I thought I was shut of the evil till Lil come along, the spitting image of my Ma. I tell you, Reverend, I've prayed for that girl. I've done everything a man could to guard her. If only I hadn't brought her here—"

"Paul! We know now that it was heaven's will."

"But now Lil's got it, Reverend. Whatever it is about this place that makes people evil and crazy, Lil's got it!"

"And we must do something about it," said the Reverend.

"What *do* they do about witches nowadays?"

❄ ❄ ❄

That afternoon Reverend Smith penned a note and took it to Calvary in Seneca, where he hid it under the mat of the tenth stair leading to the choirloft.

> *My poor Cassandra,*
>   *How terrified you must be! Rest assured, however. Your father and I will not allow anything to happen to you or the children. (Yes, my dear, I took your letter to your father. It was the best thing to do.) He and I are formulating a plan by which to trap the witches. We ask you to be brave and patient.*
>
>   *Your Servant in Christ,*
>   *Reverend Philip Smith*

The same afternoon, Curt and Emma went down to Sawyer's law office to tell Lil what they'd heard at the parlor door.

Curt patted Lil's hand. "Don't worry. This is the twentieth century. They can't do anything to you."

"Oh, Curt, that's not so!" Lil paced to the window. "Heaven only knows what laws are still on the books. I'll have to look them up. But aside from that, if word got out and people got scared…"

"Don't you think we ought to warn Harley and Mrs. Westcott and that teacher fellow?" said Curt.

Lil's face brightened. "Of course! Mr. Upjohn will know what to do."

They dropped Lil in front of the big house at Spring Farm.

"You want us to go in with you?"

"No," said Lil. "Go down and keep Cass occupied."

She didn't find Upjohn at the house. Hitty sent her to the barn, where Tobin directed her to the west pasture.

The day was warm, unseasonably so for May. Across the pasture, by the fence which bordered the Crazy Lizzy, Lil could see Upjohn. She smiled at the thought of Toynbee Upjohn driving fence posts. Yet there was no hesitation in the arc of his sledge-hammer. She found herself wondering again how old he was.

Lil approached quietly, absorbed in the incongruity of the Upjohn before her and the Upjohn she knew from the class-room. She was almost upon him before she thought to announce herself. "Hello."

Lost in his pounding, Upjohn didn't hear her. The sledge-hammer came to momentary rest, and Lil tapped his shoulder. He started, then spun, raising his arm as though for protection. His elbow plowed into her shoulder, knocking her backward onto the ground.

The force of the fall took her breath away. For a few moments she was only vaguely aware that Upjohn was kneeling beside her. "My God, Lilith, I'm so sorry!" He sat her up. "Are you hurt?" His hands moved over her blouse, brushing away grass and bits of dirt.

Lil sat still, allowing herself to be handled. "I'm all right, I think." His touch was tender and, as her equilibrium returned, she became more and more aware of it.

"I gave you quite a jab." He bent down, with one hand supporting her back, and carefully examined the shoulder. "I hit you so hard it ripped your blouse. I'm afraid you'll have a bruise." Not thinking how close their faces would be, he turned to her.

Well, he supposed he had known, but he had expected the pleasure to be his alone. When he looked at her though, she was waiting for him. And her eyes were not innocent. The surprise he felt must have shown on his face, for Lil flushed noticeably. Upjohn drew in his breath—she felt it too. But, guilty and mortified, she thought she was alone. He should release her that instant, help her up, pretend he had not noticed.

Instead, his hands—one on her shoulder, the other on her back—tightened.

Lil's eyes flew to his, the shock of realization now hers.

Toynbee Upjohn forgot what he was and why he was. With a cry he pulled Lil to him. One kiss. That would be all. One kiss to cherish—long and deep, deep and deeper.

Now he would release her.

If only she would pull away! Quickly he turned his head, touched his cheek to her lips. "Help me, my dearest. Tell me to stop!"

"Stop," Lil whispered, but she pressed closer.

"Lilith!" He took her lips again. Quickly, roughly. Then he sprang to his feet and seized the sledgehammer. He'd already driven that rail, but he drove it deeper still, swinging blindly until the rail was a splintered mess and his strength was gone. Only then did he allow himself to look back.

Lil was kneeling where he had left her, her head bowed in her hands. Upjohn touched his forehead as though it ached. Then he went to her, started to put out a hand, thought better of it. "Come, my dear. Let's sit over here on the wagon until we get ourselves back together."

They were silent for a long time, neither touching nor exchanging glances.

"I'm not going to tell you I'm sorry," said Upjohn at last, "because I'm not. And I won't claim that it was temporary insanity, as I am a most untemporary creature. I will promise that it will never happen again."

She nodded, wondering how she could ever look at him. How willingly she'd allowed—no, not allowed—how she had *wanted* him to kiss her! She wasn't sure that she would have stopped him from doing—anything. Her mind had been filled with nothing but him. Not Nick, not Harley, not guilt—only Upjohn.

"Was my grandmother that way?" she said. "A tramp?"

Upjohn smiled. "I'd flattered myself that you were responding out of some real regard or feeling for me. I didn't realize you would respond that way to any man."

"I wouldn't!" Lil met his eyes now. "It was you."

Upjohn shrugged. "Well, you could not qualify as a tramp then, could you?"

His tone gently teased her. It made things better, and Lil smiled.

Upjohn looked toward the Crazy Lizzy and the sky beyond. "Surely," he said softly, "nothing will begrudge a creature one kiss for all of eternity." He drew a long breath. "Now, my dear, tell me what brings you to the Westcott pasture."

"I hadn't taken into account that Cass might be insane," he said as she finished.

"That's a terrible thing to say!" Lil raised her chin. "You and Harley haven't been clear with Mama and me about this big campaign to 'keep an eye on Cass.' 'Overtired,' 'acting funny.' What does that mean? When she tells Reverend Smith she's a prisoner in her own home, she's not far off. You've even got Emily watching her!"

"We didn't want to alarm you," said Upjohn. "We discovered that she'd been seeing Carrie, who was supplying her with 'medicine' for Michael—a slow poison that eventually would have killed the child."

Lil closed her eyes. "How could anyone *do* anything like that? How could Carrie be so—"

"Evil?'" He smiled. "Well, these woods conceived her."

"How do you know?"

Upjohn shrugged. "The trysts of Frank and Flora in these woods were common knowledge."

Lil looked at the woods. "They almost conceived a child of Cass's and Harley's, too, didn't they?"

"Yes." That smile again. "I'd guess some stronger power prevented the conception."

"I wish Harley had known that before it was too late."

"I do too. I wish someone had had the opportunity to tell him."

Lil laughed. "How could anyone besides Cass possibly have known?" Her smile faded as she saw Upjohn's eyes. "*You* knew," she said. A shiver touched her spine. "How?"

"Don't be foolish," she heard him say. "And don't *ever* be frightened of me, Lilith."

"I wasn't," she said quickly.

He smiled. "It's these woods. Their proximity plays havoc with the mind."

He rose, looking off across the pasture. "Is that Emily?"

She was running toward them, calling, but her voice could not reach them.

Lil looked at Upjohn. The muscles of his face were tight.

Now they heard what Emily was saying. "Aunt Lil! Gramma says come help look! Michael's gone!"

CHAPTER TWENTY-FIVE

CASS REALIZED THAT she was just running, back and forth, from the edge of the orchard to the old house.

She forced herself to stop, but she couldn't calm herself. Emotion pulsed from the pit of her stomach to the hollow of her throat, gathering into knots. She listened to the others—Tobin, far down the avenue, searching the road and the orchards; Henrietta, tearful, searching the barn; Hitty, picking her way through the tall grass and burdocks beyond the big house; and from the woods behind the red house—

Listen, how *they* pretended to call. Curt, Mama, Lil, Upjohn.

Thank God Papa was there, too.

Cass sank onto a bench by the barn. "Please, God! Let us find her!" But a voice inside kept blocking her prayer: *They've taken her for a blood sacrifice.*

Like they'd taken the real Michael? No. She couldn't believe it. Even if they were witches, they were fond of Michael now. They wouldn't harm her.

Who would? God? Could God have taken her baby to punish her for not bringing religion to the Westcotts?

Crazy. No one would hurt an innocent baby, even God.

She had to think.

They'd been there in the yard with a wicker basket of wet wash—she and Emily. Naturally, always Emily.

Then Papa had come. And soon after, Mama and Curt, adding their eyes to Emily's. Michael, in her yellow puckered dress with the baby duck on the bib, had been patting sand into a high pointed mound in the sandbox by the edge of the woods.

When they got to the end of the first clothes line, Emily began to sing. "Jingle Bells." Papa laughed at "Jingle Bells" in May, and they all joined in. Cass worked down the next line, hanging sheets and towels, Michael blocked from sight by the flapping expanse.

Then Curt had left Emma and Paul, and come over to talk to her. A decoy. Yes, that would have been the time.

Cass shook her head, trying not to think what she was thinking. Someone—something—back in the woods, beckoning to Michael.

And hadn't Lil arrived with Upjohn? With her blouse torn? From creeping through the woods. Or from Michael's desperate fingers.

No! She couldn't think such things. They wouldn't do that to her just when she was beginning to love Michael! Or would they?

And which of them were *they*?

Cass rose from the bench as she saw Harley crossing the courtyard. She didn't want to talk to him. She pretended to faint. Nothing to it, just fall to the ground, keep your eyes closed, and don't giggle. As Harley carried her into the big house and put her on Hitty's sofa, he seemed far away.

When he left, she still didn't open her eyes. She cuddled against the back of the sofa and continued to figure things out.

As he left the house, Harley remembered the old well. He'd tested the boards the previous fall; they couldn't have rotted through in one winter. And that well had already claimed its life—half a century ago, when Thomas and his parents took ill from its water and Thomas' father actually died from it.

All the same he headed for the well. The path entered the woods close to Michael's sandbox, crossed fifty yards of underbrush, then stopped at a tiny clearing.

And as Harley saw the well, his heart seemed to stop. Michael was squatting at its edge, peering down into it. Two of the boards had been pulled to the side. How?

He stood perfectly still, afraid to speak, afraid to startle the child lest she slip.

Michael turned and saw him. "Big hole, Daddy!"

"Yes it is," Harley said. "Come here and I'll give you a piggyback ride."

When he had her safely in his arms, he went to kick the boards back into place. They were much too heavy. He swung Michael to his hip; leaned down and wrestled them back. Incredible that Michael had had the strength to move them. Tomorrow he'd cement the damn thing over.

Cass lay on Hitty's sofa, tracing the cut-velvet pattern with her fingers—great splotches of something, joined by curlicues and spirals. Flowers, Hitty said. They weren't. A calm settled over her. The pattern had no solution, just as there was no solution to Michael's disappearance. Michael was gone, exactly as Muriel had gone, and the world would never know what had happened to her. Cass had started to love Michael, and they'd spirited her away.

The front door opened. Tobin, Hitty, Henrietta, Thomas. Emily behind them.

"Harley found her!"

Cass looked at the pattern on the sofa and smiled.

"Come on, Miss Cass." Henrietta was pulling her up. "We've got the truck outside. We'll take you down to your house."

Still smiling, Cass allowed them to take her.

"Look, Mommy!" Emily pointed as the truck neared the house. "Aunt Lil has her."

Lil was wearing a yellow blouse, the same color as Michael's dress. But Michael was nowhere to be seen.

Yet when Tobin stopped the truck in the driveway, all the others got out and ran toward Lil, calling Michael's name. Cass followed, puzzled. Making such a fuss over Lil's blouse—

Lil's *moving* blouse, yellow with a duck on the bib. Bouncing, laughing.

Cass's eyes focused on that moving patch of yellow. It was a blouse; then, suddenly, it became Michael. She stopped, her eyes watering. The yellow jumped and flickered, from baby to blouse and back to baby.

It was wonderful. It was some witchcraft that Lil was doing!

Cass squinted, trying to change Michael back to the blouse. But the blouse wouldn't come. The lips on the Michael image moved and said "Mommy."

Cass squinted harder. "Make the blouse come back, Lil!"

Everyone turned to her.

"Are you all right?" said Paul.

They were all waiting for her to speak. And suddenly she knew. "Where did you find her?" Cass tried to make her voice seem normal.

Harley hesitated. "She was playing in the woods."

Harley was lying. The apparition in Lil's arms was not Michael. It was a demon conjured by Lil.

She looked at it, playing its part. Michael would have been pleased with her prank and gobbled the unexpected attention. The thing in Lil's arms acted accordingly. Its eyes sparkled, its fingers wiggled. Cass couldn't let them know she knew what it was. She had to react as though the thing really was Michael. Yes. *Michael* had been bad, and *Michael* had to be punished. "Put her down."

As she lowered Michael to the grass, Lil glanced at Harley. He moved forward. Cass picked up a stick. Michael began to whimper, backing away stiff-legged. With a cry Cass sprang, the stick raised. Harley and Lil closed on Cass, taking the blows themselves.

Cass struggled; her body ached to feel the stick strike the baby.

"Call Doc Barnes! She must be in shock!"

Yes, she'd pretend she was in shock. She crumpled and let them carry her into her bedroom.

And when they'd left the room—"She'll be all right when she wakes"—Cass pulled a pillow over her face to make it darker, and tried to reason. But in the warmth, the softness, it was too difficult. She drifted off to sleep, wondering what they were saying, that murmur of voices, of the enemies all around.

Harley and Lil went back to the lawn after putting Cass to bed. Paul was kneeling, halfheartedly telling Michael she'd been a bad girl to wander away.

Michael didn't seem to hear a word. She stood staring at the door where she had last seen her mother. And when Paul said that since she had been bad, she had better spend the rest of the day in bed, she preceded them to the front bedroom.

Emily's bed stood against one wall. Patty, the doll Nick had given her, was sleeping beneath the coverlet. Against the other wall was the small iron crib. Michael climbed up over the railing by herself and curled into a ball on her side. One hand began to twist at her hair. The other encircled the nearest bar and began to slide up and down.

The others tiptoed out, but Harley stayed. Michael seemed not even to know he was there.

He bent and untied the strings of her brown shoes. It would be nice to buy her some white ones, but, besides costing more, white shoes needed occasional cleaning and it was hard enough to get Cass to do dishes, lately. He slipped off the shoes, then the socks—hot and damp with the odorless sweat of babies. Harley squeezed the fat little feet, and Michael's toes wiggled back. He looked up hopefully, just in time to see a flicker of mischief cross her face, then die, like an ignition almost catching. He squeezed the feet again. Nothing happened.

Harley sighed and felt useless. His hands made a move toward Michael, then plunged into his pockets. He was no damn good at these things.

As he turned to go, his eyes lighted on Patty—made of wood, right to the short brown bob, but something to hug, even if she wasn't soft. He offered Patty to Michael. "I don't think Emily will mind if you sleep with her this once."

Michael took the doll.

Why hadn't he got Michael a cuddly cloth doll of her own? He had four dollars left in his college fund. He'd take it and get her one, today.

They all sat in the sunny blue kitchen, sipping coffee and staring at one another.

"Lil," said Emma finally, "you'd best see to their supper tonight. Cass might not be able, and Michael will need looking after."

"They'll be all right tomorrow," said Paul. He looked around. "Michael, especially. Kids bounce right back. And Cass—" He stopped. It just wasn't normal. She'd been about to kill Michael. And then his eyes moved to Lil, to Harley and Hitty, to Upjohn. Cass had been bewitched! "She'll be all right, I guess. Had a little shock, maybe a little sunstroke."

"Sure," they said. "That's it."

And all sat silent again.

"Damn it all!" Harley finally said. "It wasn't sunstroke, Mr. Bascomb! And it wasn't shock. Cass has been acting peculiar since Michael was born, and it's getting worse. She's been acting—"

"Crazy," Tobin finished.

Paul whipped around. "That's a mighty strong word, Mr. Westcott!"

"It's a mighty strong way Cass was acting," said Tobin.

"Please, Paul." It was Emma. "We got to face it. We have a problem."

"I think we ought to have a doctor look at Cass, Pa."

Paul turned and stared at Curt.

"What kind of a doctor?"

"A *head* doctor."

"No!" Paul jumped to his feet and began to pace. Curt was acting like *he* was bewitched. He turned and peered at his son. Was it possible? Looked a little queer around the eyes. And Emma. Had they gotten her, too? Good Lord! His poor Cassie was surrounded.

He leveled a finger at the bunch of them. "Any of you call a head doctor, you'll answer to me. That girl's not crazy. I'm on to what you're up to. All of you!"

Lil stood up. There had to be a showdown sometime. "Papa," she said. "I'm *not* a witch."

Paul stiffened. "What are you talking about?"

"Curt and I told her, Paul. We listened at the parlor door this morning, then went to town and told her."

Paul stared at Emma, dumbstruck.

"What's she talking about?" Harley asked Lil.

Lil told him.

Harley lowered his face into his hands. "What are we going to do with her?"

"You're not going to harm her!" said Paul.

"Nobody wants to harm her," said Curt.

"Well, it don't look that way to me! Talking about head doctors…"

"Pa, you have to admit, there *is* insanity in the family. Look at Crazy Lizzy."

Thomas slapped his knee. "I *knew* you were Paul Stockbridge."

Paul ignored him. "Your great-Aunt Lizzy wasn't crazy," he said to Curt. "She just acted strange."

"So does Cass, Pa, and it doesn't have a thing to do with witchcraft."

"That's what you think," said Paul. "I'm not so sure Aunt Lizzy's strangeness wasn't caused by some hex of my Ma's, and I'm not sure Cass's strangeness isn't caused by some hex of theirs." He pointed to Lil, Harley, and Upjohn.

For the first time Upjohn spoke. "What, sir, do you think—"

"This isn't any business of yours," said Paul.

"I beg your pardon!" Upjohn rose to his feet. "Your daughter has publicly accused me of witchcraft. She may have imperiled my life."

"Not likely," said Paul. "People don't kill witches anymore."

"You obviously have not read accounts of the Blymer case just four years back," said Upjohn. "Three men murdered a man they thought had bewitched them. Cass has imperiled the lives of everyone in this room—including *you* by association. After all, according to Cass, you are the father of a witch. Might you not be a witch yourself?"

"That's crazy!"

"No more so than to think that Lilith is a witch. Or Harley. Or Hitty. Don't you think, sir, that it is more logical to assume that Cass is suffering a temporary mental imbalance than to assume that half of the people in this room are witches and all the others, with the exception of you, are bewitched?"

Paul didn't answer. He looked at his feet; he looked toward Cass's room. He actually took a step in that direction.

Then he turned and left the house.

"I think," Emma said as she watched him ride away, "you might have given him a doubt, Mr. Upjohn. Take me on home, Curt. He'll need gentling."

Tobin, Hitty, and Thomas left on the heels of the Bascombs.

On his way out the door, Tobin touched Harley's shoulder. "Don't worry, son. We'll work things out." He drew some letters from his pocket. "Your mail," he said. "Got it out of the box when I was up by the gate looking for Michael." Again he patted Harley's shoulder and, finding no more words, he left.

Harley, Lil, and Upjohn remained. They finished the first pot of coffee; Lil put up another.

"What am I going to do?" Harley asked over and over. "How can I leave her alone with the kids after this?"

It was Upjohn who said it. "Perhaps, Harley, you should have her committed. Or at least consider the possibility."

"It's *not* a possibility," said Harley.

They lapsed into silence.

Speaking to neither of them in particular, Lil said, "You don't really think she's crazy, do you?"

Neither answered.

"Anyway," said Lil, "to commit her we'd have to be able to prove insanity, and I don't think we could. After all, what has she really done? Maybe she *was* in shock when she went after Michael. And I blame myself for the business with Carrie. I asked you not to tell Cass about her."

Harley was sorting through his mail. More rejection letters. He opened one and crumpled it. He thought again of how he had found Michael. "When you two were looking for Michael, did either of you pass the old well out back?"

"That was the first place I looked," said Upjohn.

Harley crumpled another slip. "Were the boards in place?"

"I tested them. Why?"

Harley opened another envelope, shaking his head. "I just don't understand how she had the strength to move them. I didn't tell anyone, but two boards were up and she was right on the edge—"

And then Harley forgot about Michael. He didn't see the shadow that crossed Upjohn's face.

For what he was holding in his hand was not a rejection slip, but a check. "I'm a *writer!*"

Lil jumped up and looked over his shoulder. "Five dollars!"

Upjohn looked too. "From *Weird Stories*? Well, well." He plucked it from Harley's fingers. "We'll frame it, anyway."

Harley laughed and retrieved his check. "You know what I'm going to do with this money? Buy a doll for Michael."

"What money?" Cass stood in the door of the kitchen.

"I sold a story, hon! They sent me five dollars."

"And you're going to spend it on a doll?"

Harley's grin faded. "Don't you even want to congratulate me?"

"Of course, I think it's wonderful. But the children need so many really important things."

Harley sighed and went to her. "We worried about you for nothing, didn't we?"

CHAPTER TWENTY-SIX

HARLEY DIDN'T KNOW anything about dolls, but he figured Edwards' Dry Goods Store was the place to look. The saleslady was Florence Comstock, one of Maybelle Horton's clique. Harley checked her hemline. Mid-calf. "Do you have any dolls, Mrs. Comstock?"

"Table Ten," she said in a tone that stopped just short of rudeness.

There were more dolls on the table than he had expected. He went down the line, squeezing each one—all wooden.

"Something special you're looking for?"

Harley jumped. He hadn't realized that Florence was following him. "Don't you have any dolls made of cloth?"

"They aren't fashionable anymore."

"This is for my youngest daughter. She's two."

"That's too young for a doll, she'll ruin it. You should get her a teddy bear. I'm sure if you asked your wife—"

Harley held up both hands. "Just show me a nice little cloth doll, Mrs. Comstock."

She sniffed. "How about rubber?"

"Cloth."

There was a woman at the next counter looking at yard goods. It seemed to Harley that she was paying more attention to his conversation with Florence than to her shopping. She edged down the table, the better to hear. Harley turned his back. Florence was muttering and checking the dolls. "I'm afraid you're out of luck."

"Maybe you've got something tucked away in a drawer."

Florence let out a sigh and opened the drawer beneath the counter. "This is all we've got." She began to close the drawer.

"Wait a minute!" A cloth foot stuck up among the wooden dolls. Harley grasped it and pulled.

She was a foot high and all of cloth, wearing a white grosgrain sunsuit with red rickrack and a matching sunbonnet. Her hair was black, her eyes blue. Harley grinned. "She looks like my wife. How much is she?"

"I'd forgotten about those. Mr. Edwards marked them down to get rid of them. Ninety-eight cents."

"Can you wrap her as a gift?"

As Mrs. Comstock wrapped the doll, Harley wandered; and as he wandered he became increasingly aware of the lady who'd been at the yard-goods counter. She was following him, staring. Every time he looked her way, she averted her eyes.

He turned his thought to the four dollars and two cents' change he had coming. He'd present it to Cass and tell her to do anything she liked with it—even take a singing lesson.

Of course, he could take Emily a present, too. He'd never gotten Emily a present. Casting around for an item that looked like her, he saw a china kitten, a yellow tiger with a blue bow. It looked almost like the kitten that Emily had selected for her own, from all the cats ranging the farm. Cass would never allow that kitten into the house. Maybe this china kitten would make up.

The woman from the yard-goods counter followed Harley to the cash register. "Wrap this kitten, too, would you, Mrs. Comstock?" The woman was almost beside him now, examining a fountain pen. "Excuse me," said Harley, "should I know you?"

"What?"

"You've been watching me ever since I came in. I guess I should know you, but I'm sorry, I don't recall your name."

"Smith," she said.

"Reverend Smith's wife," volunteered Florence.

She'd witnessed his wedding! "I'm sorry, I met you just once, and I was kind of nervous."

And now it made sense. She must know the contents of Cass's letter to the Reverend. She thought she was watching an honest-to-goodness witch!

He decided to meet the situation head on. "I've been meaning to call on your husband, Mrs. Smith, concerning the letter he received from my wife."

Amanda's eyes widened. "I don't know what you're talking about."

"Just tell your husband that I'll be calling on him, will you? Perhaps in the morning."

"Our parsonage is open to anyone—regardless of faith."

"Of course." Harley smiled as pleasantly as he could, took his parcels and his change, and left.

Amanda stood rooted until the door closed. "Of all the nerve!"

"Cheeky young man, isn't he?" said Florence.

Amanda rolled her eyes. "If you only knew!"

"Well, I can guess. I know his mother."

Amanda snapped to attention. "*What* do you know about his mother?"

Florence raised her eyebrows. "She's not what I'd call my kind of Christian."

Amanda drew in her breath. "I had no idea anyone else knew—the Reverend and I just found out this morning! Of course, we'd known that there were some in the village, but we hadn't known exactly who."

Florence hesitated. She was about to be privy to spice—if only she could find out *what* spice. "You and your husband have only been here ten years," she said carefully, "but we old-timers in the village—there isn't much that gets away from us."

"How have you been able to live with these people in your midst?"

"It hasn't been easy."

"Aren't you frightened? When is it the worst?"

Florence groped. "Well, the times when we think that they..."

"Like Halloween?"

Halloween. Witches. *Hitty Westcott?* Florence's head jerked.

Amanda took it as a nod. "Have they actually ever done anything to any of the villagers?" said Amanda.

"I'm not sure."

"How many of them do you know for sure?"

"Besides Hitty? Well, let's see—which ones have *you* heard about?"

"Hitty and her son, and the tutor at their house, the red-headed Bascomb girl, and Mrs. Parkinson."

"Fancy that," said Florence. Then she realized that Amanda was waiting. "Well, there aren't many more. There used to be old Crazy Lizzy." That wouldn't do any harm, seeing she was dead. "And then there's—" her mind searched the village. She certainly couldn't blacken any Presbyterian names and, seeing who she was talking to, she'd better stay clear of the Methodists. "Father Lawrence," she said.

Amanda rocked back on her heels. Such a kindly-looking man, with a smile and a hello for everyone, Catholic or no. "I wouldn't have thought it!" She stepped closer to Florence and looked around furtively, although there was not another soul in the store. "Of course, you realize the significance of the things that Westcott boy bought."

"Not really," said Florence.

"He insisted upon a *cloth* doll, didn't he? And who did he say it looked like?"

"His wife." Florence was still perplexed.

"They stick pins in *cloth* dolls. He's evidently planning to work a hex on his poor little wife. You heard him mention his wife's letter she wrote my husband begging for help."

"Mercy! What was the cat for?"

"Well isn't it obvious? They change china cats into real cats! They're called familiars. They already have *one* that we know of."

"My. And it was such an innocent-looking thing."

"Anyone want what's left of the macaroni and cheese?" Nick glanced around the table, then scraped the last of the macaroni onto his plate, taking care to get all the chewy bits from the rim. "Get a hell of an appetite working that quarry. Which reminds me, Harley, I found out this afternoon one of the guys is lighting out for California next week. Why don't you take a run up and talk to the foreman tomorrow? I'll put in a word for you."

"Oh, Nick!" said Cass. "That would be wonderful. What time should Harley be there?"

Nick winked at Upjohn and cocked his head toward Harley. "He hasn't said he's interested."

"I'll take anything," said Harley, "long as they pay me."

"They'll pay you good," said Nick. "Get there at noon. Roberts is at his best when he eats." He patted his stomach. "That was a fine meal, Lil."

Then he stiffened and looked down at the floor.

Purring, rubbing against his leg, was Emily's yellow tiger kitten. Nick flew from his chair, sending it clattering to the floor. He flattened against the wall. "Get it away from me!"

Cass dived for the kitten. It evaded her grasp and streaked for the living room. "How did that beast get in here?" she asked.

"I don't know," said Emily.

"You're lying! Get it out of here, and if I ever see it in this house again I'll kill it!"

Nick covered his face. "Don't talk about killing, Cass. Just get it out of the house!"

"I *will* kill it," said Cass.

"Stop! Nick's teeth started chattering.

Lil ran for a blanket, and bundled him up. "It's all right, sweetheart. We'll keep it away from you."

"Is it always this bad?" Upjohn asked her softly.

"Only when they get close," said Lil. She knelt with her arms around Nick, trying to warm away his chills. "I guess it's because—" She stopped, and glanced at Nick.

"Go ahead," he muttered. "I think Cass should hear it."

Lil nodded and held him closer. "He and his parents came home from Mass one night—Nick was about seven. There was a cat he was fond of. She'd just had a litter." Lil paused as she felt Nick shudder, but he nodded. She went on. "The cat had gotten into the house somehow. She was on the kitchen table eating some cheese left over from supper. Nick's father took his shotgun off the wall. Nick ran to protect his cat, but before he got there, his father fired. The cat exploded right in front of Nick's eyes, all over everything—all over him. And then his father went out and got the kittens, and drowned them in a pail of water in the sink."

"Kittykittykitty," came Emily's voice from the living room.

"Kidykidykidy," echoed Michael.

Nick was looking up at Cass now, and his eyes were gentle. "I wouldn't want your kids feeling about you the way I felt about my father. When he died, I didn't even go to the funeral."

That night, remembering how gently he had looked at her, Cass decided that Nick was her friend. Lil hadn't been able to turn him against her.

That made four she could count on—Reverend and Mrs. Smith, Carrie, and Nick. Maybe she should write to Nick and tell him what Lil and Harley were planning to do to her. But Lil and Harley might intercept the letter. They might have spies in the post office. The *whole town* might be on their side. Had they intercepted the letters to Reverend Smith and Carrie? There'd been no reply from Carrie under the stone today. Maybe it was too soon. But if there was nothing under the stone tomorrow, and nothing from Reverend Smith at Calvary on Sunday, then—somehow, she must find a way to talk to Nick.

Harley started for the quarry at 11:40 the next day. It was only a ten-minute drive, but he stretched it.

Maybe he hadn't dressed right. Not that he should have worn a collar and tie, but he'd rejected his work clothes, too. Roberts probably thought of him as a spoiled rich kid with soft hands. Work clothes might seem, to Roberts, condescension on Harley's part. Harley had finally settled on a worn pair of brown wool pants five years out of style and a gray flannel shirt that had also seen better days.

Jesus! he wanted this job. Nick was probably earning twenty-five dollars a week. What if Harley started pulling down fifteen a week steady? And then if a few more stories sold? He could go back to college, the kids could have brand-new clothes, and Cass could go back to her voice teacher.

He remembered then that he'd planned to see Reverend Smith that morning. Oh well, time enough.

He parked near the entrance of the quarry.

Harley could see Nick standing with three men near a pickup truck at the end of a dirt track. Harley checked his watch—five to twelve.

As he slowly approached the group, it occurred to him that this Nick was not the Nick he knew. His eyes didn't twinkle, he made no wisecracks. He and the other men were measuring and conferring, marking the rock with white X's. A drill bit was being set up.

Then the noon whistle blew, and Nick swung around. "Lunchtime!" He saw Harley standing there, hands in his pockets. "Hey, Westcott! Whatcha doing, slumming?" Nick clapped him on the shoulder and gave him a wink. "How about some lunch, long as you're here—I think Lil might have packed an extra sandwich. Roberts, this here's Westcott, guy I was telling you about."

"Glad to meet you, Westcott. Nick tells me you know all about handling dynamite."

Harley stared at him, appalled.

The three men burst into laughter, and now Roberts clapped Harley on the shoulder. "Don't worry, son. Nick and Clarence, here, do our dynamiting. We'll be needing you for the crusher and the shovel."

They skirted the quarry to the woods on the far side where they seated themselves on a grassy bluff some forty feet above the deepest and oldest part of the quarry. A pool of deep blue water had formed in the bottom of the pit, making their view almost picturesque. Other workmen joined them.

The men settled down to their lunches.

"Damn it!" said one. "I'm so sick of peanut butter, I could—"

"The way you keep having kids," said Nick, "I don't think Gladys has much time to think about sandwiches."

"What's kids got to do with sandwiches?"

Nick tossed the complainer one of his own. "Here. Tuna fish. Give me your peanut butter." He handed Harley a sandwich. "I think that's roast beef."

And thus the noon hour went, the men discussing the contents of their lunch pails, then stretching out on the grass to snooze and comment on the unseasonable warmth of the sun.

When he had finished eating, Nick rolled onto his stomach with his head hanging over the bluff, and looked down.

Harley sat awkwardly, wondering how he should conduct himself. Roberts and Clarence were both stretched out. But if he stretched out too, it might seem he was trying to be too much one of the group. He moved on hands and knees to Nick. "Do you think he'll consider me for the job?"

"Oh, you got the job. It's all set."

"That's great! I don't know how to thank you."

Nick's eyes grew serious. "You can thank me by making sure Cass doesn't hurt either of those kids, Harley. She alone with them right now?"

"No, but she's OK, Nick. Woke up from her nap yesterday just as ornery and normal as could be."

"Don't let that fool you." The one o'clock whistle blew. "If I were you I'd keep a pretty sharp eye out." Nick sat up, then started to stand.

They'd both been looking out over the water. Harley was to wonder, time and again in the years that followed, whether he would have recognized the danger had he seen it coming.

For it was only a yellow tiger tomcat, attracted by the scent of food, about to poke its head into the lunch pail at Nick's feet.

But when Nick saw it, he stepped backward. His foot slipped over the edge. He teetered to save his balance.

Harley made a grab, and Roberts took a step forward, but it happened so quickly.

Seeing that he hadn't caught Nick, even seeing Nick disappear over the edge and hurtle down toward the water, Harley was not afraid for him. The water was deep. Nick would be shocked and soaked and he'd take a razzing from his buddies, but damn, if he'd just been able to move faster, he might have saved Nick all the trouble.

Roberts started to laugh. "Hope he can swim."

But by then Harley was looking over the edge—and he wasn't hearing.

Nick had fallen into a shallow part of the water. There were rocks just below the surface. Nick sprawled on the rocks, staring up at Harley; very obviously dead.

CHAPTER TWENTY-SEVEN

ORISKANY FORKS HAD but one funeral parlor. Melford Collins, like his father, from whom he'd inherited the business, was liked by the townspeople. He was also disliked. For when Melford smiled and said hello, he seemed so apologetic. It was as if he knew that you knew that he knew that someday you'd pass through his workroom into the beige parlor with the floral decorations and the people tiptoeing about.

Mr. Grogan disliked Melford Collins and his funerals more each year. He sighed as he helped Nellie up the stairs. Through the open door to the vestibule, they could hear Melford's victrola scratching out a rendition of "Rock of Ages." Melford, in black suit and tie, stepped forward with the right mixture of reluctance and welcome. "So glad you could come."

Mr. Grogan looked him in the eye. "I'm glad I could, but not glad I had to."

"I know. I know." The door opened behind them, and Sheriff and Mrs. Bailey stepped in. "So glad you could come," said Melford.

The parlor was large and rectangular, rosily lit. In an irregular semicircle before the casket, their backs to the door, sat Lil and the family. Mr. Grogan was relieved. The longer he could put off facing Lil, the better.

He led Nellie to the casket and looked down at Nick on his peach satin pillow. At their feet was a stool. Son of a gun! He'd forgotten Nick was a Catholic. Were they supposed to kneel on that thing? He nudged Nellie and knelt. Nellie hastily followed suit. They remained motionless while Mr. Grogan counted to fifteen, then he tapped Nellie and got up. One more look at Nick, and they turned to the family.

Mr. Grogan couldn't see Lil's face under that veil, but the way she was sitting, it looked like she'd cried the last drop out of herself.

Cass was next to her. "Lil," she said gently. "Mr. and Mrs. Grogan."

"Awfully sorry, Lil."

Lil sat straighter. "Thank you both for coming."

"He looks so natural. Like he's asleep." Nellie hoped she'd said something comforting.

She hadn't. Melford hadn't been able to remove the look of horror from Nick's face.

Lil nodded all the same. "Yes," she said. "Thank you for your roses."

"Roses were Nick's favorite," said Cass. She gave Mr. Grogan a peculiar look. "So few people sent them."

"It was the least we could do." Mr. Grogan patted Nellie's hand. "We'd better be going."

Cass stood up as they moved toward Paul and Emma. "Don't leave till I get a chance to come chat with you," she whispered to Mr. Grogan.

She watched them move away down the line of relatives, shaking hands and making polite conversation and then stop before Harley, who sat with Emily and Michael. He was playing his role well, Cass thought. He was nearly as white as Lil, and his eyes looked red and swollen. "It must have been horrible for you," Cass heard Mrs. Grogan say. "Did it happen like they said?"

Harley just nodded. He glanced toward Lil.

Cass was well aware of the secret signals Lil and Harley had been trading all evening long. They thought to avoid suspicion by sitting so far apart. Well, they weren't fooling Cass for a minute.

Or Nick. He was silent in the casket, but Cass knew he'd forgiven her for not realizing in time to warn him. He'd been her friend, so the witches had killed him. I'll revenge you, she promised him. She fingered her medal for support. Why hadn't Reverend Smith come? Why had there been no note from Carrie? She had to find a friend.

For the twentieth time she counted the bouquets of roses among the flowers. Hers, Lil's, the Grogans', Sheriff and Mrs. Bailey's, and Reverend Smith's. Of course, Lil had sent hers for appearances. But the others? A sign from God? "I'm going to chat with the Grogans, Lil."

The Grogans were signing the guest book. "How have you two been?"

"Not too well," said Nellie. "I get these coughing spells, and then there's the arthritis. Let me tell you, once you get that, you want to give up living—" She stopped, realizing where she was. "Course that's just a manner of speaking. How's Lil taking it?"

Cass hesitated. "How does it seem to you she's taking it?"

"She looks like a rag doll with the stuffing out," said Mr. Grogan. He looked back at Lil and his eyes misted.

He *couldn't* be acting! But she had to test them. Without thinking, she took hold of her medal again. "Your roses are really beautiful."

"Well, you know," said Mrs. Grogan, "it was a funny thing. I started to get tulips, but then them roses caught my eye. They were just so pretty."

"Like a little voice saying 'Take me'?" said Cass. The medal seemed to be getting warm.

"Exactly," said Nellie. She leaned close. "Did it happen like they say?"

"How do they say it happened?" Definitely warm.

"That Nick was scared of cats and he jumped away from one and fell over the edge and landed all broken up with blood coming out of his mouth and..."

Cass had made her decision. Warmth equaled good. She'd always be able to tell a witch from now on. The medal would get cold! "That isn't the way it happened."

"Well, how *did* it happen?" said Mr. Grogan. "Your husband saw it. And a few other men, too."

"Oh, I know what the others think they saw," said Cass. "But there's one important thing. Nick wasn't afraid of cats. Not ordinary cats, anyway."

"What kind of a cat *was* it?"

"A familiar. A witch's cat."

Harley was walking toward them. Cass seized Grogan's arm. "I can't talk any longer," she whispered. "They'll kill me, too, if they know I've told you!" She moved away.

Nellie and her husband exchanged frightened glances. They nodded to Harley as he passed on his way to the men's room, and then stared after Cass, now approaching Sheriff Bailey.

"So nice of you to come," Cass said loudly, for Curt had turned and was watching. "And your roses were lovely." The sheriff, too, was afraid of spying ears. He lowered his voice as he said, "Reverend Smith showed me your letter. Do you want me to prefer any charges?"

"No! Oh God, don't do anything or they'll kill me, just like they killed Nick."

"Like *who* killed Nick?"

"Them. The witches," said Cass. Then she gasped, for Harley was re-entering the room. Without another word she returned to her place at Lil's side.

It was 9:45. Except for Melford and the Westcotts, only the Bascombs stayed to keep vigil until the announced closing hour of ten.

"I don't think anyone else will come tonight," said Mary to Lil. "Why don't you let us take you home?"

"I don't want to go."

"I know just how she feels," whispered Milly, "but these visiting hours are barbaric. Nearly put the living in the box with the dead."

Lil felt the sobs coming; she tensed every muscle and put her hands over her mouth. She had to keep them from barging in. *Don't look, don't cry, don't feel!* In a few minutes now, they'd make her go. The sobs came loose.

Milly started for her. Emma's hand shot out. "Leave her be."

Everyone lapsed into silence, ignoring the sobs, avoiding other eyes.

Suddenly Emma rose and shooed them into the foyer. "We'll be outside, honey. Take all the time you want." She closed the door.

And then Nick smiled. Just as he used to!

Lil ran to his side and touched his face.

But it was stiff and cold.

Lil patted him helplessly—stroked his forehead, touched his hair. Melford had done it wrong. "You hated your hair that way, didn't you." Tears fell on her purse as she groped for a comb. "I'll fix it."

She worked carefully, fussing with each strand. "It's soft. It won't go like it should. But don't worry. And don't you dare laugh at me, Nick.

"Nick! I've got to believe you're listening. If there's

anything in this world I know, it's that you love me. You gave. I took. Now you've got to give just once more. You've got to forgive me."

She cupped his face in her hands, waiting. But it was only Nick's body, cold and dead.

And maybe that's all she really needed. *Nick* would have forgiven her. "Hell, I knew all along you had a thing for Harley." And, "So what if you did kiss Upjohn? And like it."

Why had she never understood?

She bent and kissed him. "Thank you." She took the card from her spray of roses at the foot of the coffin, inscribed it, then broke off a rose and slipped it, with the card, into his breast pocket.

A moment later, she let herself into the foyer. "I've fixed his hair," she said to Melford. "Don't touch it."

Melford went to the body the moment the family left, and surveyed it with a professional eye. The last time he'd left a widow alone with a corpse, it had taken him half the night to get the poor man back in shape. He caught a bulge. He reached into the breast pocket.

"To *say* it, would be for the moment. This is for eternity. I love you. Forgive me for waiting until now...Lil."

Melford carefully replaced Lil's gifts.

Cass slept on the living-room couch that night. It aroused no comment from Harley, for she had slept there every night since he'd hidden her Bible.

Tonight Harley didn't really miss her. He propped himself on pillows and stared at a crack in the ceiling.

Could he have saved Nick? Could he have moved faster?

Harley tossed onto his side, stayed there a moment, then rolled back. It seemed like that crack in the ceiling was getting wider. He ought to do something about this house.

His mind wandered through the rooms, picturing the undusted bric-a-brac, the bathroom, old grayed towels used for a week, the fixtures and linoleum not quite clean. Cass just wouldn't keep anything clean lately.

Lil's bathroom had thick pink towels and carpets, powder puffs and crystal flacons. He imagined her getting out of her bath, drying herself with one of those towels, dusting herself with powder.

And Nick wasn't there anymore.

Harley's brows knit as he tried to guide his mind to safety.

What he ought to do was get everything out of this house and do the whole place over.

The image of a refurnished living room came to his mind. He sat at the desk before the fire, writing, while the children played quietly. A wind blew autumn leaves from the maples, *La Bohème* played in the background, and across the room she sat, reading, on an overstuffed down sofa. Once in a while she looked up to speak of something she'd just read and to ask how his work was going. Their eyes met in complete understanding. In the bathroom were the pink towels and the crystal flaçons. He would belong there as Nick never had.

That crack *was* getting wider! And he was going buggy just because Lil was free!

She must be beautiful to make love to; like a nectarine, smooth and cool and rosy tan. The hip bones would protrude just a bit, and the stomach would be indented. There'd be a tuck-in under the ribcage, and he'd want to squeeze her breasts to see if sweet-smelling drops actually came from the pores. He'd never be able to find enough ways to show her—

"I love her!" Crazy. He had to stop reading so much. Made him want too much. He had no college education, he'd had to get married, he still *was* married.

Cass dead. A terrible accident.

No! He didn't want it that way. He sat up, sweating.

The clock beside the bed ticked, loud. He'd shut the thoughts out. Count instead.

Ticktock. Ticktock.

He'd feel different tomorrow.

In the living room, Cass, too, was awake.

She was safe for the time being. The witches didn't know she was on to them, and they'd have to wait a decent interval before they tried to kill her, too. She might have made a mistake talking to the Grogans and Baileys though. If the witches had noticed…

What she was going to have to do was take Michael and run away. God no longer expected her to bring the Westcotts to Him. They were hopeless. But she had tried so hard with them that God had at last revealed His whole grand design.

The Truth had come in a flash of golden light. There never had been a boy Michael—only *her* Michael, so cruelly stolen from her. "Forgive me, God, I don't mean cruelly. Like Job, I submit to your will."

Tears filled Cass's eyes. What more glorious task could be set for a human being than to turn a *demon* to God? And that was her task. The demon masquerading as Michael had been conjured up by witches, but planned by God.

Cass knew now. The Michael-demon *was* her special child.

CHAPTER TWENTY-EIGHT

THE DRIZZLE THAT began next morning turned, by noon, to sheets of water pouring from an unrelenting sky. The drive home from Calvary was strained and silent.

It was just as well with Cass. She had nothing to say to Harley or the girls. It was a wonder Harley had not followed her to the choirloft, so closely had he been watching her. Under the tenth step had been Reverend Smith's letter. It rested now inside Cass's brassiere.

He had told Papa. All the while Michael had been lost, all through the funeral, Papa had known. He had done nothing to help her. He was one of them.

So they all knew now that she was on to them. They would have to kill her sooner than they had planned.

She and Michael must escape to Carrie's this afternoon. She'd send the children up to the attic after Bible lessons. Harley would be reading. She'd pretend to clean closets so she could get some necessaries packed for Michael and herself. And then...

On each side of the attic, dark, low places stretched back under the eaves. Sometimes, if she let herself think silly, the attic scared Emily. But today, with the rain on the roof, it was a friendly place.

She sat on the floor, cutting a piece of material from one of Gramma Hitty's old blouses. She gathered it with a needle and thread and attached it to the spool that was to be a chair in the doll's house Uncle Nick had made her.

She was no longer a chubby child. Her body was angular, and she was taller than she should have been at five. Both she and Michael had their hair cut short, with flat bangs across the forehead. While this gave Michael, with her big green eyes and dark, curly hair, a cherubic appearance, the severity did nothing for Emily. Increasingly quiet and thoughtful, she was quick to help and slow to anger. Her face was in between. It might turn pretty, it might turn plain.

She held up the flounced spool, examined her handiwork, and nodded. Beyond the spool she could see Michael crouched over her blocks, building something. Emily's gray eyes flickered. Daddy had told her the day he came back from the hospital that she'd like Michael. And she did. Besides, Michael looked like Mommy. She, Emily, looked like Daddy. If you looked like someone, you'd *be* like them. She was glad she looked like Daddy.

Emily pasted a cardboard back onto her spool-chair, and looked at Michael again.

The child had removed the dress and panties from her new cloth doll and was solemnly placing the doll face down in the rectangular framework she'd built with her blocks. Unaware of Emily's attention, she went to the box of dress-up clothes and returned with a piece of peach-colored fabric. She tucked it tenderly around and over the doll, leaving nothing protruding but skimpy cloth buttocks.

"What's that?" said Emily.

Michael jumped. "Body," she said. "Tapudina groun'."

"You mean like Mommy said they'd do with Uncle Nick?" Emily came over and looked at the buttocks. "He didn't look like that."

"Mommy said!" Michael pointed to the buttocks again. "Body. Tapudina groun'."

Emily tried to figure it out. She'd heard Mommy say "body" lots of times. *Cover your body, Emily. Keep your dress down, Emily; it's not nice to show your body. Grampa Frank's body is all sore from laying in bed so long.*

Michael was right—a body was a *behind*! They must have to slice it off with a knife.

"Did Mommy say why they do it?"

Michael shook her head. "Tapudina groun'."

"Oh! The rest must be what goes to heaven. They cut the body off because heaven doesn't want it."

Michael's face began to pucker.

Emily was envisioning Uncle Nick with his body cut off. "It must be awful to die."

Michael began to whimper. "Donwanna!"

Emily looked at her. "*You're* not going to die."

Michael's whimpers built to frightened gasps. "Mommy says."

"But why?"

"Secret." Michael was crying.

Emily looked into the shadows about them. "Let's go downstairs."

Michael scrambled away. "Fraid!"

"Of who?"

"Daddy!"

Then Michael realized that she'd told the secret. She stopped crying.

"Why are you afraid of Daddy?" said Emily.

"Kill Nick!" said Michael. "Mommy said!"

Emily gasped. "He did not! That's a lie! You're wicked!" A look of terrible hurt crossed Michael's face.

Then there was a sound at the door of the attic—a footstep. The hair at the back of Emily's neck prickled as she turned slowly to look.

It occurred to Harley that the house had been silent for some time. "Cass?"

He put his book aside and went to the window. The rain hadn't lessened. He wondered if there were men working with shovels right now, digging Nick's grave. The funeral was set for ten o'clock tomorrow morning. They'd never get the grave dry by then.

He looked at the clock. Three. Tonight's visiting hours started at six. He dreaded sitting in front of that casket another night.

"Cass?"

He walked to the kitchen, and stopped—not really knowing why an upside-down laundry basket should arrest him. Then he realized; there were always clothes in that basket; most often, lately, dirty.

He walked to the basket and lifted it. Underneath was a burlap bag, outfitted with a drawstring. In the bag he found clothes that belonged to Cass and Michael, galoshes and an oilcloth to protect them from the rain, two peanut butter sandwiches, two dollars, and Cass's Bible.

Harley started to call for Cass again, but the silence of the house stopped him.

He moved to the base of the stairs and listened. Nothing.

He slipped off his shoes and mounted the stairs, avoiding spots where he knew there were creaks.

The door to the attic was open. He looked in.

Cass was kneeling, her back to him. She was dressing Michael in winter leggings, coat, and hat. Emily was nowhere to be seen.

Harley stepped into the attic. "What's going on?"

Cass spun around. "Heavens, you frightened me! Nothing to concern you, Harley. I just wanted to see if Michael is outgrowing her winter clothes."

"Where's Emily?"

"Downstairs."

"I didn't see her."

Cass shrugged. "Maybe she went to her room for a nap." She rose, taking Michael's hand. "Come downstairs, Michael. I'm going to let these leggings out."

"Emily?" Harley called.

'Harley! Stop shouting and come downstairs."

But Harley's call got a response—a thud from the trunk in the corner.

In an instant Harley had the trunk open. He cried out—Emily was bound and gagged like a mummy in layers of rags and clothes from the dress-up trunk. Harley snatched her from the trunk and began to tear at the wrappings. "Why'd you do this, Cass?" He had to get those awful rags off Emily. He tore them from her face and unwrapped her mouth. She was crying, not saying anything, just looking at him. "Don't, sweetheart. Don't cry."

Then Emily screamed.

Harley started to turn. Cass was almost upon him, a heavy Civil War bugle raised above her head. He threw himself backward, rolling, but Cass followed. Emily dived at her mother and managed to knock her off balance. The blow missed Harley's head; the bugle struck the floor by his ear.

For an instant he couldn't see clearly, but Emily was screaming again. And when Harley could focus his eyes, he saw Emily struggling to hold Cass back—protecting him.

He leaped to his feet and pulled Emily away. She'd had hold of Cass's medal. The chain broke and the medal flew across the attic.

"My medal!" Cass screamed. She swung the bugle. Harley ducked, feeling the pain as it grazed his head. He came up fast and sank his fist into her jaw.

He hadn't meant to hit her that hard. He hadn't meant to hit her at all. But there she lay, unconscious at his feet, blood trickling from her mouth.

"Emily." His voice was barely a whisper. "Run to Gramma's. Tell her to call Doc Barnes. Bring Grampa and Mr. Upjohn."

When Emily had gone, he bent and lifted Cass. "We've got to put Mommy to bed, Michael." He carried Cass down the stairs, barely aware of Michael following behind him.

He made Cass as comfortable as he knew how. Then he turned to explain to Michael.

She wasn't there. "Michael?"

The only answer was rain slapping against the windows.

Harley raced back to the attic. He skirted the edge, peering into the dark places beneath the roof. "Michael, baby, where are you? Please don't scare Daddy this way!"

On the floor was Cass's medal. He picked it up and put it in his pocket.

Then his eyes found the trunk in the corner. It was closed. He hadn't closed the lid when he took Emily out. He walked to it slowly. "Michael, I know you're in there. Please come out."

There was a scuffing sound.

Tears stung Harley's eyes. How could he ever explain what had just happened to a two-year-old? He couldn't even explain it to himself. "Michael, Emily is helping Daddy. She's gone to get a doctor for Mommy. I need your help, too. We've got to tuck Mommy in so she'll get all better."

He opened the trunk.

Michael began to scream, a frantic ball in the corner of the trunk; her head between her knees and her arms over her head.

Harley reached for her. She lashed out, beating him with little fists and kicking. He endured the blows and carried her downstairs to the bedroom. Cass was still unconscious. He pulled back the covers and put Michael in bed with her.

Michael's cries became howls of grief. She buried her head in Cass's breast. "Mommy dead!"

"No, baby. She's fainted. She'll wake up soon."

"Dead!" sobbed Michael. "You!"

Cass was so still; her face, beneath the drying blood, so white. A thought from the previous night came back to Harley. *Cass dead. A terrible accident.*

No! Anyone could have those thoughts from time to time. But why was she so still?

He listened for a heartbeat. Michael's head, beside his on Cass's breast, turned. "Pud me ina groun too?" she said.

And then Harley cried. He hadn't wanted to; he'd wanted to be strong. But he felt weak—and frightened. The world was disintegrating around him, and he didn't know why, or how to stop it. He climbed beneath the covers and, as Michael was clinging to Cass, he clung to both of them. Together on Cass's breast, he and Michael sobbed.

Cass's eyes flickered open, confused. She started to speak. Then her eyes cleared and, before either Harley or Michael had noticed, closed again.

"What happened?" Doc Barnes asked as he removed his dripping sou'wester. "Hitty didn't make much sense on the phone."

"I hit Cass," said Harley.

Barnes came to the bed, took Cass's pulse, and felt her jaw. "Why?"

"She tried to kill me with a bugle."

"Must have been quite a spat."

"No spat," said Upjohn. "Cass tied and gagged Emily and locked her in a trunk in the attic."

Barnes, rummaging through his bag in search of smelling salts, stopped. "'What'd she do that for?"

"You're the doctor," said Tobin. "We been waiting for you to tell *us*."

Barnes frowned. He had the smelling salts in his hand now, but he put them back and motioned with his head. They followed him into the living room. Barnes glanced into the kitchen, where Hitty was reading to the children, and spoke low. "This the first time Cass ever done anything queer?"

Harley hesitated, but Tobin and Upjohn had no compunctions.

"Tried to kill Michael the other day," said Tobin.

"She's written to the Methodist parson accusing people of witchcraft," said Upjohn.

Barnes gave Harley a sharp look. "Well, I'd better get in there and wake her up. Make sure she's OK structurally, so to speak. Then I'll give her a good strong sedative and call Dr. Hershfeld at the state hospital."

"Now wait a minute—"

"Just for a recommendation, Harley." Barnes opened the bedroom door, then stopped. "She's gone out the window!" He made for the front door.

It was too late. The engine of his car roared to life just as he gained the porch. The wheels spun, and Cass was off, skidding on the muddy road.

"The truck!" yelled Tobin. But the truck was going nowhere. Cass had taken the key.

Sheriff Albert Bailey was working at his desk when Dr. Barnes called, studying three files; an old one, "Muriel Moore"; a more recent one, "Satyendra Singh"; and a brand-new one, "Nicholas Clunycourt."

"It all ties together," he'd muttered to Edna as they left the funeral parlor the night before. He'd been up most of the night with those files, and returned to them immediately after breakfast. "A ring of killer witches, Edna. Men have been made governor for solving cases like this."

As she heard Albert talking to Burt Barnes, Edna came to his side. From the elation on Albert's face, their niece Ruth must have had her baby.

"I'm on my way. Good-bye."

"Boy or girl?" said Edna.

But Albert was buckling on his gun. "Harley Westcott just tried to kill Cass."

"Burt saw it happen?"

"No. Harley's got him believing some cock-and-bull story, and Cass has run off."

Edna watched Albert put his Stetson on his head and slip into the coat with the brightly polished star. He looked so proud. He wasn't the same man who'd shot it out with Jack Jenkins twelve years before, but Edna hoped he'd never find that out. "Drive carefully," she said, and smiled, as always.

The rain poured down, turning the afternoon to night.

"In the land of San Domingo, lived a girl named O-By-Jingo, yah dah, yahdedadedahdah, ommpah, ommpah, ommpah, ommpah." The song kept time with the windshield wipers. Cass wished she could drive without those wipers. She couldn't think and sing at the same time.

"From the fields and from the marshes, came—"

Over the crest of College Hill shot the lights of a car racing toward her. Lil!

Cass's eyes glittered as she spotted the red blinker. What a clever trick! They'd figured she would go to the sheriff. They were trying to make her pull over, thinking the sheriff had come to help her. Well, she'd show them! She took the car out over the center line, and pressed the accelerator to the floor.

Through the rain Sheriff Bailey saw the car tearing up the curves. Must be Cass. Driving too fast. He began to honk his horn, but the distance closed. They were on the straightaway, and the oncoming car was not giving way. They were going to crash head on! With a cry, the sheriff spun his wheel, careened through the ditch, crashed through a wooden fence, and came to a halt straddling a huckleberry bush.

Couldn't have been Cass—Cass would have stopped. It must be Harley, making a getaway! Sheriff Bailey threw the car into reverse.

Once out of sight over the rise, Cass slowed down and massaged her jaw, wondering if Harley had loosened her teeth. She was too young to lose any teeth.

Catching sight of Sheriff Bailey's flashing red light in the mirror, she gasped and hit the gas.

They raced down College Hill.

At the town limits, Cass was still well in the lead, but the flashing red light stuck to her rear-view mirror as though pasted.

And the way it was wailing! *Not* Lil, but some monster from hell.

She skidded onto Elm Street and took as much speed as the car would give down the straightaway. Only two more blocks to the sheriff and safety.

She was out of the car almost before it stopped.

But the monster was still coming, a block away; shrieking and blinking. She stumbled to the door and banged with her fists. "Sheriff! Unlock the door! Help!"

"Who is it?"

"Mrs. Bailey? It's Cass! Let me in!" Then the headlights caught her. She flattened against the door and started to scream.

The door opened, and she tumbled into the room. "Good heavens!" said Edna.

The red light stopped outside and the wail died. Cass scrambled to her feet and slammed the door. "Where's the sheriff? Get his gun—it's after me!"

"That's Albert now." Edna tried to open the door.

"No, it's not!" Cass threw herself against the door. "Don't open it!"

Rapid footsteps crossed the porch. The doorknob turned, then rattled angrily. "Edna? Are you all right? Open up!"

"It's Cass Westcott, Albert. She won't let me open the door."

"Cass! You almost killed me back there. Open this door!"

Cass smiled at Edna. "See how clever it is? It really sounds like the sheriff. I think you'd better get Albert's gun so we can kill it."

"Kill what?"

"The monster! It chased me all the way from College Hill, because now I don't have my medal to protect me."

Edna heard the kitchen door open. "Aren't we lucky," she said. "I just heard Albert come in. He'll know what to do about the monster."

Albert appeared in the door of the living room, his clothing dampened, his pride askew. "Would you two mind telling me what's going on?"

Edna took his arm. "There's a monster on the porch, Albert. It chased Cass all the way from College Hill. It was pounding on the door, pretending to be you. Could you shoot it, please?" As she talked, she kept squeezing his arm and making broad facial signals.

Albert pulled his arm free. The trouble with Edna was she had no subtlety.

"What kind of monster?" he said to Cass.

"I thought it was Lil at first. Then I realized it was one of their demons, pretending to be your car."

Albert nodded. She *was* acting strange. "Stand back," he said, and he took out his gun.

It was a good thing the street was empty when Albert opened the front door. Otherwise he would have felt an utter fool as he took aim and fired a bullet into the old tire that housed Edna's gladiolas.

Cass had been put to sleep by a glass of warm milk laced with cough syrup. "Do you think she's crazy?" said Edna.

"Not at all," said Albert. "Just temporarily unbalanced from fright."

Of course, if the witches insisted on claiming she *was* crazy, he'd have to go along with it, so as not to tip off how much he knew. It would be hard on Cass, but he'd have this case solved in no time, and then he'd bail her out.

"Albert? Maybe she *is*. Maybe she's been crazy all along, and all the things she's been saying—"

"Edna, you just don't understand these things. Harley's own aunt claims he's the head of a pack of witches and that they killed her husband. Think she's crazy, too? Of course not. And even if Cass *was* crazy now, it's them would've driven her crazy." He picked up his coat.

"Where are you going?"

"To the Westcott place. Then up to talk with Carrie again."

"You're *not* going to leave me alone with Cass. Please!"

"All right. Get the Grogans to come over. But don't you go telling them about any of this business."

"Of course I won't, Albert."

But of course she did. And naturally, despite Mr. Grogan's admonition, Nellie Grogan called Clarenza Edwards the minute she got home from the Baileys' that night. Clarenza first called Florence Comstock, who offered Clarenza the cloth doll story, and then Florence called Maybelle Horton while Clarenza was calling Eleanor Woodin...

Mabel Wheelman grew frantic trying to listen to all the conversations at once.

Nick's funeral was the biggest in the history of Oriskany Forks. People began arriving at Melford's two hours before the service.

Lil was glad she'd allowed Doc Barnes to give her a sedative. It stopped her from thinking the thoughts that had kept her pacing the night before. Could what they were saying be true? Did she really have some kind of power? Strong enough to kill Nick and drive Cass crazy? Did Upjohn? Did Harley?

The sedative also kept her from thinking about the prying eyes that watched her every expression throughout the service.

"Well, I was in the funeral parlor and I can tell you that girl wasn't putting on an act. She loved her husband, and I don't believe any of this talk."

"*I* didn't see her shed a single tear. What kind of love is that?"

"Do you suppose Father Lawrence was casting spells when we thought he was talking Latin?"

"I saw her look at Harley Westcott and smile!"

The funeral cortege, a half-mile long, started for the Catholic cemetery on Dugway Road. Midway, vehicles began to pull ahead.

When Melford reached the gate, he found the one small driveway blocked. He, the family, and friends parked on the road, shouldered Nick's casket, and pushed through a crowd which parted reluctantly and closed immediately, each member afraid he'd lose his place.

By the time they reached the grave, the floral pieces, hurriedly arranged by Melford's men, were bedraggled from feet splashing mud on them.

This was not, Father Lawrence decided, an occasion for long prayers. The few Catholics in the crowd knew that he was rushing, stumbling even, to get the thing over with.

"...Ashes to ashes, dust to dust." He threw the first fistful of mud onto the casket and nodded to Lil.

The tears Lil had so successfully hidden began to flow. Once she threw her share, they would all do the same. Nick would be covered up "No!"

The crowd began to buzz.

"It's all right," said Doc Barnes. "You don't have to."

But they were construing her refusal in some horrible way! "All right, I will." She stooped and dug her fingers into the mud. "Ashes to ashes." It spatted onto the coffin.

And then—nobody could or would say afterward who had thrown the thing. "It just came out of nowhere" was the consensus. Lobbed into the air with marvelous precision, it arched over the heads of those nearest the grave and thudded onto the casket.

A dead yellow tiger tomcat.

Lil jumped, slipped, slid down into the grave and onto the casket. She seized the stiff animal and hurled it back in the direction it had come from. "Nick's afraid of cats!" She clawed at the side of the grave, trying to climb out. "Get away from him! You monsters!"

The crowd began to pull back. Lil was up and out without the help of her family. She scooped up a mass of mud and flung it at her persecutors. "Ghouls! You didn't even deserve to *know* a man like Nick!" More mud. The pace of the exodus quickened. "You think I'm a witch? You people don't need witches to curse you. God will do it! God damn you! God *damn* you!"

They slunk away, Lil's mud on their faces, her oath in their ears. Soon only the Bascombs, the Westcotts, and a few friends were left.

And Sheriff Bailey.

They couldn't shake the sheriff. He had gall if nothing else, Harley thought as the Baileys made themselves at home with coffee and cake in Lil's kitchen.

The Bascombs and the Westcotts, along with Robert Sawyer and Burt Barnes, were gathered for post-funeral refreshments—but no one was rehashing the funeral. They were waiting for Dr. Hershfeld to arrive from Seneca, from Cass's bedside in St. Elizabeth's.

"I don't care *what* he tells us," Paul kept saying. "My girl ain't crazy." He fastened a baleful stare on Barnes. "I think it's awful funny you whisking her away to the hospital and not letting any of us see her."

"The hospital was the best place to contain her, Paul."

"What do you think she is, a pail of milk?"

"Paul," said Emma. "I'm sure Cass is in good hands."

"What's this doctor's name?" said Paul. "Goldstein?"

"Hershfeld," said Doc Barnes.

Paul nodded. "I always heard those Jews was witches."

"For heaven's sake, Papa, don't be such a sap!"

Paul turned and stared at Lil.

There had been no tears from her since the cemetery. With her head high she'd picked up the dead cat and marched back to the car. Once home, she had asked Curt to bury the cat in the backyard, then excused herself to take a bath. She had sung in the bathtub, and emerged smiling.

For a bit of Nick had climbed out of the grave with Lil that afternoon. Slinging the last handful of mud at the last running heels, Lil could swear she'd heard Nick's voice: *That's my girl! Give 'em hell!* She never had been Nick's girl. Now she was. It felt good.

"I take it," she said now, "that you and Cass still think we're all witches. Right, Papa? So naturally we'd hire a witch doctor!"

"No daughter of mine has ever talked to me this way," said Paul.

"Well, that's all right," Lil said softly. "I'm not really your daughter, Papa. I'm some sort of a visitation from hell."

The doorbell rang, and Lil went to answer it.

"Reverend and Mrs. Smith! Just in time, come in. We're going to desecrate a Eucharist and have a cup of blood!"

Reverend and Mrs. Smith glanced nervously toward the kitchen. "We can't stay more than a minute," said the Reverend. "I wanted to pay my respects and explain why we didn't come to the funeral. I felt, since a Roman Catholic was presiding—"

"Oh, weren't you there? You missed a regular circus. For a finale we threw mud and dead cats...or have you already heard?"

"Well, no."

"My goodness, the phones must be out of order. You're acquainted with everyone here, aren't you, Reverend?"

"I think so, except—"

"Reverend and Mrs. Smith, Toynbee Upjohn. The fourth witch."

"Lilith!" Paul sprang to his feet. "Have you gone crazy?"

"No, Papa. I've gone sane. After today I'm certain the whole town knows what Cass wrote to the Reverend, as well as what she told the sheriff."

"We'd better go," said Reverend Smith.

"Why?" said Upjohn. "You and your wife have done a great deal of talking behind our backs, sir. Don't you have the courage to say it to our faces?"

"We've exercised utmost discretion," said Reverend Smith.

"Then it must have been Sheriff and Mrs. Bailey—" said Lil.

"Not us!" said Edna. "We didn't say a word."

"Leave it to me," said Hitty. "Sunday, when I go to church, I'll find out who told what to whom. I'll bet that knobby-kneed Maybelle Horton started the whole thing."

The doorbell rang again.

"That," said Lil, "must be the witch doctor."

Arthur Hershfeld was large and gentle, with sober brown eyes and straight black hair too sparse for his age. His diagnosis was dementia praecox. "…Specifically, what Dr. Freud of Vienna sometimes calls 'paranoia.' I would oppose you most strongly if you refused to commit Cass."

"Then you better start opposing," said Paul. "What would people say?"

"Papa!" said Lil. "We've got to decide what's best for Cass, not what the neighbors will say. They'll say it anyway."

"Seems to me," said Sheriff Bailey, "you're mighty anxious to see your sister declared insane."

Lil turned. "The field day that accompanied my husband's burial this afternoon was the direct result of your meddling," she said. "Yours and Reverend Smith's here. Any more incidents, and I'll initiate legal proceedings against the both of you.

Now if you insist on remaining for what is strictly a family discussion, keep quiet." She turned back to Paul. "I just buried Nick today, Papa. I don't want to bury Cass. And that's what we'd be doing if we kept her here. We'd have to watch her all the time. She'd be scared to death, thinking we were going to kill her. If she's got any kind of chance, it's with a man like Dr. Hershfeld."

"Besides," said Sawyer, "it's up to Harley. He's the only one who can commit her."

Paul turned on Harley. "So that's the way it is," he said with all the contempt he could muster. "The father's got no say in it at all."

Harley met Paul's eyes straight. "I'm a father, too, Mr. Bascomb. Yesterday Cass tried to kill one of my daughters and run away with the other." He turned to Hershfeld. "Dr. Barnes tells us you run an experimental wing at the hospital—not what we've heard state hospitals are like."

Hershfeld's face lit with gentle enthusiasm. "There's only one other unit like it in the state. We deal exclusively with dementia praecox. Beds for just forty patients, clean sheets, daily personal therapy. In our first year we've had most heartening results. And if we can prove our methods—"

"You telling us you wanna use our little girl as a guinea pig?" said Paul.

"Have you ever visited a state hospital, Mr. Bascomb?"

"Of course not." Paul's anger faded. "Just heard tales of what they're like."

"What you've heard is pale beside the truth, sir."

"Does she think you're a witch?" said Tobin.

"No. She thinks Harley has paid me to kill her—with the five dollars he got for his story."

"But I bought a doll and a china cat with that, and I gave Cass the change!"

Hershfeld smiled. "You secretly met me and gave me the

five dollars. Lil supplied the doll and the china cat. The change you gave Cass was counterfeit."

Amanda Smith gasped. "But I was there and saw—" She glanced at Reverend Smith and fell silent.

Hershfeld's brown eyes narrowed. "For some years now," he said, "Cass has been living in a world increasingly out of touch with reality. If she has tricked any of you into sharing her delusions, I suggest you rethink everything in light of the fact that the girl is insane." He smiled. "Persuasive and charming, but insane."

Sawyer interpreted the committal papers for Harley. "This agreement is by no means to be construed as a committal to any state mental institution. She is committed only to Dr. Hershfeld and his experimental unit. Once you sign, you give Dr. Hershfeld complete authority as to medication, treatment, length of stay, and visiting arrangements. If, for any reason, the wing is discontinued by the state, legal responsibility for Cass will return to you."

It was so simple.

Cass dead, he'd thought. *A terrible accident.*

Not exactly.

He should be upset, sorry to lose his wife.

He wasn't. He didn't know what he felt, but he didn't feel sorry. And he signed.

CHAPTER TWENTY-NINE

THE WEEKS THAT followed Nick's funeral were unprecedented in the history of Oriskany Forks gossip.

Mrs. Keats made frequent public mention of Lil's mysterious piano-playing. "Just came to her natural," she said.

The fifty-year friendship of Violet Baxter and Binny Wesley, senior members of the Methodist choir, came to an end when Violet, over Binny's objections, began to tell the whole town how she heard Cass say to Lil, "You got Mr. Keats sick instead of Mrs. Keats." How Charles Keats had, indeed, awakened with diarrhea that morning, and how Cass afterward had told Mrs. Keats that Lil was a witch.

Nathan Gifford, the Westcotts' neighbor, described the mysterious white animal he had seen following Harley around. "Like a little horse," he said. "With a horn in the middle of its forehead. And last time I saw it was right before my dad's cattle got sick!"

Then Nathan reminded everybody of Harley's miraculous emergence from Tobin's burning barn. "Wasn't no normal human being could of come out alive. Look at Sailor—burnt to a crisp!"

With it all, Harley found that Stanley Roberts had hired Nathan Gifford for the job at the quarry.

Hitty was the one who stumped the gossips.

"But you know, she's got a cat. And there's a wild bird she calls Genevieve that eats out of the same dish with the cat. Ever heard of a cat eating with a bird instead of eating the bird?"

"How about Hitty's perfume? Same as that tutor man wears."

And in Toynbee Upjohn the townspeople found an endless subject. Since they knew nothing about his background, they assumed it must be evil.

"Could be Satan himself. His eyebrows are kind of pointy!"

It all stood to reason. Harley had been raised under Toynbee's influence. So, at the end, was Lil. And, with Frank sick, Toynbee had ample opportunity to bring Hitty under his sway.

"The nurse says they do all sorts of spells over Frank."

"Do they ever take their clothes off?"

As for old Mrs. Parkinson on Elm Street, she had been "queer'" for years. In her seclusion she became the only person in Oriskany Forks who did not know that Mrs. Parkinson was a witch.

Father Lawrence was not so fortunate. He found out, the day a rock crashed though the window of the rectory, that he, too, was suspected of witchcraft. A note was attached to the rock: "Satan worshiper," it said. "Remember Salem."

In the eye of the storm, the Bascombs and the Westcotts went about their business. The only change was the attention lavished on Emily and Michael. At least once a day, a Bascomb came visiting—Paul with chocolate-cream pains, Emma with feed-bag clothing, Curt to play hide-and-seek, and Helen to bake and cook and clean and clasp the children to her breast.

Even Hitty and Tobin paid attention. Tobin welcomed the girls into his barn. Hitty allowed them to watch her curl her hair and clean the boarders' rooms, and taught Emily to play chess. "The poor little thing has to learn to conceal her brains or she'll never get a husband," she told Harley. "She's already beaten me twice."

The children accepted the situation without comment. "Mommy is very sick," they had been told. "She had to go to a hospital for a long time."

Yet Harley worried. Not about Emily—she had the equilibrium of a cat. It was Michael. And it wasn't anything he could put his finger on.

June arrived, and with it hay to be mowed, raked, loaded into wagons, and transported to the barn before it got rained on. Though Harley and Tobin feared they would be shorthanded with only Chuck remaining, they ended up with plenty of help. Emily was on hand, ineffectual but eager, Upjohn and Thomas pitched in—

And so did Lil.

It was wet work. Clothes clung, and hayseeds stuck to the skin. On Lil it looked good, for the perspiration molded her Levi's and open-throated blouses to her body, and the spot where hayseeds seemed to want to gather was in the dampness between her breasts, just at the top unbuttoned button of her blouse.

Harley caught Upjohn looking at those hayseeds one afternoon, and grinned. He'd thought Upjohn was above all that.

Then Upjohn stole another glance at Lil.

Harley frowned.

Hell, no. Upjohn was old enough to be Lil's father. He was just enjoying himself. No harm in that.

He wished, though, that Lil would button her blouse.

"Aunt Lil, what's a crazy house?"

The day's haying was finished, the men had gone to the evening milking, and Emily and Lil were on their way to pick up Michael at Hitty's.

"Where did you hear that?"

"Nathan Gifford. He lives up the road. He said my mommy's in the crazy house."

Lil smoothed Emily's hair. "I'm sorry you had to hear it that way, Emily. Do you understand what 'crazy' is?"

"Is it how Mommy was when she put me in the trunk?"

"Yes. And it's not Mommy's fault. She didn't stop loving you. She couldn't help getting crazy—she just caught it like a disease."

Emily nodded. "Then I guess Michael's caught it, too. That must be why she does that thing with her doll, and why she thinks you and Daddy killed Mommy and Uncle Nick, and that you're gonna kill her, too."

"Poor Michael," said Hershfeld when Harley came that evening and told him. "Can you bring her over here tomorrow? We've got to let her visit with Cass."

"I didn't know Cass was ready to see any of us."

Hershfeld shrugged. "Neither did I."

Cass sat on the edge of her cot, watching the doorway. They'd taken her dress. To wash and iron it, Nurse Stokeham had said. Cass didn't believe it. When Michael came, they'd force her to go downstairs in her bedgown. "Look how Mommy's dressed,"

they'd say to Michael, "she's a crazy person!" And the Michael-demon would believe them.

And maybe it was all a lie. Maybe Michael wouldn't come at all.

She heard footsteps and crawled under the bed.

"Cass?"

Cass peeked.

"All starched, washed, and ironed." Stokeham was holding her dress. "Go get showered, and when you come back, we'll comb your hair and put on some lipstick."

Cass found herself running down the hall, stripping off her bedgown.

There were fresh towels, and a new bar of soap. She stepped into the shower and raised her arms to the spray. Would Harley come? And maybe Emily?

Then she dropped her arms. Why was she so excited? Why should she care? They'd only want to kill her.

But she *did* want to see them.

Was it possible the doctor had been telling her the truth?

Suddenly she was lathering frantically. She had to get clean. She'd be clean and sweet and sane, and Harley would be there. "I want to go home!"

Were they down there? Waiting? To see Crazy Cass?

She stopped her lathering and stared into the stinging spray. How had she gotten herself into this? They were right. She *had* been crazy. How could she convince them she'd gotten well?

She raised her arms as though to push a lid off herself, and she heard screams from somewhere.

Then she was lying in a corner of the shower, and knew the screams were hers. "Help me, someone! I'm not crazy. I want to go home!"

"Yes, dear. It's all right. Don't be afraid."

"Miss Stokeham! I'm not sick anymore. I can go home! Tell the doctor. Please!"

In the office next to Hershfeld's, Harley paced. Hershfeld had been right. It was best for him not to see Cass. But he couldn't forget the look that had come over Michael's face as he left the room. She thought she'd been brought here to be killed.

In the next room Michael sat watching the doctor. He was talking, but she wasn't listening. She was looking for an ax like Uncle Curt used to cut off chickens' heads, or a gun like Grampa used to shoot woodchucks.

Then the hall door opened and a lady in white came in. "Ready?"

The doctor nodded.

Michael stiffened. *She* was going to do it. "Someone is here to see you, Michael," said the lady.

A lady in blue came into the room. "Michael," she said, and started toward her.

Michael slipped out of her chair and backed away. That wasn't Mommy. Mommy was dead.

The lady kept coming. Michael kept backing. She was against the wall and the lady was reaching for her, like all the things that chased her in dreams. Michael began to scream.

On the other side of the wall, Harley stopped pacing.

Hershfeld tried to lift the child. "It's your Mommy. Don't be afraid."

"No!" Michael fought him off. "Mommy's dead!"

"I'm not!" Cass stretched forth a trembling hand. "Touch one, darling. I'm real."

"Daddy! Daddy!" Michael screamed.

Cass put her hands to her ears to shut out the sound and to stop the feeling of crumbling inside her head. She'd been tricked. She ran behind Hershfeld's desk. "That's not my baby. That's the demon. Make it stop screaming!"

It did stop—because the door opened and Harley was there. Michael ran to him, and he lifted her and comforted her. He smiled uncertainly at Cass. "Hi."

He'd come so suddenly, Cass wasn't sure. Maybe it was another trick. She smoothed her hair.

"Why was Michael screaming?" said Harley.

"To drive me crazy."

Harley almost grinned. He didn't know what he had expected, but not this. "You look pretty."

Cass reddened, and looked prettier still.

Harley joggled Michael. Her face was buried in his neck. "Hey, honey, what's the matter? Why're you screaming at Mommy?"

"Not Mommy," said Michael.

"Then who is it?"

"Dunno."

"We seem to have new problems," said Hershfeld. He closed the door, motioning Nurse Stokeham to position herself there. "Take a chair, Harley." He turned to Cass, who had the look of a cornered rabbit. "You can sit at my desk. No one will come near you. Coffee, Harley? Would you do the honors, Miss Stokeham? And I'm sure that Cass would like a cup, too."

"No!" said Cass.

"Even if Miss Stokeham fills the cups in front of you so you can see there's no poison in yours?"

Cass's eyes flashed. She hated Hershfeld. He always knew what she was thinking; he was always prying, picking, pulling her mind apart so that she had no place to hide. "I'll take a cup."

"And what do you say?"

"Thank you."

Hershfeld nodded. "Our problem is, Harley, each of these young ladies," he indicated Cass and Michael, "refuses to acknowledge who the other is. I just don't know what we're going to do about it." He turned his attention to Michael. "Where'd you get that pretty dress?"

Michael pushed her face into Harley's shirt. "Gramma Bascomb," she whispered.

"It certainly is pretty," said Hershfeld.

Michael made no answer.

Cass raised her head. "Michael! What do you say?"

"Thank you," said Michael. She gave Cass a long look.

"Will you be going to school this year, Michael?"

Michael looked at the doctor as though he was really stupid.

"Uh-uh."

"Will Emily be going?"

"Mm-hm."

"Emily misses her Mommy, too, doesn't she. I'll bet you both wish she'd hurry up and get well and come home. Why don't you tell your Mommy you hope she'll get well soon? I'll bet it would make her feel a lot better."

Michael buried her face in Harley's shoulder again.

"Say," Hershfeld turned to Cass, "open that left-hand drawer, will you? There's a box of chocolate-covered creams. Maybe Michael would like one."

Cass stared at the drawer. Another trick!

But she hadn't had a chocolate-covered cream in a long time.

She jostled the drawer. Nothing happened. She pulled it open an inch. Then another, and another, until she could see inside.

Chocolate-covered creams! Surely the doctor would let her have one if he let Michael have one.

"There, Michael, your mother has the candy," said Hershfeld. "Why don't you go get some?" Harley set Michael on the floor, but she didn't move. "Cass, how many may she have?" asked Hershfeld.

Cass, shocked to find herself called upon to make a decision, bit her lip. Michael shouldn't have more than two; they were bad for her teeth. But if she only gave Michael two, then she, herself, would have to be content with that number. She looked up, a hopeful smile on her lips. "Has Michael been a good girl, Harley?"

"Quiet as a mouse and twice as helpful," said Harley. "Emily's taught her to dress herself. She can't tie bows, and she always gets buttons cock-eyed, but she tries."

For a moment Cass forgot the chocolate-covered creams. Her eyes went to the child at Harley's feet and she blinked back tears. "I'm missing all the growing up, aren't I?" She looked back at the candy. "You may have three candies." Her voice broke. "For being such a good girl."

Michael came, shyly, both hands stretched forward.

Of course that was her baby! No demon. Just Michael, frightened and confused. They said children didn't remember long at this age. Cass's hand shook as she counted out three candies.

Then she stopped, horrified at the candy she'd put into her baby's hands. She fought the disintegrating thought. Someone was trying to close a door on her. It had been so good to be out!

A test. "Harley. Do you want a candy, too?"

His dear voice. "Sure."

She couldn't hide the tears now. She counted another piece of candy into Michael's hands. Then another. "Give one to Daddy, and one to the doctor, and the rest are for you. And tell the doctor 'thank you.'" She touched Michael's hair as the child turned away; she watched the three of them put the candy into their mouths and begin to chew. She'd been crazy to imagine that it might be poisoned. It had been so long. Papa. She took a piece.

But they were still trying to close the door on her. If the candy wasn't poisoned, it might still be a trick of some sort.

No. They'd never let her go home if she kept thinking that way! She put another candy into her mouth. Papa. She had to be alone to figure out this terrible new plot. No—she had to stop thinking there was a plot.

She took another chocolate and chewed vigorously, her cheeks bulging, comforted by the growing mass of sweetness that was Papa.

She stopped chewing, grabbed two more chocolates, and crammed them into her mouth. She wouldn't chew anymore. She'd just hold the whole sweet mass in her mouth and let it dissolve slowly. That way she could keep Papa with her.

"I have a patient coming down in a few minutes. You'll have to say good-bye now, Cass."

Cass turned and stared. It couldn't be over already! There were so many things she'd meant to say to Harley, and now she couldn't because she had to keep Papa in her mouth.

She swallowed just a bit of sweetness. "How's Emily?" She must look awful with her mouth all full.

"Fine. She sends her love."

Miss Stokeham was starting toward her. No! She wanted to go home with Harley. But if she told them, she'd have to swallow all of Papa and then, if they made her go back upstairs—

She stuffed more candy into her mouth, slapped Miss Stokeham's hand away, and dived beneath the desk, trying to think what to do.

There was a murmur of voices. Cass peeked under the front panel of the desk and saw Harley and Michael going out the door. "No!"

The door closed.

Miss Stokeham whispered to the doctor for a minute, then left. The doctor turned and smiled at Cass. "You've been holding out on me. Miss Stokeham tells me you were being a very sensible girl when you took your shower. You wanted to go home."

Cass scrambled from beneath the desk. Was he going to call Harley back?

"Take some more candy," said Hershfeld. "I think we ought to talk about *why* you want to go home."

What, Cass wondered, was *this* new plot?

CHAPTER THIRTY

HARLEY DIDN'T DRIVE home through Oriskany Forks. He took the long way home, rather than see people turn and stare.

Harley, you been holding out on me? Did you catch one of them unicorns? Thomas had been perfectly serious. *Jake Burmaster says Nathan Gifford saw you riding one.*

Idiots. If they believed he rode a unicorn, what wouldn't they believe?

Yet, were they any worse than he? Didn't he believe his aunt had magic powers? Hadn't it occurred to him today that she might be responsible for Cass's madness?

It *wasn't* crazy! He had to believe that Frank's sickness, the barn burning, the calves dying, the cows being shot and Tobin broken, were all Carrie's doing. That he couldn't get a job because no one would hire a witch. Why not add Cass's insanity to the list? And what about Michael? Was she in danger, too?

Muster the forces of good, Upjohn had said. For the first time, it occurred to Harley that maybe Upjohn was crazier than Cass.

Pacing the living room, Harley could hear Michael puttering with blocks in her room. Still building caskets. Carrie *was* destroying them all!

Then Harley stopped pacing.

Was she? Was there any tangible thing that had ever happened to prove Carrie was behind everything?

Or was it only Upjohn who said so?

If he could only believe all that happened had been fate and not black magic—if he could believe there was a chance of getting out from under—!

The day that Frank choked, Harley had been so convinced. He'd felt the malignancy of Carrie and Satyendra. With his own eyes he'd seen them goad Frank until he began to choke, then feed him that medicine. But analysis had shown it was only blackstrap molasses.

The barn burning? The closed and locked doors? Wet hay, misplaced keys, fallen debris, wind.

The calves? Bacteria, drafts.

The cows? Rotten luck.

Cass's insanity? It had been building for years.

The cold spots. Had they ever really existed?

The poison Carrie had given Michael—that had been tangible. No, he'd taken Upjohn's word that it was poison. As a matter of fact, Upjohn's suggestion that it had come from Carrie was the only basis for his belief that Cass had been seeing her.

Could Carrie be innocent of all he had ever believed of her—guilty only of hatred for the name Westcott?

He had to go to her. He had to find the truth.

Harley, my boy, you seek the impossible. Truth lies at the bottom of a well. You will see only your own image—your own truth.

Wasn't that, after all, what he was seeking?

It was nearly dark when Harley left the phantom hooves behind and came out of the woods onto Carrie's road. Her house, looming suddenly before him, was like a shape perceived in a darkened room just before sleep; disproportionately large, and ominous.

No lights. That didn't mean she wasn't home, though.

He stopped at the mailbox, relieved. The box was full— weeks of letters and circulars. Carrie was off on one of her trips.

He swung down, pulled the mail from the box, and shuffled through it, straining his eyes in the failing light. Nothing, He stuffed it back, took Polly's reins, and grasped the saddle.

But he didn't mount. He looked back at the house, checked the road in both directions, and led Polly to Carrie's garage.

He was going to break and enter, and he didn't want anyone happening along, spotting Polly.

Somewhere in there he'd find something, some little thing that would tell him whether Carrie was a monster—or innocent.

There was no lock on the garage. He swung the door open and started to lead Polly in—Carrie's *car* was there!

Could she have gone away without it? He left Polly ground-tethered, strode to the front door, and knocked. No answer. "Aunt Carrie?" He continued to knock until his knuckles were sore. "All right." He stepped back. "If you won't open up, I'm coming in!"

He tried the windows; then he scaled the garden wall, thinking perhaps the back door was unlocked.

It wasn't. He knocked one more time, then smashed the glass with his shoe and stepped into—

A kitchen. No sound, not even the tick of a clock. "Aunt Carrie?"

His ears strained for a breath, a rustle, a thump. There was nothing. He groped around the wall; no light switch. Maybe a kerosene lamp on the table? Yes. And matches in a cup at its base.

He'd never realized how feeble the light of one kerosene lamp could be. No matter how high he turned the wick, there was a whole house in darkness beyond the kitchen door— waiting, like Carrie.

He started toward the hall, then stopped, looking at the cellar door. Perhaps he shouldn't leave any unknown quantities behind him. He opened the door.

"Aunt Carrie?" He started down.

There was almost nothing there. A few rows of jars, some canned goods, some kind of fungi growing—

No windows! If Carrie was tiptoeing toward the cellar door to slam it on him—

He scrambled back to the kitchen.

Silence.

He closed the cellar door and went to the hall.

Shadows raced ahead of his light and hovered, waiting, in corners and on the landing of the stairs.

"Aunt Carrie?"

He had to go on. The day Michael was born, he'd sworn to be strong.

An odor penetrated his senses, and his mind searched for a possible source. He walked—slowly, deliberately—to the only other doorway in the hall. The shadows regrouped at his entrance, rushing away before, closing in behind.

Books. That must be what he'd smelled—damp, and God only knew how old.

That left only the upstairs.

"I'm coming up," he called, as if she didn't know.

Two doors off the landing, both closed. Behind the one to the right was a sitting room or office—surprising in its charm, with none of the clutter of the book room. On the walls were framed photographs: Hitty and Tobin's wedding picture, Frank and Flora, Jason Cole, and Harley, as a child, on his first pony.

Harley moved closer. There was a patch of brighter wallpaper within the faded whole. A photograph had been removed.

He went to the desk and opened the one drawer. Empty, save for writing paper and a pen.

Then he realized that everything in the room was coated with dust. He *was* alone in this house.

With no fear now, he crossed the landing and opened the other door.

The light from his lamp struck a bureau, a chifferobe, a washstand; and all in one moment he was stepping into the room, placing his lamp on the bureau, and realizing what the odor had been, for it rushed at him now. He flattened himself against the wall and looked in horror at the bed.

Carrie. Propped on her pillows, her eyes open, staring straight at him, her body in an advanced state of decay.

The house was no longer silent. A thousand creatures began to scurry and scratch, bony hands reached for him, wings fluttered, and Harley's legs gave way.

Silence returned with Harley's strength. He got to his feet, keeping his back against the wall, and looked at his aunt's face.

It was strange how, dead there on the bed, her once-fine features bloated, she resembled the father she had consigned to a vegetable existence in another bed.

He felt he should say something to her.

"I'm sorry," he whispered.

More than ever it was necessary to find a solution to Carrie's mystery among the objects in her house.

He took a deep breath—and began to search.

The chifferobe held her dresses and coats—nothing in any of the pockets. The bureau yielded scarves, gloves, handkerchiefs, underwear. The small top drawer where he had expected to find jewelry and small personal items was empty except for a camera with no film, some silk hose, and a clothes brush. On top of the dresser was a bottle of hand lotion.

There was nothing to do except descend into the darkness below, to the books. Patiently he riffled the pages. *You can tell a lot about a person from his books.*

Not from hers. There were no bookmarks, no forgotten letters. And as for inscriptions and underscoring, the pages they might have been on had been torn out! Almost as though—

The kitchen, too, seemed empty of anything that might help—until Harley opened a Nabisco tin sitting on a shelf.

Tucked into the gray powder which filled it was a paper. Harley drew it out, dusted it off, and held it to the light.

Just a hand-drawn map of Spring Farm, the Bascombs', the woods...Harley frowned. No way to tell if Carrie was the one who'd drawn the thing. Funny place to keep it, in that Nabisco tin.

He folded the map, put it in his pocket, and pumped some water to wash that gray dust off his hands.

Then he went back upstairs to Carrie, and returned her blank stare with a thoughtful one.

Everyone left things in coat pockets from time to time. Everyone had keepsakes in dresser drawers, correspondence in desks, junk in the kitchen, even Carrie. Someone had painstakingly removed every trace of her past from this house! They'd missed only the map, and he couldn't see how that would help him.

He bent down to close Carrie's eyes; he had to search *her*, too, and he didn't want her watching.

He closed her right eyelid and reached for the left, exerting the same downward pressure as he had with the right. Then he cried out and wheeled away. The eyelid had come off; one piece now rested on Carrie's puffy cheek, another on Harley's finger.

Violently, he flung it off, then forced himself back to her, folded down the coverlet, examined the decaying flesh. There seemed to be no trace of violence on the front of her, and he wasn't about to turn her over to check the back.

No use, anyway. He was sure now that whatever had killed Carrie would not be evident externally. Maybe not even internally.

Harley turned his back on Carrie, and went for Polly, not caring now whether he was seen. "We hadn't heard from her in so long," he'd tell the sheriff, "I got worried and went over. When I saw all that mail—"

Tonight Harley was grateful for the company of the phantom hooves and for the full moon lighting the way. He tried humming "Making Whoopee" to the rhythm of Polly's hooves, syncopated by the echo.

Suddenly he thought he heard the phantom hooves miss a beat, come in late with a double clop as though they had stumbled. But Polly hadn't stumbled.

Harley swung sharply.

Did he really see it? Yes! He felt sure it wasn't his imagination. Only partly hidden by saplings—white, horselike, with the tail of a bull and a mane sweeping toward the ground. And in the center of its forehead—he was sure—one straight slender horn.

The animal's eyes seemed to meet his. It leaped into the air, cleared a log, and was gone into the depths of the wood.

Harley spurred Polly in pursuit. He was sure he could hear it, crashing through the underbrush just ahead; but no matter how Polly lengthened her stride, he could neither close the distance nor catch a glimpse of the flicking white tail.

And, where the woods ended in Westcott pastureland, even the sound of the crashing hooves ended, leaving only

Harley, Polly, Artemis tracing her lonely path across the sky, and a scent—

Musk.

Harley pounded on Upjohn's door.

It opened a few moments later. Upjohn was tying the belt of a robe, looking moist, as from a bath.

Harley walked past him and slumped into the armchair. "I've just come from Carrie's."

"You went there alone?"

"You're perspiring. Have you been out for a run? Never mind. You wouldn't give me a straight answer anyway."

The numbness that had at first shielded him from the shock of finding Carrie's body was gone now. His hands were trembling. "How about some brandy?"

Upjohn obliged. "Drink it right down."

Harley did. And through the chill, through the warmth, he watched Upjohn's face. It showed only concern.

"Who went with you to Carrie's?" Upjohn refilled Harley's snifter.

"You did," said Harley.

"I?"

Harley stared at him for a long moment, then downed the second brandy. "OK. We'll play games. I found Carrie's body. Don't bother with a big scene. I don't know how you killed her, but I know you did. You're the only one that would have—besides me. And you're the only one who would have got every last bit of incriminating junk out of that house. Because if they found out Carrie was a witch, it would clinch the case against us. Right?" Harley took the map from his pocket. "Here. You missed this. Go ahead. Take it. It's no help to me."

"Harley, you should never drink brandy so quickly," said Upjohn. He took the map, gave its contents a brief, expressionless glance, and tossed it onto a table.

"I guess maybe I should thank you for killing her," said Harley. "From the looks of her corpse, she died just after you found out she tried to poison Michael—or maybe the day Michael got lost. Just like Satyendra died right after we killed the cows, so I guess they did have something to do with that." He pushed his glass forward and watched Upjohn pour. "Every time I go into those woods, you're along. You came here when I was six and got my first pony and started going into them. Is it because they *are* evil? You going to watch after the girls, too? You were a little slow, the day Michael was lost—I found her first—but you'd been off somewhere with Lil, now that I think about it."

"You're drunk, Harley."

"I'm making perfect sense!" Harley took a deep swallow of the third brandy and leveled a finger at Upjohn. "Who the hell *are* you?"

"Your friend."

"Am I gonna be a unicorn, too, when I'm older?"

"Go home, Harley. Sleep it off."

"*Now* I know why your forehead sweats when there's poison around. Everyone knows a unicorn's horn sweats near poison!" Harley rose, chuckling, and lurched to Upjohn's bathroom. He flipped on the light and looked at the tub. "Dry as a bone. You weren't taking any bath!"

"I don't recall telling you that I was."

"Of course not." Harley wheeled. "You never really commit yourself, do you? You never get caught in a lie." He closed his eyes. "You're not gonna tell me a thing, and now I never *will* know whether Carrie was evil or whether you're just crazy." He sagged against the doorsill. "Unless you tell me."

Upjohn poured himself a brandy. "What I have not told you need not be told."

"Oh, hell." Harley turned toward the hall. "I'm gonna call the sheriff and tell him I found my dear aunt's body. That OK with you?"

"Of course," said Upjohn. Gently he reached for the snifter in Harley's hand.

Harley let it go. "What about Nick? You're so good at killing people and making it look like an accident. I've seen you looking at Lil. You get Nick out of the way so you'd have a clear path to her?"

Upjohn's face hardened. "I've seen you looking at Lil, too, Harley. Were *you* responsible?"

Harley blanched.

"Forgive me. That was cruel, but so was your remark. Neither of us was responsible."

Harley nodded, feeling sick. "I suppose if I told you I'd seen a unicorn up on the Crazy Lizzy just now, you'd tell me I was drunk before I got here."

Upjohn swirled his brandy and sniffed the bouquet. "*Did* you see a unicorn?"

"Yes."

"What a shame,'" said Upjohn, "that you did not have a camera along."

CHAPTER THIRTY-ONE

CARRIE WAS LAID to rest in the Parmalee plot at the town cemetery, with little fanfare and with few to sincerely mourn, save Flora.

Where, Harley wondered, were the things that had been taken from Carrie's house? In Upjohn's dresser drawers along with the map? Burned, most likely. And the missing photograph too—Philimentha, Harley reasoned. Upjohn had surely burned that.

When they returned from the cemetery, Flora insisted on going to Frank's bedside and telling him Carrie was dead. He was conscious—much better since Carrie's death, Harley realized suddenly. Though he said nothing when Flora told him about Carrie (for he could now say "Yes," "No," and "'itty"), tears squeezed from his eyes.

An hour later he was dead.

"Just too many people dying in that bunch to be natural."

"'Course, Jason's curse killed Frank. But Carrie? That was murder if ever I saw it."

"Not a mark on her though. Bedcovers were neat as a pin."

"Well, that's suspicious right there. Too young to be dying of a heart attack."

"Do you suppose they used Lil Bascomb's cat again?"

Mr. Sawyer dissolved his partnership with Lil the following Monday. He was reluctant and embarrassed. "You have no idea the calls I've been getting," he told her. "It's taken me twenty years to build up my practice."

"You've been good to keep me as long as you have."

"Do yourself a favor, Lil. I'll give you a recommendation that will set you up in any law office in the country. Get out of this town."

That night all the front windows of Lil's house were broken. There must have been several throwing arms involved, for it seemed that all the windows shattered at once, leaving a variety of litter on Lil's rugs—rocks, clods of dirt, tin boxes spilling horse manure, a dead rat. Around its neck was a note: "Witches die like rats."

Lil telephoned Sawyer. He and his son, Carl, were at her door in five minutes. Carl stayed to guard the house, and Mr. Sawyer followed along as Lil drove to Curt's farm.

"This enough to convince you?" he said before he drove back. "You have to get out of this town."

Lil found no sleep that night.

She'd told herself she couldn't run out on Cass, but she could never help Cass, only hurt her. She'd told herself Emily and Michael needed her; she was only using that as an excuse to see Harley. She was ruining his family with her selfishness. If she went, the Westcotts could live peacefully.

Wishful thinking. Accusations didn't get forgotten in a town like Oriskany Forks.

She should make them leave with her—Harley and the girls and Upjohn. The others would be all right with them out of the way. They'd just load some things in her car and go.

Then what would they do? Sell potions for a living? Wasn't that what witches were supposed to do?

The next day she sent Curt to Spring Farm with a message for Harley. It would be better for her not to be seen going there. Better for Harley to ride Polly through the Crazy Lizzy and meet her at the house in the woods so they could talk privately.

She left right after Curt's buggy rolled away. Harley might not be home now, she might have to wait up there for hours. But she wanted to think.

"Where are you going?" said Helen, following her to the driveway. "You're not going into the woods, are you?"

Lil left Helen at the mulberry bush by the road, her face forlorn behind her spectacles.

How long ago seemed the day that she, Cass, Muriel, and Janet had first entered these woods. Janet had married a farmer from New Devon just the week before. She was the best off of the bunch; neither missing, insane, nor persecuted as a witch.

Ahead, in its patch of sunlight, was the house—no longer frightening, for today Lil was going there not as a stranger but as a part of it. Her grandfather had built it—for her evil, rusty-haired grandmother.

You must always be good to little sisters. Philimentha, too, had had a little sister who had gone mad. Lil thought now that Philimentha must have loved and mourned Lizzy—must, like Lil, have been plagued by guilt.

What had she looked like, Mad Lizzy?

Hair the color of Lil's, Cass had said, and Muriel had nodded. *Tall and beautiful.* But that was a description of Philimentha. Maybe the two sisters had looked alike.

Yet Papa blamed Lil for looking not like Lizzy but like Philimentha.

There was a sound off to the left beyond the trees, like a hoofbeat. "Harley?"

The woods kept about its secret business.

Into the patch of sunlight that held the house, the small green things of the forest still crowded. Lil sat down, evened the laces of her saddle shoes, then rolled onto her back and stared at the sky, trying to relax. But something in her insisted on staying alert. Again she thought she heard Polly's approach. "Harley?"

Silence.

Hearing things, as she'd heard things that first day. She smiled, remembering how she and Harley had romantically assumed that witches were hiding in the upstairs room.

She glanced at the house. The front door remained comfortably closed. There had to be a way up to that room. *I've searched the downstairs rooms a dozen times,* Harley had said.

So the entrance was not in the house.

Lizzy seemed to have gone to the carriage house one day—

Lil rose and walked to within fifteen feet of that building. There didn't seem to be any way to reach the door, now; it was completely choked by raspberry bushes. Then, beneath the branches, she spied a natural arch. Thankful for her Levi's, she dropped to her knees and crawled forward, thinking that there would be just room enough next to the door to stand and shove it back on its trolley.

"Lilith." It was a voice like a bell!

She halted and looked up through the branches. Another sound: a *rasping* sound. The rusted hardware of the carriage house door had given way—the door was tottering! Lil screamed and scrambled backward, through the brambles.

A crash. A crunch.

Then the clearing returned to silence.

And Lil lay staring up at the door; its top caught by the bushes at a harmless forty-five-degree angle over her head. But had she been closer to the base—

Lil closed her eyes and felt sick. What agonies Lizzy must have endured, pinned beneath that door.

She remembered, then, the voice that had called her. Harley? Harley never called her Lilith. "Is anyone here?"

Of course there was no one there. The "voice" had been her own senses, anticipating danger.

She extricated herself from the thorns and crawled back to the clearing. With the door down and its weight flattening the bushes in front, she could see inside. It was obvious that the falling door had been an accident. It was also obvious that the carriage house could conceal no tunnel entrance. It had space for two horses and a carriage, a grain box, a floor of closely packed dirt, and walls so thin it was hard to see how horses could have survived a winter.

Oh, well. At least it was out of the sun—a good place to wait for Harley. She climbed over the door and into the shed, sat down on the grain box, and began to swing her feet idly.

But the curiosity kept gnawing. If she left Oriskany Forks, she might never come back. And she wanted to see that round room, just once.

Her glance swept the dirt floor. There was a pattern in the dirt, like the tracing of an arm as it makes an "angel wing" in snow—as though something had, again and again, swung outward from the wall on a hinge.

She stood up. One edge of the grain box corresponded exactly with the curve cut in the dirt. She stepped to that side and pulled. The box swung out, and Lil found herself staring into gaping blackness.

She fell to her knees, hardly daring to breathe. There was a ladder by which she could descend, but—

She wished Harley would hurry.

She patted her pockets. She had a book of matches for light, and she did so want to see that room...

"Lil?"

It was Helen, climbing over the door. "I swore I'd never go into these woods, but I couldn't let you come into them alone."

Then Helen stopped. She saw the shaft, looked at Lil, started to look back at the shaft, and froze.

For Lil's face wore a grin, and there was a gleam in her eyes.

"No!" said Helen. "Whatever you're planning—"

But Lil was already onto the first rung of the ladder.

"I'm not going down there," said Helen.

"Yes, you are," said Lil. "You won't let *me* go down alone."

She could hear Helen climbing down the ladder above her, but as the light faded, so did Lil's bravery. How far down did the shaft go? Why did she suddenly have the feeling—

Then there was no more ladder. Lil was down, and standing on something that crunched and disintegrated like a dry stick. She stepped aside onto something else, which also disintegrated.

Lil knelt and lit a match. Its light flared into the darkness and lit the face of a woman. The jaw opened in a slow grin of welcome.

As Lil screamed and fell backward, the match went out.

"What's the matter!" Helen was down and beside her now.

Lil didn't even hear. The woman was getting up, moving forward, reaching for Lil's throat!

Lil grabbed Helen with one hand and struck out with the other, swinging with all her might. But the air was empty, and only Lil's feet met resistance: more of those dry rungs crunched underfoot.

With a wave of nausea Lil realized what she was standing on. She groped to light another match.

As it flared, Helen cried out.

Muriel Moore sat propped against the stone wall. Moldy yellow hair and a dotted bandana still framed her skull. What Lil had been trampling on was Muriel's legs.

"Murdered," breathed Helen.

"Sshh!" Lil held up her match to see further into the darkness. Hanging on a nail at the side of the ladder was a lamp. Lil jiggled it. Kerosene splashed.

"If no one's been down here for years, the kerosene in that lamp should have evaporated," said Helen.

Lil lit the wick. The light thrown by the lamp revealed a curve in the shaft—the tunnel entrance. And leaning against the wall, Muriel's bicycle.

"Helen," said Lil, "We've got to get out right now. I think there's someone down here. The carriage-house door fell over on me before you came. I'd thought it was an accident. But now—"

Helen's hand slipped into Lil's. "Where does the tunnel go?"

"To a round room on the second floor—where my grandmother's coven used to meet."

"What do you suppose it's like?"

"Dark, probably. Every surface will be painted with ripe things. Like the maturity of a pregnancy. That's what they worshiped. Artemis and her horned consort are gods of fertility."

"I could worship that," said Helen. She turned to Lil, her homely face lit with hope. "Lil. Are you really a witch? If we went up there together and prayed, maybe Artemis and the god with the horn could help me get a baby."

"Oh, Helen!" Lil blinked back her tears. "I wish I were, but I'm not. It's a religion, not a genetic state. I don't know how they pray."

"Would you try?" Helen's eyes pleaded. "Maybe you're wrong. Maybe you inherited a talent you don't even know you have.

Maybe they really are here, Artemis and the god with the horn. That might be the funny feeling of this place. Lil, I'll get down on my knees to *anything* if it will bring Curt and me a baby."

"Helen, you're forgetting there might be someone hiding in that tunnel. We could get killed!"

"Artemis and the god with the horn will protect us."

Lil stared. Helen sounded exactly like Cass. "No, Helen. We're going back up and wait for Harley."

And, with the thought, Lil looked up the ladder toward the mouth of the shaft in the carriage shed. Something stood there, watching them. She gasped. Helen was right—the god with the horn did guard this place!

"Lilith, my dear. Are you all right?" And Toynbee Upjohn emerged from the silhouette that had seemed to be a horned animal.

Suddenly Lil was climbing upward. "I'm so glad it's you! Is Harley with you?"

"No. I was out for a stroll."

A minute passed, Lil telling all that had happened, before she realized that Helen had not followed her up the ladder.

"Helen!"

The call echoed into the darkness.

"Oh my God," said Lil. "She's going up to the room by herself. She's got some crazy idea it will help her get pregnant!"

Upjohn was already on his way down. "Stay, Lilith. I'll get her."

"No!" Lil followed him. "I think there's someone down there! You might get hurt."

"Lilith, you'll only complicate matters." Upjohn took her shoulders in the darkness as she reached the bottom. "There is more danger to you than to Helen, and none to me. You *must* wait here."

"I don't understand!"

"Let me get a light." He moved away in the darkness.

"Toynbee?"

"I'm still with you." Beyond the bicycle, and around the corner, matches flared. Upjohn returned with two lighted lanterns. "Here. Take one. I'll be back shortly."

"Wait! Please tell me what's going on."

"Let me find Helen and then we'll discuss it." He paused at the bend. "You mustn't try to follow me, Lilith. It's easy to lose oneself down here." And then he moved off, calling Helen's name.

Lil crept to the turning. The tunnel was not man-made, nor did it run in a single direction. It was a maze of subterranean caves. The silhouette of Upjohn against his lamp grew smaller, then he turned a bend and was gone, only his voice drifting back. "Helen?"

Lil glanced at Muriel and shivered. She felt as she had felt the night of the party when Upjohn left her in the closet—and forgot about her.

No. She refused to be left this time! She started after him, then stopped, frowning at the confusion of passages. She wasn't sure which one he'd gone into. For a moment she considered going on anyway. Then she turned and went back to sit beside Muriel.

It was obvious to Upjohn after only a minute that Helen had, by dumb luck, found the way to the house, else she would certainly have answered his calls. He came to a dead end, roofed by beams of the house, and hurried up a tiny spiral staircase to the second-floor room.

Helen was there, kneeling in prayer just to the right of the trapdoor in the center. She looked at Upjohn and smiled, but there was no recognition. She returned to her devotions.

Upjohn held his lantern aloft and scanned the circular room, swirling with abundance on every surface; even the chairs, tables, and chest around the perimeter smothered in ripe things.

He glanced at Helen once more. "Helen?"

She didn't answer. The giddiness that was inescapable in this room had taken hold of her mind. She, no doubt, felt a part of the harvest. He smiled.

He tiptoed to the chest against the wall and tapped on the lid. "How are you today, my dear?" There was no sound. Upjohn knelt and peered through one of the chinks in the side. "I know you're there."

"I can't come out," was the furtive whisper.

"I understand perfectly. I suppose you've noticed the lady praying in the center of the room?"

"Couldn't hardly miss her. She's a ghost. I seen her haunting the meadow house nights I've been there. She decided to haunt here now?"

"She's not a ghost, she's Curt Bascomb's wife. She's praying for a baby."

There was silence in the trunk. Then, "She must not eat right. I was sure she was a ghost. Tell her, stop praying and start eating, she might get a young'n. You bring my vittles?"

"Not today. I'll come Sunday, as usual."

"I'm plumb out of molasses."

Upjohn sighed and leaned closer to the trunk. "The people who visited you today—I do hope you understand that they are my friends. I don't think they'll ever bother you again, but if they do, I'd take it as a special favor if you would not attempt to harm either of them."

"Won't harm them if they don't harm me," said the voice. "Only you-know-who. I'll kill her every chance I get."

"Yes. Well, it's been nice chatting. Shall I leave a lamp on?"

"No matter. Just don't forget my molasses."

Upjohn went to Helen. "We'd better go back," he said. "Lilith will be worried."

Helen did not even hear. Her eyes were shut and her body swayed.

Upjohn put his hands upon her head. "Your time of barrenness has passed, Helen. You will conceive a child within the year. Keep that thought in your mind, as will I. Together we'll see your thought bear fruit." He lifted her to her feet and led her gently down the stairs.

❀ ❀ ❀

Lil heard them coming and ran to meet them. Upjohn was assisting Helen, who seemed not at all interested in what she might stumble over. "What happened to her?"

"Nothing," said Upjohn.

Helen reached out and patted Lil's face. "It was just like you told me, Lil. You really ought to go up there sometime."

"I don't seem to know the right people," said Lil. She shot Upjohn a look. "I do hope you're intending to have that discussion now."

He smiled. "Now that I'm not worrying about anyone's safety, I'll be happy to oblige."

They turned the corner, leaving the natural tunnel behind. The light from their lamps fell on Muriel propped against the wall. "I guess," said Lil, "we should tell the sheriff about her right away."

"I suggest we leave her here," said Upjohn. "She makes an admirable scarecrow."

He met Lil's shocked eyes. "We can't help Muriel by reporting this, Lilith, but we could do a great deal of injury to ourselves. Someone will discover her someday, but let it not, officially, be a Bascomb or Westcott that does."

"Lil?" It was Harley, starting down the ladder. "What's going on?"

"Especially *that* Westcott," whispered Upjohn. "Not a thing," he called to Harley. "Go back."

But Harley had already seen.

❀ ❀ ❀

A few minutes later, they reascended the ladder. "I'll answer all your questions," Upjohn had promised. "But let's make ourselves comfortable out in the sun."

Helen stepped off the ladder first, then Harley, then Lil—and found Albert Bailey and two of his deputies waiting, guns bared. "Harley, Lil. You're under arrest," said Albert. There were tears in his eyes. "I knew if I waited long enough, you'd lead me to Muriel. Now you're gonna pay for the killings you done."

Lil glanced back down the shaft. Upjohn must still be there. But if they'd all been followed, watched as they must have been watched, hadn't the watchers seen Upjohn arrive?

"No use looking down there," said the sheriff. "No one there but Muriel. Let's take them into town, boys."

❀ ❀ ❀

It was lucky for Albert Bailey that Marve Whipple, the deputy who'd been assigned to follow Upjohn that day, had, like all the "Upjohn" deputies before him, lost sight of his quarry just after Upjohn entered the woods, had sneaked around trying to find him, and had gotten himself thoroughly lost.

Marve finally sat down to rest on the edge of some sort of circular pit. He'd hardly had time to untie his shoelaces when he heard a scraping and scuffing just below his feet. Marve stood up, drew his gun, and was ready when Toynbee Upjohn emerged from the tunnel dragging a bicycle and the crumbling remains of Muriel Moore.

CHAPTER THIRTY-TWO

AT THE GRAY granite courthouse in Seneca, a sense of carnival prevailed that day in late October. The case of the mass-murdering "Crazy Lizzy Witches" had gotten extraordinary circulation; even New York papers had carried interviews with Albert Bailey. "A good man," people were saying. "He ought to run for office."

Today the street was filled with balloon men, hot-dog carts, vendors with witch masks and hats—and vendors with cushions, for the crowd was too large for the courtroom.

Folks from Oriskany Forks, who had foreseen the mobs of Senecans at the trial, were bitter about it. After all, weren't *they* the ones in danger of their lives, and therefore the most entitled to know the facts? Sheriff Bailey requested preferred seating for the locals; the court politely refused.

Led by Nathan Gifford, Oriskany Forks got up a transportation pool. Conveyances met at the village green at five a.m. that morning, loaded themselves to the running boards, and started for Seneca.

They were not, however, first in line. The Bascombs and the Westcotts were there in front of them. Mr. Grogan was with them. And Burt Barnes. And—a murmur of surprise— Father Lawrence.

Of the three defendants, only Upjohn had posted the thousand-dollar bail and roamed free these months. "You and Harley will be safer in jail," he'd told Lil in a smuggled note.

"What about you?" she'd answered.

"I'm in no danger," came the reply, "and I have work to do."

"Besides," said Sawyer, "you kids can't put up that bond. You'll need what money you got to pay Bellman's expenses."

Joseph Bellman was a "fancy New York lawyer" who had earned his reputation by successfully defending one murder suspect after another. To Mr. Sawyer's surprise and relief, Bellman had phoned his office one afternoon and asked if Sawyer might like help with the witch case. When told that the defendants could not afford him, Bellman replied, "I've been meaning to get out into the country and get a little fresh air anyway. Can they manage my expenses?...Fine. I'll be there Friday."

But when Bellman showed up, Sawyer couldn't help feeling disappointed. Bellman's face was cherubic, his eyes as guileless as a baby's. Most disheartening of all, he was an invalid on crutches.

Bellman smiled at Sawyer's crestfallen face and waved one crutch. "These will work in our favor," he said. "Mr. Roosevelt is getting so popular, the jurors like me without being quite sure why."

When Judge Engel called his court to order on that first morning of the trial, Bellman had not arrived. "Why has the defense counsel not put in an appearance?"

At that point, with a great many bumps and pardon-me's, Bellman made his way down the aisle, smiling as if to assure the audience that while progress was painful, it was bearable, and he was content with his lot in life. "Forgive me, your Honor. I was unable to obtain a taxi. I found it necessary to walk from my hotel."

Engel watched Bellman seat himself, spread his papers before him, clasp his hands, and raise his eyes to the bench. "Let the record show," Engel said then, "that defense counsel made an admirably dramatic entrance due to lack of a taxicab."

Bellman nodded sweetly.

District Attorney Anthony Scala was nervous at the thought of confronting the famous Bellman, but he took his role in the case of *The People of the State of New York vs. Westcott, Clunycourt, and Upjohn* with the utmost gravity. His own grandfather had died a horrible death back in the old country after a witch gave him the evil eye. Scala carefully avoided the eyes of the defendants as he proceeded to establish the motive of witchcraft for the murders of Satyendra and Carrie Singh, Nicholas Clunycourt, and Muriel Moore.

"Reverend Smith, when did you first become aware of the fact that the defendants were involved in strange activities?" Scala glanced at Bellman, who was preparing to object. "I'll rephrase that. When did you first become aware of the *possibility* that the defendants were engaged in what *some* might call strange activities?"

"When I received a letter from Cassandra Westcott saying they were witches."

Scala ignored the rumble from the spectators. "Reverend Smith, the defense will make much of this later, so let's discuss it here and now. Cassandra Westcott is now in a mental clinic, regarded by some to be insane—"

"I had no cause to think she was insane when she wrote the letter and I still don't."

"Tell us why, Reverend."

Reverend Smith recounted Cass's first and subsequent visits to him. "The girl is a saint, Mr. Scala," he finished. "One of God's anointed—worthy, pious, truthful." Reverend Smith inclined a learned head toward the jury. "This is not the first time that a saint has been persecuted as insane by those of lesser vision."

Bellman hoisted himself up by the table edge, got his crutches under his arms, then hobbled to the front of the defense table, and grinned at the jury. "Well!" he announced. "Seems like the district attorney would have started out by establishing a motive for the crimes my clients are accused of. But so far I haven't heard a word about any motive, or any crimes, or even the supposed victims. All I've heard—"

"Objection," said Scala. "Defense is orating."

"Sustained."

"I'm sorry," said Bellman. "But the thing that the district attorney seemed to be trying to establish through you, Reverend Smith, is that my clients and some other people are witches—which, of course, wouldn't make them criminals even if it were true, because being a witch is no longer a crime in these United States. Be that as it may, it seems important to the district attorney to establish that *you* think they are witches—"

"Get to the point, Counselor."

"I just got there, your Honor. Now *you*, Reverend Smith, think my clients are witches because you trust the word of Cassandra Westcott, is that so?"

"That is so."

"You mentioned some really marvelous qualities this girl's got." Bellman consulted his notes. "She's 'saintly, one of God's anointed, worthy, pious, truthful.' Now as to a female 'saintly' person—would you also rank chastity as a prime requisite?"

"Why no! Cassandra is married. God's law does not require—"

"I mean before marriage, Reverend. Would you say chastity *before* marriage was a prime requisite for a woman to be saintly?"

"I would. But Cassandra was a virgin when she came to me, Mr. Bellman. I had her word for it."

"That's right, I forgot that truthfulness is one of the prime virtues of a saint. Well now, Reverend." Bellman consulted his notes. "Oh yes, Reverend Smith, what is a witch?"

"What do you mean?"

"Are witches old and ugly with warts on their noses?"

Reverend Smith glanced meaningfully at the defendants. "Some are young and quite presentable.

"Then you can't tell a witch by the way he or she looks. How *do* you tell them?"

"By their evil deeds, mostly. They wish their fellows ill."

"Don't witches ever do any good deeds?"

"Never."

"Wouldn't that make a witch pretty conspicuous? Going around doing all those evil deeds? How do you suppose witches manage to live among us for years and never get found out?"

"They hide their evil by pretending to be good."

"Reverend, how can you 'pretend' to be good? If I nurse you when you're sick, the deed is done—and it is good."

"Well, I suppose witches sometimes do good deeds—but only for ulterior motives."

"Why are *you* good, Reverend?"

"Please, Mr. Bellman. That should be obvious!"

"It is. You're good because, if you're not, you think heaven will *punish* you. So you, right along with witches, have an ulterior motive for doing good deeds. Tell me, Reverend, in the secret of your own heart, have *you* ever wished another human being ill?"

"Objection, your Honor! Reverend Smith is not on trial."

"I find this line of questioning of interest," said the judge. "Please answer, Reverend."

Reverend Smith sat silent, staring down at his fingernails. "Yes," he said at last.

"Thank you, Reverend. So far, you've described a witch as a person who may be young or old, or pretty or plain, who does good deeds for ulterior motives and who sometimes wishes other people ill. You fit the description perfectly. Reverend, I call you a witch."

"That's ridiculous!"

"Yes, it is," said Bellman. "And so are the charges you and other unthinking people have caused to be brought against my clients. It might interest you to know, Reverend Smith, that this morning my clients filed suit against you and certain others for defamation of character and creating a nuisance dangerous to life and limb. You may step down."

❀ ❀ ❀

"Tell me, Mrs. Keats," said Bellman when Scala had finished with the organist, "why do you keep Kaopectate at home?"

Mrs. Keats drew a quick breath. "I don't believe that's any of your business."

"I admire your gentility, Mrs. Keats, but the lives of three people are at stake here. You keep Kaopectate at home because your bowel movements are often loose, is that correct?"

"I'm a lady. It's Charlie gets it, not me."

"How often? Once a week?"

"Couple of times a month."

"So it didn't take witchcraft that morning for Charlie to get diarrhea. Now, Mrs. Keats, how long have you been playing for the Methodist choir?"

"Ten years."

"And in that time have you ever, besides the day in question, forgotten to bring a piece of music with you?"

"A few times."

"Without, I presume, witchcraft. We come now to your final reason for thinking Lil is a witch. She played the piano for her sister, and she was not known to play well. But she played, you said, 'just like Beethoven.' Mrs. Keats, when did you hear Beethoven play?"

Mrs. Keats sniffed. "That was a figure of speech. I meant she played better than *I* could of played!"

"Thank you, Mrs. Keats. Now, isn't it true that you have a great deal of difficulty with new pieces? You take them home and you practice for days and you still miss notes and tempos."

Mrs. Keats' eyes misted. "I try so hard!"

"Of course you do. We're not complaining. The point is, if Lil played better than you, how well did she really play? She had been taught basic chords by Mrs. Hopper, had heard phonograph records of concert pianists, and was suddenly called upon to display her abilities. Don't you think that might explain Lil's performance that Sunday?"

"No! No natural human being could just up and play like that."

"Mrs. Keats! I'm sure you've read about men like Mozart, Mendelssohn, Schubert, Chopin, Brahms. Each of these gentlemen, at an age much below sixteen, sat down at a piano and began playing—often with *no* lessons—but they did quite well, even, in some cases, composed melodies. Would you call all these august gentlemen witches?"

Scala didn't even call his next scheduled witness. Violet Baxter's testimony could only repeat the shambles of Mrs. Keats'. Looking through the evidence against Harley, he called Florence Comstock.

"I've found your testimony very interesting," said Bellman as he approached the witness stand to cross-examine. "Mrs. Smith sure put a bee in your bonnet that day, didn't she?"

"I'm not sure I understand," said Florence.

"You didn't know that Harley was a witch until Mrs. Smith told you he was, did you?"

"Well, no, but—"

"So we're back to our friend Cassandra again, for Mrs. Smith's assumption was based on her husband's assumption, which was based on what that young lady had told him. And you, Mrs. Comstock, lost no time in telling your friends the exciting news, am I correct?"

"I'm not a common gossip."

"I'm sure you rank with the best of them. You are under oath, Mrs. Comstock. Isn't it true that you repeated all that had passed between Harley and yourself and Mrs. Smith to a number of your friends?"

"I guess I did tell a couple of people."

"I guess you did. I don't suppose you would recognize the doll and the cat you sold Harley that day?"

"I most certainly could."

"Good," said Bellman, "for the doll, if it has been stuck full of pins, will show pinpricks. Your Honor, may I have these two objects brought into the courtroom?"

"Of course," said Judge Engel.

Bellman signaled to Sawyer, by the side door.

But what appeared in the door was not an assistant with the doll and the cat. It was Emily, leading Michael by the hand.

"Your Honor!" Scala leaped to his feet. "I object. Counsel is using the basest sort of trick to sway the jury."

Michael had been promised she would see her Daddy. She found him and broke into a grin. "Hi, Daddy."

"Hello, darling." But Harley was pale. Bellman had not warned him.

"Your Honor," said Bellman, "the prosecution is trying to say that Mr. Westcott did not buy the doll and the cat for his children, but for some base purpose. I maintain that the only two people who can answer the prosecution's charges are *these* two people, Emily and Michael Westcott."

"Your Honor!" said Scala.

But Judge Engel was smiling at the girls, leaning over the bench. "Come here, Emily, dear—and Michael, is it? Let's have a look at your pretty toys."

Scala again looked through his list for a witness—any witness—who could establish the motive of witchcraft.

Nathan Gifford had never liked the Westcotts—you couldn't tell him that Tobin didn't milk with a quart of cream hidden in his pant leg to raise his butterfat test, and he was positive that Harley and his familiar had more than once jinxed the Gifford cattle.

"A unicorn," he explained. "I seen it following after him a couple of times."

"Mr. Gifford, the attorney for the defense will hold you up to ridicule for this story. Are you certain of it?"

"He can say anything he likes. I know what I seen—and there ain't nothing going to talk me out of it."

Scala turned to Bellman. "Your witness, Counselor."

Bellman was drawing curlicues on his pad. "I don't think I have any questions for this witness. Why don't we let him go?"

Scala blinked. "You may step down," he said to Nathan. Then, "I call to the stand the grandfather of one of the defendants—Thomas Westcott."

Thomas was surprised to find himself called as a hostile witness, but not unhappy to find himself the center of attention.

"Mr. Westcott," said Scala, "you've just heard the testimony of your neighbor, Mr. Gifford. What do you think about it?"

"Don't think much of anything about it."

"Don't be cagey, Mr. Westcott. Mr. Gifford has told me all about what you confided to him."

"I confided a lot of things to Nathan Gifford. Which one you want to know about?"

"The unicorn, Mr. Westcott. Do you think Mr. Gifford is mistaken in thinking he saw a unicorn?"

"No. There *is* a unicorn in them woods! There's no trick to seeing it—you just gotta be looking in exactly the right spot at exactly the right second. Why didn't you come out and ask me?"

"How many times have you seen this unicorn?"

"Just the once I told Nathan about."

"Would you tell the court the circumstances of that sighting?"

"Sure. It was the day Harley was born. Harley was a long time coming—when he did come, Doc thought he was dead. He tossed him on a chair and kept working on Hitty. Then, all of a sudden, Harley lets out a squall. The Doc called Tobin to come help him. It was way past chore-time, and the cows were bawling, so I went out to do the milking. I come out the back door of the house—and there was that unicorn, right at the edge of the trees, looking at the house. It was the prettiest thing I ever saw—something between a horse and a deer, though its hooves and tail were more like a bull's, and it had this great long horn in the middle of its forehead. It disappeared in such a wink, I almost got to thinking I hadn't really seen it. But I did. I know I did."

Again, when it came time to cross-examine, Bellman just looked up from his squiggles and smiled. "No questions, Mr. Scala."

❀ ❀ ❀

Scala should have been elated. The spectators and jury were now convinced that Harley, at least, was a witch. If only he knew why Bellman was not cross-examining. But what could Bellman do, after all, except try to convince those two men that they hadn't seen what they'd seen? Nothing could break the impact of that testimony, and Bellman knew it. That must be why he was not cross-examining.

Feeling confident for the first time that morning, Scala pushed on.

He called Janet Martin and questioned her in detail about the day in the woods; most specifically about the fight.

"Then, Janet, Lil hated Muriel Moore. And over some silly girlish quarrel, she flew into a murderous rage and tried to kill Muriel."

"Objection, your Honor!"

"Rephrase it as a question, Mr. Scala."

"Did it seem to you, Janet, that Muriel was in danger of her life? That Lil Bascomb was, at that moment, capable of murder?"

"Yes. It did."

Scala turned to Bellman. "Would you like to cross-examine *this* witness, Counselor?"

"I never pass up the chance to talk to a pretty young lady," said Bellman, struggling with his crutches. "Besides, I was beginning to think you'd never get around to mentioning any of the 'murder victims,' Mr. Scala. Now, Janet, why do you think Lil didn't like Muriel?"

"I guess—well, Muriel used to tease Lil a lot. She'd call her the Ugly Red Duckling and make remarks about her flat chest."

"Did she by any chance say something like that to Lil immediately before the fight?"

"Well, she said Lil was gawky and stupid and would never get a husband."

Bellman smiled at the jury, then back at Janet. "That throws a different light on things, doesn't it? Janet, when you witnessed the fight, did you think Lil was a witch in a murderous rage? Or a girl who'd had enough of insults."

"Well, I didn't think she was a witch, but—"

"That will be all, then." He looked at his notes. "Oh. Just one thing. You were describing how Harley and Lil went outside the house and whispered together, and Muriel teased Cass and said, 'You'd better watch out, I think Lil is trying to steal your'—and then Mr. Scala interrupted you."

"Objection, your Honor!"

"I must admit," said Engel, "that my curiosity was piqued, too, Mr. Scala. The sentence was so nearly complete that I think we'll consider it fair game for cross-examination. Please finish it, Janet."

"Well, Muriel just said it looked like Lil was trying to steal Cass's boyfriend."

"Cass's boyfriend?" said Bellman. "You mean Cass *liked* Harley?"

"Sure she did. And right from the first day they met, you could see that Harley liked Cass, too. Muriel teased Cass about how wonderful it would be if she could marry Harley, and how we'd all come visit her in her big house and have afternoon tea."

Bellman turned to the jury. "It has been testified here today that Cass said she did not like Harley—that she married him only because she was ordered to do so by an angel of God."

Janet's laugh faded as she caught the expression on Scala's face. Somehow she had betrayed her team.

❀ ❀ ❀

Court recessed for early lunch at Scala's request. Bailey was waiting in Scala's office, and Scala lit into him. "Damn it, Albert, I can't get past first base! I can't *prove* they're witches, and if I can't do that, I can't establish motive for murder."

Albert sighed. Scala would never be more than a small-town district attorney. All mechanics, no vision. "I thought we'd agreed to start with our eyewitnesses and our tangible evidence and forget about motive."

"It's not strong enough."

"It *is*. We got Muriel's body—"

"So what? So Upjohn got caught carting her off. That might make Harley and Lil accessories to the disposal of evidence, and what does it make Upjohn? Can't prove he killed her. No sign of violence on the body. Besides the nurse and her meditation story we've got nothing else to say about the man."

"That's just it!" said Albert. "No sign of violence on the corpse. Witchcraft. A man with no past. *Everyone* has a past. We turned this country upside down with every alias we could think of. Did Upjohn appear out of thin air? Like he disappeared *into* thin air every time he went into those woods? *Use* it, Tony! You got to be bold. Give them the tangible in each of the deaths, then pile on the intangibles with a shovel. And watch the faces of the jury. What you think is *no* evidence in this case is what's going to win your conviction. Those are good people in that jury box, Tony. Just like the judge that gave up the indictment, they'll smell the dead rat and you'll never once have to prove there's a body."

❀ ❀ ❀

Scala called Stanley Roberts, the quarry foreman, right after lunch. He established the fact that, as far as Stanley was concerned, Harley had seen the cat at Nick's elbow before Nick did and had done nothing to warn Nick. He also drew from Roberts the admission that he could not be absolutely sure that when Harley reached out to "catch" Nick, he hadn't, in fact, given him a push.

Then, obeying Albert's instructions, he began to shovel. Had Roberts ever seen that cat—any cat—around the quarry before the day Nick died? No. Had Roberts seen the cat since? No. Had he heard that the cat matched the description of the mysterious cat that had followed Cass Westcott? Yes. What happened to the cat after Nick fell?

"It just disappeared?" repeated Scala, watching the faces of the jury. "Your witness, Mr. Bellman."

"Mr. Roberts," said Bellman, "according to your testimony, you, like Harley, saw the cat before Nick did. Were you aware of the fact that Nick was afraid of cats?"

"Well, I guess he had mentioned it."

"Why didn't *you* warn Nick?"

"It all happened so fast, I didn't think to."

"Neither did Harley," said Bellman. "Now, you told Mr. Scala you can't be sure Harley didn't push Nick. Can you be sure he did?"

"No."

"About this cat, now. You're a busy man—what with dynamiting and such—do you think you'd notice if a cat did happen to wander into a noisy place like your quarry?"

"Probably not."

"Was there noise and confusion after Nick fell?"

"Yes."

"So the cat, like any sensible cat, got frightened and ran away. Mr. Roberts, if you saw the cat again, would you recognize it?"

"Maybe."

Bellman turned to the judge. "Your Honor, I have an assortment of yellow tiger tomcats outside—"

"Your Honor!" Scala leaped to his feet. "You *can't* allow this!"

"I don't see why not," said Engel. "You brought up the subject of cats, Mr. Scala."

The cats were brought in—four of them, protesting loudly. Roberts eliminated one. "Too small."

"What about the others?"

"Could be any one of them."

Bellman turned to the jury. "These cats were gathered yesterday from four farms, all within a mile's radius of the quarry where Nick died. So much for the district attorney's 'mysterious' yellow tiger tomcat."

❊ ❊ ❊

Cyrus Hamlin was the prosecution's next witness. Scala was pleased with himself for having called him—Bellman would never have thought of the librarian, he'd be unprepared. Yet, Scala was uneasy. Cyrus, at first, had declared himself hostile, then, for some reason, had changed his mind. The evidence was simple. Cyrus wrote and filed neat, individual cards each time one of his precious books got borrowed. Toynbee Upjohn had read all three of the library's books on witchcraft; Harley, two. Lil had read just one, but she had renewed it.

Bellman began his cross-examination by establishing a distinction that Scala had failed to consider. Two of the books were definitely *anti*-witchcraft. "Still," said Bellman, "reading three books on witchcraft is unusual."

"Yes," said Cyrus. "The only others who read all three are Reverend Smith and Sheriff—"

"Your Honor!" Was there nothing Bellman had failed to anticipate? "I demand that the remark be stricken from the record!"

"Jury will disregard."

But the jury was still tittering. Bellman excused Cyrus and took his seat. "Your Honor," said Scala, "may I examine the cards in evidence?" He examined the titles, smiled, and asked permission to redirect.

"Mr. Hamlin, the book that Lil borrowed and renewed—was it one of the two *anti*-witchcraft books?"

Cyrus glanced at Bellman. "No, but—"

"That will be all."

"Permission to re-cross, your Honor...Mr. Hamlin, is the book she read actually *pro*-witch-craft?"

"It's just a study," said Cyrus. "It doesn't draw a moral conclusion one way or the other."

Sheriff Bailey was to have been the next witness, but, despite having won at least a draw, Scala decided to give the jury time to forget their amusement over the fact that Bailey had read all those books. He called Frank Parmalee's nurse and spent an inordinate amount of time discussing the meditations.

Bellman had only one question. "Did anything *bad* ever happen to Frank as a result of these meditations?"

"No, he just got better."

Bellman turned to the jury and smiled at one particular lady. "I'm sure there are some people in this courtroom who find that fact anything but strange—I mean, of course, those persons with a background of Christian Science."

"Sheriff Bailey," said Scala, "how did you happen to get in touch with Caroline Singh?"

"I'd been suspicious of Harley and Lil since the day Muriel disappeared—they showed up at Spring Farm together, claiming it was a big surprise to them that Muriel was missing. Anyway, along about the first of this year, I began remembering how Harley's uncle died when his car went through a guard-rail near his home. On a hunch, I went up to have a talk with Carrie." Albert took a breath and said the next very quickly. "She told me that killer witches led by Harley had killed her husband and were after *her*."

Scala waited for the "hearsay" objection from Bellman. None came. "Tell us about your next visit to Mrs. Singh."

"It was the night of Cass's breakdown." Sheriff Bailey described the events preceding that breakdown. "Her behavior was just too much of a coincidence not to be the work of the witches. I went to Carrie, hoping to get more information. I found her dead."

"What else did you find, Sheriff?"

"Well, first of all, the place had been cleaned out. Everything of a personal nature had been removed from Mrs. Singh's effects—even her mailbox was empty. The killer missed just one thing. A letter, pinned inside Mrs. Singh's nightgown, over her heart."

The letter was placed into evidence and read by the bailiff. Scala watched Bellman's face.

He's killing me. I dreaded this. From the moment I saw him, I knew he was the one who'd been working against me all these years. I know now it was he who killed Satyendra. I can only guess at what he is, so incredible is his power. I am too weak to fight now, but my hatred will gather strength beyond the grave. I go to my God—and I call upon Him to avenge me. I lay this paper over my heart. My God, hear my call. My hatred, destroy my killer—and destroy all the Westcotts.

Bellman actually frowned! Scala immediately asked if the defense would like them to validate Carrie's handwriting. There was the deed to her house, and postcards she'd written to her mother—

"Defense will concede that the note is in Mrs. Singh's hand," said Bellman.

Triumphantly Scala turned back to Sheriff Bailey. "Why didn't you report Mrs. Singh's death immediately?"

Albert sat back, smiled, and angled his body so that his star flashed at the jury. "Mr. Scala, there are people who know, just from standing in a certain spot, that there's water hidden beneath them. I got the same talent when it comes to sniffing out the truth of a crime. I had the whole thing figured out, but I had to bide my time. If that body went unreported long enough, the killer would be drawn back to see what had happened or maybe to work some spells on it. I put a twenty-four-hour watch on the house."

"And the killer came back?"

"Harley Westcott."

Even Judge Engel glanced at Bellman, expecting an objection.

"Did he perform spells on the body?" asked Scala.

"Yes, he did. He tore her eyelid off."

A shudder ran through the spectators.

"Why did you make no arrest at that point?" said Scala.

"Because I knew they'd killed Muriel Moore, too. I had every one of them followed by deputies. Sure enough, Harley and Lil led me to Muriel's body—out in a cave under Crazy Lizzy's place."

Scala turned to the jury. "The same sinister spot where Lil and Muriel had their fight. I think we're beginning to understand about that house."

"So you're the famous Sheriff Bailey," said Bellman as he approached. Albert gave a modest smile. "Nothing gets people chuckled up like a pack of witches, does it, Sheriff. Everybody with his eye on high public office—"

"Objection, your Honor! Counsel's slur on the integrity of the sheriff is reprehensible."

"Cross-examine, Mr. Bellman, don't smear."

Bellman nodded, sweet again. "Sheriff, you just gave testimony composed almost entirely of hearsay, opinion, and pomposity. If I'd objected to everything I should have, we would have been here till midnight. You say you went to see Mrs. Singh 'on a hunch' because her husband had died in an automobile accident. I happen to have the coroner's report, and your *own* report of that death. It was a dangerous corner. Before Mr. Singh's, there had been four accidents there in as many years, resulting in one death and five injuries. What made you, years later, decide to seek another answer to that death?"

"Well, like I said, it was a hunch. First Muriel, then Singh, and later Nick. Too many strange deaths around those people."

"Strange? Mr. Singh was an obvious accident, and I think we have established that Nick also died accidentally. Muriel we'll get to presently. Now about this note you found on Mrs. Singh's body—oh, by the way, I have the coroner's report on *her* death, too. Malnutrition. She didn't take care of herself. But her note says, '*He's* trying to kill me.' Why didn't Mrs. Singh make the destruction of her killer certain by naming him outright?"

"She'd already told me who it was."

"But why didn't she make your job easier by being explicit in the note? Might it be because it was not meant for you? Might not the note have been some sort of curse leveled by a woman mistaking her sickness for murder—the raving of her unsound, hate-filled mind?"

"Mrs. Singh seemed perfectly sane to me."

Bellman smiled. "Cass Westcott seemed perfectly sane to you, too, didn't she?"

"Well, now, I—"

Bellman rescued him. "That's all right, Sheriff. We all make mistakes from time to time. As the case stands, Mrs. Singh was undoubtedly of unsound mind. The careful clearing out of personal effects was probably done by Mrs. Singh herself, knowing her end to be near and wishing to take all trace of her past with her. We found the remains of a good-sized bonfire in the woods behind her home.

"Now. You found the poor woman's body, and instead of seeing it got decent burial, you left it to putrefy for months, hoping to catch some imaginary killer. And who did you catch? Her nephew, going to see her on family business, alarmed at the piles of mail in the mailbox, knocking, deciding finally to break in and see if his aunt was all right. Which brings us to that missing eyelid. Sheriff, when you first found the body, were the lady's eyes open?"

"Staring like she was alive," said the sheriff. Then he realized his mistake.

Bellman smiled. "And when you entered the house after Harley's report of her death, one of her eyes was closed." Bellman told the court what had happened when Harley attempted to close the second eye. "That boy's simple, brave act of respect has been rewarded by the accusation that he was performing some impious rite. Sheriff Bailey—for *shame!*

"Now, what does that bring us to? Ah, yes. You 'knew,' then, that Harley and his friends had killed Muriel Moore. I'll be presenting affidavits as to their whereabouts that day, but Sheriff, please tell me what, besides ambition, gave you the ridiculous idea that Harley and his friends had killed Muriel Moore?"

The sheriff stared at Bellman. "It just had to be, that's all! It didn't take half a brain to—"

"Ah!" said Bellman. "You've explained the whole thing."

During Whipple's testimony on the capture of Upjohn, Bellman sat squiggling. He did not cross-examine.

At five o'clock that afternoon, the prosecution rested its case.

That evening Bellman went first to Harley's cell, half an hour later to Lil's; and then to his hotel, where Upjohn was waiting. They conferred for an hour, and went their separate ways.

At eight o'clock Bellman arrived at Spring Farm. The Bascombs were staying there that night. And outside, four Pinkertons, paid by Bellman, patrolled the darkness.

Bellman asked to speak with Tobin privately.

CHAPTER THIRTY-THREE

THE MORNING PAPERS were heartening; some of the reportage favored the defense. And though most of the spectators remained surly, Bellman saw a few smiles of encouragement being directed toward Harley and Lil as they were brought in.

Harley looked drawn. He'd left Tobin stoop-shouldered in the hallway. "I'm going home, son. I just can't sit through the story again. Bellman's doing the right thing, and he had to tell me. Don't worry."

But Harley couldn't stop thinking of Tobin heading home alone, tortured by grief and self-reproach. He motioned to his brother-in-law. "Drive my mother home, will you, Curt? Tell her to stay with my dad. Tell her not to let him out of her sight."

Lil, too, agonized for her father. Everyone had begged Paul to stay at Spring Farm, warned him he'd hear things that would hurt. He'd insisted on coming. And now he sat, church-pew straight, refusing to acknowledge Lil's glances.

Scala was tense through the testimony of the first defense witness, Dr. Hershfeld. All damaging. But damaging enough? If Bellman had nothing worse in store—he and Albert had worked into the wee hours on Scala's summation. He had to hand it to that Bailey. It was going to be a spellbinder worthy of Bellman himself.

"What kept Cass from breaking down long before she actually did?" Bellman was saying.

"Probably the medal I told you about," said Hershfeld. "The one she says she got from a unicorn."

Scala sat forward as Bellman hurried on to other subjects. He must be hoping Scala hadn't noticed.

Scala rose to cross-examine. "So, Doctor, Cass Westcott is insane—the witches merely her imagination. Yet I heard you speak of a unicorn. What does Cass 'imagine' she saw?"

Hershfeld told him.

"And you consider this fantasy?" said Scala.

"Of course."

"It might interest you to know, Dr. Hershfeld, that Cass is the third person to have seen a unicorn in those woods. Doesn't that strike you as quite a coincidence? You must admit, Doctor, that among the fantasies of North Americans, unicorns are rare. Yet three separate people who knew the defendants have seen a unicorn—first following Harley Westcott, and now following Lil Bascomb. You may step down."

Bellman seemed unperturbed. "I call to the stand George Folger."

Harley lowered his head into his arms as the bailiff admitted a man in his sixties, small, with nervous hands and a twitch—a man immune from prosecution in return for the evidence he was about to give.

"Where do you live, Mr. Folger? And what is your occupation?"

"I'm a veterinarian. From Pennsylvania."

"Would you tell the court how you happen to be here to testify for the defense?"

"My cousin saw a piece in the paper a few weeks ago about this trial. She's Alice Bascomb, Lil Bascomb's aunt. And when she saw what Lil and Carrie's nephew were being charged with, she told me I better testify or else." Folger glanced at someone in the crowd of spectators, and Paul Bascomb turned. Alice nodded hello. Quickly Paul's eyes returned to Folger—his unknown cousin.

"Because it's not the defendants who was witches," Folger was saying. "It was Mrs. Singh."

Bellman let the hubbub die.

"You see, Mr. Bellman, my sister and my Aunt Philimentha, Alice's mother, were involved in some bad stuff—worse than witchcraft. They practiced black magic, making people sick and such. Called themselves MS.D's.—that's a degree they used to give in medieval times, Doctor of Metaphysical Sciences."

"And how did Carrie come to be part of this group?"

"Well, when my Aunt Philimentha was just a girl, she married a man named Stockbridge, and they moved up here to Oriskany Forks. Stockbridge finally threw her out. She was practicing witchcraft, her and some others, and one of them was

Carrie's grandfather, Jason Cole. They'd kept in touch, and when Carrie ran away from home, Jason sent her to Aunt Philimentha. By this time Aunt Phil was into the real bad stuff, and she taught it to Carrie."

"Are *you* a practitioner of black magic?"

"No! They tried to get me into it, my sister and their friends—Mr. Singh, he was one of them—but I told them I didn't like it. Besides, my wife is a real God-fearing woman, and if she'd ever found out, she'd have left me. Anyway, when Carrie figured she was powerful enough at her spells, she went back to Oriskany Forks. Aunt Philimentha was going to come along. The two of them was going to make all the Westcotts sick, give them bad luck, and finally kill them. And Carrie's father, Frank Parmalee, too."

"Why did your aunt agree to help Carrie in this undertaking?"

"Aunt Philimentha had been real close with Jason Cole, who'd put a curse on Frank Parmalee, and she wanted to see it got carried out. Besides that, the reason her husband tossed her out was the real serious affair she was having with John Westcott—Harley's great-grandfather. John had promised her if her husband ever found out about them, he'd go away with her. When the chips were down, he refused to do it. Aunt Phil swore then she'd get every last Westcott with her hexes. Always claimed she actually did get John."

"Where is she now?"

"She disappeared. She was supposed to meet Carrie in Oriskany Forks, but she never showed up. So Carrie worked by herself for about six years. She was real patient, but after a while, things were going slower than she'd planned. It seemed as though everything she tried to do got stopped. Like there was a counterforce working against her, she said. Finally, Singh went up to help her. When he died, Carrie was fit to be tied. She kept feeling this good force working against her. She got desperate and decided she had to do things besides spells. I mean physical things, like she and Singh had already done when they burned the Westcotts' barn down."

A murmur swept the Oriskany Forks contingent—farming people mostly, with hay-filled barns.

Bellman placed into evidence the map Harley had found in Carrie's Nabisco tin. "Do you recognize this, Mr. Folger?"

"Yes. It's Carrie's map. She carried it around with her, and I saw her looking at it lots of times. One day she was sticking a pin in it, and when I asked her why, she laughed and said the map was an old friend, and it had already done her good service. That's when she told me she and Singh had burned the Westcotts' barn."

"Objection," said Scala. "Hearsay."

"Overruled," said Engel.

Bellman smiled. "Go on with your story, Mr. Folger. How did you become actively involved with Mrs. Singh?"

"Well, one day, about three years ago, Carrie shows up at my house. I told her I wouldn't help her. She says I'd better help her, or she'll put a curse on the wife and me, and kill us both. Well, the wife is in poor health anyway—you understand how it is—I just couldn't risk having Carrie down on us. And I didn't realize till I was in too deep what Carrie was up to."

"And what was that?"

"She tricked Tobin Westcott into thinking his herd was tuberculin and had to be shot."

The spectators sat stunned for a moment. Then a sound, almost a growl, swept them.

Folger's hands fluttered.

"Don't be afraid," Bellman said. Engel silenced the court. "How did Carrie manage it, Mr. Folger? A man doesn't just shoot a prize herd."

"She'd been planning it for over a year. First she got a job at Mr. McCullock's office—he's the Regional Commissioner of the Eradication Program. Carrie put Tobin's name on a list of herds to be checked, put my name on the list of accredited vets, and saw to it that I was the one sent over to Tobin's."

"Were any of the cattle, in fact, tubercular?"

"No. I faked the reports. Carrie put the paper work through, and Commissioner McCullock signed the order to have them killed. He didn't have cause to suspect anything."

"Didn't the herd have to be appraised for indemnity?"

"Tobin's herd was so well-known, wasn't any question he should get maximum price. Carrie wrote out the requisition and the commissioner just signed it." Folger shrugged. "It was all so simple. And Tobin was never the wiser. Just at the end he phoned McCullock's office. The secretary he talked to told him that there wasn't a bit of doubt his cattle had to be shot. But, of course, the secretary he talked to was Carrie."

There was no sound in the courtroom except the clumping of Bellman's crutches as he paced to his table and then back to the box. "Mr. Folger, that's a pretty sad tale. Why did you help Carrie when you realized what she was up to?"

Folger gave a short, tense laugh. "I'd seen what Carrie and her like could do. I mean, when Carrie threatened to kill us, it was no idle threat!"

"Mr. Folger, all these other things you knew of and assumed to be the result of magic—are you sure they weren't coincidence?"

"Coincidence, my foot! Her magic's *still* working. I wouldn't put it past her to kill herself and accuse Harley, just so this would happen to him. And now look what I've had to testify to. This is all part of Carrie's plan—she was going to tell Tobin, eventually, what she'd done. She expected the news to kill him. Look at his son sitting over there!" Harley sat as with the weight of a hundred years. "You just told him about all this last night. If you think it's hard on him, what do you think it's doing to Tobin? I tell you, Carrie's just as much alive as if she sat in this courtroom!"

Scala had no questions for George Folger.

❊ ❊ ❊

"I call to the stand Toynbee Upjohn," said Bellman.

Had Bellman gone mad? Scala turned and stared as Upjohn crossed to the witness box. A defendant left open to cross-examination? A defendant who had been caught red-handed?

"Mr. Upjohn, are you a witch?"

"No."

"Are you a practitioner of black magic, or a Satanist?"

"No."

"To your knowledge, do Harley and Lil fit into any of those categories?"

"No."

"To your knowledge, were Harley and Lil in any way involved in any of the deaths of which they are accused?"

"No."

"Were you?"

"Yes."

Scala rose to his feet without even knowing he'd done so. Lil cried out and reached for Harley's hand. The courtroom was a bedlam. Judge Engel pounded his gavel. "Silence!" Spectators were clapping each other on the back. *"Silence!"* Engel sighed and mopped his brow. "Go on, Mr. Bellman."

"Tell us how you were involved, Mr. Upjohn."

"I was involved in the death of Muriel. My sin was missing a Sunday—if I hadn't, she'd probably be alive today. I also failed to report the whereabouts of her corpse."

"As Sheriff Bailey failed to report the whereabouts of Carrie's," said Bellman. "Now, were you, in fact, caught red-handed attempting to escape with Muriel's body and her bicycle after Harley and Lil were arrested?"

"I noticed no change in the color of my hands, but I *was* carrying the articles you mentioned when a gentleman with a gun apprehended me and insisted on applying handcuffs."

"Why were you attempting to make off with those articles?"

"To save the two people I love most in this world from exactly what has come about."

Bellman clumped back to his table. "Your witness, Mr. Scala."

Scala sat shocked, trying to decide what to do. He glanced at his assistant. The assistant shrugged.

It was a trap. He'd fool Bellman. He'd let the testimony stand.

But maybe Bellman had *figured* he'd let it stand. Maybe *that* was the trap.

How had Upjohn come off? Nobly. He'd sacrificed himself. But he hadn't admitted murder. Scala glanced at the jury. They were as confused as he was.

He rose. Take it easy, he thought. Probe. Stall.

He glanced at his notes. The examination had been so limited—

"Mr. Upjohn, you say you're not a witch. Why then have you read all the library's books on witchcraft?"

"I am a teacher, Mr. Scala. If you checked with Mr. Hamlin, you would find that your question should more properly be, 'Why have you read *all* the library's books?'"

"All?"

"Cyrus may have some new things I don't know about yet."

Scala turned away, wishing he'd gone into medicine. Bellman there, with his baby face. Just waiting.

He turned back to Upjohn, met Upjohn's eyes and stopped, an odd feeling flowing through him. Upjohn's eyes were without fear, without rancor. They were—replete with understanding. This man couldn't have killed anyone. No—

The man *was* a witch! That's why Bellman had put him on the stand—to mesmerize him into losing the case!

"Mr. Upjohn, you were a difficult man to trail. You went into those woods often, and Sheriff Bailey's men always lost you. You simply disappeared. How do you explain that?"

"Since I never saw any of the sheriff's men, I assume they were forced to follow at such a distance that it was impossible *not* to lose me once I walked into those trees."

"Very clever, Mr. Upjohn. Here's one you won't be able to get around. *Why* did you go into those woods?"

"Most often for a stroll. Sometimes to visit the house where Muriel's body was found."

"And why did you go to that house?"

"To take care of the old lady who lives there," said Upjohn.

Scala backed away. He refused to look at Bellman. "No further questions," he muttered, and sat down to wait.

"Your Honor, before calling my next witness, I must explain to the court that the person whose name will be circumlocuted in the testimony is Philimentha Stockbridge.

"I call to the stand Eliza Stockbridge, sometimes known as Crazy Lizzy."

Paul Bascomb cried out and sat forward. In the doorway of the waiting room stood a small, frail creature with tangled gray hair, wearing a spotted skirt and a bodice from a bygone age. As her eyes swept the spectators, she turned to flee.

Toynbee Upjohn rose. "Eliza," he called. He went to her and took her by the shoulders, speaking words of encouragement. Finally, throwing panicked looks about her and clinging to Upjohn's arm, she allowed herself to be led to the witness box. She sat, at Upjohn's command, but refused to release his hand.

"If the court please," said Bellman, "the witness has not seen this many people in one group for many years. She will be more comfortable if her friend Mr. Upjohn remains beside her."

"Mr. Upjohn may stay," said Engel.

"How old are you, Lizzy?"

Lizzy eyed Lil. "I was born long about '46."

"Well, Lizzy, there are a lot of people in the courtroom today who are surprised to see you. They thought that house in the woods was deserted. They thought you were dead."

"Not dead. Just minding my own business."

"Then the woman they found under the door at your place was—"

"Don't say her name! Toynbee promised you wouldn't! The evil in that name's as bad as she is."

"Of course. We'll just refer to her as your sister. She's the one who had the terrible accident with the door."

Lizzy tossed her head toward Lil. "Does *she* have to be here?"

"I'm afraid so."

"Makes me nervous," said Lizzy. "You can never be sure when you-know-who's got possession of her."

"You mean you think because Lil bears a resemblance to her grandmother—your sister—that your sister can take possession of Lil's body?"

"I don't think. I know."

"But your sister is dead."

"Bad ones like her never die."

Scala rose. "Your Honor, this woman is obviously insane. Her testimony is inadmissible."

"Your Honor," said Bellman, "Lizzy believes her sister's evil spirit is strong enough to survive the grave and search her out. The district attorney and many others here believed that Lil and Harley and Mr. Upjohn could cast spells to give people diarrhea, sicken cattle, conjure cats from porcelain statues, and keep a unicorn for a pet. If Lizzy is insane, then so are half the people in this courtroom!"

"Overruled," said Engel.

Bellman smiled. "Now, Lizzy, what makes you think that your sister can take possession of Lil's body?"

"Well, just look at her," said Lizzy indignantly.

"We understand that Lil is the spitting image of your sister. But have you ever *seen* Lil do anything bad? Cast spells, or work magic?"

"No."

"Did you ever see your *sister* cast spells or work magic?"

"Seen her plenty."

"Had Paul ever seen his mother work spells?"

"Yes."

"Lizzy," said Bellman gently, "if Paul was familiar with his mother and her ways, why do you suppose that after all these years of seeing Lil day in and day out, *he* never saw anything to make him think his mother was taking possession of Lil?"

Lizzy blinked and stared at Bellman.

Lil turned and looked at Paul. There were tears in his eyes, and he would not look at her.

"Do you suppose, Lizzy, that it's because your sister is really and truly dead and never does take possession of anyone or anything? Do you suppose maybe it's your own imagination that's kept you living in terror all these years?"

Lizzy shook her head stubbornly. "Bad ones like my sister never die." But her brow furrowed in thought. "Can't rightly understand how Paul never saw it."

Bellman sighed. "All right, Lizzy. Do you recognize that young man sitting beside Lil?"

"I seen him lots. He used to come by on his horse."

"Did you ever see him doing anything bad or witchy?"

"Not witchy. But I seen him fornicating with a girl once." She pointed to Lil. "The other look of her—the little one with the dark hair."

"You mean Lil's sister, Cass?"

"If that's what you want to call her. They was fornicating in broad daylight, right in front of the house."

"Was that before Harley and that same girl were married?"

"I dunno. When were they married?"

"December 30th of the year Paul moved back to the meadow house."

"Well, then, it was before. We hadn't had a snowfall yet when I seen 'em fornicating."

"The girl you saw fornicating told Paul and her pastor that she didn't even like the young man," said Bellman. "She told them she only wanted to marry him because an angel ordered her to."

"Wouldn't no angel come to the likes of her."

"But maybe Harley *forced* her to fornicate. Maybe—"

Lizzy cackled. "He was on his horse all set to ride away! She grabs him and says, 'I love you. You can do anything you want to me.'"

"To your knowledge, Lizzy, was that the only bad or suspicious thing you ever saw Harley do?"

"Yes."

"If he was a witch, you, being familiar with witches, would have spotted it?"

"If he was a witch, the creature that guards the woods wouldn't have nothing to do with him."

Bellman went on quickly. "Now, Lizzy, there's just one other thing we've got to clear up. Harley and Lil here have been accused of murdering several people. One of these people is a girl named Muriel Moore. She disappeared about five years ago. Pretty, with blond hair—and when she disappeared, she was wearing a yellow dress and a dotted scarf. Have you ever seen a young lady like that?"

Lizzy sat silent.

"Lizzy," said Bellman gently. "Are you going to make me put Mr. Upjohn on the stand again?"

Lizzy pouted. "You'd tell them, wouldn't you, Toynbee."

"I'd have to," said Upjohn. "I'd be under oath. And so are you."

Lizzy sighed and looked down at her worn old hands. "The first time I seen her, a whole pack of 'em come up to the house. Her and the redhead and the fornicating look of the redhead and another one. You remember, Toynbee? You were with me."

"It's been testified that doors opened and closed by themselves that day," said Bellman.

"Doors always open and close by themselves in that house. It's her—my sister's magic that does it."

"When was the last time you saw Muriel?"

Lizzy fussed with her skirt. "Well, I didn't rightly see her at first. I heard her, calling out for help. She must've climbed down into the tunnel and lost herself. She was way down one of the passageways—and I was afraid. I figured it was my sister trying to trick me into going down there and getting lost. And when I found her bicycle, I thought that was part of my sister's plan, too. So I just dumped it down into the tunnel and went and hid." She glanced at Upjohn. "Toynbee found her the next time he came by. He'd missed a Sunday. He usually comes Sunday at least, brings my food and we visit. He was real mad at me, but it was too late by then. She was dead."

"Why didn't you report Muriel's death to the authorities?"

"Toynbee was all set to, but I begged him please not. He finally allowed as how it wouldn't help the girl none to report it. So we left her."

Bellman turned to the jury. "Until she was found quite accidentally by Lil and Helen and Harley. Your witness, Mr. Scala."

Scala rose slowly. "Lizzy—you mentioned a creature that guards the woods. What does it look like?"

"A little white horse with a horn on its head.

"And you've seen this creature fraternizing with Harley?"

"Doesn't fraternize with anybody. It's powerful shy."

"But you've seen it following Harley?"

"Yes."

Scala took a step closer to Lizzy. "Why are you trying to shield your niece?"

Lizzy looked confused. "Who's that?"

"Lil, of course."

Lizzy shook her head. "Alice is my niece."

"Well, your great-niece, then."

"I suppose she is. I never thought about it."

"Didn't Mr. Upjohn and Mr. Bellman put you up to this?"

"Objection!" said Bellman. "The witness has told the truth and now the district attorney is badgering her."

"If it is the truth," said Judge Engel, "all the badgering in the world will not shake her. Witness will answer the question."

Lizzy looked at Engel. "What was it?"

"The district attorney wants to know if Mr. Upjohn and Mr. Bellman put you up to telling this story."

"Oh, sure," said Lizzy.

"You mean," said Scala, "they dictated a false story of Muriel's death and made you come to this courtroom and lie under oath?"

Lizzy got to her feet. "It ain't no false story! All Toynbee done was to tell me someone was being accused of the murder of that girl. He said if I had any decency left in me, I'd come down here and tell you the truth. So that's exactly what I done. Now I got to find another hiding place, and I'll never find one as good as the one I had. I shan't go to all that trouble just to be accused of lying by a whippersnapper like you. Toynbee, take me away!" And Lizzy stepped out of the box.

"Witness has not been excused!" said Scala.

Engel smiled. "You have my permission to force the witness back into the box, Mr. Scala—if you can."

❀ ❀ ❀

"I call the final witness for the defense—Dr. Giles Townsend." Bellman watched the jury as the tall, white-haired man was sworn in. Dr. Townsend, the first questions revealed, was a professor of ancient history at the University of Ottawa. He's also the author of a book—*The Living Unicorn.*

Scala sat back helplessly. This was why Bellman had baited him to cross-examine unicorn references.

"Dr. Townsend, what qualifies you as an expert on unicorns?"

"Well—no school gives a doctorate. However, unicorn legends have fascinated me since my youth, and I've read everything available on the subject."

"*Is* there such a thing as a unicorn, Dr. Townsend?"

Townsend smiled. "That depends on the plane of being you're referring to."

"I don't understand."

"There's the weighted and measured plane of reality that science demands nowadays, and then there is the plane that science has taken from us—faith and spirit and imagination. It has nurtured man's finest achievements, among them the unicorn. He, as far as I'm concerned, is more real, more worthy of my devotion, than any scientific entity could ever be."

"But what is so special about the unicorn?"

"To me, the very fact that the human mind was able to conceive a creature—absolutely good, absolutely pure—and to keep him that way for over four thousand years. Even the gods we dreamed up quarrel—they're vengeful, they kill, they scatter hardship willy-nilly—in short, they are just as ignoble as ourselves. But not the unicorn. He seeks only good, he does only good. He proves there's nobility in the soul of man, though man himself has not discovered that nobility as yet."

"What about Christ, Dr. Townsend? Christ is pure."

"So are Buddha and Confucius. Those three men are the closest the human mind has come to the perfection of the unicorn. But the triumph of the unicorn is greater. Unicorn legends, in varying forms, seem to have been spontaneous worldwide, not an idea of just one people of one region. And, by the way, since you bring up the subject of Christ—the unicorn was used for centuries as the symbol and personification of Christ."

"Hasn't the unicorn ever been associated with witches?"

"If you're referring to witches of popular imagination, no. But real Wicca worship centers around Artemis. And that's where the association might arise. The consort of Artemis is a horned hunting god. And yet, later, with the decline in the need to hunt, the horned god might have come to be thought of as the unicorn, or the unicorn the horned god. But as to his being a 'familiar' of 'wicked' witches? Absolutely not. As a matter of fact, the unicorn is thought to be a devil-fighter."

"Tell me, if this unicorn had put in an appearance at the birth of a boy, and had later been seen to follow that boy around—and if this unicorn had been observed making a gift to a young girl—what would you say about that boy and that girl?"

"People actually saw this?" Townsend stared at Harley and Lil. "Did you ever hear its voice? It's supposed to have a voice like a bell."

Lil gasped and turned to Harley. Harley stared straight ahead.

"You can speak with them later, Dr. Townsend. In the meantime, what would you say about a boy and a girl who drew the unicorn's attention?"

"I can tell you what the Chinese would say—their unicorn, or *Chi-lin*, over four thousand years old, comes from heaven on very rare occasions to herald the birth of someone great and good."

"What might explain the unicorn's following the boy and giving this gift to the girl?" Bellman went to his briefcase and produced the medal.

Dr. Townsend smiled. "Mercury, the metal of the Moon. The clog, the serpent, the unicorn—the straight object here is certainly the horn of a unicorn—they're symbols for the phases of the moon. The six-pointed star is a symbol of fertility. If I were a unicorn, I could think of no more representative gift."

"Why do you think, Doctor, that this unicorn—and we're granting just for the moment that such a being from another plane of existence might have been glimpsed by some lucky people— why do you think this unicorn was hanging around this particular woods, and why do you think he tried to give Lil this medal?"

"Well, one of the properties of the medal is protective, and the unicorn himself is a protector. This unicorn might be on assignment, so to speak, guarding worthwhile individuals from an existing evil."

"In your opinion, could the young man and the young woman accused here today of witchcraft and murder possibly be guilty? Could they possibly be evil?"

"No," said Dr. Townsend. "Not if the witnesses really saw a unicorn."

"Perhaps we might go into the woods and trap the unicorn, to prove to ourselves that he does exist."

Townsend smiled. "Mr. Bellman, man has pursued the unicorn for untold centuries. He has never, save for fantasy, entrapped him. The unicorn remains—as he must remain— solitary and beyond our grasp."

At two o'clock that afternoon, Lil, Harley, and Upjohn were free.

CHAPTER THIRTY-FOUR

ALTHOUGH HARLEY WAS worried about Tobin and anxious to start home, he, Upjohn, Lil, the family, and witnesses remained in the deserted courtroom for hours. The crowd waiting outside had refused to disperse, and their mood, the police felt, was too uncertain for safety.

George Folger spent his time in a corner of the courtroom picking at his nails; Paul Bascomb paced with rigid steps and glared at Emma, who chatted amiably with Alice.

Paul spoke only to his aunt. "You ought to be paddled, Aunt Liz, starving up there all these years and never letting me know."

Lizzy had kept a firm hold on Upjohn's arm throughout the wait. "I never starve," she said. "Toynbee sees to me."

"Toynbee!" Paul stalked away.

Upjohn smiled across the room to Lil. He had been avoiding Harley's trusting glances, but not hers. He glanced down at Lizzy's iron grip and beckoned to Lil with his head.

She rose and came warily toward her great-aunt.

"I don't believe you and Lilith have been formally introduced, Eliza."

Lizzy turned away. "Do you really trust her?" she whispered.

"Implicitly," said Upjohn. "I want you to shake her hand."

Lizzy stiffened.

"Would you at least allow me to step away and have a few words with her?" asked Upjohn.

A pout formed on Lizzy's lips, then she folded her arms. "Only because I trust *you*, Toynbee." She gave Lil a look. "I'll give you two minutes—and I'll be watching her all the time."

They walked to a back row of the courtroom. "It's hard to believe she's done murder," said Lil, and she saw from Upjohn's eyes that her assumption was correct. "How did she pin my grandmother under that door?"

Upjohn looked back at Lizzy and nodded reassurance. "Philimentha arrived in Oriskany Forks a week ahead of Carrie," he said softly. "I'm sure she thought Eliza was dead. But, through the peepholes into the downstairs, Eliza knew when Philimentha began to paint herself. She knew she'd come to the upstairs room, and she set the trap. She's deceptively strong for such a tiny thing. She lifted the door off its track—"

"And pushed it over when my grandmother got close enough. Exactly as she tried to do with me."

"She was confused no end by that fiasco." A twinkle lit his eyes. "She was sure you were Philimentha back from the dead. She forgets the bushes are there, and since the door didn't fall all the way, she decided that you'd cast a spell to stop it." The twinkle faded. "She's not responsible, Lilith—any more than Cass would have been responsible if she'd succeeded in smothering Emily that day."

"I wasn't thinking of turning her in."

"I know you weren't. I just wanted you to know why I've taken such pains to protect her. It was difficult for her to come here today—to expose herself to you and the 'evil' she's been hiding from all these years...Quite gallant, really."

"So are you, Toynbee. Gallant." Lil looked up into his eyes. "That's what I wanted to say. Thank you for all you tried to do—and did."

Upjohn's fingers closed over her hand. "Our two minutes are up," he said. He rose and went back to Lizzy.

"Mr. Upjohn." Dr. Townsend was waiting. "I've been meaning to ask. Have you ever seen a unicorn?"

Upjohn realized Harley had edged closer and was listening. "Unicorns have reality only in the imagination," he said. "If I had seen a unicorn, I would have been seeing a phantom of my own mind."

"I won't dispute that," smiled Townsend. "But have you ever seen one?"

Upjohn returned the smile. "You've enough witnesses already."

Townsend shrugged. "Mr. Bellman tells me that you were the one who told him about my book. Do you own a copy?"

"Yes."

"It's sold very little. Not a common purchase."

"I'm not a common reader, Dr. Townsend."

At 7:15, under the protection of darkness and the three policemen who were to accompany them home, they were taken out the delivery entrance to cars waiting a few blocks away.

By the time they'd gone a block and a half, the sound of hurrying feet told them they'd been sighted. Harley glanced back. Most were strangers, but here and there he saw a friendly face—Mr. Grogan, smiling encouragement; Mr. Meiklejohn, the butcher. But there were others, men who had been friends— Nathan Gifford, Jed and Phil Cummings, Jake Burmaster,

Roland Young. On their faces was something more frightening than fear or anger.

It was as Bellman had said. They were never going to understand. So maybe Harley and his bunch weren't witches— Harley was still followed by some supernatural creature, and the defense had admitted that some of his and Lil's relatives *had been* witches.

The police kept the spectators back as the party climbed in. Mutters were heard, then shouts. A fist hit the window by Harley's face. He looked up into the eyes of Nathan Gifford, who was running alongside. "Get out of Oriskany Forks! We don't want you queer bastards around!"

"Get out," echoed the call. As the cars outdistanced Nathan and the others, objects thudded against the trunks and rear windows—apples and eggs and bottles from lunch pails. Lil put her face in her hands and began to cry. Screened at last from hostile eyes, Harley put an arm around her and tried to give her the comfort he did not feel. He kept looking at Upjohn— imploring, trusting him completely now. But Upjohn just sat, impassive.

❀ ❀ ❀

The convoy, three cars in all, took Hershfeld to his car and Folger to his train, then started for home, Bellman and Townsend having elected to spend the night at Spring Farm.

They took the long way round, bypassing Oriskany Forks, and drove up Bascombs' Road past the darkened house to let Lizzy out at the perimeter of the woods.

"I got to find me a new spot to hide right away."

"But Aunt Liz," said Paul. "There's no need for you to hide. You've got relatives and neighbors—"

"I seen some of my neighbors tonight," said Lizzy. "You can keep 'em!" Then she grinned. "When the bunch of you decides to go into hiding too, I might show you some good spots. Toynbee will know where to find me. Alice, it was fine to see you again." And she disappeared into the darkness of the trees; the wraith Lil and others had so often seen gliding these fields at night.

They started back down the road, heading for Spring Farm where, it had been decided, the Bascombs would continue to stay until things simmered down. They had nearly passed the Bascomb barn when Paul touched the arm of the policeman driving the car. "Long as we're here, let me run in and check things over."

"Oh, Paul, you don't have to do that," said Emma.

"Makes me nervous leaving the stock unattended." He heaved himself out of the car and started for the barn.

Thomas stuck his head out of the following car. "Where you going, Paul?"

"Take a look at the stock. And I don't need *your* help."

They heard the door scrape back on its track; saw a flicker as Paul lit a kerosene lamp.

Lil leaned listlessly on Harley's arm. Her eyes traveled the yard; the two granddaddy maples, the open shed, the outhouse. She thought of dear, crazy Cass, baiting Muriel and Janet on a bright summer day so long ago: *We heard the little door between the bedroom and the loft open, ever so slowly. Then we saw—her!* Lil's eyes filled with tears. She had to leave this place, these people. She'd brought them nothing but grief. But she couldn't leave them in danger. She'd convince them to leave, too, and when she'd gotten them safely away, she'd just—

Her eyes jerked across the road to the chicken coop.

Upjohn and Harley had seen it, too: the bumper of a car, protruding from behind the coop.

"Stay here!" Harley was out of the car and running toward the barn, Upjohn beside him. Harley couldn't see Paul's light. "Mr. Bascomb? Watch out—there's somebody here!"

He was into the barn before he knew it—into blackness. The cattle were stomping in their places. Harley stopped and groped. His hands fell upon a shovel; he lifted it and advanced. "Mr. Bascomb!"

Someone hit him from the side. Upjohn dived at the attacker, and the blow glanced off. Then there were matches being lit at the door of the barn and the glow of lanterns. Thomas and two policemen ran toward Harley; the attackers scurried up the stairs to the haymow. And lying on the floor at the edge of the lantern-light was Paul Bascomb, a pool of blood beneath his head.

"He must've surprised them getting ready to set fire to the barn," said Officer Foley. He held up a can of kerosene and some torches he'd found.

"They're in the haymow," said Harley. "One match is all it takes."

"You guys get Mr. Bascomb out to the car," said Foley. "We'll take care of them."

Harley, Thomas, and Upjohn lifted Paul gently. Lil was there suddenly, holding Paul's hand and talking to him.

There were shouts from the haymow. A shot rang out, then another, as Paul was borne to the car. Foley joined them, Nathan Gifford in tow, Nathan with a gun wound in his shoulder. "The rest of them got away," said Foley, "but at least they're out of your barn." He handcuffed Nathan to the steering column of his car and addressed the third cop. "Get these two to the doctor, Jip. McCrea and I'll stay here and keep an eye out. Better call the station and get more men. These people are going to need protection tonight."

As the two cars sped toward Spring Farm, Harley knelt over Paul and tried to stay the blood with his wadded coat.

He kept waiting for Upjohn to tell him what to do. Upjohn just sat.

They turned down the avenue of maples; Harley peered ahead, eager for the sight of house and barns. They were there, intact.

Curt and Henrietta ran onto the porch at the sound of the motors. Harley was out of the car immediately. "Is Burt Barnes here?"

"In the house." Then Curt saw his father being lifted from the car. "Oh, God!"

Emily and Michael came running. "Daddy!" They quieted at the sight of their grandfather's blood and followed, clutching at Harley, as Paul was carried to an upstairs bedroom.

Harley touched Upjohn's arm then. "We've got to get things organized."

Upjohn nodded, not taking his eyes from Paul. "You'd better begin."

Harley backed away, feeling betrayed. He glanced at Emily and Michael, so frightened and confused. He led them out of the room, then knelt and hugged them.

"What's a mattera Grampa?" said Michael.

"He fell and hit his head," said Harley.

"Can we help?" said Emily.

"Yes." Oh, God! he had to keep them safe. "I want you to stay in one place so I can find you if I have to—because there's going to be a lot of excitement around here for a while. Why don't you go into Gramma Hitty's room? You can play with her chessmen."

Michael ran off eagerly, but Emily lagged. "What's really the matter, Daddy?"

No getting past Emily with half-truths. "We're afraid that men are coming here tonight to do mischief, Emily." He tried to keep his voice steady. "It's very important for you to keep

Michael in Gramma's room. Whatever you do, don't go outside. Not even to the porch."

"You can count on me," said Emily.

Harley touched her face, loving her. "You're not scared, are you?"

Emily looked up into his eyes. "Not now that you're home, Daddy."

Harley watched her go.

He tried to organize his thoughts. Tobin. He hadn't seen him or Hitty.

But first the Pinkertons and Chuck should be alerted. He started down.

The policeman called "Jip" was standing in the foyer with Nathan Gifford. "Where's the doctor?"

"Top of the stairs, first on the left down the passageway."

"Soon's I get this guy up there and cuffed to something that won't move, I'll call the station house."

Someone stepped from the door of the parlor. "Is there anything I can do, Harley?"

"Father Lawrence!" Tears stung Harley's eyes. "What the hell are you doing here?—excuse me, Father."

"Perfectly all right. I came straight up with Dr. Barnes after the verdict. We knew your father must be in distress."

"How is he?"

"Not well, Harley. Dr. Barnes gave him something to sleep. Your mother is with him. What about Mr. Bascomb?"

Harley laughed at the irony. "I think maybe he could use some of your Catholic prayers."

The priest started toward the stairs.

"Father. There might be a lot of trouble here tonight. You'd be safer if you went home."

Father Lawrence smiled. "It's terribly dull at the rectory, Harley. I'll stay."

It was warm for late October, but the full moon kept hiding behind clouds. They needed light.

Harley found Chuck and two of the Pinkertons near the barn. Curt and Thomas trotted up; Upjohn walked behind them. They all looked to Harley.

Harley took a breath. "Well, I think we need all the lights on, in every room of every building. Let's not give them a place to hide. Grampa, you and Curt station the cars and the trucks around the house and barns, pointing out at the fields so we can turn on the headlights and see what's out there. Chuck, you and I will turn the bulls into their runs. That way, if there's a fire, we'll only have to open the gates to the pasture. We'll put the calves into the calf yard, and the cows in the barnyard."

"The cows are in the pasture," said Chuck. "It was so warm tonight, I figured I'd let them stretch their legs. They'll be coming down for the eleven o'clock."

"What about the red house?" said Curt.

Harley hesitated, still thinking about the cows. "Forget it. It's too far away from the center to defend."

"Lord!" said a Pinkerton. "You sound like you're getting ready for Gettysburg."

Harley passed a hand across his face. "I don't know what I'm getting ready for. Maybe nothing."

"How many men have we?" said Upjohn.

Upjohn could count. Why was everyone expecting *him* to do the thinking? But he closed his eyes and figured. "The four Pinkertons, you, me, Curt, Grampa, Jip, Chuck, Father Lawrence in a pinch, and Townsend. Bellman won't be any use. Doc Barnes—"

"The doctor will have to stay with Paul," said Upjohn softly.

Harley was silent, then he turned to Curt. "How about *my* Dad. Can he help?"

Curt looked away. "No."

Harley wanted to turn and run to his father's bedside. He glanced at Upjohn, imploring, but Upjohn wouldn't meet his eyes. Harley wiped his palms on his trousers. "All right. I don't want anybody alone unless they're within easy shouting distance of the house and inside the lights. How many guns have we got?"

"You're going to use *guns?*" asked the older Pinkerton.

"Only for self-defense," Harley assured him. "Give Curt one of your guns now. Round up your other two men and station them by the house. Then come back and help us turn on lights. Grampa, Curt, get going." Harley turned to Upjohn. "Go back to the house. Send Jip out to help us. Take Father Lawrence with you, and turn on every light from attic to basement. Get the shotguns from Dad's office. See that everyone is in one area of the house, and don't let anyone go down to the kitchen alone. The girls are in Mom's bedroom. Take them in with the others. Do you think you can manage that?"

"I'll do my best, Harley. But the important thing is that you'll do *yours.* " Upjohn touched Harley's shoulder and walked away.

Chuck and Harley moved quickly into the barn, turning on lights as they went. They drove the calves into the calf yard, then tackled the bulls. Jip arrived and went to the haymow to turn on lights. "The station's sending help."

All around them was the roar of motors, as Curt and Thomas stationed the vehicles about.

Then they heard other motors—automobiles, two of them, coming down the drive. A Pinkerton ran up. "You expecting company?"

Harley took the Pinkerton's gun and advanced. There were eight or nine men climbing from the cars. "Stop where you are or I'll fire!"

"You do and we'll be mighty sore," answered Mr. Grogan.

Harley ran to embrace the old man. With him were Mr. Meiklejohn, Gillespie Hamlin, Jeremy Cole, Gillespie's sons, Jeremy's sons—and Cyrus Hamlin.

"We come to sit with you," said Mr. Grogan.

"Do you mind if I put you to work first?" He told them about the attack on Paul and the attempt to burn the Bascombs' barn.

Gillespie shook his head. "Florence Comstock called my wife and told her that *you'd* shot Nathan Gifford. Dead. I'm afraid that's the news that's making the rounds."

"Jip, you get Nathan and handcuff him by the phone. Gillespie, you get on the phone and call your wife. Tell her what really happened, and tell her to call everybody she knows and tell them. Then start calling everybody *you* know. Put Nathan on and make him talk if you've got to break his arm to do it. The rest of you, come with me."

Harley set them to filling every container they could find with water. Soon a car arrived with three more policemen. Mr. Sawyer arrived. Spring Farm blazed with lights. Shouts filled the night.

At last Harley could go back to the house. He went upstairs and stopped at the room where Paul lay. Ignoring Upjohn, he beckoned Lil into the hall.

"How is he?" said Harley.

"Dying." Her voice was flat. "It's time, really. Mama once said that the evil wouldn't die until he did. Maybe with him and me both gone—"

"What are you talking about?"

Lil took his hands. "We've all got to get out of here. Now. Tonight."

"We've got no place to go."

"We can *make* some place. Maybe Professor Townsend will help. Or Mr. Bellman."

"We can't just leave everything!"

"*I* can." There were tears in her eyes. "I've got to. That was the reason I wanted you to meet me that day in the woods, Harley. To tell you that I'd decided to leave. I was going to ask you to come. You and the girls, and Upjohn. But now everyone is in danger. We've got to get them *all* to leave."

It was impossible. There was Cass to think about. But—Lil gone? What if he did go with her? Maybe she was right. He had two children to think about. And now that Helen was going to have a baby...

"But my father!" Tobin's hard-won new herd. Of course, Gillespie and the others could see to them. And with Tobin senseless from Barnes' drug—they could load him into the car—

No! It would kill Tobin. And, Harley realized suddenly, it would kill *him*, too. You couldn't rip up the roots of a lifetime in an hour. His own, Tobin's, Hitty's, Emily's, and Michael's roots. That would be the completion—no, the perfection—of Carrie's vengeance. Tobin and Hitty packed into a car with a couple of valises and driven off to God-knows-where with everything they held dear left to be slaughtered or burned or auctioned off to Nathan Gifford!

He turned and walked down the hall to his father's room.

Hitty, beside Tobin's bed, didn't look up as he entered. "I think we've lost him, Harley."

Harley ran to his father. Tobin's pulse was steady and strong. "He's all right, Mother."

"No, he's not. When I got home this morning," she smoothed Tobin's hair, "he was on his knees out there, digging with his hands. We couldn't stop him—me, nor Curt, nor Chuck. He just dug till he found a skull and some bones. He hugged them and rocked them—he thought it was Pontiac Lass."

"My God!"

"He kept telling her he was going to make her well and

she'd have all the alfalfa she could eat. He made Chuck dig up more bones. He put them in a row—called this one Topsy and that one Agatha, or Laura Beets, or Locust. And he sang to them. 'Hi diddle diddle, the cat and the fiddle, the cow jumped over the moon.' Then he began to cry, just lying on those bones and hugging them. That's how he was when Doc Barnes came." Hitty kept patting Tobin, gazing down at his face. "I'll never forgive myself, Harley. I always meant to tell your father how I loved him—loved him from the first. Now he'll never know."

Harley sank to his knees and looked into the quiet face with the high forehead and the shock of dark hair so unfriendly to combs. There was a lot of gray in that hair now, and the face had lines that Harley did not remember.

And Hitty? Her eyes were dead.

So Carrie had won.

Suddenly Harley was up, out of the room, down the hall past Lil, and into Paul's room. "Upjohn! Emily!" He went to Helen, gathered Michael into his arms, and led them all back to Tobin's room. "'We need some minds in concert," he said. He sat Michael beside her grandfather and took Hitty by the shoulders. "Come on, now! He's going to be all right. Carrie isn't going to win!" He leaned over Tobin. "You hear that, Dad? I'm going to see that she doesn't!"

"What should *I* do?" said Emily.

"What Mr. Upjohn tells you. You're going to help make Grampa well."

He turned to Upjohn—met his gaze, gripped his hand.

That hand was warm and strong. Harley squeezed, holding for that first and last instant; then he released it. "My *father* needs you now."

"Only for the moment, Harley. After that, it will be enough for him to have you." Upjohn's gaze faltered. He turned away. "Come, Mehitable. We must all concentrate."

Lil was still waiting beside Paul's door when Harley came into the hall. He walked to her and stopped. There were things he wanted to say; if she was going away tonight, perhaps they were best left unsaid. Yet that was exactly why he had to say them. "I'm staying for a while, Lil. I've got to look after things until they're right. I'm not sure how long that will be." He reached out, meaning only to take her hand, but somehow he moved toward her and she toward him; they kissed, and felt each other's tears. "I'd hate to lose you again," he said as their lips parted. He turned and went down the stairs.

"Chuck?"

Chuck appeared from around the barn, followed by a policeman. Harley beckoned. "I've decided to go up after the cows. Where's the truck?"

"In the orchard," said Chuck. Harley started off, Chuck and the policeman trotting after him. "It's 9:30, Mr. Harley. They'll be coming down by themselves soon."

Harley shook his head. "They ought to be here where we can keep an eye on them."

He climbed in, started the motor, and switched on the headbeams. For an instant they lit freshly dug earth and a row of bones; then Harley turned the truck and started up the wagon road.

The moon was out of the clouds now, clear and full. They reached the top of the hill and began to search for the spots of white that would be the herd. At last they saw them, near the fence where the pasture met the Crazy Lizzy.

Then the policeman riding the back of the truck shouted. "I see a man! Two—no, three!"

Harley saw them, too. He pressed the accelerator to the floor, hit the horn, and kept hitting it. The cattle began to mill, and the figures among them jumped out of the way. One cow lay motionless on the ground. "God damn them!"

The figures had vanished into the darkness of the Crazy Lizzy by the time the truck stopped. Harley leaped out and ran to the stricken cow. It was Korndyke King's Mary, one of Tobin's best new heifers, heavily pregnant with her first calf. Her throat had been cut.

Harley wheeled on the Lizzy. "Come out and fight! Forget old men and cows! Fight *me* if you've got the guts."

The Lizzy answered with silence.

Chuck was kneeling beside Mary. "And her not a week from calfing."

Harley looked down at the cow—still warm, blood still pouring from her neck. "Give me your knife, Chuck."

"What for?"

"Give it to me!"

And in the glare of the headlights Harley knelt beside Mary. He dug the knife into her belly—hard at first, to rip through the tough, protecting layers; then gently, probing among the innards. He found the womb, sliced it open, and widened the slash. He could see the calf now, complacent in its liquid, still drawing life from the mother it did not know was dead. As he pierced the sack, the juice gushed out, watering the blood to pink. He grasped the calf and pulled. It came all in a piece, still curled, unaware of so easy an exit. And then it lay in Harley's lap, its warmth turning cold in the night air, connected to what had been its mother only by the umbilical. Harley stripped off his shirt and began to rub the calf, forcing its jaws, wiping the mucus from its mouth. It lay there, unwilling to give up its automatic life and to accept the air. Harley jabbed its ribs. It coughed. It kicked the man who had given it life.

And he fell upon it, tearing the umbilical, laughing to hear the cough, delighting in the pain of stabbing hooves.

He stood then, the small beast cradled in his arms, and for a long moment he stared at the darkness of the Crazy Lizzy. Then he headed for the truck. "Come on, Chuck. We'll get the herd down to the barn, and come back for the carcass. We'll be needing that meat."